MARKED

JOSHUA HEDGES

zombiesnackllc@gmail.com

Cover art design by cheriefox.com
Map by Joshua Hedges

Book Interior and E-book Design by Amit Dey | amitdey2528@gmail.com *for Liam,*

So you can always dream of dragons
with your father.

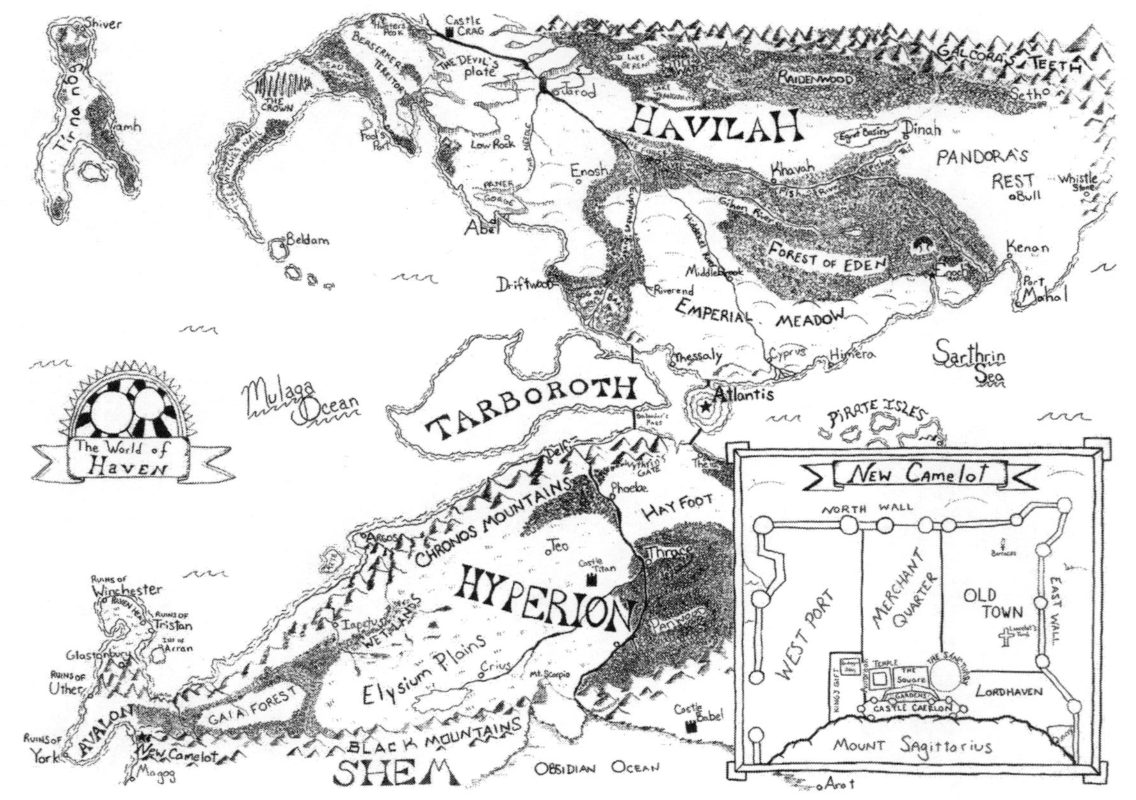
The World of Haven
Tir na nog
Shiver
Niamh
Beldam
Mulaga Ocean
Castle Crag
Berserker Territory
The Devil's plate
The Crown
Fool's Port
Low Rock
Abel
Tarod
HAVILAH
Galcora's Teeth
Raidenwood
Setho
Egypt Basin
Dinah
Pandora's Rest
Bull
Whistle Stone
Enosh
Khavah
Fish River
Gihon River
Forest of Eden
Kenan
Port Mahal
Driftwood
Riverend
Middlebrook
Emperial Meadow
Thessaly
Cyprus
Himera
Sarthrin Sea
Atlantis
TARBOROTH
Pirate Isles
Delf
Phoebe
Hay Foot
Chronos Mountains
Teo
Castle Titan
Thrace
HYPERION
Iapetus
Wetlands
Elysium Plains
Crius
Mt. Scorpio
Castle Babel
Gaia Forest
Black Mountains
SHEM
Obsidian Ocean
Ruins of Winchester
Ruins of Tristan
Isle of Arran
Glastonbury
Ruins of Uther
Ruins of York
Avalon
New Camelot
Magog
Arot
New Camelot
North Wall
West Port
Merchant Quarter
Old Town
East Wall
Lordhaven
Castle Caerlon
The Square
Temple
Gardens
The Sanctuary
King's Gift
Mount Sagittarius

1

Avalon

Freedom is wild. Untamed excitement still pumped through her heart. She'd never forget the first step she took to defy the Emperor. He had the power to punish thoughts and actions. The power to ensure absolute obedience. A single lingering thought of disobedience didn't go unpunished and a step in defiance was a step into the grave. The Mayan slaves named it the "Mind Curse."

For centuries the Mind Curse governed their every action. When they had thoughts that didn't please the Emperor, pain lashed their minds like a cruel master's whip. Deviants were punished with death. The Mind Curse was the most powerful of curses, a blood curse, passed from parent to child.

Three hundred years ago, a boom of Mayan immigrants crippled the city of Enoch, throwing it into chaos. Alejandro Vega offered the Mind Curse to help the King of Havilah restore order. The king gave him access to the dungeons. Almost overnight, Vega turned Enoch's hardened criminals into obedient hard workers. But Vega didn't stop there. With the thieves and murderers under his control, he had the power to force the Curse on the rest of the city. Within a year, he had imprisoned the minds of the entire city of Enoch. Like wildfire, he sent the Curse though the Kingdom of Hyperion and their great capital, Atlantis. It even spread to the southern Kingdom of Shem. In a few years, he had conquered three of the four kingdoms of Haven. He killed the King of Havilah and Shem, and dissolved Hyperion's republic. Then Vega declared himself Emperor and lord of their lands. In three hundred years the curse had become so widespread, Emperor Vega took lordship over their minds.

Then one night, she found that the Mind Curse couldn't hurt her anymore.

She dreamt of running away. She ran toward a city with tall towers and high walls. She could be safe there. Running through rolling green fields she found her freedom.

That night when she woke expecting the Mind Curse to deal her a punishment, it never came. In the days that followed, she learned to dream while she worked. Ideas washed in on a high tide of thought. She dreamed of a world without the Emperor. In that world she could read and write. Instead of wiping crumbs from the emperor's table, she sat and dined with kings and queens.

Then the bump came. It wasn't long after she could dream that she noticed it. She wanted more for her baby. She wanted her child to grow up to live dreams and feel the wild excitement of freedom. She wanted her baby to never know slavery and be given more than a number.

She traced a finger through her slave number burned into her forehead. 1289. Her name.

She needed to take her child where it could be free. There was only one free city remaining in the four kingdoms. New Camelot, the seat of Avalon.

The Emperor sent countless slaves off to war to take control of New Camelot. None returned. 1289 served the Emperor's house all her life. She'd overheard stories of the city. It was built out of the side of a Black Mountain. The Black Mountains held unspeakable perils, yet the fearless Avalonians built their city in their midst on top of the remains of an ancient Elven city. Within their walls was the Aurorean temple where the Council, the practitioners of light magic, studied and trained. The Avalonians fortified the city by rebuilding the legendary impenetrable walls designed by the Elves and guarded those walls with their soldiers. It was magnificent. She'd seen it too. In her dream.

She knew her baby would be safe there.

1289 rode on horseback down an old road leading from Atlantis to New Camelot. The road had once been wide enough for a wagon. Tall grass, ferns, and trees grew in the path. The road was now a small walking trail just wide enough for a horse or two. Over the centuries, the feet of soldiers were the only force preventing the forest from reclaiming its lost ground. She didn't worry about covering the number burned into her forehead or changing from her slave rags. A Mayan slave alone and so far out of Enoch was uncommon, but the Mind Curse protected her in a way. Mayan slaves had no free will. They were the servants of the emperor. Commoners assumed she was on the Emperor's business. She'd even galloped through the Emperor's army advancing toward New Camelot. No one stopped her.

As she crossed the bridge dividing Hyperion and Avalon, the wild sense of freedom pounding in her chest intensified.

"Soon, we're almost there," she said, comforting her unborn.

1289 hadn't noticed that a single raven trailed her like a shadow from the gates of Enoch. It followed her across Havilah. More ravens joined in Hyperion, south of Atlantis. As she got closer and closer to New Camelot, their numbers multiplied. She saw them hovering behind her like an ominous storm cloud.

The suns set, vanishing beneath the rim of the western sky. The smaller of the two, set first. Then the greater, followed. Twilight turned to darkness. 1289 watched the black ravens blend into the cloudy starless night leaving only the flutter of a thousand wings as a reminder of their presence.

The baby kicked, making 1289 jump in her saddle. Gently, she patted her belly to calm the child and sang a lullaby.

Long ago Elves lived in the woods,
With pointy ears, fair skin, and hoods,

They sang all day,
And even at night,
They were masters of magic, truth, and light—

She paused when the forest fell silent. The fluttering stopped.

From the first spark,
They came out of the dark,
It's said they'd learn more than they should,
Some say their trial was for their own good,
The gods knew they would betray,
So they took them away,

A twig snapped in the forest. Then another. And another.

Filled with fear, she kicked her horse to a gallop. It didn't budge. She tried again and a pain shot up her leg from the horse's firm muscles.

"GO!" she cried, shaking the reins. Nothing.

She tilted herself to look over the horse's shoulder into its blank eyes. The horse had stopped breathing. It stood completely still, frozen in place. It was dead.

Another twig snapped behind her. She whirled around on her stone steed to search the darkness. Only the darkness looked back. More twigs snapped to her left and right.

The full moon peeked out from the clouds, leaving a puddle of moonlight in her wake. Then she saw it, in the middle of the road looking back at her.

A pale white face hovered in the darkness. Its eyes were black voids. It was staring right at her.

The creature moved toward her.

As it got closer, she made out a body. It wore a black-feathered cloak that was nearly invisible in the darkness. The black void eyes glinted like beetles in the moonlight.

She'd seen their kind in the Emperor's army. They were fallen dark mages. Doya.

"We've been watching you," it said in a deep, throaty voice.

Faces appeared out of the darkness. They surrounded her.

1289 wrapped her arms around her womb. Her chin trembled as she looked from face to face.

A Doya came out of the darkness. Its savage black eyes flickered up her as it ran its oily black tongue over its sharp rotting teeth.

"Isn't it strange that a Mayan slave, a sworn servant of the Emperor, would be traveling on the road to New Camelot?" The largest Doya spoke Mayan.

Unlike the others, it wept tears that carried a blackness so thick it made the dark, starless sky look gray. It wept Doya blood.

There was no use running. She was trapped on her horse.

"You must feel brave, walking out of Enoch like that. So brave that you even stole one of the Emperor's horses."

The Doya ran its bone claws through the dead horses mane petting it as if the horse were still alive. He was so tall he could look her in the eye.

"The Emperor wouldn't approve of a slave stealing one of his horses."

His black, searching eyes made the hairs stand on the back of 1289's neck.

"You're fleeing, cursed and fleeing to your Emperor's enemy. Fascinating."

The Doya around her hissed what 1289 interpreted as a chuckle.

1289 clenched her teeth to stop her chin from shaking. She knew what was coming. They wanted what she couldn't give.

"Denounce Emperor Vega. Denounce him as the Emperor of the four kingdoms."

1289 shook her head. She reached deep inside for the courage to speak.

"No."

The blood weeping Doya yanked her off her horse and backhanded her. Her lip split and she stumbled backwards. Doya surrounding them shoved her back. Holding his claw to her face, the Doya prepared to strike her again.

"Denounce him. Prove to us that you've broken the Mind Curse."

Holding her bloodied lip, she refused. Ruthlessly, he threw her to the ground. Two Doya yanked her back up. He slapped her repeatedly.

Still she refused.

"I am Sarod. The Prince of Darkness. Don't mistake me for a mere Doya, you feebleminded fool."

With a flick of his wrist, he drew a magical symbol in the air and prodded his claw into her neck. In an instant, she felt her insides swell. Her skin strained to hold her body in. She looked down at her hands. They looked normal, but it felt as if the fibers of her skin were straining and, at any moment, she would burst. Her screams filled the night.

Still she refused.

Infuriated, Sarod reached for her large belly with another spell.

"No! Not my child!" she pleaded.

"Denounce the Emperor!" he demanded once more.

She let the words escape.

"Yes. I denounce him. I denounce the Emperor. His filthy curse has no power over me."

A wry grin spread across Sarod's face.

"How? How could such a stupid worthless creature escape a spell that took so many of my followers?" Sarod leaned in close. His rancid breath made her want to vomit. Then he placed his pale cheek on hers. His tears burned like acid. He whispered softly to her.

"I am going to cut you open and examine you piece by piece."

Her dark skin turned pale. A cold sweat made her shiver and she slipped into unconsciousness.

1289 woke up strapped to her undead horse by an invisible force. Unholy magic animated the horse's legs, moving her along at a slow trot, while its head hung low to the ground. Her captors surrounded her and she knew where they were going. The Doya only inhabited one region, The Black Mountains.

She'd heard the Emperor speak of the Black Mountains. He described them as a snake with a sharp spine that rose and dipped out of the land. Sometimes streams of red lava bled from the ground. The Emperor sent the Branded there to bring back Doya. Once they were captured, he forced their obedience with the Mind Curse. The Doya had no moral boundaries they would do things, horrible things, that most men would never do, even to save their own lives.

Hours passed. A dark mass towered over the forest. 1289 knew it was the Black Mountains. She'd never seen them, but nothing could be that big and black. As they got closer, she shrank on her horse, fearing the darkness might stomp her out. Moonlight escaped over the jagged peaks as the mountain range marched over the moon. Soon they would leave the road and enter the dark caves. Is that where she would leave her child? Is that where she would die?

She didn't know much about magic, but she knew the difference between the Aurorean and the Aphotic. Just as the Aurorean took their power from the light, the Aphotic took their power from the darkness. Doya were fallen followers of the Aphotic.

Doya loved fear and darkness. During the night, they were gods, and during the day they sucked their power from nearby shadows and whatever terror they could create. It was just after midnight, a time when an Doya's power was unparalleled.

A raven landed on Sarod's shoulder and whispered into his ear.

"The Branded are less than a league behind us," Sarod warned.

"Move faster!"

1289 knew of the Branded. They were the Emperor's elite force. Most were light or dark mages led by Lady Black, a killer that even the Doya respected. The Branded were a formidable threat to a small group of Doya, but they never marched alone. They led an army of at least ten thousand Mayan slave soldiers.

When the city of Enoch swelled with more slaves than the shacks and pits could hold, the Branded marched armed slaves to the walls of New Camelot. There they would watch slave armies battle, breaking like water on a rocky shore. It was a way to clean the capital while searching for weak points in New Camelot's defenses.

If the Branded caught them, 1289 would be forced into battle or carried captive back to Enoch. Either was a better fate than being at the mercy of the Doya.

"Far-utha-dom"

Sarod spoke words of power. He waved his arms like a conductor ending a symphony. The air hummed. 1289's ears popped. Dozens of trees uprooted flinging dirt into the air. Branches snapped and the ground quaked as the trees fell to block the road.

The other Doya cast a spell to speed up the dead horse.

Sarod snatched up 1289's arm and used the point of his bone claw to cut into her wrist. She tried to pull away, but he was too strong. He squeezed her wrist to extract her blood and licked the wound with his oily tongue. She didn't know what he was doing, but from the waving of his claw and his odd rhythmic chants, she knew it was magic.

"Impossible," he scowled.

Sarod grabbed her arm and leeched more blood, but none of his spells revealed the nature of the woman's ability to defeat the Mind Curse.

"You're just as cursed as the next human!" he spat.

1289 knew her blood was infused with the Curse. It was only a matter of time until the Curse took her once more. Overcoming it hadn't been her doing.

The forest shook. Trees dropped their dry leaves as twenty thousand feet marched down the road.

Sarod was still mulling over her blood when the baby kicked.

1289 couldn't hide her discomfort. Sarod was staring right at her.

"The child. It's the child!" he exclaimed, but it was too late. The army was nearly upon them.

Sarod grabbed her arm. 1289 kicked him away. He reached for his magic, but the other Doya snatched him. The army came into view just as the Doya pulled Sarod out of sight.

1289 climbed off the horse. The spell keeping it upright dissipated and the horse carcass toppled into the road.

Slaves flowed past her as if she were a rock in a stream. Countless faces passed, not even turning to look. They were focused on the Emperor's command. Attack New Camelot. Any wavering brought the punishment of the Mind Curse.

The last of the slave soldiers passed and 1289 came face to face with the Branded.

They were a strange collection of soldiers. Some were ruthless warlords carrying impossibly large weapons. Others were Aurorean and Aphotic mages wearing the black and gold colors of the Emperor's banner. At their center was Lady Black. She was a tall woman with a noticeably long neck. Her armor was dull black, and a serrated obsidian sword hung from her waist.

1289 couldn't look her in the eyes or speak. It was unheard of for a slave to address a Branded, unless she was spoken to.

She said a silent prayer to the gods. 1289 couldn't see Lady Black's face under her black velvet hood, but she could see the glint of her bright green eyes.

"What is this?" Lady Black said sharply.

One of the warlords spoke up and pointed to the dead horse. "Her horse has the Emperor's brand. She must be one of our scouts."

1289 couldn't look, but she felt Lady Black loom over her like the long shadow of a headsman.

"Where is the Enchanter?" Lady Black asked.

"I'm here," Alaric responded. He was a man in his fifties with dark, thinning hair and a crooked nose.

"You're new to the Branded," Lady Black said. "What should we do with scouts that run their horses to death?"

Alaric winced and shielded his nose in his sleeve. He could barely stand the stench of 1289's sweat-drenched rags.

"Dear gods, woman. I think you'll smell better dead."

The Branded belted out a hearty laugh.

1289 stared at the dirt. She wouldn't let them see her cry.

Alaric held out his hand. He had a symbol branded on his palm.

"You know what this is?"

Careful not to make eye contact, she glanced at his hand. It was the silhouette of a bullhead.

"Its the Emperor's seal," she responded.

"What does it mean?" he asked.

"That you speak for the Emperor."

Alaric looked at the brand as if he held the world in his hand. Then he issued his command.

"It's the Emperor's will that you take the city of New Camelot or die trying."

"Yes, my Lord," she replied. 1289 kept her tear-filled eyes on the ground as she joined the rest of the slaves in their march.

She was on the same road heading to the same city, but with the Branded at her back, everything had changed.

Her wild heart withered. She needed to get inside New Camelot before her baby was born. It would take a miracle just reach the main gate.

She would rush the wall unarmed and pray that the arrows wouldn't find her.

2

Avalon - New Camelot

The buildings lining New Camelot's walls were built in tiers, one roof slightly higher than the next. Archers would take to the rooftops and fire arrows down on invaders. Together, the city guard and the Elven walls created a defense that had protected the city from the Emperor for two hundred and fifty years.

New Camelot lacked a southern wall. Instead, it used the cliff face of the black mountain, Mount Sagittarius. The palace, Castle Caerleon, stood in the shadow of the mountain. To the West was the Mulaga Ocean where they could get supplies should they fall under siege. The city was open to attack only from the north and the east.

When ten thousand slaves armed only with farm tools and makeshift spears attacked New Camelot's battlements from the north, the city's archers waited at their rooftop stations and fired on command. Countless arrows vanished in the early morning darkness before screeching down on the invading army. Each lethal volley eliminated hundreds of advancing slaves, creating heaps of bodies on the battlefield.

Few of the invading army's slaves made it to New Camelot's walls. Those that did erected siege ladders that were promptly destroyed by New Camelot's swordsmen on the wall. The slaves' spears took out a few soldiers, but for every soldier to fall in New Camelot, one hundred slaves were either cut down by their arrows, leveled by their ballistae, or slaughtered by swordsmen. The brave slaves fought and died, others were killed by the Mind Curse as they tried to flee.

Not a single slave breached the wall.

The Branded lined the hills just out of range of New Camelot's archers and watched until the last slave died in a merciless shower of arrows.

Lady Black applauded the bloody performance.

Warlords underestimated the skill and number of New Camelot's archers. They watched which lines fell first and what walls they reached. In the end, they came to the same conclusion as with every battle before: New Camelot was impenetrable.

Leaving the Emperor's banner atop a hill, they galloped off.

Rain began to fall and wash the air of the bloody stench of battle. Puddles erased the final steps of the fallen slaves. Arrows held firm in mortal wounds or sunk deep in the mud, never to be used again. Wounded slaves, unable to continue the fight, had been struck dead by the Mind Curse.

The battlefield was silent.

New Camelot's city garrison mourned their hollow victory. Guards lined the great walls while a battle still waged in their consciences. Guilt brought some to their knees, while others would drown it in ale. In their waking nightmares, the faces of the dead would join those they had killed in the past and live on to haunt them. It was a heavy price to pay for freedom.

Ravens circled the battlefield. The desolation enthralled them. Their black eyes gleamed over the heaps of carcasses. They gathered in a horde and flapped their wings in a dance of both pleasure and excitement.

Cries of agony from a slave woman broke the eerie reverence of the fallen army.

A pregnant slave lay hidden among the dead. She had dark skin and wide cheekbones. Her long, wavy, black hair was caked with dirt and blood. Sweat ran through the scars of a number burned into her forehead. 1289.

She shook from labor pains.

"Help me! Save my baby!"

She sucked in a sharp breath against her cramps. Her insides were in knots, but she found the strength to pull herself out of a pile of bodies. She stumbled toward the city. 1289 wrapped her arms around her womb to shield her unborn from each painful fall. Gradually, she moved toward the main gate.

Mathus Ward, a squire, watched the woman from the North Wall. He wore an odd mismatched collection of used armor. His curly, light brown hair hung to his shoulders. He was easily the stature of the other soldiers, yet he was no older than fourteen. He stood at his post and followed the woman intently with his eyes. Impatiently, he waited for the guard to raise the gate.

"Shall I gather a rescue party, Sir?" he asked.

The woman fell again. He wondered if she had the strength to get back up.

"It's a trap," Sir Cador replied.

"But Sir? The Branded have gone. Their army is dead."

"She'll be dead soon enough. If the archers don't get her the Mind Curse will."

Step by step the woman pulled herself toward the gate. Her sweaty, gray rags clung to her body. Mathus thought she looked more like a rat than a person. A rat trapped in an impossible maze of human corpses.

The ravens had stopped circling. With the screams of hell, they descended in a mass. Mathus was still watching as the woman looked up, eyes white with terror.

"Sir!" Mathus shouted.

Sir Cador eyed Mathus as he would eye a roach.

"Know your place, squire!"

"We have to do *something!*" he blurted.

Sir Cador grabbed Mathus by his curly hair and directed his eyes to the battlefield. He forced him to look over the wall. A pile of bodies heaped at the base of a broken siege ladder. Ravens picked at their open wounds.

"Imagine yourself in that bloody heap. Mercy for the enemy, that's what will get you there. This is war! We die or they do."

The woman swatted at the mass of birds and slipped in a puddle, nearly impaling herself on a broken spear.

Mathus struggled under Sir Cador's grip. Unable to break free he recited the oath. An oath every guard took.

"...Strength to those that protect, and above all, Honor to those who forgive."

It deflected off Sir Cador's iron heart.

"It's a nice sentiment from the great King Arthur. But kings don't win wars. Soldiers do." Sir Cador's voice turned icy cold. "She'll die like the rest. I'll not risk my men for one of the Emperor's bitches."

Mathus' anger gave him the strength to pull his head free. He twisted and threw his fist. His knuckles crashed into Sir Cador's face. The Knight's nose crunched and blood came bubbling out.

"You little shit! I'll have you whipped and thrown back in the gutters where I found you!"

Mathus brought his armored elbow crashing across Sir Cador's face. The blow knocked him out cold.

Mathus looked out on a crowd of archers lining the wall. With their bowstrings taught, they aimed at the advancing slave.

Mathus imitated Sir Cador's voice.

"HOLD YOUR FIRE!"

The archers on the lower tiers fell for his trick and repeated the order down the wall.

The sound of hurried footsteps came from the tower stairwell. Mathus stood over the unconscious knight, unsure of what to do.

A soldier walked into the tower. "What is this?"

Mathus bolted for the door, but the clever soldier caught him by the breastplate before he could escape. Mathus' fingers fumbled for his breastplate buckles. Unclasping them, he slipped out, leaving the soldier holding only a metal shell. Mathus tossed his heavy gauntlets and sword to make him lighter and sprinted across the wall.

Within moments he had lost his pursuer. Mathus dashed through lines of soldiers while keeping an eye on the woman. He could see the ravens still clawing and snapping at her. She was alive. He still had time.

Four ravens flew apart from the horde. Instead of attacking the woman, they watched like generals from above. There was something different about them. Their heads didn't jerk like normal birds, instead they moved fluidly. The other ravens were ever aware of their presence. The slightest tilt of their wings caused the entire horde to change course as if the four were directing them.

The four ravens tilted into a dive and dropped out of the sky. They hit the ground with incredible force. They squawked and contorted, tucking their heads under their wings as their bodies grew. Bones snapped and joints cracked. White, bald heads extended out from under their wings. Soulless black eyes void of light and color opened like holes directly to hell. Raven-like features melted away into raven-feathered cloaks. They held their heads low like vultures and stretched, revealing gangly arms. These ravens weren't just birds. They were Doya.

The Doya were hunting her.

The pregnant slave fell backward. She opened her quivering mouth to scream, but her voice retreated somewhere inside. Her mind told her to run but, in her terror, she couldn't feel her legs. She tried to crawl away but ended up at the feet of the largest of the four Doya. Unlike the others, his arms were muscular and his chest was broad. She thought he looked impossibly tall. Her stomach sickened at the sight of the creature's pale white, veiny legs coursing with black fluid. Under his tattered, feather cloak, he wore a grey, bloodstained loincloth and a necklace made from black stones, strands of human hair, and teeth. Their eyes met and she saw black tears streaming down his face.

It was him. She remembered how to scream.

New Camelot's garrison watched with awe and fear at the events unfolding before them. Even Mathus couldn't open the gate now. He knew the Doya would enjoy nothing more than to kill every man, woman, and child in the city.

Mathus beat his fists on the portcullis. He cursed for more time.

"Mathus." A compassionate hand grabbed his.

She was the one person who would follow him into hell itself, his older sister, Ele. She had his curly hair, wore heavy clothes instead of armor, and carried a Cogbow as long as she was tall.

"I saw you running, so I followed. I heard you order the archers not to fire?"

"I...I thought I could save the slave woman. I'm too late." Mathus leaned heavily on the portcullis. And like the rest of New Camelot, he watched the woman scream.

The first sun broke over the horizon. The large Doya, the leader, absorbed dark power from the long shadows. It wasn't enough energy, but using the woman's fear he could amplify that power. He gathered the energy he needed and reached out with a bleached white claw and touched the woman's forehead. He licked his lips and drooled tar on her bulging stomach. He sensed the strength of an innocent heart inside her, beating so hard to stay alive. The Doya placed his other claw under the woman's belly and suspended her in the air. His claws squirmed in dark magic as they burrowed into her womb. Like ink in milk, darkness poured into her eyes.

She convulsed, foam spewing from her mouth.

He pushed the point of his claw harder into her skull. Somehow his spell wasn't working. Then he could feel it. The dark magic he poured inside her found the child. Soot fell from his mouth as words of power hissed out. He pulled at her head and stomach. The woman felt her midsection tighten. Her muscles strained as they tried to hold her together.

"Don't watch." Ele tugged on his arm.

Mathus' hardened face made him look like a statue. His resolve defied reason. He had to do something.

"Ele, give me your bow."

Ele took his arm and tried to pull him away. He wouldn't budge. She'd seen the fire in his eyes. The fire that fueled him. The fire that defined him. No matter the cost, he would see justice. She'd seen it before.

It was the same fire he had used to protect her.

Ele reluctantly handed over her bow.

"You know you can't stop them?" she cautioned.

"I know," his voice was distant. Mathus pulled an arrow from her quiver and climbed to the top of the city wall.

He nocked an arrow and drew the bowstring. The cogs turned at the bow's extremes.

Click. The cogs completed a revolution.

Each revolution pulled the bowstring tighter giving the arrow more power. Mathus eyed his target. He needed at least three revolutions to close the gap.

The ground shook as soldiers marched down the wall.

"Seize that boy!" shouted Sir Cador. His broken nose made him a frightful sight.

Click.

"What's going on!?" Ele insisted as the guards charged toward her brother.

Mathus didn't take his eyes off his target. He took a deep breath and let it out slowly.

"I'm showing mercy."

Click.

Calculating the distance, he adjusted his aim to pierce the woman's heart.

He had the shot.

A guard ripped the arrow from his bow. Mathus shoved the guard back. He tried to wrestle the arrow out of his hands. It snapped. Another guard grabbed him, and twisted Mathus' wrist, he sent the Cogbow skidding across the floor. Weaponless, Mathus landed a punch, knocking the guard over. A third guard tackled him to the floor. Mathus tried to kick him off, but the guard clamped himself around his leg. Mathus crawled and reached for the bow. He cried out in pain as his fingers crushed under the force of the Knight's heavy steel boot.

Mathus looked up at Sir Cador's raging face.

"If I were Lord Marshall, I would toss you out with the bitch!" the Knight erupted.

Click. Click. Click.

An arrow loosed from the castle wall. All eyes watched as it crossed the gap between the garrisoned guards and the Doya.

The arrow soared through the air. It peaked in the sky and plunged down, striking the Doya leader in the back. The arrow protruded out the front of his chest, stopping right before the woman's bulging belly.

The city stopped. Nothing moved. Nothing breathed.

The Doya looked down at the arrow. His was face painted in amusement. Thick inky blood poured down his abdomen. His three Doya companions cackled. He grabbed the arrow by its head and pulled it through the front of his chest. Like pulling a stick from mud, the flesh sucked closed, filling the wound with black scar tissue. He bellowed deep laughter and licked the arrow with his tar-covered tongue. A layer of oily saliva mixed with his ebony blood. The arrow dripped with greasy slime. Soot oozed from the Doya's mouth as he imbued the arrow with dark magic. He raised the arrow and released his grip. It flew from his hand with vehement force, crossed the battlefield, and hurtled the city wall.

The arrow found its mark in the archer who'd fired it.

"ELE!" Mathus broke free of his captors.

Ele looked at Mathus. Her lips trembled in wordless confusion as her small hand clenched the spelled arrow that stuck in her chest.

"I was just trying—" Ele fell into his arms.

"Shhh. Don't speak. I'll get you help," Mathus said. He gently scooped her up into his arms. "I'm taking you to the Healer's Sanctuary."

Sir Cador didn't try to stop him.

Mathus felt the icy sting of dread. In his mind, he pleaded to the One God, please don't let her die. He bounded down the stairs and through an alley that opened into the outskirts of town. Ele's face turned pale. Mathus' eyes welled with tears. With all his stubborn bravery, he couldn't summon the strength to let her go. Ele had to live.

"The Healers can help you, but you need to hold on," he told her. He could see the red dome of the Sanctuary in the distance, in the heart of the city.

Blood saturated her thick clothes. Her bottom lip quivered as she held tightly to his shoulder. Like all the dying, she spoke of the wisps.

"I can see them. They dance in the Afterlight. It's so beautiful."

"Stay with me, Ele," he pleaded.

Mathus could see the Sanctuary doors. They were incredibly tall but looked so small. They were still so far away. Ele was slipping. Desperately, he searched the nearby streets.

"Help?! Someone. Anyone. I need a Healer!"

Mathus felt Ele's tense muscles relax. The small hand that had been clenching the arrow went limp. Her arm fell dangling at her side. Her head rested softly on his shoulder, eyes open. She was dead.

Puddles of red turned the battlefield into a marsh of blood. The garrison watched the Doya through the steady rain. The leader of the Doya snatched 1289 by the throat. His dark eyes focused on her belly.

"It's true. The child protects her. Even from my magic," the leader said. The other Doya surrounded her. Black drool dripped from their wide toothy grins.

"Now. It's time to peel you open."

Extending a sharp claw, the leader pressed it under her rib cage. She could feel her skin split as he started to cut.

New Camelot with its mighty walls, tall towers, and an army of archers watched helplessly. No one dared to fire more arrows. And four Doya could kill hundreds of soldiers before the soldiers could even reach striking distance.

Alpha, the first sun, rose higher in the eastern sky. Soon the second, Omega, would break the rim of the skyline and the Doya would lose the dark morning shadows.

The great portcullis at the main gate rattled. Its clanking chains echoed throughout the city.

An Aurorean mage rode out on the back of a white horse. He had fair skin and thick arms. His long hair looked like tarnished silver and he had a short, neatly-kept beard. The man didn't look old enough to merit his graying hair, but the wisdom in his eyes was limitless. His muscular upper body just fit in his brown robes. The robes weren't elegant. They had a single purpose, to warn those who would oppose him that he wasn't just a mage. He was a Warlock, an Aurorean knight trained in the fast kill. They were masters of quick spells and deadly blades.

The Warlock had a long, golden sword hanging from his sword belt, and he hoisted a steel spear above his shoulder, ready to strike.

Doya scowled and cursed at the sight of the fast-approaching Warlock.

"Kill him," the Doya leader commanded.

Doya grabbed their throats and hissed out a spell. A thick black cloud shot out their mouths, followed by a blast of blue fire. The horse reared between the flames. The closest Doya swallowed and prepared to cast the spell again, but the Warlock threw his spear. It hit squarely in the creature's neck. The Doya fell to its knees. It tried to dislodge the blade, but the Warlock uttered a spell. The spear shattered. The creature's black, syrupy body gushed in every direction. Shocked, the three remaining Doya watched their companion splatter them.

The Warlock jumped from his horse. He drew his golden sword and severed the nearest Doya's head from his shoulders. The next Doya spoke words that made soot fall from its lips and small lightning bolts crackle through its claws. The Doya lunged and tried to grab him. But the Warlock spun out of the way and decapitated him from behind. Only the leader remained.

The Warlock recognized the Doya by his black tears.

"Sarod," he spat.

The dark mage dropped 1289. Shouting a magical word, he sucked a scythe from one of the dead slaves. His black eyes scanned the Warlock. Sarod knew him.

"Vallan. Do you still call yourself that?" Sarod growled.

Doya blood boiled off the Warlock's golden blade.

"You've crawled from the grave, again."

"You knew I would. Killing me only postpones the inevitable," Sarod hissed.

Vallan, the Warlock, gripped his sword with both hands.

"Have you come for revenge?" Vallan asked. He stepped closer, sword ready.

"I'm here for the child."

"This city is protected by the Order, and the suns are rising, Dark Prince." Vallan replied.

"I do not fear your Order, old man. Have you forgotten that I know what you really are?"

A wry grin spread across Sarod's face. "Leave the child with me or I'll tell them. All of them." Sarod pointed to the city. "What would they do if they knew what you really are? Would they protect you, or feed you to the evil that would devour this city?"

"You can't talk without a head." Vallan swung for Sarod's neck. Sarod blocked the blow with his scythe.

Sparks flew as their blades clashed. The Doya was abnormally tall. His long arms made it difficult for Vallan to get close. Vallan could feel the morning sun and its abundance of power. Soon the shadows of the battlefield wouldn't be enough for Sarod to cast even the most basic spells.

Sarod raised his right hand and made a fist. A flock of ravens surrounded Vallan. They clawed at his arms and snapped at his eyes. He shielded his face in the crook of his elbow. He shouted words of power and produced an enormous fireball. The birds immediately tore into the sky. They didn't get far before Vallan threw the ball of fire into their mass. The birds flailed and collided as the sticky flames spread like honey between them.

The garrison watched from their safe-hold. They pounded their weapons on the city wall creating a slow, dull beat.

Vallan twirled his sword as he circled Sarod.

"This will end, as it has so many times before," Vallan said.

He watched for an opening to take the Doya's head. Sarod tripped and tumbled into a pile of bodies. He thrust his arm under the corpses, finding shadow and darkness. Using power hidden in the shadows, he primed his magic, but there wasn't enough energy. He needed more. To amplify the power of the darkness, he searched for fear. He found it in 1289, who still quivered on the ground. Red-hot embers glowed under his milky skin. His arm emerged a raging inferno. Sarod exhaled a column of soot and thrust his fist into the ground. A wild trail of flames stampeded across the battlefield colliding with Vallan. His robes burst into flames. He dropped to the ground and rolled through a puddle. The flame smothered in the water and Vallan kicked himself to his feet. Smoke twisted as it rose from the charred patches in Vallan's robes.

Sarod's head cocked to the side.

"I've had centuries to wait between life and death. Centuries to wonder: What would happen if I took your head? Would your soul travel to the afterlife? Do you even have one?"

He lunged at him, arm ablaze, ready to burn Vallan's flesh from his bones.

In a blink, Vallan brought his sword down through the Doya's flaming wrist. Vallan's golden blade cut his hand clean off. Sarod shrieked, his own spell backfired and flames pumped through his veins. The pain sent Sarod into a fluttering fury. The muscles in his arms jerked. His arms and legs contorted. Feathers sprouted out of his skin as he transformed into a raven and vanished into the horde of birds.

1289 trembled on the ground, covered in scratches. Sarod's grip left deep holes in her stomach and a bloody gash on her forehead.

"Please, take me to New Camelot. Please save my baby," she pleaded.

Vallan scooped the slave woman up into his bulky arms and placed her on his horse. Once they were safe inside the city walls, the portcullis crashed shut.

"You!" shouted Master Durakos. He was an extraordinarily tall, rough-looking mage with burn scars covering his face and arms.

"You—You killed three. You might have started a war. And for what? An enemy slave? When the Council hears of this—" Durakos' voice drowned out as the guards cheered for Vallan, the Doyaslayer.

Vallan wandered through the streets, searching for the Healers.

A crowd of Healers recited prayers over a bedroll where Ele laid lifeless in the street. Mathus gently kissed her head and folded her arms as if he were posing a doll.

"She always liked the rain," he said to no one. Ele's skin was fair, even in death. Her mouth hung open, but he remembered the smiles that had once crossed her face. Her cocky smile always reminded him of their mother.

He would never see her smile again. Soon she would be a memory. Would he forget her face? Her smile?

Mathus took out a dagger and cut a lock of her curly hair.

"Can we move her?" the Healers asked as they made room for the slave woman.

Mathus saw Vallan approach, carrying the pregnant slave. Tears filled his eyes. He looked to Ele and then the slave. Anguish pulled at his insides.

Somehow he found the courage to nod.

Vallan placed the woman on the bedroll and moved aside so the Healers could gather.

"Wait," the slave insisted.

"My lady?" Vallan responded in Mayan.

"Will you stay? Stay with me until I die?"

Vallan nodded.

Healers knelt around the woman and placed their hands on her stomach. Using a collective ability, thoughts ran through the Healer's joint mind like ripples in a pond. United in thought, they each chanted different threads of magical words. Their tone and sequence weaved a complex spell. To the ears, it was more of a hymn than magic.

Mathus watched the last of the Doya blood boil off Vallan's sword. He held the spelled arrow that killed his sister in his hand. It still dripped with the same black blood.

"That arrow shouldn't be touched," Vallan said.

He tore a piece off his robe and carefully took the arrow. Vallan waved his fingers and a spell beaded the Doya blood off Mathus' palm and onto Vallan's golden sword.

"Doya use their corrupt bodies for dark magic. Their blood can mask vile spells." Within moments the Doya blood boiled on the sword until it disappeared.

"Did you kill their leader? The one that killed my sister." Mathus asked.

"No, Sarod still lives," Vallan responded. "Doya don't give up. Like darkness, they linger and wait."

"They'll be back?" Mathus grit his teeth, pushing back the tears.

"Sarod always finds his way back."

Mathus watched the guard carry his sister away. He clutched the lock of hair he'd taken between his fingers.

"Teach me how to kill them and, I swear, I will fight with you till my dying breath."

Vallan thought for a moment. The boy was young and rash. He didn't have the gift of magic. He wasn't even a proper soldier. But he had heart.

"Were your sister killed by a man, I would tell you to find it in yourself to forgive."

Mathus' voice was hoarse. "She was murdered by a monster."

Vallan saw the anguish in his grief-stricken face. The boy blames himself, he thought. Vallan knew his grief, evil had taken what was most precious to him.

There are some pains that even time can't heal.

The Grandmaster Healer, Daynin, helped administer to 1289. He was a heavyset man dressed in a long white robe with a beautifully embroidered Aurorean symbol on the chest.

As Vallan approached the group of Healers, Daynin turned his back to the woman.

Vallan surveyed his troubled face.

"How is she?" he asked.

Daynin opened his bloodied hands in a gesture of helplessness.

"The baby is tangled in the life rope."

Vallan looked over Daynin's shoulder at the woman. He saw the holes in her stomach. Holes from Sarod's dark magic. Without realizing it, he tightened his hand on his sword.

"The mother is too weak. We cannot save the child without killing the mother." Vallan could hear the pain in his friend's voice. Daynin understood what it was to be Aurorean, to cherish light and life.

Vallan found an empty spot and sat beside the woman.

"What is your name, fair lady?" Gently, he stroked the top of her hand.

"1289," she moaned.

"1289 isn't a name. Can I give you a name?"

Her eyes brimmed with tears. But not from childbirth. Her voice cracked.

"A name is such a precious gift. My child is safe thanks to you. You're too kind."

"Nonsense."

Vallan thought for a moment.

"You remind me of a beautiful queen from long ago named Asteera. She forsook everything for her child, just as you have. Does that name please you?"

She beamed.

"Then Asteera it is." Vallan pushed her sweaty hair from her face.

"Asteera?" Daynin addressed her.

"Yes?"

"Your baby is tangled. We can't save—"

"Many of my people are dead," she interrupted. "They were forced to attack your city or die. I was given the command. Yet the Mind Curse didn't harm me."

Vallan exchanged an intrigued glance with Daynin.

"I have no master. I dream. I walk on my own path. His Mind Curse has no power over me. But it wasn't my doing."

She lovingly rubbed her tummy.

"My child angel gave me dreams. This angel protects me from the Curse. Even now, I feel the Curse. It's trying to harm me. When my child is born I will be punished. I'll die."

Asteera's chin trembled, but not from pain.

"I'm here. I made it. In New Camelot, my child has a chance."

Vallan tried to respond, but labor took hold of her.

Daynin pulled a sharp knife from his Healer's bag.

"This child is immune to the Emperor's Mind Curse. We've been trying to break it for centuries."

There was only one way to save the baby. Asteera welcomed Daynin's knife.

She bore a son.

A crowd of common folk, guards, Healers, and mages gathered. The boy took his first breaths as Asteera watched her child squirm and cry. Vallan handed her the infant, so she could hold it before she died. She refused. Asteera could feel the power of the Mind Curse surface and reclaim her.

Her defiance couldn't go unpunished. She screamed and swatted at her head as she tried to shake off some invisible beast. The Healers watched helplessly. She writhed and shrieked. Then death silenced her. Daynin said a hushed prayer for her spirit.

Vallan used a towel to clean the baby. The tiny dark-haired infant opened its big eyes. The child looked up at him. A shiver when down Vallan's spine.

The child had black Doya eyes.

Something had gone very wrong. It was still a child. An infant. The innocent little face with its tiny nose and helped him look past the dark voids peering up at him.

"Oh, what a world to be born into, little one," he whispered.

Vallan washed and wiped the baby, but, for some reason, the baby wouldn't come clean. Then he realized the marks weren't going to come off. Gasping, he almost dropped the child. Vallan's face turned white. He focused on the baby's gentle face. There were strange marks under the infant's eyes. It was the symbol of the Aurorean order, but broken in half under each eye. He knew the sign. Everyone did.

It was the mark of the Doomseeker. The one prophesied to open the gates of hell and release the great demon. The one who would take the throne of darkness. The one who would kill the greatest of the sun gods.

Vallan took the child and ducked into the shadows of an alley. He called for Daynin to join him.

Daynin opened the blanket and saw the marks. He tried to stay calm, but couldn't keep his hands from shaking. As the knowledge crossed the channel of the Healers' Collective mind, they stopped tending to the wounded soldiers. Protests rang out as the injured and their families requested their assistance. Every Healer ignored the cries for help and crammed into the alley.

The child's big black eyes made Daynin squirm.

"I pray the child's soul isn't as black." Daynin wanted to look away. "There isn't a home in the city that will take a child with Doya eyes."

Daynin looked around at the other Healers. Vallan couldn't hear the words crossing their channel of collective thought, but he knew the child's black eyes were trivial compared to the marks he bore.

"He's marked. The Order will never let him live," Daynin said.

Vallan's voice became sober. "If they find out that we hid him, they *will* punish us." Vallan looked long and hard at Daynin. "They'll come for me and they'll come for you. The Council will rule us traitors."

"He's only a baby." Daynin ran his fingers across the infant's chubby cheeks. He wished to the gods the marks weren't there.

"The Emperor was a baby once. This isn't simply a marked child; there are two lesser marked. This is the Doomseeker, their leader. The ancient scriptures prophesy of the terrors he will bring," Vallan said. Daynin could hear the conflict in his voice.

They had just saved a damned child.

The Healers' collective feelings, thoughts, and opinions flowed freely to converge in Daynin. As the Grandmaster Healer, Daynin spoke for the Collective.

"Our Collective will bring him no harm." Vallan scanned the Healer's faces. He knew why they wouldn't kill the baby. The shattered conscience of one murderer shared across their mental connection would tear them apart. It wasn't much of a promise.

"The best of Auroreans, the Archmage himself, would murder this child, thinking it was justified to save our god and us from destruction," Daynin said.

Daynin looked out to his brothers and sisters in the Collective. A thought bubbled up from a Healer in the crowd. Daynin verbalized the words.

"Sharing a mind with hundreds has taught us that we are defined by our actions. Not thoughts or expectations. Not even prophecies. The Gods put us here to make decisions and this child is here to do the same. Who are we to question the wisdom of the gods?" The Healers nodded in agreement.

Daynin continued. "Give him a chance. Don't let him become that monster. If he chooses that path, we know you have the power to do what needs to be done." Daynin glanced at Vallan's sword. With a heavy nod, Vallan agreed.

Vallan put his index finger in the baby's tiny hand. The baby gripped it tightly. Vallan didn't know why, but, for some reason, that made him smile. Daynin pulled the blanket to cover the infant's face.

The assembly of mages attracted a crowd eager to see what the fuss was about.

"He needs a name," Daynin said. The second sun, Omega, had joined the first high in the sky, both shined brightly on Vallan's face, sparking an idea.

"The child shall be named Apollo. He is the first Mayan to breach our walls in two hundred and fifty years. In the womb, he has done the impossible. May he serve Avalon with that same audacity. Let him be a beacon of light in these dark times." The people of Avalon ignorantly cheered for the birth of Apollo. The birth of the Doomseeker.

3

Avalon - New Camelot

Apollo strained on his tippy toes to peek out the window into the side street. It was early and the people of the city were about their daily business.

First came Pots, or that's what Apollo called him. Yesterday morning he had pushed his handcart of clay pots through the alley. Apollo was pleased that he had decided to take his road again today. After all, it was a nice little street and Pots was an interesting man.

Pots' skin was darker than Apollo's, almost black, and when he smiled, which was quite often, he would flash his golden tooth. Vallan wasn't born with a golden tooth and neither was Apollo, so Apollo thought that Pots must have been very special. Pots seemed to know everyone, every time he saw someone he said: "Shlama," and they would reply: "Good day."

A metal man marched by next. His armor clanked with every step. His name was "Guard." Apollo had heard someone call him that. Everyone in the metal seemed to have the same name and they weren't very happy. They especially hated Sleepy Peat.

Of course Sleepy Peat wasn't his real name. Apollo wasn't really sure what his real name was. People called him Lazy, Stupid, Street Rat, Drunk—Apollo couldn't remember them all, and since there were so many, he chose to name him for what he did all day, Sleep, and Peat because that was the name of the street he slept on.

Sleepy Peat needed a bath. Apollo couldn't smell him from the second-story window, but he knew what dirty was and Peat was a very dirty man. The Guards didn't like him much. He never harmed anybody. Peat didn't do much of anything but sleep, of course, and rattle a cup with coins in it. Once one of the guards spit in his cup. Peat didn't like that. It was mean. The Guard shouldn't have done that.

"Apollo?" Vallan said sternly.

"Yes, father?"

Apollo turned from the window and looked up at Vallan with two wide, jet black eyes.

"What did I tell you about the window?"

Apollo slumped his head.

"You said not to look outside."

He was five years old and had never played in the daylight before. His only visitors were Daynin and Vallan and two old wooden beds in the corner and the rickety table by the stone hearth.

"Why can't I go outside? There are boys and girls out there. I want to play with them. We could play knights and dragons." Apollo puffed out his chest. "I could be a knight." He reached to his rope belt and unsheathed his wooden sword. He twirled in a flurry of swings and jabs that made Vallan smile.

"We talked about this."

Apollo lowered his weapon and ran a finger over one of his marks.

"Maybe I could scrub them off? You know, like that time I knocked over your ink bottle and it went everywhere. My hands turned purple, but we scrubbed them and look."

Apollo held his little hands up.

"They aren't purple no more."

A knock came at the door.

"Quick, into your bed."

Apollo hung his head.

"Quickly now."

Vallan gave him a nudge and Apollo plopped into bed and pulled the covers over his head.

When Vallan saw that Apollo's face was safely hidden, he cracked open the door.

The Land Lady, a short fat woman with three good teeth and a bun of wiry grey hair, peered in. She carried a tray with a few hard rolls, some butter, and a watery bowl of thin broth that smelled like chicken.

She bowed her head and tried to sound dignified, but it came out all wrong.

"How...how are you Master Warlock Vallan, sir?"

Vallan folded his arms. "I asked to not be disturbed."

The Land Lady shifted uncomfortably.

"Well...um...you see...You said your boy was sickly and...well...we thought, that is all of us, my brother and my uncle. When we're sick, we eat soup. It's not very good, but it will go down easy. I made it myself."

Vallan smiled graciously.

"Thank you."

He took the tray and set it on the table. As he did, the Land Lady stepped past him.

"Is that the poor dear?" she asked.

Apollo lay still under the covers. She could make out his outline in the sheets.

She cupped a hand over her mouth.

"He's just a little one," she gasped.

"Keep your distance," Vallan warned.

"Does he carry the plague?"

"No, but his fever is scorching, and the boils—"

"Boils?" She winced.

Vallan gently took her by the arm and escorted her to the door.

"He has terribly itchy boils as big as your fist." He balled up his fist and held it out to her.

"Oh, poor thing, that's wretched," she said with a shiver that made her chins wobble.

"The Healers said not to let people around him. I think it best if we took their advice."

The Land Lady nodded so profusely that her cheeks wobbled.

"We will pray for the poor dear."

As soon as Vallan closed the door, Apollo leaped out of bed.

"I don't have boils!" he blurted.

Another knock came at the door.

"Back to bed," Vallan said.

Apollo huffed and dove under his sheets.

Vallan opened the door, expecting to see the plump Land Lady once again. Instead, Daynin waited in the hall.

Vallan greeted the Grandmaster Healer with a traditional Aurorean greeting by placing his palm to his forehead and bowing.

"There is no need for that," Daynin said, slapping him on the back as he passed.

He lumbered through the doorway and took a seat at the table. Vallan bolted the door and joined him.

Daynin patted one of the empty seats. "Apollo, come sit."

Apollo barreled out of bed and leaped up into the chair. He snatched up a bit of hard roll from the tray and ripped off a bite that hung awkwardly out of his mouth.

"Master Daynin," he said through a mouthful. "What are boils?

"Boils?"

Daynin raised an eyebrow and Vallan shrugged.

"It's boils this time? You're running out of infirmities and quiet inns. You can't hide him away forever," Daynin said.

"I know," Vallan admitted.

They both looked at Apollo, who'd given up on the half-eaten hard roll. He took a spoonful of soup, smelled it, and then dropped it back in the bowl.

Apollo's skin was lighter and he had softer features than other Mayans. They'd guessed his natural father, whoever he was, had to have been of a fair-skinned race, which made his marks stand out even more.

"They caught another one of the Emperor's spies today," Vallan said.

Daynin nodded, "That's ten this year, but the Mind Curse kills them before they can be questioned. The Lord Marshall is certain the spies are looking for weaknesses in our defenses."

"What does the Council think the Emperor is after?" Vallan asked.

Daynin folded his hands on the table.

"Vega knows one of his slaves escaped. We've learned that much from our whisperers. The Emperor is having the three kingdoms reswear their allegiance. The Mind Curse is at the height of its power, yet Vega fears his curse is weakening."

"Is it?" Vallan asked.

"No, not from what I've learned from Apollo. Whatever power is in Apollo's blood is his and his alone. The Emperor's power is still as mysterious and absolute as ever."

Daynin leaned back and gave the room a critical look. The floorboards were warped and the walls mottled with pink and green paint. The window was wide and beams of sunlight shown through the thin grey curtains to illuminate grains of dust floating through the air.

"It's not much, but it's the last inn outside of Westport that doesn't know us," Vallan said.

"Have you thought about what you're going to do?" Daynin asked.

"We will stay here a few moon turns then move on again," Vallan answered.

"To where? Westport is no place for a boy to grow up, and people are starting to talk about the Mayan boy who never goes outside. There isn't room for secrets in this city. Rumors and lies are the bread and butter of New Camelot."

Vallan leaned back in his chair. Apollo had his wooden sword out and was about to attack a hard roll when Vallan snatched the sword away.

"Hey?" Apollo complained, but Vallan shot him a look that made him quiet down.

"I'd thought about heading South. The sandmen of Shem move throughout the desert never staying in one place too long. Our enemies would never think to look there. Many of the Sheminites still cling to the god of their fathers, and do not know of the Doomseeker prophecies."

Daynin nodded pensively.

"They're barbarians. They would take a Warlock to strengthen their tribe, even if he had a peculiar child," Daynin agreed, but there was hesitation in his voice.

"However, the desert is no place to raise a child. How can you teach Apollo right from wrong when your tribe is murdering for goats? And what of his gift? He doesn't show signs of it now, but the prophecies say he will be gifted, and gifted children need the direction of the Order."

Vallan raked his fingers through his silver hair. "There isn't a good answer. I have a boy that needs protecting and a world that wants to hurt him. I must keep him hidden and I can't hide him in this city much longer."

"There are different ways to hide," Daynin said.

He fished into the pockets of his robes, pulled out a tin, and slid it across the table to Apollo.

Apollo dropped the roll he was trying to tear apart, grabbed the tin and twisted it open; inside was brown clay.

Daynin's voice was almost boastful. "I call it Thetus Mud."

Apollo looked at it, smelled it, and set it aside. "Thank you for the mud," he said awkwardly and returned to his bread.

Daynin picked up the tin and set it in front of Apollo again.

"This is special mud. It makes it so you can go outside."

Apollo looked up wide-eyed. He glanced at Daynin's smiling face and then to Vallan's furrowed brow and then back to Daynin's grin.

"I can go outside?" he asked Daynin.

Vallan tried to interrupt.

"Give me a moment," Daynin insisted.

Daynin searched through his robes until he found a small mirror. He gave it to Apollo. Then he scooped up a wad of Thetus Mud on the end of his finger.

"Hold still," he said.

Apollo curled his lip as Daynin pressed the moist mud into his cheeks.

"It's the color of his skin and damp enough to last several hours without cracking. No one will ever be able to tell he's wearing it."

Apollo looked in the mirror. His mouth dropped. He turned his head left and right to inspect both marks. His cheeks were brown and smooth.

The marks were gone.

Apollo ran to the window and threw open the curtains.

"I'm going to play outside!"

Vallan instinctively jumped up from his chair and hurried to the window. He thought to scold him, but the excitement in Apollo's face stopped him short.

"You said that I can't go outside because they think my marks are scary."

Apollo held the mirror up high so Vallan could look in it.

"See, they're gone. I'm not scary anymore."

Daynin got up from his chair and went to the door.

"The mud will have to be reapplied every couple hours," he said.

Vallan wore a fragile smile.

"There are going to be a lot of questions. It will be dangerous and not just for Apollo—"

"Healers swear to protect life. I haven't broken any oaths. We're not just protecting Apollo; we're protecting the Council from a hard decision. They will get to know Apollo and maybe in time, they will learn to accept him. Then there will be no more secrets," Daynin said.

"How will I explain his eyes or where he came from?" Vallan asked.

Daynin shrugged.

"The Collective and I swore an oath to keep Apollo's secret. There are over a hundred of us, that's quite a task. I created a substance that covers Apollo's cheeks like a second skin. It's odorless and the perfect pigment. There isn't an apothecary in a thousand leagues that can do that. I think you can come up with a believable story for the boy."

Daynin turned the doorknob and paused.

"Start with the mother. You fell in love with her and had a son. You fought the Doya to save her. Memorize it, believe it, and see that Apollo does too."

Vallan turned back to Apollo, who was staring up at him.

"Can we go outside now?"

Vallan knelt so he was eye level with Apollo.

"You've been sick, but now you're better. Remember that," he said.

"Yes, I had marks, but now they're gone. I wished them gone—"

"Never speak of them," Vallan interrupted. "If you do, then you'll have to be locked up in this room again for your own good."

"I will never tell anyone," Apollo agreed with a nod.

"Now, you've been sick in bed. That's why you've never been outside," Vallan insisted.

"With boils!" Apollo chimed merrily.

"With the ugliest boils," Vallan laughed.

Vallan opened the door and Apollo rushed out. He wondered if Pots was still selling his clay pots in the street.

"Wait!" Apollo ran back into the room.

"Leave your sword," Vallan said.

"No, not that," Apollo whined.

He climbed up on a chair and grabbed one of the hard rolls. He tucked it under his arm and ran back to the door.

"Sleepy Peat might be hungry."

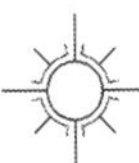

A fire breather upended a bottle of oil in his mouth and spit into his torch. A long stream of fire flashed over the crowd.

"Look at that!" Apollo exclaimed. "He's a dragon. A real-life man-dragon."

The crowd clapped enthusiastically. The fire-breather bowed to the left and to the right. Then he belted out another stream of lively flames that twisted through the air.

Apollo kept on clapping even after the crowd had stopped. He'd never seen a man do something so fantastic before. The fire-breather took another swig from his oil, turned to face Apollo, and nearly choked.

For a moment, the five-year-old and the stocky, red-faced performer looked at each other with an equal degree of astonishment. The performer stared into Apollo's black eyes and Apollo watched the clear oil leak out of his mouth.

"Is that how he does it? Is that oil?" Apollo asked Vallan, but he was too busy watching the Guards in the crowd to listen.

A monkey ran by. Its little feet were blurs on the street's cobblestone. Apollo forgot about the fire-breather. His attention was stolen by a gray monkey with a white beard and a ridiculous mustache. The monkey had stolen his trainer's cap.

The monkey trainer, a spindly woman in a fancy coat, chased him through the crowd and swatted at him with a crop. The monkey got a hard smack on the butt.

"That's what you get!" cried the trainer.

The monkey surrendered her hat, but just as she was about to take it, he threw it on the ground and jumped on it until it went flat.

"You little monster!" the trainer growled.

Apollo giggled.

"Did you see that?" Apollo asked Vallan. "What's that furry thing?"

The monkey trainer caught Apollo staring. She forgot about her unruly companion for a moment and stared back.

"What's he looking at?" she asked Vallan.

Vallan didn't answer.

"Hey, I'm talking to you," the trainer shouted.

Vallan tugged on Apollo's hand and they lost her in the crowd.

"That was a Bearded Monkey. It came from the Pirate Isles in the far east," Vallan said.

Apollo looked over his shoulder. He tried to spot the monkey, but there were too many people. He gave up and turned back to Vallan.

"I want to go there. I want to see islands and pirates and boats and people. I want to see everything."

"You might, you just might," Vallan said and playfully ruffled Apollo's hair.

They walked past a merchant booth selling herbs and another that sold candles.

"We're almost there. I want to show you the Temple. You can't go inside, but we can watch the great torch burn on the top."

Apollo wasn't listening; he was too busy waving at all of the people. There were so many more people here than on his street. He had to smile and wave to every one of them; that's what Pots would do, and Pots had a lot of friends.

The people in the crowd were starting to stare like the fire-breather and the monkey trainer had. They were probably staring because Apollo was new. After all, he had stared at Sleepy Peat the first time he saw him.

This moment, with the crowd staring and wondering where he'd been, was just how Apollo had imagined they'd greet him day after day from the windows of the inns he'd called home. He knew they'd be happy to see him. They passed a Guard who stopped his march to gape. He waved back at Apollo but didn't smile. Guards never smiled anyway. Apollo figured it was all of that metal they had to wear, it had to be heavy. He was sure that if he had a cup to shake at the guard; he wouldn't spit in it like a guard did to Sleepy Peat. After all, he was clean. He'd just suffered through a bath that morning.

"What's wrong with him?" a woman whispered.

Vallan gripped Apollo's hand tightly.

"Look at his eyes," said a young man.

Then the guard stepped in their way.

"What is this?" he demanded.

"This is my son, Apollo," Vallan replied.

The guard in the metal clothes examined him. Apollo wore a simple pair of pants and a loose brown shirt. He liked to wear brown. Warlocks wore brown; it made him feel tough like father.

The soldier kept glancing back at his eyes. Apollo waved again. He saw the metal man had a sword on his belt. He would've shown him his wooden sword, but it was back at the inn.

"Is there a problem?" Vallan asked.

"What's wrong with your boy?" the guard asked plainly.

Vallan hesitated. Apollo didn't.

"I was sick, but I'm better now," he said.

"Liar!"

A man scurried through the edges of the crowd on one good foot, a peg leg, and a crutch like a three-legged spider. He pointed a gnarled hand in Apollo's face. Apollo flinched.

"I know this boy," he said. "And I know *him*," he hissed at Vallan. "I saw him take the boy's mother from the Doya years ago."

Vallan felt the eyes of the crowd on him, he didn't know what to say.

The peg-legged man continued: "You can't hide a Mayan boy in this town. I'm a bloodhound to their slave stench. One of their spears took my leg. I was a soldier, a respectable one, now look at me."

The man waved the nub of his leg stump in front of Apollo.

Apollo gasped and clung to Vallan's leg.

"That's *enough*," Vallan protested.

"We kill Mayans, we don't take them in." He pointed his crutch at Apollo. "It's clear to me what this boy is. Look at him. His mother was the Doya's whore."

Vallan reached out to snatch the man by his collar, but the Guard blocked him.

The cripple straightened his hunched back and puffed out his chest.

"I won't stand for it. This city isn't a nursery for the bastards of our enemies!"

"He has the eyes of a devil," a woman whispered.

"Don't look in its eyes. It's bad luck. They can steal the soul right out of you," said one of the street artists.

"He is my son," Vallan retorted, but his words were nothing. The crowd started yelling and reaching out for him.

"Best be on your way," the soldier said, placing his hands on his sword belt.

"Take your monster with you and go far, far from here," the cripple spat.

Apollo's eyes welled with tears. This wasn't how it was supposed to be. They were supposed to be happy to see him. He was to be greeted like he'd seen from his window. A smile and a wave, that was all.

Apollo looked up at Vallan's tight jaw. He was angry, so angry.

"I am a Warlock of the Aurorean order. This is my son," he barked. "We are both citizens and we have every right to be here."

Everyone was unhappy, and Apollo knew it was all his fault.

Apollo got a lump in his throat. Warm tears ran down his cheeks. He couldn't let them see him cry. He had to be brave. He had to get back to his room. He would be safe there.

The soldier pointed back the way they'd come.

"Mind your brat."

Vallan looked down to where Apollo had been hugging his leg, but he was gone.

Apollo ran as fast as he could. He had to get back to the inn. He'd be safe there in the dark, peering out the window. There the people couldn't see him. Tears streamed down his face. A lump caught in his throat.

Why were they so mean? What was wrong with him? Why did they say such mean things about his mother? He wasn't sure what a "whore" was, but it sure sounded like a mean word. Why didn't his father make the bad spidery man leave?

The thought of the man's face made Apollo run even faster.

He turned down an unfamiliar ally that curved until it ended in a courtyard. The inn was around here somewhere.

Apollo ran through the courtyard. He passed hearty chestnut trees and found an enormous building, bigger than the inn, bigger than anything in the whole world.

"Apollo?" shouted a woman in a white robe. Her robes were just like Daynin's.

Apollo stopped running to catch his breath. He sniffed away his tears, but they kept coming.

"I don't know you, go away," he cried.

The Healer captured him in her arms.

"Let me go!" Apollo cried.

He tried to wiggle free.

"I know you. Daynin wants you to be safe. He told me that," said the Healer.

Apollo stopped squirming. "He did?" Apollo sniffled.

"I know everything Daynin knows," she said. "Where's your father?"

Apollo hung his head; a tear fell off his chin.

"Are you lost?" she asked.

"No."

"Then, where are you?"

Apollo folded his arms and looked around.

"I'm away from the mean people and I'm not going back there, not ever."

The Healer gave him a doleful look and scooped him up.

Apollo threw his arms around her neck and laid his head on her chest. The tears had stopped, but he couldn't catch his breath. He wiped at his eyes.

"Don't wipe. You don't want to smudge your face," she said.

The Healer examined his cheeks. She pushed the mud on his cheeks around, Apollo could feel her re-spreading the remaining mud over his marks. She checked him a final time, and carried him into the massive building.

"Do you know what this place is?" she asked.

Apollo looked up from the Healer's shoulder. The walls were all stone and bigger than him. The ceiling was painted with a picture of a sleeping man with a Healer and an angel standing over him. The angel's wings cradled all three of them and on its head was a bright ring that sent beams of light outward.

"Who's that?" Apollo pointed up at the angel in the mural.

"That's an angel. Do you believe in angels?" she asked.

"Do they really have wings like that?" Apollo gave the wings a suspicious look.

"I don't know, I've never met one," she answered.

In the next room, Apollo spotted another angel, but this time it was a female with strands of silky, white hair and her eyes were white, completely white like Apollo's were black. She was tending to a crowd of people. At their head was a man in a crown surrounded by metal men with brightly color shields.

"That's King Arthur and his Knights. They built this place. It's called the Healer's Sanctuary. You are always safe here," said the Healer.

She took him down some stairs to a room of never-ending, stone pillars. Torches illuminated small parts of the vast chamber.

"Listen," she whispered.

"Good day!" she shouted. The words echoed back.

"Good day...Good day...Good day."

Apollo looked over her shoulder. Then to the left and to the right the sound came from everywhere.

"It's an *Echo,"* she said.

"Echo...Echo...Echo," the chamber repeated.

"Is it magic?" Apollo whispered.

The Healer laughed. "Go on, you try."

Apollo hesitated for a moment, and then he shouted.

"GOOD DAY!"

"GOOD DAY...Good day...Good day," the chamber repeated.

A girl peeked out from behind one of the pillars.

"Good day," she said.

Apollo's mouth dropped open.

The girl's blonde curls bounced as she skipped out from behind the pillar. She was older than Apollo and wore a petite Healer's robe.

She walked right up to him and placed her hand on her hip.

"I'm princess Clara and this is my castle," she announced in a sing-song voice.

The Healer gave Clara a warm smile and put Apollo down beside her.

"Princess Clara, I'm entrusting you with Apollo, the Knight of Peat Street. He's a very just and chivalrous knight, see that he's treated with honor and all sorts of knightly respect."

Apollo straightened and bowed chivalrously.

"I am honored—"

She interrupted him.

"You may kiss my hand, Knight of Peat," she said, holding it out to him.

Apollo puckered and went to kiss it, but just as he got close enough, she giggled and snatched her hand away.

"Hey! Wanna go catch bugs with me?" she blurted and ran off into the chamber.

Apollo watched her run off. He gave the Healer a look of uncertainty.

"Well, go get her," she insisted.

Apollo ran into the dimly lit chamber. Clara jumped out from behind another pillar.

"They have glow bugs down here. Big ones!" she squealed and took his hand.

She dragged him through the chamber to a seat where the pillars were covered in green stuff and water pooled on the floor.

"Sit here," she instructed.

Apollo sat down beside her without argument.

"Don't talk. If you talk they won't sing for you,"

"Sing for me?" Apollo repeated in a reverent tone.

"Shhh!" Clara clapped Apollo's mouth shut.

The echoes stopped mumbling.

"Listen," she whispered in the tiniest voice.

Faintly, in the distance, Apollo could hear a low hum. A green light flashed and the high pitched ting of what sounded like a knife tapping on glass followed. Then the light and the sound were gone.

"Wow!" Apollo exclaimed.

"Be quiet stupid, you're going to scare them away."

A red light flashed with a lower tone, then a purple one with another, a pink one, a yellow one, and soon the whole chamber was blinking light and filled with a wild song of erratic notes.

"Sometimes I catch them and they sing just for me," Clara whispered.

"Clara?" Apollo asked.

"Princess Clara," she corrected.

"Princess Clara," Apollo shifted nervously. "Aren't you afraid of my eyes? Aren't they scary?"

"Scary? No, they're not scary. My father was scary. He's gone now. He can't hurt anyone anymore. They say my mommy isn't scared of him anymore. Daynin said she is in a better place where no one can hurt her."

"You know Daynin?" Apollo asked.

"Of course I do," Clara replied.

"Daynin doesn't think my eyes are scary," Apollo whispered.

"I don't think they're scary either, I think they're neat. I had a dog with two legs. He was neat too. We called him Sweep, because as long as we had him we never had to clean the floor. He was my favorite dog."

"Clara, will you be my friend?" he asked.

"Sure!" Clara grinned.

Apollo's smile brimmed. Not only did he have a friend, but she was also the most interesting person in the whole world.

"Hey, wanna know a secret?"

"Yea," Apollo nodded.

"I'm only pretending to be a princess, but I have the gift. I think that's better than being a princess. They thought I was sick because my heart hurt so much, but then the Healers taught me to make magic."

"Really? I wish I could do that," Apollo said.

"Yeah, it makes me more special than you. It's okay, though. Not everyone can be special, otherwise, nobody would be special. That's what special is."

"Can you do magic? Can I see it?" Apollo asked.

Clara rolled her eyes.

"You don't know anything about magic. I can't do it down here. It's too dark. I need light. I'm going to be a Healer. If I was a Healer, I could've saved my mother and she wouldn't be with the gods right now. She'd be with me."

Apollo thought of his mother. He'd visited her place in the catacombs. Vallan took him there once a year to talk to her. He'd always wondered what she was like.

"Do you think my mother is with the gods?" he asked.

"Is she dead?" Clara asked bluntly.

Apollo nodded.

"Well, good, she can't be with the gods if she's not dead. Did she die well?"

"I think so. She died when I was born."

"You have to die with the gods in your heart to get to heaven. The Sun God has to like you, too. That's what Grandmaster Durakos told me." Clara pulled a dangling curl out of her eyes and tried to tuck it behind her ear. "I'm going to live with the gods too. Well, when I die. I have to. My father is in the Otherworld and I don't want to see him again. He's mad at me. Hurting a lady is bad, don't you think so?"

Apollo nodded. "I want to be a Warlock. They're good too and they get to go anywhere they want. They even get to see monkeys. I know, my father is a Warlock, he's seen everything."

Clara's eyes went wide.

"Your father is a Warlock?"

Apollo puffed out his chest proudly.

"Yep, he's got a brown robe the same as my shirt and he has a sword too. I have a sword. It's only wood, but I can swing it really fast."

Vallan's voice came from somewhere behind them. "Apollo?"

The song of the light bugs died and the light in the chamber returned to yellow torchlight.

Vallan reached the side of the pool.

"Is that your father?" she whispered.

Apollo nodded.

Clara hopped to her feet and curtsied.

"Good day Sir. Be kind to him. This kingdom only has one knight to protect my pool and my glow bugs, and there are quite a lot of bugs," she said and marched off.

Vallan sat down and put his arm around Apollo. When he spoke, he wasn't angry. There was softness in his voice.

"I know I'm not your real father, but I'm trying. The people out there. They're wrong about you. You know that, right?"

"Am I evil?" Apollo asked.

Vallan pulled the tin of Thetus Mud from his pocket and gave it to Apollo.

"My eyes are different, and no one else has to hide marks."

"Do you remember the story I told you of your mother?"

"That man said she was a 'whore.' What's a whore?" he asked.

"That man said a lot of awful things. He didn't know your mother. He was just trying to hurt you. Sometimes people try to hurt others because they're unhappy."

"He didn't look very happy," Apollo agreed.

"I knew your mother. She was a brave woman. She stood up to Sarod and she didn't have a sword or magic," Vallan said.

"And you saved her from Sarod. You were a hero like Wythrin, the elf king. You fought Sarod, the Dark Prince. That was brave. I want to be good like that."

Vallan picked Apollo up and set him on his lap.

"You saved your mother from the Mind Curse. It's a blood curse, an evil curse that no one in hundreds of years has been able to break. You, little baby Apollo, saved her from it."

That made Apollo smile. The mud on his cheeks was starting to crack off. Vallan pulled open the can of mud and reapplied it.

"You defied the evil Emperor. Doesn't that make you like Wythrin, the golden knight, who freed his people from Sarod's reign?"

Apollo's beamed up at him. Vallan ruffled his hair and grinned.

"See you're a hero. The world just doesn't know it yet."

4

Avalon - New Camelot

Sunlight came pouring through the arched window. Vallan unbuttoned the top buttons of his Warlock robe and peeled the sweat-soaked cloth open to let air in.

The two suns were their hottest this time of year and the nights were shorter. The People of Avalon had two seasons; the farmers named them Sow and Yielding. It was the third moon of Yielding, and a time to pray for rain. The crops were nearing harvest. Those who prayed to the One God would plead for blessings and a reprieve from famine. The many who prayed to the Sun God would pray that their crop would honor him. The more devout even offered up portions of their crops as burnt sacrifices.

Vallan took his seat by Apollo's bedside. He was seven now.

Time had always seemed like a burden to Vallan. He'd lived so long that he had felt like a rounded stone in a riverbed. Time flowed by, people lived and died, and none of it seemed to matter. He had been a rock, apart, constant, unmoved.

Then Apollo had entered his life and Vallan felt as if he'd been pulled from the riverbed and skipped across the surface of the water. Time moved by too quickly now. Apollo was seven, and it had seemed like yesterday when Vallan had saved his mother from Sarod.

Over the past seven years, he'd convinced himself that he'd done the right thing. Now, looking down at Apollo sick and suffering in his bed, he wasn't so sure.

Apollo had been through a lot for a boy. Even with time, the people of the city hadn't learned to accept his Doya eyes. He'd spent most of his youth apart from the townsfolk, either with Vallan or Clara. He was a dreamer. He'd read every book he could on the four kingdoms, the pirate isles, distant lands, and magical creatures. Vallan didn't know if Apollo was simply curious or if he longed for a place where he would be accepted.

Apollo grabbed at his chest and his face twisted in pain. Sweat dripped down his brow.

Breathing was a struggle.

His heart was drawing power from the light and the darkness. So much that his heart was straining under pressure.

If Vallan taught him to control that power, he could use it to fulfill his destiny. Was he failing again? Could he bear to lose another son?

Vallan thought of his son, his own blood, from days long past, and his wife, a radiant beauty with the most exotic green eyes he'd ever beheld.

He could still feel the venom in her words: "I'll *never* forgive you. You did this. You took my son from me."

The door creaked open and Daynin stepped in. He pulled out a vial of liquefied Hawthorn root and dripped its contents between the gap in Apollo's lips. Apollo coughed and swallowed.

"Thank you," he wheezed.

Daynin glanced over at Vallan. "He's going to be all right. Hawthorn will help slow his heart."

Vallan's frown was chiseled in his face. He was a gargoyle at Apollo's bedside.

"He needs to be trained to control his gift," Daynin said.

"You know what you're saying. The nights are the worst." Vallan tried to push the curtains back farther so more sunlight could enter the room. He crossed his arms, sat down in a chair, and stood back up.

"He's a dark mage," Daynin stated. Vallan winced, he didn't like hearing the words said aloud.

"Some still believe in the old ways when light and dark mages worked side by side." Daynin continued. "The Council believes he's your son, born from a Mayan woman that you met on your travels. This would just be another secret, and with Apollo, lies are easier than truths."

Vallan nodded. He dabbed Apollo's head with a damp rag and reapplied a thick layer of Thetus Mud to his sweaty cheeks. He spoke with wistfulness in his voice.

"I'd thought if he didn't have the gift, then the prophecies haunting him couldn't be real."

Daynin scratched his chin.

"We all fear for Apollo's future. The gods can be wrong."

"The gods have never been wrong," Vallan said.

Vallan searched Apollo's seven-year old, sunbathed face as if the answers to his doubts were hidden on it.

"I'm afraid that one day I will have to be the one to stop him," he said.

"I believe in the prophecies as well, but you can't forget there is a reason for his birth and for our laws. The gods gave them both to us. All we can do is try to teach him how to live and hope for the best."

Vallan pulled a Garatha from the bedside table and thumbed through it.

"Do you know what the next prophecy is?"

Vallan held the book out to him. Daynin read the verse out loud.

The fire will know him. The throat of hell will swallow him, and in hell, he will face one of the lost children of the Gods. He will battle that fiend, and when his blood is spilled on the ground, what was strong will become weak, and what was prized will be lost. In that day, you will know that it is the beginning of the end of the laws of the Great Sun God.

Daynin stopped abruptly. The door pushed open and Clara stepped in. She pulled back the hood of her white Healer's robe and shook out her blonde hair. She was only nine and still learning the basic forms of medicine and magic, yet she insisted on tending to Apollo.

"Are you still giving him the Hawthorne root?" she asked.

Daynin handed her the vial. Clara snatched it and leaned over to examine Apollo.

She bit the inside of her cheek as she thought. After a moment, she looked in his mouth and nodded, pried open one eye, and nodded again.

"He should be drinking this every half hour," she said.

Grandmaster Miriam stepped through the open door. She squinted in the bright room and located a chair by Apollo's bedside.

Grandmaster Daynin reached for her arm to help her across the room.

"I'm old. I'm not a cripple," she growled.

Miriam's knees cracked as she lowered into the chair. Her green Oracle robes hung off her shoulders like a sheet draped over a sapling.

"He doesn't look well," Miriam said.

"He'll be fine," Clara snapped.

"I've seen a mage's heart burst. It's a gruesome specticle. Let me meditate with him awhile. I will teach him a simple spell to relieve the pressure in his heart."

Vallan looked to Daynin for an answer, something to stop all of this.

"You can't suppress the gift," Daynin said. "Miriam understands his sensitivity to the darkness. She's here to help."

Apollo's face was twisted, chin trembling. Vallan couldn't lose another child. He would make this right.

"I will train him, he's my son."

5

Avalon – New Camelot

"What do you mean you want to see one?" Clara asked.

"I want to see a Doya, a real one," Apollo said.

"I've seen what they can do." Clara prodded Apollo in the chest. "One flick of their claw can cut you open so fast, you'll see your own heartbeat before you die."

"Stop being such a mouse," Apollo teased. "They're in a cage. It's not like they can get out. There are guards everywhere."

Apollo's mother had faced a Doya to save his life. It had been fifteen years and Vallan still told the story of his mother's courage with fervor. He wanted to understand what she faced, what the world thought he was.

Apollo and Clara passed wagons piled to the brim with barrels and goods. Clara had to hold her breath as they passed a wagon that stunk of fish. They passed a wagon completely filled with animal skins, and another with twenty barrels of apples. When they reached the back of the caravan, they saw the prisoner wagon. It was an iron bear cage with wheels attached.

They walked in a wide arc around the iron cage. It had a single door in the back locked tightly with a thick steel padlock. The carriage was constructed of heavy iron bars and hay was scattered on the cage floor.

He saw a person on the far end of the cage with a black cloak pulled over his head. As far as Apollo could tell, he looked normal.

Clara pointed to a man in the cage. "There you've seen one. Are you happy?"

A woman fell from the top of the cage. Clara grabbed onto Apollo, who watched as the woman twisted and with cat-like agility land in the hay. Hunched, with her head cocked, she studied him curiously.

She was dressed like a noble in a white dress with a crimson sash.

She walked seductively toward him, swinging her hips with each step.

Apollo's heart pounded in his ears. He should run, but he didn't want to. He needed to know what evil did to a dark mage. He wanted to see her.

"She's corrupted," Clara whispered to Apollo.

The Doya got closer. Her hair was in knots and her dress was open, so her breasts were nearly hanging out. Her skin was pale and she had the darkest brown eyes Apollo had ever seen.

"I am called Cat," she purred. Inky dribble came from the corner of her mouth. She wiped it away with her hand.

She had black scars on her hands.

"Look at her hands," Clara said. "She cuts herself."

"My fingers itch," Cat pouted. She pushed her hand through the bars. They were dainty things, scarred, but not unsightly.

Cat used a finger to bid Apollo to come closer. "Come here, Black Eyes. You belong in here with your kind. Come in the cage with me."

Cat strutted back to the cloaked man. She bent over and ran her hand across his shoulders.

"Cedric here is so serious. He's no fun. If I'm going to the Chasm forever, I want to have some fun first," Cat said, pointing to the man at the back of the cage.

Cat tilted her hips in Apollo's direction.

"She's disgusting, let's go," Clara insisted. She grabbed Apollo by the arm, but before they could leave, Lord Marshall Mathus appeared at the head of a group of three soldiers, all in red leather armor. He pointed to Cat and Cedric.

"Keep them quiet. We don't know what spells they can conjure." The soldiers beat a fist to their chests in a salute and took positions around the cage.

"What did she do?" Apollo asked.

Mathus walked right up to the cage. The man called Cedric watched him from the shadows of his hood. Cat spun and hissed.

"They're murders. Their words are filth, poison to the mind. Given a chance, they'd kill us all."

"Not all of you," Cat purred. "I like Black Eyes, he's different, he's pretty." She decided happily.

Cat ran her finger down her face and between her pale breasts. Apollo tried not to look. Clara's lip curled.

"Keep away from them, the Corrupted are just weaker Doya. There's no good in them. The King ordered them sent to the Chasm."

Apollo looked at Clara and then Mathus.

"They do not have eyes like me. I thought that they would." Apollo admitted.

"Apollo," Clara tugged on his arm. "You're a good man. Black eyes and all."

Apollo nodded.

"Can I have a moment with him?" Mathus asked Clara.

"Be careful." Clara gave Apollo a quick hug. She shot a glare back at Cat and left.

"Vallan trained us," Mathus turned away from the cage and put his hand on Apollo's shoulder. "You're my brother. I know the face of darkness. I've seen it. It's not you. Vallan thinks it's important to take you to the Chasm. Be careful. It's a pen for these demons."

Barrels jostled in the wagon beds as the caravan rumbled down the uneven road. They'd already stopped to fix one broken wheel, yet they were still making good time. With a little luck, they'd be nearing the border by nightfall.

Apollo rode alongside the group. He wasn't much of a rider, he'd only ridden a horse a time or two before. He'd spent most of his time in the city. Vallan took a caravan to the Chasm every year. He never talked about it. Apollo didn't know why Vallan was taking him this time, but he wasn't going to argue. There was a whole world out there to see and he'd never gone out of sight of the city gate.

The Black mountains glistened like an onyx stone to the south and the Gaia forest decorated with vibrant yellows and reds surrounded them. Rolling hills gave the forest a fiery brilliance, as brisk winds shook the trees, waving the glowing pigments like the flicker of flames. Warm sunshine came through the forest canopy as the caravan traveled down the old, dirt road.

The smell was different here, Apollo thought. In New Camelot, the city streets carried the stink of chamber pots and the people smelt of sweat. Before each meal, bakeries and kitchens cooked up an aroma that mixed with the odor to make the stink more bearable. Out in the woods, the air was crisp. Apollo took a deep, savory breath.

In the distance, to the north, Apollo could barely make out the edge of the Chrons, a mountain range named after Chronos, the mighty titan. He'd only seen the Black Mountains. Apollo had read about the Chrons, and even seen them on maps. He'd always thought all mountains were black. The Chrons looked almost blue on the horizon; it was difficult to tell where the sky ended and the mountains began.

Grandmaster Rhean and Vallan were riding at the front of the group. Rhean, the Small Giant, was so large that his horse looked like a mule underneath him; his reins were as small as shoelaces in his hands. Rhean had to be nearly seven feet tall, Vallan had to incline his head just to speak with him.

Grandmaster Rhean and Vallan had been good friends for as long as Apollo could remember. They'd often sparred together in the temple courtyard. Their styles of fighting were practically opposite. It was Rhean's strength and reach against Vallan's speed and agility. Their duels always attracted a crowd. Some even took bets on who would win. Games of chance were against temple rules, but that didn't stop Grandmaster Miriam from being the temple bookie.

Rhean waved his arms, they were arguing. Vallan was adept at making his leaders angry, but Apollo wondered what Vallan could've said to make Rhean so upset.

Apollo drew closer to listen.

"The Gods warned us for a reason. We have prophecies. Is there greater proof than the words of the prophets?" Rhean spat.

"We don't always understand prophecy," Vallan responded respectfully, but the edge of his voice told Apollo he was reaching the limit of his patience.

Rhean shifted rigidly on his horse.

"The Council wants answers. They want to see the Marked for themselves."

Apollo's jaw dropped open. What kind of answers? He didn't have any. Did they know who he was? He dabbed his fingers under his eyes. The Thetus Mud still covered his marks.

What would the Council do to him if they knew the truth?

He had to get control of his fear. He knew skilled mages could sense emotion almost as easily as they could feel the sunlight. It was a tool they used to amplify their Well Energy.

Fear was a potent emotion, one that Doya thrived on. Master Warlocks could sense it with pinpoint precision. Apollo tried to push it away. He tried to think of anything else. His lessons, the Chrons, Clara's smile.

"The Archmage wants them dead or alive, but it doesn't matter. If I don't kill them the Council will," Rhean muttered.

Apollo felt a shiver run down his spine. It all but screamed to the mages. Rhean and Vallan halted their conversation and turned to confront him.

"I…um…I was just," Apollo said.

Rhean's glare bore into him.

"What are you so afraid of boy?" he asked. Rhean scanned his face.

Vallan nudged his horse between them and gave Apollo a stern glance.

"My son has never been this far from the city."

"Your fear stinks, boy." Rhean spat. "Get a handle on it. Doya are hard enough to fight as it is. We don't need a coward feeding them."

Apollo returned the Grandmaster's contemptuous stare. Rhean was bigger and more powerful, but at that moment it didn't matter. Apollo's oily black eyes flared open like an endless abyss prepared to devour Rhean whole.

Apollo was no coward. Rhean didn't know what it was like to wake up every day and be a dark mage with a grim destiny. He didn't have to hide from zealots just to survive. He didn't study scripture only to learn of the atrocities the gods expected him to commit.

Vallan gave Apollo an order before he could say something he'd regret. "Apollo. See to Grandmaster Miriam. She's falling behind." Vallan pointed to an elderly Sheminite woman beyond the wagons at the rear of the group. Apollo halted his horse and waited for Miriam to catch up, refusing to drop his venomous stare.

Apollo had known Miriam since he was seven. They'd become good friends over the years. She instructed him in ancient scriptures almost as fervently as Vallan instructed him in magic. Together, Vallan and Miriam had taught him how to control his gift despite their inability to use dark magic.

Apollo knew Miriam to be a wise yet stubborn old woman. She had her way of doing things and that was, of course, the only correct way things should be done.

When Apollo saw her sour expression and heard the curses she was muttering under her breath, his mood lightened. Miriam shifted bitterly in her saddle, hopelessly searching for a comfortable position.

"Dragon spit! How do you sit on these rock hard beasts all day?"

"You've never ridden a horse?" Apollo asked.

"Well, of course, I've ridden a horse. It's just been a long time."

"How long?"

"Long before you were born," Miriam huffed. "The last one I rode was when I left Shem and came to New Camelot."

Apollo's eyebrows went up. Miriam was old, very old. Most of the Grandmasters were. Powerful Aurorean mages lived much longer than normal humans. It was the use of light magic that rejuvenated their bodies. The more power they absorbed, the slower they would age. The head of the Council, Archmage Lorad, was just under three-hundred years old. Apollo had no idea Miriam was even older than him.

"You left Salem when the Emperor conquered it. Wasn't that three hundred years ago?"

"Yes, and I swore I'd never ride another one of these flea-ridden, smelly creatures again," Miriam snorted.

"The Chasm is still a long journey. Vallan says it can take weeks with these wagons, but only a few days on horseback. The road gets a lot rougher north."

"Then it's a good thing I'm not going to the Chasm," Miriam said.

Apollo's brow furrowed. "I thought we were all going to the Chasm? Why *did* you leave the library?"

Miriam didn't answer.

"The road is an odd place for the Grandmaster Oracle," Apollo added.

"The road is no place for an Oracle." Miriam agreed. "We belong in the library with a pile of books and hot tea. If the Archmage hadn't requested that I go on this journey, then that's where I'd be. In a book with nothing but silence and a cup of hot tea." The thought made Miriam smile for the first time all morning.

Apollo watched Wislan, who rode only a few strides ahead. He was a Warlock with the blonde hair and blue eyes of a Pendragon and the royal pompous attitude that came with it.

"You're traveling with Rhean and Wislan?" Apollo asked.

Mirium nodded.

"Why would the Archmage send an Oracle on a journey with two Warlocks?" he asked.

Miriam gave Apollo her crooked instructor's smirk. He knew it well. It meant he'd asked the right question.

"Curious indeed. Archmage Lorad promised them the company of the Oracle with the most knowledge of the old prophecies. In particular, the prophecies concerning the Marked."

Wislan pulled his horse to a grinding halt. Miriam's steed slid to a stop behind him, nearly knocking her off.

"That's enough, Miriam," Wislan warned. "The Archmage swore us to secrecy."

Miriam's lively, brown eyes assessed him. Stewing in Wislan's disrespect, she forced a smile through her clenched teeth. "Secrecy, bah, what is an Oracle but a pioneer for uncovering secrets?"

"Despite our callings, Warlock or Oracle, we took an oath of silence. It's understandable. You probably don't remember. It's a wonder you can remember anything at your age." Wislan kicked his horse to join Rhean and Vallan at the front.

"That's GRANDMASTER to you!" Miriam shouted indignantly.

Her mouth ruffled into a sneer. "That little snot-nosed, pink-eared coddle! He crawls up from an Apprentice and thinks he can tell me what to do. *Me*! The Grandmaster Oracle. Can't remember anything! I recall more in a day then that straw-brained twit will ever learn. If Rhean wasn't so fond of him, I'd cast a spell to mess with his feeble mind. Why I'd have him on all fours barking like a mutt and smelling every ass from here to Atlantis."

Apollo chuckled at the thought.

"What's in Atlantis?" Apollo pried. Miriam quickly changed the subject.

"Do you know why I became an Oracle?"

"No."

"I considered the other branches of the Order. I never had the patience to become an Enchanter. Working for several years just to make a trinket didn't interest me. Healers, like your friend Clara, must join the Collective mind. Sharing my thoughts with others would probably cause more harm than good."

Apollo agreed with her on that.

"Sorcerers are far too serious. The idea of casting spells for hours at a time didn't appeal to me. And Warlocks…" Miriam held out her skinny, brown arms. "Could you see me in a battle with these muscles? I've seen more meat on a chicken leg."

Miriam giggled at her own joke and continued.

"I almost became a Creator. Writing new spells and studying old ones fascinated me, but as time passed, I realized what I really enjoyed was books. I love the feel of their ancient pages, their smell, and above all, the endless possibilities waiting in their texts. When I discovered the prophecies, I never stopped reading. Each is so complex and dependent on so many factors that I found it intriguing that an ancient prophecy had never been wrong.

No magic is as certain or as old as prophecy. It takes many years to acquire knowledge to reveal the secrets hidden right before us. As an Oracle I would have the ability to train my mind to recall my preciously learned knowledge. That's why I became an Oracle."

"Can you really recall *all* that knowledge, everything you've ever learned?"

"Not everything. I can't recall things I learned before training my aura."

Most of Apollo's training had taught him how to listen to his aura. Gifted or not, all creatures have an aura.

The un-gifted understood the aura as a voice of warning, or a subtle prompting of danger or misfortune. The aura of the gifted is much more complex. The use of the aura is the only skill that separates one branch of Aurorean Magic from the next. Every lesson Vallan taught focused on it.

For a Warlock, the aura was a type of magical intuition capable of warning of complex dangers. Master Warlocks, like Vallan, could even use their auras in combat to anticipate the physical actions of another. It keeps them one step ahead, which makes it nearly impossible for Apollo to best him in a duel, but that doesn't keep him from trying.

Apollo caught a glimpse of the prisoner wagon. It was in the middle of the caravan, which was a good ways off. One of the prisoners was watching him. He used his hand as a visor to block out the sunlight.

It was Cat. She was standing upright against the bars. Watching him, waiting. They'd only met briefly. What did she want?

6

Avalon

The night sky ushered in a theater of lights. Countless stars in a rivalry of brilliance only to be upstaged by the moon, which glowed like a flawless white opal flooding light into the blue forest. Frigid gusts of wind brushed through the trees startling the group with a late evening chill.

The river Bassas, the barrier between Avalon and Hyperion, was only a few hours up the road. But camping on the border would only bring trouble.

They'd planned to separate in the morning. The road forked with one route leading east and the other north. Vallan, Apollo, and the caravan would be taking the northern route, while Rhean, Miriam, and Wislan would take the eastern route that crossed into Hyperion and to Atlantis.

Apollo touched the Thetus Mud under his eyes to ensure it was still moist and hadn't flaked off. From the bits of information he gathered from Miriam and Rhean, Apollo knew their journey had something to do with the Marked.

The mages built a small campfire and huddled around, vying for a warm spot away from the smoke. Vallan opened his pack and pulled out a loaf of rye bread and a hunk of cheese.

"It's not often that Warlocks travel in the company of the Grandmaster Oracle." Vallan said with a respectful bow. He offered her a piece of bread and cheese before passing it to the others. Miriam graciously accepted.

"Its been a long time since I've sat around a campfire." Miriam scooted closer to save herself from the night's chill.

"It's the perfect night for a tale, is it not?" Vallan remarked. "Grandmaster Oracle, do you recall the tale of the three wonders of Wythrin?"

"Of course I do." Miriam brightened.

Miriam closed her eyes and took a deep breath. A natural peace brushed across her ancient face as she meditated. Miriam invoked her aura. In her mind, she stood at the edge of a river of pure golden knowledge. There, the words of thousand upon thousands of books, every book she'd memorized with her aura, rushed by in wild rapids. Kneeling at the river's edge, she sipped the water taking in the words she needed for her story.

Then she opened her eyes and began her tale.

"Long ago, in the time of the Elves when Haven was still young, there lived a king, King Galandor Tarbor, who was given two enchanted stones. A white stone was from the Aurorean Dragon Raiden and a black stone was from the Aphotic Dragon Pandora.

The white stone was named the Urim, or Truth in Primoris, the first tongue. This stone held power to see all things good. The black stone was named the Thummim, or deception, it contained the power to see all things evil.

Under the instruction of the creator dragons, the Elves forged a golden breastplate. Upon the breastplate, they attached twelve gems, one for each Elven clan. When the breastplate was complete, King Galandor set the white and black stones in the base of the neck creating the Breastplate of Decision, a relic that could answer any question, past, present, or future.

Word of this power rallied the twelve Elven clans under the rule of a single king. Elves, with their obsessive desire for perfection, couldn't resist the promise of an all-knowing ruler.

Galandor received answers to his questions in form of mental rapture. In his mind's eye, he could see vivid details as he watched the answer unfold right before him. The breastplate helped him see the crimes of the accused, making his judgments perfect. He chose his allies based on his knowledge of their pasts and possible futures. Using the foresight of the breastplate, Galandor even chose Asteera, a common elf, as his queen. He'd seen an illustrious vision of the golden king Asteera would bear. In that vision, he saw an era of peace and prosperity unlike the world had ever known.

Asteera bore a son and named him Sarod. Galandor gave him every comfort a prince should have. As the boy grew, he deviated from the principals of his father. By the time he became a leader, his unsympathetic justice stained

Galandor's just society. Elves were sent to their deaths for petty crimes. Beggars were dragged out of the streets and tossed into dungeons. Despite Galandor's fervent pleas, Sarod dominated the Elves with brutal demonstrations of his power terrorizing them into subservience.

Knowing his son to be a tyrant, Galandor used the power of the Breastplate. Praying that he would see his son have a change of heart, Galandor foresaw his intentions. He saw Sarod's hunger for power and his followers pledging secret oaths of fidelity. Sarod would collect those loyal to him, kill Galandor, and take the throne and the breastplate. As king, Sarod would rule with an iron fist. In that vision, Galandor saw his legacy of justice end.

With a heavy heart, the king chose to spare himself and his son from the grim future. Galandor stripped Sarod and his followers of their titles and banished them from his kingdom.

Shattered by grief, Galandor asked the breastplate of his heir once more. He wanted it to show him the golden king he'd seen in that vision so long ago, but the breastplate's power was limited to answering a question a single time. Infuriated, that it had shown him a future he couldn't have, Galandor lost his trust and locked the breastplate away, avowing to never use its deceitful power again.

Sarod roamed the world. The memory of the fallen son of Galandor faded into story and song. For hundreds of years, Sarod hunted for a power strong enough to take his father's throne and exact his revenge. Wandering to the north, he heard rumors of corrupted dark mages that preyed on fear and rage. Filled with hate for his father, Sarod found the Doya.

He learned to use hate to turn the darkness he absorbed into a potent power. Over the years, his lust for that power changed him. His body was overtaken by corruption. Then his eyes turned black and he became the Doya's leader.

Elves live for centuries, but even they must die one day. After years of hope and prayer, Asteera was with child again. Galandor would have an heir.

Sarod and his Doya army fell upon his father's kingdom in the night. Like ghostly shadows, the Doya moved from one soldier to the next slaughtering the king's army. By the time the alarm was raised, the Doya had nearly conquered the city.

That night amidst the battle, in secret, Asteera bore Galandor's second son. Galandor feared for his family, so he broke his oath and used the breastplate's power of knowledge to escape.

King Galandor led his wife and their newborn outside the city through the breastplate's vision. But Galandor couldn't forsake his throne. He couldn't understand how his great kingdom could fall in a night. He wanted to see the face of his enemy, so he asked the breastplate to showed him the invaders. The breastplate showed him the pale, white face and oily, black eyes of his son Sarod, now a monster of the darkness. Visions of the breastplate showed Galandor what would happen if he escaped. There was nowhere he could hide. Sarod and his demons would hunt him to the ends of the world.

Galandor returned to the palace to face his first-born. He instructed the guard to take his wife and heir and place them under the protection of their allies, the wisps and fairies. So long as Sarod never learned of his newborn, Galandor knew the Elves would one day have a righteous king.

Sarod slew every member of Galandor's house, down to the servants. When he reached the throne room, Galandor was waiting. He offered Sarod the throne in exchange for compassion for his people. In response, Sarod slew his father. Before Galandor's blood was cold, he took the breastplate and the throne.

Sarod used the boundless knowledge of the breastplate to unlock magic forbidden by the gods. Abandoning the business of the Kingdom to the Doya, Sarod spent most of his reign in the caves underneath the rocky spires of the Crown, in the far north. The knowledge of the breastplate showed him darkness he could create. An everlasting evil unlike the world had ever known.

Asteera and her newborn son Wythrin lived among the wisps and fairies. Wythrin grew up in hiding. Decades passed and he became a legendary Enchanter. Using his masterful skills, he created a suit of golden armor carrying such a powerful enchantment that the sight of it could weaken any Doya. Girded in his armor, he rallied the Elves and took back the kingdom.

Sarod was consumed by his work and ignored the rebellion. The power of a king was nothing compared to the power he would have when he finished his quest for ultimate power. He had the knowledge of all things, but not power over them. With the aid of the breastplate, he would give himself the abilities of a god.

Wythrin marched every elf able to carry a sword or wield a spell and surrounded the Crown. Sarod's forces were no match against Wythrin's numbers.

Sarod beckoned the breastplate to find a means of escape. There was only one. The breastplate taught the Doya how to take raven form.

Wythrin fought at the head of the army in his enchanted armor. His armor shined with such splendor that it burned the eyes of the Doya, blinding them in battle. He cut through the lines of Doya like a single ray of sunshine piercing through a storm cloud. Hundreds of Doya died at his hands.

Wythrin led the army through the spires of the Crown, where Sarod watched the battle. Barreling through the door, Wythrin was engulfed in a wild wave of ravens clawing at each other to escape. When the birds cleared, a single raven remained. The raven looked deep into Wythrin's eyes. Its jet pupils glinted with dark rage when it saw Galandor's crest, a white dragon head, engraved in his golden armor. Wythrin felt the raven's dark presence. Rushing toward the creature, he swung his sword in a swift stroke, but the raven slipped by him and vanished into the sky, leaving him alone standing above the breastplate.

Wythrin took the breastplate, and with his knowledge of magic, used its power to open his mind. With it, he enriched his knowledge of enchantments.

Using the boundless knowledge of the breastplate he took his army and erected his first wonder, the mystical city of

Tarboroth. Once complete, he enchanted it with a spell to call out to all Elves. Elves traveled from distant lands and united to build a kingdom under the rule of their king, King Wythrin Tarbor. The Elves entered their golden age. Wythrin ruled much like his father did, fairly and as a servant to his people. As Wythrin's knowledge of enchantments grew, Tarboroth became a place of rare wonders.

The breastplate was a magical instrument. After a century of practice, Wythrin mastered its power. He learned ways to ask the same question more than once. He'd even learned to ask it questions secretly through his mind. Galandor and Sarod were common bards compared to the genius of the magical composer. The wondrous Enchanter became so in-tuned with the breastplate that his mind readily accessed its power, creating a flow of knowledge that only he and the gods could fathom.

The power ultimately alienated Wythrin from the Elves. Though his judgments were just, most of his subjects were too afraid to enter his presence, fearing their thoughts might offend the king. Many thought it a crime for the king to see their past and their futures when they could not. Some rose up and spoke against the king, they believed that molding the future was too much power even for a just ruler. Others remembered the days of Sarod and readily defended him. Tarboroth teetered on the brink of civil war.

Wythrin could see into the hearts of the Elves. As a humble servant to the people, he consented to give up the breastplate for their confidence.

A relic of such great power couldn't be locked away, nor could it be given to another. He feared his brother Sarod might get his hands on the breastplate, so Wythrin used his full knowledge and searched for a way to destroy it.

The breastplate showed Wythrin a chasm deep in the Chronos Mountains. The chasm was so deep that lesser magical objects could be cast into its depths and safely destroyed. Wythrin removed the Urim and Thummim from the breastplate and cast the breastplate into the chasm. It fell to the bottom and shattered, releasing a magical force that shook the mountains with a violent fury.

Wythrin opened the Chasm to all Enchanters to help rid the world of their mistakes and relics of evil. Wythrin's Chasm became known as the Enchanter's second wonder.

After the breastplate was destroyed, Wythrin still possessed the stones. They held far too much power for even the chasm to absorb. Fearing that someone might try to recreate the breastplate, he erected the Aurorean temple. Wythrin enchanted the structure to draw from the rich energy of the Urim. Its power created a barrier to block any intruder from entering the temple. The Aurorean temple became the third of Wythrin's wonders."

Apollo was intrigued by Miriam's tale. He posed a question. "What about the Thummim? Did Wythrin create an Aphotic temple for the dark mages?"

The corner of Mirium's mouth curled up into a thoughtful smirk.

"It's uncertain. Wythrin was a light mage and incapable of drawing power from the Thummim. But the ancient texts spoke of an Aphotic temple, the dark twin of our Aurorean Temple."

"Did anyone ever find it?" Apollo asked.

"I've spent a century searching my books for the location of the dark temple. It would be a great discovery, and might even force the stubborn Purists to believe Wythrin worked with Dark Mages. There is nothing evil about dark magic, corruption is the evil, that's what turns dark mages into Doya."

"That's enough," Rhean ordered. "We don't need you filling Apollo's head with absurd ideas. Haven is much crueler outside the comforts of the library. I'd slit a Dark Mage's throat just as fast as a Doya's."

Apollo winced.

Rhean groaned and climbed to his feet.

"They're all the same," he growled. "When their back is against the wall, they'll use whatever fear, hate, lust, or greed they can find and they'll stab you in the back with it." Rhean marched away.

When he was out of earshot, Miriam couldn't help herself.

"Is it absurd to think Wythrin would instruct a dark mage to perform the task for him?" she murmured.

"Yes." Wislan spat. "It's daft to think Wythrin would have anything to do with a Dark Mage!"

Miriam had enough of Wislan's disrespect.

"*Stupid, stupid boy.* In Elven times, Dark and Light Mages fought together." Miriam's contempt made Wislan even angrier.

"No true Light Mage would have anything to do with a Dark Mage." Wislan rounded the fire with his fists clenched and towered over ancient Miriam. "Miriam, you best not spread such ideas. One word to my Uncle, the King—"

Miriam shot up and in a swift motion drew a magical symbol. Before Wislan could react, she jammed her finger into his temple.

Wislan's body wrenched upward. Eyes bulging with shock, he watched his arms move freely. He tried to call out to Grandmaster Rhean, but before he could scream, his own hand clasped over his mouth. His other hand reached for his sword. Wislan watched the long blade slowly leave its sheath.

Miriam's eyes glinted in the firelight. Vallan made no move to stop her. Apollo watched in awe. She'd conjured a powerful spell, with only the help of firelight.

Wislan had no choice. He brought his sword point to his chin.

Miriam's tense voice got Wislan's full attention.

"I am the Grandmaster Oracle. You will call me Grandmaster Miriam, do you understand?"

Miriam used magic to lower Wislan's hand from his mouth.

"Yes, Grandmaster." Wislan quaked, watching his other hand gripping the sword.

"I have power over the mind. Especially one as simple as yours. I can haunt your dreams with nightmares. I can make you feel as if your skin was melting from your bones. I can make you forget your own name."

The caravans reached down the middle of the road. Torches and campfires burned down their path to illuminate the camp.

It was Apollo's watch. He paced down the roadside close enough to the fires so that bandits could see his Warlock's robe. Even at night, bandits didn't dare attack a caravan guarded by Warlocks.

The slope to the closest Black Mountain was only a few hours march. Vallan had told Apollo to keep a careful eye to the south, and even though it was his watch, he didn't doubt that Vallan and Rhean were awake, watching him pace up and down the group, searching the sky for ravens, and the shadows for Doya.

Apollo kicked a stone. It skidded through the dirt and off the road into the forest underbrush. His rusty broadsword was in his hand, shining dully in the firelight.

"Watch the flames squirm," whispered someone.

Apollo stopped and felt compelled to do what the voice said. He looked into the campfire, the flames looked like red snakes escaping from a nest of firewood.

"Even fire is scared this close to the Dark Prince," said the voice.

Apollo looked up and into the iron cage. Cat was at the edge of the cage with her arms curled around the bars. Her brown eyes reflected the firelight. There was excitement in her pale face.

Apollo tried to ignore the way she pushed her breasts through the bars as she leaned against them, seemingly trying to get closer to him.

"Where are your guards?" Apollo looked around the cage. He spotted Cat's companion in the cage with her. His hood was still pulled over his head, but from the way he laid limp against the cage wall, Apollo guessed he was sleeping.

Cat kept watching the fire.

"One of them is sleeping. He drank too much. He's off in the shadows over there." Cat pointed. "Can you see him?"

Apollo squinted against the firelight. He thought he saw a man hunched over puking, but wasn't sure.

"He's supposed to be watching me while the other one waters the trees. I think he drank too much too. But I'm not worried, I have you here to protect me."

Cat crouched down and slipped her legs between the bars of the cage to sit. Her long, slender legs nearly touched the ground. Her dress came up, exposing more of her thighs. Apollo felt his cheeks flush.

"Do I make you uncomfortable?" Cat asked with a coy smirk.

"A little," Apollo admitted, face turned.

"I can't have that," Cat said.

She scooted back some and pulled the hem of her dress a tad bit lower.

"Is that better?"

Apollo looked back. She smiled that smirk again as he looked down her body to make sure she'd covered up.

Apollo pointed to the hooded figure in the cage.

"Cedric doesn't do much," he said.

Cat leaned back on her elbows and gave Cedric a bored glance.

"Cedric doesn't like people. If he was awake, he'd kill some."

A breeze made the fire shift to one side, and the door to the iron cage creaked open. Apollo hadn't noticed it before, but the iron lock was cracked in half on the ground.

"Your door is open!" Apollo gasped.

A shiver of dread went up Apollo's spine. Cat felt it.

"Have you come to tickle me with emotions?" Cat asked.

"How did it get open?" Apollo asked.

"I opened it. Would you like me to close it? Would that make you more comfortable?"

Cat drew a symbol and the door pulled shut, the iron lock lifted off the ground and melded back together in place, securing the door.

Cat blew out a puff of smoke. "Thank you for that."

Apollo's face flushed. It felt awkwardly intimate seeing her feed off of his fear.

"It's dark, and your guards are gone, why didn't you escape?"

Cat swung her feet whimsically off the edge of the cage. She held her breath for a moment, and Apollo got the odd impression that she was bashful, which seemed utterly absurd.

"I wanted to see you again, Black Eyes," she admitted. She searched Apollo's face for a reaction.

Apollo's brow furrowed. He hated being called that. "Me? Why me?"

Cat ran one leg down the other.

"I think you're interesting. Your eyes. You're a dark mage among the lights."

Apollo stepped closer to the fire and closer to Cat.

"I'm not a dark mage," Apollo contested.

"You can't fool me. I can see it in you. Dark mages know one another, and I want to know you."

Apollo glanced around to see if anyone nearby could hear.

Cat playfully dragged her finger across the iron bars, letting a finger catch on each bar before breaking free to get caught on the next.

"Your secret is safe with me. Do you have a lot of secrets? I am good at keeping secrets. Dark Mages, like us, we like secrets. Isn't that what the dark is for, hiding things?"

Cat let her finger slide down one of the bars and caress her thigh.

Apollo couldn't help taking a long look at her legs. They were fair and curved, the sort of legs that he'd heard men describe in the tavern back in New Camelot. He knew he shouldn't be looking, but if her legs could escape the confines of an iron cage, wasn't it his duty to make sure they didn't get any farther? Was there harm in patrolling them with his eyes?

"You have such wondrous eyes," Cat said.

That broke Apollo out of his trance. His eyes were an abomination. There was nothing wondrous about them.

"My eyes are a curse," Apollo answered firmly.

Cat jerked her hand back and gripped the bars.

"No, they have power. I know what they can do."

Apollo turned away. When he did, he saw one of the Night Guard standing behind him. How much had he heard? Apollo opened his mouth, but before he could find words Cat spoke up.

"He didn't hear our secrets. I will keep them, we will keep them together."

7

Havilah – Enoch

Emperor Vega lounged in a great hall at the head of a mahogany dinner table carved with symbols in Primorius and accented with sculptures of golden dragons. His bloodshot eyes looked like slimy boiled eggs. Dead, veiny flesh draped off his skull like cave moss and open sores seeped yellow puss from his cheeks. The skin around his jaw stretched like dry rotted ropes ready to burst. A muscle thumped in his left cheek, making his whole face twitch.

Cooks swiftly marched in from the kitchen. Their footsteps echoed in the cavernous hall as they heaped the dinner table with an extravagant feast from the four corners of the world.

The first cook served chunks of Atlantean lamb wrapped in thick, fatty bacon. Bananas from the pirate isles were served diced and mixed with rare pink kiwi from the South and tart strawberries from the North. The smell of warm Havilalonian bread and pungent cheese rivaled the scent of pork fat drifting through the air.

The meal's centerpiece was a turkey the size of a boar. Its crispy golden skin glistened in the firelight. Fragrant steam poured out as the Emperor's cooks cut and served the moist bird.

Next to the Emperor sat Cain. He was a hulk of a man with long white dreadlocks, a midsection as thick as tree trunk, and arms so large they made the two-handed war hammer hanging from his belt look like a toy. A brutal scar split his ear and crossed his throat.

Cain was one of the few thousand pure blood decedents of Enoch left. Over the centuries, Enoch's ancestors had mixed with the other nations of men. Only a few secluded Northern villages and wealthy families could claim such a high honor. Many envied the people of Enoch for their longevity. Cain was half the Emperor's age, yet naturally looked no older than fifty.

The giant of a man refused the fresh cuts of turkey offered to him. Instead, he reached across the table and snapped off one of the prized turkey drumsticks.

Emperor Vega pulled a glowing pouch from his pocket. He reached inside and pulled out a flailing fairy. He plucked off its wings and dropped it in his mouth, his face soured at the awful taste as he crunched the fairy's bones in his teeth.

The Emperor's old decrepit body renewed itself on the power in the fairy's blood. Within moments, the twitch in his left cheek relaxed. His sores closed. The skin holding his face together softened, and his wrinkles smoothed out. Cain watched the Emperor, a man of over three hundred and fifty years, turn from a near skeleton into a man no older than thirty.

"Do you know what masks the taste of Fairy blood?" Vega grumbled before taking a big bite out of a block of soft goat cheese.

He swallowed, paused, and then used his fingernail to pick out a fairy bone lodged between his teeth.

"Nothing makes them palatable. Imagine the taste of swamp water mixed with skunk musk that nothing, not even the harsh flavor of Sheminite Blood Mead, can mask." Vega took a long swig of wine, swished it around in his mouth, and spat it on the floor. Almost instantly, a Mayan slave hurried in and wiped it up.

"If only I was born a son of Enoch. Then I would have a long life and not have to eat those vile creatures," Vega said. He gave Cain an icy stare.

The last cook to serve them was a Sheminite woman in a cobalt dress. She had neatly braided charcoal colored hair and long eyelashes. When she reached the table, she emptied her arms of a brass bowl and a bottle of amber rum. She took the lid from the bowl and released the aroma of dry roasted almonds and cinnamon. She popped the cork off the rum and poured a generous amount in with the nuts, and mixed them. Once the almonds were coated in a thick, syrupy layer of rum, she lit it with a candle. A dazzling fire whooshed upward, and a sweet, smoky scent followed. When the fire died out and the bowl cooled, the cook offered the cooked almonds to the Emperor.

Vega carefully selected a nut and tasted it. He gave a nod of satisfaction and waved for her to offer the bowl to Cain.

"That's squirrel food," he said.

Cain took a deep bite into his greasy drumstick. Like a dog, he tore the meat off the bone and let it dangle from his chin.

"The bird is good," Cain said as he inhaled his food.

"Your table manners are dreadful," Vega frowned and tossed him a cloth. "For god's sake, clean yourself up. You sicken me with your lack of etiquette."

The cook awkwardly collected her utensils and rum. She tried to retreat to the kitchen, but Cain grabbed her by the arm. He picked up the corners of her dress, and wiped his chin, leaving an oily stain in it. She trembled, bowed to the Emperor, and bolted to the kitchen.

"I should've taken my meal in the barn with the pigs," Vega grumbled.

Cain kept his eyes on the kitchen. He sucked the last of the meat off his drumstick while he waited for the woman to return.

"She's a fine dish, you should brand her so I know her name," Cain said. A grisly smile crossed his face as he rubbed a finger over the ridges of his split ear.

"She's not a slave. I had her brought here all the way from Salem. She's one of the best cooks in Haven," Vega boasted. He leaned forward in his chair and grabbed a handful of nuts.

"She cooks the best Fire Nuts I've ever had."

Cain rolled up a sleeve of his cotton shirt, revealing hundreds of slave numbers tattooed on his arm.

"Maybe, I'll give her a number," Cain said. "Maybe I'll put her here," he pointed to an empty spot on his wrist.

"Fine!" Vega conceded. His bottom lip curled in frustration. "But don't break any of her bones. She's too good a cook to waste on your bizarre carnal urges."

"You know me too well," Cain said. His mouth twisted into a cocky smile.

The thump of Marcus' walking stick announced his arrival before he even entered the great hall. He was a tiny, elderly man who wore a gray cloak embroidered with the Owl of Athena, the symbol for the Atlantean Society of Science. His cloak was speckled with ink blotches from writing quills, and he had bags under his eyes from the sleepless nights he'd spent delving through books in the palace library. He didn't mind the seclusion. He didn't have time for research back home. In Atlantis, he held the position of the Pillar of Science, and he was constantly interrupted with matters of law.

"My Lord, you look to be in good health," Marcus remarked pleasantly. He clung to his walking stick with both of his jittery hands.

The Emperor gripped his chest as he watched Marcus fall to his knees to bow. When he heard the old man's joints crack, a rush of nausea hit his gut.

"This better be important. Your old bones have ruined my appetite."

The Emperor shoved his plate across the table and rose from his chair to loom over Marcus.

"Of course, Your Grace. Alaric just arrived from Atlantis with the final gem. He's prepared to oversee my work," Marcus said.

The Emperor watched the wrinkled man struggle to get to his feet. His shaky hands strained to keep hold of his walking stick as he tried to pull himself up.

"Do you need a hand up?" The Emperor asked.

"Oh that would be most appreciated, my Lord." Marcus reached a desperate hand toward the Emperor.

"Not me, corpse!" Emperor recoiled. Vega covered his mouth and backed away as if age were infectious.

"I don't know why Alaric thinks he needs your sack of bones. If those shaky fingers so much as scratch one of my gems, I'll have Cain cut those weak, disgusting things off and feed them to you like dried carrots."

Marcus felt cold sweat run through the wrinkles in his brow. He was about to apologize when Vega turned to Cain.

"We're going to the summit. Get this rotting piece of carrion on his feet."

8

Havilah – Enoch

The Emperor looked down from the summit of his palace as a god would look down from the heavens. Below him was his creation. His city was a living organism of order and precision. The high outer wall was the skin. The streets were veins and the hundreds of thousands of slaves were the blood moving from place to place. Each slave had a task. They were prompt, focused. He was the brain that commanded their actions. Any and every command the Emperor spouted to his agents, his Branded, was carried out with uncanny precision. He was the creator, their god, the keeper of order.

Order, the thread that holds society together. Some of the oldest Havalonians still remember the chaos they had endured under King Erin's rule. Tangled up in his own incompetence, he had let the great plague, Death's Whisper, spread and wipe out over half the kingdom. Erin had ruled a land drowning in its own dead. The wealthier members of society had fled or had shut themselves away. The poor were wiped out.

The Mayans were a people without a homeland. King Erin had endeavored to repopulate his cities by promising the Mayans the homes and lands of plague victims.

King Erin had thought to control the savages. He had expected them to obey his laws and rebuild his nation, but he hadn't known the Mayans like Alejandro Vega did.

Lifetimes ago, that's who he was, Alejandro the explorer, the last of the conquistadores sent to the New World by royal decree to bring Order to these savages. What would the King of Spain say of Vega's Empire? He'd wanted the last of the Mayans hunted down, but circumstance brought him to this world across the stars. Here Vega had tamed the Mayans, he'd saved them.

King Erin would've never let the Mayans into his kingdom had he seen the savages perform the bloodletting or sacrifice their own babes to their Sun God. Alejandro had been inside the temples of their homeland. He'd seen the human sacrifices. He'd attended the festival of Ixchel, where they had celebrated the moon goddess by flaying their finest woman and prancing around in her skin. Alejandro Vega had seen the worst of their untamed beliefs and it filled him with revulsion.

But the gods gave him the power to change all that.

When he had discovered the power of the Mind Curse, he had recognized his calling. He was to be their God. He had given them commandments and punishments. Their obedience had tamed them to be more than the lowest form of human waste. The Gods had created the Mayans to be ruled.

When the suns reached their parallel peaks in the sky, heavy iron bells rang through the city. Every man, woman, and child stopped to face the palace. They knelt, prostrated themselves on the ground, and started to pray. The extreme height of the palace and strong winds prevented their voices from reaching the Emperor's ears.

Cain reached the top of the stairs with Marcus limping closely behind.

"Do you remember my prayer, Marcus?" Vega asked.

Standing on the cusp of the summit, Vega was poised with a haughty dominance as if the height of the tower let him transcend his mortality. The powerful gusts of the high winds made his yellow silk cape flap to one side. His crimson doublet tightened on his chest, held shut with gold buttons. Even the Emperor's long black hair lashed in the wind, flicking like a black flame.

Marcus bowed his head and joined the distant rumble of voices chanting a memorized prayer.

"I take every breath by Your Grace. If I am to die this day, let it be in your name. For both my body and soul are yours to command. From eternity to eternity, I follow your command with an open and willing heart. I heed every command of yours and your servants the Branded. Let your wishes be carried out with exactness, for on the throne of heaven sits Emperor Vega and he is my judge."

The Emperor raised his chin. He inhaled the words of his followers like fresh morning air.

Marcus rose to marvel at the view of the countryside. To the west, he could see the rolling hills he'd crossed. Somewhere beyond those endless fields of grass was Atlantis, his home. To the south were the cold blue waters of the Sarthrin Sea. They were so vast. He knew it was impossible, but the water looked as if it fell off the edge of the world. When he faced north, Marcus saw the Forest of Eden. Its imposing face took up his entire vision. The forest was large on a map, but it was more massive then he could've imagined. At its center was a group of trees the size of a small mountain. To the east, he could see the sails of the ships in Port Mahal, and past the forest and flat plains were the points of snow-peaked mountains. The distance was deceptive. The mountains appeared as if they could fit in the palm of his hand.

Cain ran a finger over the scar in his neck. A devilish grin spread over his lips. There was a wildness in his eyes that made the hairs stand on the back of Marcus' neck.

Cain called out over the summit's edge. "Giblet!"

A dragon ascended from the ridge of the summit. It flew upwards with the grace of a pelican. With each stroke, it opened its immense bat-like wings and pushed itself higher into the sky. The motion made sapphire blue muscles ripple across the beast's shoulders with the same awe-inspiring beauty of a prized horse flexing in a canter. When the beast's chest flipped toward Marcus, he got a better look at its body. It had a triangular head, much like a great newt. Its eyes were wide and yellow with the elongated pupils of a snake. It had a body shape that resembled a blue crocodile with a fat neck, a long wide midsection covered in hard ridges, and short stubby legs. As it flew, the dragon tucked its four stocky limbs close to its body and clenched its sizable talons. The creature's reptilian tail was nearly twice the length of its body and curled like a ribbon in the wind. The dragon turned into a glide and circled the palace summit, casting a dark shadow as it descended. It landed next to Cain and left its wings wide open. Their mass dominated Marcus' vision like the shoulders of a blue giant.

Marcus cowered in their shadow.

"That's…a…that's a…dragon," he stuttered.

Giblet recognized the word and bore a hundred razor-sharp teeth in a bone-chilling smile.

"Never seen a dragon up close before?" Cain's wicked grin pushed at the limits of his cheeks. He pulled out a dagger and ran the blade over his palm. Blood trickled out. Giblet opened his mouth and Cain dripped blood inside. The dragon's scales shivered in delight.

Cain took a few steps toward Marcus. Giblet followed, swaying like a crocodile.

Marcus quivered. The dragon's breath was a gust of winter wind that pushed through his robes. Cain's bloody hand dripped and the dragon flicked its long tongue to snatch the droplets out of the air.

"Giblet is just over a month old. Blood is like mothers milk. He still has his baby teeth." Cain pulled back on Giblet's lips to show Marcus another row of teeth just starting to push through his clear, veiny gums.

"They're sharper than his adult ones, but they're not as strong. His adult teeth will snap bones, even crush steel. These little ones are for nourishment. They're for ripping flesh." Cain watched the wrinkles on Marcus' face shake as he trembled.

"He's already shed his first scales. Though they were thinner than parchment. In time, they'll grow in and be harder than stone." Cain flaked off a thin scale from Giblet's back. It was so thin that Marcus could see right through it. When Cain held it in the air, the wind snatched it away as easily as it would whisk away a fallen leaf.

"He breathes a bitter cold. When it comes to blue dragons, there's one hard and fast rule." Cain tossed his iron dagger downwind. In a single fluid movement, Giblet retracted his wings rolled over and enveloped the dagger in a dazzling, freezing cloud. Paces away, Marcus felt the air in his lungs chill. He watched the frosty dagger hit the ground. There was a high-pitched "ting" and the blade shattered into pieces.

Marcus' eyes went wide and the Emperor gave the dragon sluggish applause.

"The smaller the dragon, the colder the breath," Cain said. He waved Giblet back to heel at his feet. "Giblet has mutt blood. He'll never talk like the Highborns. Maybe a word or two." Cain and Giblet advanced another step. Cain reached out, Marcus flinched and Cain wiped his bloody hand down the front of Marcus' robe.

"What? What have you done," he said, nervously.

The winds changed. The whooshing flaps of dragon wings rumbled around them. The palace peak shook as dragons ascended from below. They streaked through the sky, creating a blue tornado around the summit.

"See the might of Dragon Fang Castle," Cain shouted. He held his arms up high and marveled at the sight of his pets.

Every dragon was blue, but they ranged in size. Some were half the size of Giblet and staggered around, trying to dodge the older, larger dragons. The older dragons were three times Giblet's size with slightly more elongated bodies and thin shale-like scales. They flew with such command of their wings that they made the smaller dragons look clumsy.

Each dragon differed in strength, size, and shade of blue, but they had one frightful thing in common. They were all staring at Marcus.

"Dragons love the scent of blood," Vega said, stepping toward them. "Cain has trained them well. Any normal dragon would have you ripped to morsels by now."

Cain pointed up into the storm of dragons. "Do you see the scales? They bristle along the neck to show their dominance."

Marcus counted four larger dragons with their scales bristling, ready to swoop down and knock Giblet aside, then they would eat him. Giblet had no scales to bristle; his skin rippled into folds, he wasn't going to let his meal be taken. One bite and he'd snap in half.

Giblet's nostrils flared as he pulled in long intoxicating breaths of air. The dragons swirling around them did the same thing. They smelled a new, savory scent.

Alaric stood at the top of the staircase. He was a wry old man in his seventies with a thin boney frame. He wore the purple robes of an Aurorean Enchanter. What little hair he had was long and stringy and hung from the sides of his head, leaving his scalp completely bald.

In his hand, he held a piece of cloth torn from his robes. He drew a dagger and put one hand firmly around the blade. Alaric cringed and pulled the blade through his palm, soaking the purple cloth in dark blood.

Every dragon started to growl a deep heavy rumble that made the tower shiver. The attention of the army of dragons rested on Alaric's bloodied cloth.

Alaric stepped to the edge of the summit. He shook the cloth. The dragons growled. Giblet opened his wings to gain momentum and dashed toward Alaric. The mass of dragons flowed after him in a rushing rapids of claws and teeth.

Alaric tossed the bloody rag from the summit and dove into the stairwell.

The scores of dragons threw themselves over the ledge toward the blood-soaked cloth. Giblet caught it in his teeth, but the runner up bit him in the tail. The lead dragon twisted and snapped back, but lost the rag to another who swooped by and snatched it up. Like a horde of starving crows fighting over a worm, the dragons disappeared in a ferocious battle somewhere near the base of the Fang.

Marcus released a heavy sigh of relief. Cain's face twisted in disgust.

"Mage blood, it's like damn catnip," Cain grumbled.

Alaric picked up an iron mold from the stairwell and placed it on a silver table in the center of the summit. The Emperor snatched his hand.

He examined the fresh cut in Alaric's palm. It had sealed, leaving only a black scar.

"Interesting trick," Vega said.

"Thank you, Your Majesty."

Alaric examined the bloodstain on Marcus' robe, "Are you alright?"

Marcus' face was still trembling. He couldn't get out a word, so he nodded.

"Dammit, Cain. You idiot! I need him to complete my work," Alaric spat. Cain flung his dreadlocks over his shoulders and reached for his warhammer.

"What did you call me, mage?" he said.

Alaric was a twig compared to the beastly Cain, but the hate in his expression was colder than dragon's breath.

"That's enough!" Vega ordered. "Cain, you've had your fun. Let them work."

Marcus huddled over the silver table in the center of the summit. He couldn't control his shaking hands.

"They were going to eat me," he said to Alaric.

"Let's finish what we came to do," Alaric insisted.

Marcus took a deep breath and agreed with a heavy nod.

Alaric called over Marcus' shoulder to the Emperor and Cain.

"We're ready to begin."

Alaric unrolled a scroll in front of him and prepared to read instructions to Marcus.

"Get on with it," Vega ordered.

Marcus placed a leather strap around his head. He then took a leather wrap from his belt and unraveled it on the table. Inside was a collection of simple hand tools, including a small hammer, tweezers, an assortment of needle files, and many small magnifying glasses of varying sizes. He selected the largest of the magnifying glasses and attached it to his leather headband, so it rested just over an eye.

Alaric lifted a flat golden plate from an iron mold. On its face were fourteen fittings designed to hold precious stones. At the base of the fittings were small grooves. Marcus took a file from his tools and gently rubbed off the excess gold left from the casting process. He took out a tiny metal tool and measured the depth and width of the groves. Once finished, he took a cloth and wiped the breastplate clean.

"Now we attach the twelve gems," Alaric instructed.

Alaric read the scroll over and over to ensure his translation of Primoris was correct. Then he pulled a flat diamond from his pocket.

"The final gem," he said, holding it out for the Emperor's approval.

Vega took the diamond from Alaric and held it up so it shimmered in the sunlight. It was nearly flawless. It hadn't an equal in his entire treasury.

"You are quite the jewel thief," Vega said.

Vega untied a pouch from his belt and handed it, and the diamond, to Alaric.

Alaric emptied the pouch into a bowl on the table. Gemstones poured out. Each was about the size of a walnut and unequaled in cut and clarity.

Marcus took the first gem from the bowl. Alaric pointed to one of the fourteen settings and Marcus placed it and tapped each of the four prongs into place to grip the gem. They continued until each stone was affixed to the golden plate. Marcus measured the distance between the stones and double-checked the rough diagram drawn on Alaric's scroll. Once the stones were set precisely, Marcus nodded and stepped away from the table.

"The breastplate is ready for the enchantment," Alaric said.

He gripped it tightly in both hands.

"We will join the silver, the element that conducts darkness, to the gold, the element that conducts the light, by speaking the words of the creator dragons."

Marcus took a crucible containing melted silver from the forge. Alaric raised his hands up to the sky. He coiled his fingers as he opened his magic well to absorb power from the suns and closed his eyes to focus on absorption.

A minute of silence past. The winds whistled. Alaric's purple robe wafted and went taut. His few strands of hair danced in the wind like the legs of a jellyfish. His face contorted in pain. The energy he drew from the suns felt heavy. Sweat ran down his temples as he held in the power and gathered more.

"Pour the silver," he said.

Marcus poured the liquefied silver evenly into the breastplate's tiny grooves, while Alaric spoke the words of the ancient dragons.

"Far culmon eda trai a vidi elves gib ebgon athu roks athu dragons."

"I ordain this work of mortal hands to be the keeper of the stones of the gods."

As Alaric spoke, the silver started to glow red.

"Gib hu pow a vidi hia pai ola da."

"To be the tool of time both past and future."

"Co al pow hu Gara farthum vidi gara, bera tal urim ola thummim. "

The silver converged and ran behind each stone, connecting them in a web of glistening melted metal. Along the edges of the breastplate, the silver filled in a word. Alaric read it aloud.

"Gara."

With his finger, he drew a magical symbol on the breastplate. The first gem started to glow.

"Gara," he repeated.

He drew another symbol. The second stone glowed to join the first. Alaric continued the pattern until all twelve stones were glowing.

When the silver cooled, the gems lost their luminance. Alaric attached the ends of a golden chain to the breastplate.

"Your Majesty, I present the Breastplate of Decision." Alaric placed the chain around the Emperor's neck.

"You followed every detail of Sarod's instructions?" The Emperor asked, admiring how seamlessly the gold and silver joined together.

"I understand Primoris better than any of your servants. The design and enchantment fit Sarod's description," Alaric assured him.

Vega waved to Cain.

"Burn the scroll," he commanded.

Cain snatched the scroll from the table and tossed it into the forge. The old parchment burned up like dry leaves.

Vega's attention turned to Marcus.

"What do we do with you old man? I can't have you making another breastplate," he said.

"Your Majesty, I would never, I could never betray you," Marcus said.

Cain stepped between Alaric and the Emperor. He held out his palm. Marcus saw the Emperor's brand burned into his skin. A line from the Emperor's prayer stuck in his mind: "I heed every command of you and your servants the Branded."

"Throw yourself from the summit," Cain commanded.

Marcus' stomach turned. Alaric pushed past Cain to confront the Emperor.

"Your Majesty, Marcus is a member of the Atlantian Senate. The Hyperions will not like this," Alaric said.

"I don't care what the Hyperions think," Vega growled.

Alaric helplessly dropped his hands to his sides. The destruction of the scroll and the old man's death were inevitable. He knew that. The Emperor was too smart to leave a man with intimate knowledge of the Breastplate alive.

"Alaric, I'll need you to help procure the steer stones."

The Emperor turned his back to them.

"Marcus has outlived his usefulness."

Cain waved his hands with his palms down, motioning for Marcus to hurry up.

The Mind Curse was a hot poker prodding at the back of Marcus' skull. He looked to the ledge and the pain receded a little. He took a step toward the edge of the summit, and relief came almost instantly.

Marcus saw the city. The people were insects at this height. Marcus fell to his knees to stop himself. The Curse ripped into his mind like never before.

Alaric pulled Marcus to his feet. Marcus backed away. The Mind Curse punished him. Searing pain went through Marcus' head. Blood trickled from his nose.

Alaric's face was blank, emotionless.

"Die well, old friend," he said.

Alaric yanked Marcus back and secretly slid his dagger through the old man's armpit into his heart. Marcus jerked and died. Alaric shoved his body from the summit.

The Emperor and Cain watched his body flail in the velocity of the fall until it splattered in the streets.

"A brave man doesn't scream at the face of death," Alaric said. He bowed his head while hiding his bloody dagger in the folds of his robe.

"You're right, Cain. The Atlantians do fall faster," Vega observed.

"It's those big heads of theirs. Smarts are heavy," Cain said.

Vega ran his fingers through the two empty positions at the top of the breastplate. The lines of silver reached downward from them to touch every gem.

"Alaric, you will go back to Atlantis and continue your research to bind the Urim and Thummim to the breastplate. Lady Black will bring you the seer stones. Then you will come to me and complete the breastplate."

Alaric peered down at what remained of Marcus.

"It's difficult to be motivated when you are rewarded and punished with death." Alaric watched the young dragons fight over Marcus' broken body. They pulled it apart until only a puddle of blood remained.

"You don't have a choice," Cain argued.

Alaric couldn't hide his hate for Cain. He held his tongue, but not his glare.

The Emperor adjusted the golden headband on his brow.

"Alaric understands the power of the Curse. He could refuse and die. Is Alaric, the great Enchanter, prepared to die today?"

Vega searched Alaric's tight face for a speck of fear, but he only found resolve.

"I am glad to see that after so many years we understand each other," Alaric replied.

"Those years haven't been kind, have they Alaric? Well, not kind for an Aurorean mage." The Emperor focus glossed over Alaric's deep wrinkles and balding head.

"No, Your Majesty, my taste for magic has soured," Alaric admitted.

"When you complete the breastplate," Vega paused to swallow. "I will release you from the Mind Curse."

"You are too gracious sire," Alaric said, stonefaced.

Vega dismissed him with a wave and returned to the edge of the summit. His attention rested on the mountainous tree in the center of the Forest of Eden, the Evertree, home to the Whisps and Fairies, a place forbidden to man.

He ran a finger across the brim of the golden breastplate.

Soon he would have the answers to any question he could think of.

"What do you think the fruit of the Evertree tastes like? Is it as bitter as a green lemon or sweet as a strawberry?" asked the Emperor.

"I'm told the fairies are fond of sweet fruit. There is no sweeter fruit than one that gives eternal life," Alaric answered.

Alaric turned and descended the stairs, leaving Cain and the Emperor alone.

They looked out across the north to the forest of Eden. Even though the suns were high in the sky, the density of the trees made the forest look unnaturally dark. Grey ironwood trees shielded the perimeter with trunks and roots so entangled that it was impossible for any creature larger than a mouse to pass through. Despite the density of the woods and the forest's thick darkness, flashes of wisp light still broke through the canopy. Brilliant blues, bright yellows, sharp greens, nearly every color traveled though and illuminated different parts of the shadowy forest.

At the center of the forest were four enormous trees that twisted together to form a wide base and a narrow peak. From a distance, the trees resembled a mountain.

Just outside the city, thousands upon thousands of Mayan slaves cleared a pass through the forest.

"How long until we reach the Evertree?" the Emperor asked.

"The forest is thick. The trees are like mountain rock," Cain said. "And the Wisps and Fairies—"

"How long?" Vega interrupted.

"A month, maybe two. The wisps slow our work. The ground we don't guard grows back. If we could use the dragons, we might be done sooner."

"Not even I can persuade a dragon to attack them," Vega said.

"You have the Mind Curse," Cain replied.

"If the Mind Curse worked on dragons, I wouldn't need you to train them. The Mind Curse has no power over Witching creatures," Vega said.

Cain looked back, confused. He knew nothing of magic. Vega forbid the use of magic in all three of his kingdoms, and as a result, mages and arcane knowledge had become extremely rare.

"Fairies, Wisps, Dragons, Imps, creatures that get their magic from birth, Witching creatures, can't be influenced by my power."

Cain's eyes glazed over. The Emperor sighed, frustrated. He'd reached the limit of Cain's attention span.

"Your job isn't to think. Just chop the forest down. You have weeks, don't try my patience. What good is a breastplate to show me the secret of how to enter the Evertree if I can't reach the Evertree?"

"It will be done," Cain conceded.

Cain glanced over his shoulder back at the stairs.

"There is something else," he said.

"What?" the Emperor asked.

"Alaric has refused the help of the soldiers," Cain answered.

The Emperor scanned Cain's face.

"As long as my orders are carried out, I don't care how it's done. You should know that. You and Lady Black have controlled the Mayan population with how many failed attacks on New Camelot?" The Emperor's face soured.

"He doesn't travel alone," Cain hesitated. "Well, he's alone, but…" he tried to find the right words.

"If you're so curious, have some men watch him and see what he is up to," Vega said.

"I did. I sent my best. No man has returned," Cain said.

Vega turned back to the forest, but this time he wasn't staring at the Evertree but mulling in his own thoughts.

"Alaric is no fool. He's sharper than a dagger, given the chance, he'll put that dagger in your back." The Emperor interlocked his fingers and cracked his knuckles as he thought.

"He's cursed. He can no more harm me than a moth can harass a hawk. Unless…" a nervous look crossed Vega's face. "Once he completes the breastplate, he'll be expendable."

The high winds atop the summit whisked a strand of the Emperor's hair into the air. It tumbled and turned, higher and higher, turned gray, and then white before crumbling to dust. Vega ran a hand through his scalp. Clumps of dry, wiry hair broke free to expose a gaping bald spot. He looked down at his now wrinkly hands. Bags formed under his eyes. The breastplate around his neck was heavy. His knees buckled and Cain caught him.

"My body wants to die," he wheezed. "Soon, even the flesh of the fairies won't be enough."

Vega fumbled through his robes. He pulled a small glowing sack from his pocket and emptied its contents into his mouth. A tiny fairy scream escaped on the wind.

"Gods, I hate the taste of fairies!" Vega scowled and spat out a mashed clump of fairy wings.

In moments, the wrinkles on his hands receded and his long black hair filled in as his youth returned.

"You may release me now," he said, pushing Cain away.

Emperor Vega straightened his clothes and centered the breastplate on his chest. He ran a finger through the two empty fittings in the breastplate, the positions for the Urim and Thummim. He looked out across the horizon to the Evertree.

A bite of its fruit was all he needed to rule forever.

9

Havilah

For those who didn't recognize his purple Enchanter robes, Alaric looked no more significant than an elderly peddler riding a mangy, draft horse. It was old, broad shouldered, and some might even call it a runt for its height.

Alaric followed the western road as it cut a jagged path through walls of yellow grass. The suns were high, but the air was cool.

Behind him, he towed a magnificent stallion. Its long, lean muscles rolled like shiny onyx ridges that glistened in the sun. The horse's neatly-brushed, white mane fluttered in the wind with the grace of an angel's wing, and its white tail was tightly braided so that it hung above the ground.

Just as a king wouldn't walk in the shadow of a peasant, Alaric's ancient horse looked odd escorting the prized stallion.

Alaric squinted against the sunlight. On the horizon, he saw Rinn, his companion, waiting on top of the first peak where the prairie ruffled into the hill country.

Rinn's cloak had the splendor of a storm cloud. It was made of rare spider silk that appeared to be as light as smoke. Rays from the suns glinted off Rinn's oiled, blue leather armor.

As Alaric got closer, he counted the thirteen knives tucked into the folds of Rinn's armor. His handsome face was framed with chin-length chestnut hair. He looked no older than twenty and clean despite the stubble on his chin. Alaric's attention went to the eye patch clasped tightly around Rinn's head by a silver chain. It was the first thing everyone saw when they looked at Rinn. His missing eye was his only physical flaw. He had the eye patch specially made from silver to perfectly match his gray eye.

The most peculiar part of Rinn's armor, a relic of Alaric's own handiwork, was a pair of Hyperion Gauntlets. They were made from Argos steel, and tailored much like Elven armor with smooth surfaces brought up into tall ridges, not unlike the mounded peaks of ocean waves. The gauntlets weren't perfectly shaped, yet a skilled blacksmith could no more criticize their imperfections than he could call a tree ugly for its natural, disproportionate shape. His right gauntlet contained rubies, they decorated the armor as if they were gliding on the waves of a metallic sea. His left gauntlet was an impossibly perfect copy of the right, but instead of rubies, blue sapphires swam through the wavy metal. The gauntlets were exquisite enough for a prince, yet the Argos steel made them strong enough for a warrior.

"No one has seen you?" Alaric asked.

"Do you need to ask?" Rinn replied.

Alaric still looked at him expectantly.

"No, no-one saw me," Rinn said, rolling his eyes.

Rinn heaved a pair of saddlebags off the ground and placed them on his stallion. He walked around his horse and picked up each hoof. He inspected the new iron shoes and ran his fingers through the stallion's gleaming coat, admiring the smell of Jasmine oil and the texture of the horses' neatly brushed hair.

Rinn untied the towrope, gripped the stallion's leather saddle, and mounted the horse. He clicked his tongue and the stallion quickened its pace to trot alongside Alaric.

"I do miss the city. What is my reward up to now?" Rinn asked.

"Thirty thousand gold pieces," Alaric answered.

"Insulting, I've stolen a gem worth twice that. Tell me they have a new picture of me, that last depiction was frightful, I didn't even recognize myself."

"No, the Emperor has more pressing matters to deal with than a thief."

"I'm not just a thief," Rinn corrected. "I'm the Shade. There are songs about me."

"So you've said," Alaric huffed at the spider silk cape floating from Rinn's shoulders. "You could wear something less conspicuous," Alaric said.

"Then no one would recognize me."

Rinn gave Alaric a sharp smirk.

"How many gems have I stolen for you now? Eleven? Twelve?"

"Just, give me my amulet," Alaric demanded.

Rinn pulled a green vial from his saddlebags and tossed it to Alaric.

"Careful!" Alaric scowled. "Bane blood is rarer than diamonds!"

Alaric snatched the vial from the air and clutched it close to his chest.

"So you've said, but you don't see anyone else making necklaces out of it. I'd rather be carrying witch piss. At least *it* would smell better."

When the vial got close to Alaric's body, the green blood took on a faint, hazy glow. He relaxed his mind and let his rebellious thoughts run free; sudden ease settled on his face. Alaric closed his eyes and gave into an array of mental images.

Bane blood was the only thing that could dampen the effects of the Mind Curse.

Alaric's mind was a loom and each decision a string that weaved a complex mental tapestry. He carefully plotted and placed each thread. Every color represented a different facade he used to inspire trust, greed, sympathy, or hate. Allies and enemies were used like stitches, entering abruptly and cut off when they fulfilled their purpose.

For Alaric, it wasn't that easy. For the first thread of Alaric's masterpiece, the stitch that held the whole tapestry together was a deal. The knowledge needed to recreate the breastplate could only be given by one old enough to have worn the original breastplate. Sarod was the only being with intimate knowledge of it. Of all the threads, his deal with the Dark Prince was the most costly.

Alaric stopped at the top of the road's tallest hill and turned to look back at Dragon Fang Castle. In the misty distance, it was a tiny thorn poking out from the horizon. Sullen, his face turned as still as a lizard trying to blend into its surroundings. His empty eyes didn't move as he stared into his past.

He remembered himself as a complicated young man. Everyone knew why he caused so much trouble, but no one would speak of it. When his village was massacred by Doya, he had been hiding from his chores on the outskirts of town. He was the only survivor.

He had traveled to the nearby city of Atlantis and lived on the streets for a few years. He stole and begged to get by. Then he fell sick. A doctor with secret ties to Aurorean Order recognized his symptoms as signs that he was gifted. The doctor then had him smuggled to New Camelot, where Alaric could be trained by the Order.

Alaric relished enchantments. He enchanted his first object, a dagger, when he was only eight. He was a prodigy. A stern, but fair Enchanter, Master Durakos saw his potential and took him as his apprentice. Alaric's apprenticeship lasted only four years before he insisted on leaving the city and the Order. He confided in Durakos. Alaric told him of his plans to leave and join the Emperor in his quest to place the four kingdoms under the rule of a single king, one that could ensure obedience and peace. A king powerful enough to control the Doya.

Alaric set out for the Fang shortly after learning that Durakos had revealed his wishes to the Council.

When Rinn saw Alaric's long stare, he pulled his horse to a halt alongside him.

"Why do you always stop here?" Rinn asked.

"It was here that I burned the flesh from my mentor," Alaric said. He made a bitter grimace and spat into the grass.

"He was my trainer. My friend. But I knew his intentions. He thought to stop me from serving the Emperor even if it meant my death," Alaric continued.

"What did he do?"

"He hesitated," Alaric said. "In that moment of hesitation, I triggered a fire enchantment that I hid in a medallion I'd given him as a gift for his hundredth birthday."

Alaric swallowed as if trying to push the truth down like vomit. "When I stand here, I can still hear his shrill, skin-peeling screams."

"There is nothing that you can do about it now," Rinn said flatly.

"I'm a traitor and a murderer. The damned quickly grow an immunity to regret." Alaric's face was void of emotion, but Rinn could tell from his tone that the old mage couldn't even convince himself. Inside Alaric was a blackened soul unable to wipe itself clean.

"I've never let anyone stand in my way. Not then, and not now. The Emperor and Cain betrayed me and I've waited long enough for my vengeance."

Rinn matched Alaric's low, cautious voice with the same eerie severity.

"I'm in this for one reason. Me. You better get this through your twisted brain. I'm on your crusade because you claim to have the one thing I can't steal," his voice was on the brink of shouting, Rinn paused for a moment to calm himself.

"You'd better hope your fancy breastplate works," he finished.

Alaric nodded coolly.

"You'll get your answers, but not until after we kill Cain and the Emperor—" Alaric hunkered over in pain, unable to finish his sentence. Verbal treachery brought a punishment that even a vial of bane blood couldn't dispel.

The Curse felt like a sharp pitchfork pulling at his brains. His hands shook. He fumbled for the cap of the vial tied around his neck. Alaric yanked the cork off and dipped a finger into the slimy liquid and dabbed it under his tongue. Almost instantly, the Mind Curse's punishment diluted to a dull, steady ache.

Alaric took a determined breath.

He needed the Seer Stones. The Urim would be the easiest to steal, at least he knew where it was. With a little luck, he'd retrieve it before Lady Black and Sarod. He just hoped the Order had taken the bait he'd left them. If it worked, Aurorean mages would be in Atlantis to confront them. How could they pass up the rumor that one of the Marked is hiding there? Would they send Durakos? Alaric had wondered what his mentor would say if they came face to face again. No, they wouldn't send him. It would be a fighter, a Warlock, and of course, an Oracle. They always sent an Oracle when it came to matters of prophecy.

Alaric's horse startled at a clumsy rustle in the tall grass.

A ragtag gang of highwaymen stepped out of the grass and blocked the road. There were four; each was dressed in a mismatched assortment of elegant clothing that was worn and stained with blood or dirt. All but their leader had a face gaunt from starvation.

Three scrawny men lingered behind the leader. Instead of armor, the highwaymen carried their own odd collections of loot. One had dozens of Atlantian timepieces hanging from his coat, another wore soft furs, and the last donned extravagant necklaces of polished glass.

Their leader was a pudgy man in a tight yellow coat that squeezed him like a pastry. On his head, he wore an iron helmet. He rested his arm across his gut, and used his fat to help hold up a silver sword that was designed more for show than combat.

"This is a loot'in. Give up your valuables," he shouted.

Alaric cursed under his breath. His vial of Bane blood weakened magic. Without his magic, he was just an ornery old man armed with a dagger and a sharp tongue.

Alaric shot a glance at Rinn. He caught a glimpse of him just before Rinn jumped off the far side of his horse. The gang moved to intercept him, but they never saw his feet hit the ground. They checked the road and nearby grass, but Rinn was gone.

"What?! Where did he go?" the leader demanded.

Alaric's confronted the leader with a chilling, tenacious stare. He was a hawk eyeing a fat mouse. The leader couldn't look back. He took a few paces backward to put his gang between him and Alaric.

"Find the coward!" the leader ordered. "Those gauntlets of his are worth a fortune."

Tick, the bandit with the assortment of clocks, picked up each of Rinn's bags and listened for the subtle mechanical chime of his passion. The bandit with a fur fetish, Pet, lustfully ran his fingers through his stallion's white mane and over its black coat.

"You're all going to die." Alaric's voice was as eerie as a church bell chiming in a ghost town.

"Keep your eyes on him," the leader said, nervously. He mustered the courage to look Alaric in the eyes.

"So the piggy has a backbone," Alaric said.

The leader raised his blade to Alaric's chest, fat pudgy fingers wrapped tightly around the handle. Alaric discreetly reached for his dagger, but with the height of the horse, his only target was the fat man's helmeted head. Alaric had a strong blade, but the helmet was made of thick iron.

"What kind of rich man doesn't own a single watch!" Tick grumbled and tossed the last of Rinn's things onto the ground.

Alaric tilted his ear toward their leader.

"Pig. Is that a clock I hear ticking in your pocket?" Alaric asked.

Like a hound sensing an intruder, Tick rose up out of a pile of Rinn's blankets and crept toward the gang leader.

"That's a pretty shard of ruby glass that you hide around your neck," Alaric said. Shiny dropped what he was doing to lurk in the background. A coy grin spread across Alaric's face.

"Hold your tongue! What would I do with that worthless junk?" The leader's voice weakened as he watched Tick and Shiny close in on him.

"Is that soft rabbit skin lining your helmet?" Alaric felt the sharp point of the leader's sword dig through his robes.

The leader held his sword in one hand and used the other to pull his head out of his iron helmet. He revealed two biscuit sized cheeks and a mouth drawn up into a snobby pucker that almost hid his double chin.

"Look! See! I don't have any of your crap," he exclaimed and tilted his helm to show them the iron shell.

"This old man is a liar!"

Alaric smiled a wicked, crooked grin.

"I am the worst of liars," Alaric said.

In a flash, he swatted the leader's sword away and pulled his dagger out from under his robes. With a powerful stroke, he drove his blade through the leader's naked scalp. The fat man fell like a puppet cut from its strings.

The gang's mouths dropped. They looked at their dead leader and then up at Alaric. They were about to flee when Pet caught a glimpse of the Emperor's seal burned into Alaric's palm.

"He's one of the Emperor's Branded!" he exclaimed.

Tick, Shiny, and Pet pounced on Alaric. He swung his dagger, but they were too quick. They dragged him from his horse. Shiny grabbed for his vial of Bane blood. Alaric dropped his dagger and clutched the vial tightly between his fingers.

"One of you bastards burned my village," Tick growled.

"And killed my mum!" Shiny charged.

Quaking with frustration, Shiny stomped through the dirt and took the leader's sword and thrust it through Alaric's shoulder. Alaric cried a high pitched squeal and rolled to his side.

"Look! He bleeds black!" Pet shrieked, pointing to the blood seeping from the wound.

Dizzy from the pain, Alaric wanted to use magic to crunch their skulls one by one like rotten peaches, but he knew it was no use.

The three highwaymen stood over him, contemplating their next move.

"Pet, you should kill him." Tick said. "They took your wife from you."

Pet ran his fingers through a lock of hair sewn into his furs and nodded. He pulled a long sword from under his furs and rested it on Alaric's throat.

"Rinn?!" Alaric cried, helplessly.

Pet raised the sword.

"Rinn, you'll never find the Doomseeker. The answers to your questions will die with me." Alaric tried to move out of the way, but Tick seized the sword sticking from his shoulder.

"Do it!" Shiny ordered.

Pet swung at Alaric's neck. The cry of steel on steel rang, and Pet's sword stopped in mid-air. Vibrations ran down the thick blade as Pet struggled to keep hold of it.

In a blink, Rinn materialized before them, blocking Pet's next blow with his gauntlet. With his head hung and his black hood pulled up, he looked like the reaper come to take them.

Rinn's labored breath made his black hood shake. He panted as if he'd been running. Sweat dripped from underneath his hood and leaked between the metal of his gauntlets.

The three highwaymen stared aghast.

"He's the Shade," Tick gasped.

Rinn put his hands on his hips and puffed out his chest.

With his captors distracted, Alaric pulled the silver sword from his shoulder. He got to his feet and jammed the point between Tick's ribs. Alaric grunted as he pressed it up into his heart. Tick looked down at the sword poking out of his chest. He tried to scream, but only blood came out. He fell to his knees and watched as the hole in Alaric's shoulder crept shut, leaving only a black scar.

"Kill them and be quick about it," Alaric ordered.

Rinn flicked a wrist. A click came from a gauntlet and a serrated, curved blade folded out its side and sprung to his hand.

Pet swung to take off Rinn's head. Rinn blocked. He snatched Pet's sword in his armored fingers and yanked Pet toward him. Pet stumbled and Rinn's dagger opened his throat.

In a breath, Rinn was gone.

"Where did he go?" Shiny gasped. He was alone. He looked down at his companions lying in their own blood. He spun around, terrified, unsure of where to point his sword.

A sharp pain shot through his chest. Shiny saw blood dripping from his coat. It saturated his glass necklaces in crimson blood. A moment later, Rinn appeared before him with his curved dagger in his chest. Shiny fell dead.

Rinn stood over his fallen enemies. He ripped his hood back and gasped for air. Sweat dripped from his chin and down his neck, drenching him in a musky, salty stench. Rinn stumbled. He couldn't hold himself up. He fell into the road. Alaric hurried to his side and placed a hand to his chest. He could feel Rinn's heart pound in a wild, erratic rhythm.

"My gods! You absorbed too much light," Alaric gasped.

Alaric hurried to Rinn's belongings strewn about the road. He rummaged through them until he found a bottle of Hawthorn elixir. He popped the cork off in his teeth and dumped the potion into Rinn's mouth.

"Drink it. All of it." Alaric said.

Rinn coughed between gulps. His hand reached for his chest. He strained to speak.

"I'm...getting...stronger," he said with a triumphant smile.

"Quiet! Your heart is nearly ready to give out."

10

Avalon

Never be afraid. Never be angry. Never be seen. Mathus' three rules cycled through his head, over and over.

Never be afraid. Never be angry. Never be seen.

They were the rules to hunt Doya. He didn't have the gift. If he was going to kill, it had to be swift and quick.

Do not think. Act. Do not hesitate. Bludgeon their brains. Cut off the head. Wound them with gold. Make their heads roll.

Vallan's lessons paraded through Mathus' mind.

The breeze moves through you. Your feet leave no marks. You are a shadow in the darkness. Sound is your enemy. Death is your gift.

Vallan had started teaching him with the sword and when Mathus had mastered it, he taught him how to track them, what they smelled like, the powers of their blood, the limits of their healing, where to cut them, where to crush, and when to run.

They cannot see colors in the night. Reflections will attract their attention. Textures can fool them.

Mathus tightened the laces in his leather breastplate. The leather was bright red and soft. Iron plates were sewn in for protection and bark had been pressed into it to mimic the texture of a tree trunk.

Mathus leaned with his back to a tree. His soldiers crowded around. They wore the same type of armor, pressed in the bark to conceal them and dyed in cow blood so that he could easily spot all twenty of his men in the moonlight.

Captain Willow led the group to the road. She was taller than the others, even Mathus. On her back was a quiver of short spears. Her rigid cheeks and pointed chin made her features striking. Willow's thin lips didn't smile, nor did they frown. Her face was tense, yet still like a cat before it bares its teeth to growl.

"Someone's coming," Willow whispered. She pulled a golden tipped spear from her quiver. The muscles in her forearm flexed as she drew it back over her shoulder.

A man in a coat of green wool sprinted down the road. When he saw the soldiers approaching in their blood armor, carrying bows and crossbows, he waved his hands over his head.

"Don't shoot!" he commanded.

The man pulled his hood back. His mop of straight black hair fell out and his round, frog eyes bounced between the crossbows pointed at his head.

"Hold you're fire. It's only Dirk," Willow ordered.

"Lord Marshall," Dirk saluted Mathus with a fist to his chest.

Mathus' face looked to be made of pale steel in the moon's light. "Did you spot the Doya?" he asked.

"They're approaching from the east, they're a league out," Dirk answered.

"How many?"

"Three."

"Are they in raven form?"

Dirk shook his head adamantly.

"I watched them change to men."

"Doya aren't men," Mathus said flatly.

Dirk winced. "I saw their bones pop and crack. I was going to have chicken tonight. They can't turn into chickens, can they?"

Snails, a chubby brown-toothed man, stepped out from behind a rock.

"Tonight they might," he laughed. Snails threw his arm around Dirk.

"You can keep your chickens. I have a stomach for ravens. They have fatty meat; it's tasty. Fat is good for you. I say the body knows what it needs, and what tastes good is always best."

"You eat snails," Dirk said, shrugging his arm off.

"*I told you,*" Snails prodded Dirk's chest with one of his brown fingernails. "I don't eat them. I rub a bit of them on my skin. Snails ward off magic."

"Who told you that?" Mathus asked doubtfully.

"The witch who sold me my Snails," he shrugged. "But she didn't get the best of me. When I asked what made them snails so special, she said it was their mystical food, so I had the witch sell me their food. I can make my own snails, sometimes I even eat the powder."

Snails pulled out a pouch and dipped his finger in it. Then he dabbed it under his tongue.

Captain Thar, a short, stocky man with an ax over his shoulder, stepped up beside them.

"The way I figure is if I smell like snails and I eat the powder, then I will be mystical too," Snails said.

Thar slapped Snails over the back of the head. "When you were a babe, your mother dropped you on your head."

Snails held the bag out to Dirk. Thar batted it away.

"Don't be poisoning the boy with your worm dung. You don't need to be mystical. You just need a little bravery."

Thar pulled a wineskin from under his armor. He popped off the top and took a long drink. "Meade from Tír na nÓg, the strongest there is, it will make you brave." He took another long drink and winked, "Watch this bravery."

Thar patted his hair flat and straightened his beard. Then he cut in front of Willow and gave her the widest grin his round face could muster. The top of his head only came up to her shoulders.

"Willow, you're looking very...um...round tonight," he said.

His eyes didn't leave the small bumps that were the thin woman's meager breasts.

Willow's fists clenched. "Are you speaking to my breasts?"

"Yes I am, and have some decency. You're interrupting our conversation. The left one was just saying how the right one is bigger and I can't rightly tell with them all bound up in leather."

Willow punched Thar so hard that he fell on his butt.

Thar laughed and rolled to his side to face Dirk.

"See! I wasn't scared at all." He rubbed his jaw where Willow hit him. "My face burns a little, but good mead does that to a man."

"Willow, Thar," Mathus called to them.

Captain Willow and Captain Thar jogged up beside him.

"Willow, your soldiers in the front. Thar, keep yours in the middle, and I'll charge down the road."

Mathus examined the road. "We will fight them here." Mathus pointed to a tall tree at the top of the hill.

"Willow, I want you in that tree. The Doya will step over the hill. We'll have the lower ground, but we'll hide." Mathus pointed to felled trees on both sides of the road. "Our crossbowmen will take position behind those logs. You will let two Doya pass. When the third one passes, you will take it down. Archers and crossbowmen will fire when you throw your first spear."

Mathus turned to the far end of the road and pointed to a patch of bushes tangled up in a clump of trees. "I will hide there. When the other Doya turn to look at who's attacking them, I will charge down the road with my swordsmen."

Mathus gestured to the tree line along the side of the road. "Thar's men will shoot from there and then join us in the fight."

Mathus looked between them. Willow nodded her approval. Thar glanced at the tree line and scratched his chin.

"Fine, but if my men kill them first, you're buying the drinks."

Mathus laughed and gave Thar a friendly jab. "It's a deal."

Willow and Thar gathered their soldiers and hurried to their positions.

"Dirk and Snails, you're with me," Thar ordered.

Dirk drew his crossbow.

"That's a fine weapon there. Does it have a name?" Thar asked.

Dirk looked back confused.

"Well, all good weapons have names." Thar patted the ax resting on his shoulder. It was a lumber ax made from simple iron.

"This here is Hag. She's cold and cruel. I don't much like her, but we've been together so long I've just gotten used to her. I want a new one, but it wouldn't feel right casting her aside."

Thar held out the ax head and pointed to a notch in her blade.

"That is from a Doya's skull. My first kill. Split the creature in two. I wasn't sure if it would die like that, so Hag and I spent a long night under the stars waiting for the damn thing to stop moving."

Mathus called out to all the soldiers from his position in the patch of tangled bushes. "Remember, they're not dead until their heads roll."

Willow stood in the tall tree facing toward them. In her hand was a golden tipped spear, and to either side of the road, hidden behind log and crouching in the tree line, were archers with their bows drawn and crossbows cocked.

Mathus drew his Aureate dagger from his belt. It was a crude weapon. Its original handle had broken off. Now it was a rough blade with a wooden handle wrapped in black leather. He'd paid a fortune for it. It was the only Aureate weapon in the whole group.

"Good luck, Sir," a soldier whispered.

Mathus nodded to the soldier. He pulled out the lock of Ele's hair that he'd tied around his neck. He gave it a soft kiss and tucked it back under his armor.

Mathus drew his broad sword in his other hand.

Willow signaled that she was ready. Now, they only had to wait.

The moonlight cast the forest in an eerie gray. When the light hit the tree bark, the trees took on the pale, wrinkly skin of an old corpse.

The crickets did not sing and there were no birds in the trees. Somewhere in the darkness of the forest a Barreled owl made a whooping growl that sent rodents scurrying through the underbrush.

A white, bald head came over the crest of the hill. Its eyes were blacker than the night, and tar-like drool leaked off its chin. It moved slowly with its back hunched. The Doya didn't sway as it walked. It moved evenly like a bird in a run. Its raven-feather cloak flapped behind it.

No black tears and it had both hands. It wasn't Sarod, but there were still two more.

The next two came up side by side. Their skin was just as pale as the first, and their eyes were just as black. They hunched as well, unlike Sarod, who stood upright. He was strong, the strongest of them all, but he wasn't there.

Mathus wouldn't have his revenge tonight.

They stopped under the tree. Willow was just above them.

"What are they doing?" Mathus growled.

The Doya in front sniffed at the air.

"Come on, keep moving," Mathus whispered.

Willow crept away from the trunk. She dropped to her belly and slowly, silently slid out on a limb.

Mathus' heart pounded. This had to be right, no mistakes. They'd never taken three before.

The Doya looked around. They gazed to the side of the road where Thar was hiding, nodded, and started walking again.

Mathus released a sigh of relief.

The Doya were approaching the logs. Once they stepped beyond them, they would see the crossbowmen.

"Now, throw the spear. What are you waiting for?" Mathus whispered. They were going to be late. The timing couldn't be off. Timing was everything.

Mathus spotted Willow standing on the limb of her tree, frozen. Why hadn't she attacked? Then Mathus saw movement beside her. A flutter of wings. A bird. No, a Raven was staring right at her.

"Mathus—" a soldier whispered.

"Shhh! I see it."

"I can hit it," the soldier turned his crossbow from the Doya on the road to the Raven in the tree.

"No, you'll give us away."

The Raven screamed a gurgling cry. The Doya spun around and looked up into the tree.

Willow's spear flashed through the moonlight. It made a moist thud in the nearest Doya's chest. The Doya growled and ripped the spear out and tossed it aside. Blood oozed from its chest. Arrows came flying through the air. One got it in the leg. It stumbled and another caught it through the temple. Willow leaped down. Her sword flashed and parted the Doya's head from its shoulders.

The other two Doya reeled.

"What have you done?" one screamed as it watched a pool of black blood flow from the head-less Doya's neck. "You'll die for that."

It drew a fist and a surge of lightning went up its arm. It threw a bolt. Willow ducked. The bolt crackled and flashed over her. The ground shook when it blasted away half of the tree trunk behind her. Flames emerged from the trunk, the tree teetered, and the Raven disappeared into the sky.

Mathus barreled down the road. His legs were a blur of strides. Behind him, his men tried to keep up. There were no battle cries, no screams. They were a silent, red gale of steel and muscle.

Before the Doya knew they'd charged, Mathus' broadsword was already through one of their necks.

Crossbows loosed. Bolts and arrows rained into the last Doya. The Doya deflected the bolts on one side with a pressure spell, the ones on the other missed.

This was the Doya that concerned Mathus. It had time to think.

Thar charged out, wielding Hag. He slashed and cut. The Doya took in a deep breath and drew a spell. Thar rolled out of the way. A gust of frost shot from the Doya's mouth. It caught Dirk's arm. He cried out in pain. The frost spread up his arm and bled into his skin like frost on a windowpane. When it reached his lungs, he choked.

"Dirk!" Thar cried.

Dirk's legs froze; he stumbled and hit the ground. His frozen body cracked in half at the waist. His eyes filled with tears, but he couldn't scream; his mouth had frozen.

The Doya laughed. His inky smile spread across his face.

"Look out!" cried Willow.

The Raven dove out of the night sky. With the force of a meteor, the Raven crashed to the ground behind

Mathus' men. It tumbled through the tall grass. As it spun, it started to grow; its bones cracked and contorted.

"Get it before it transforms!" Mathus cried.

Soldiers charged the Doya. They hacked at it, but they were too late.

A blast threw two of his soldiers beyond the road and tumbling into the woods.

The Doya fighting Thar waved its fingers and his likeness split into ten visages.

All ten went in different directions.

"Ah hell, I haven't had that much to drink," Thar muttered. "Kill them all; one of them has to be real."

Another volley of bolts and arrows zipped through the air. They passed through the visages like an arrow through fog. One caught in the real Doya's arm. It was close enough to Thar. He swung Hag at the Doya's head. The Doya caught his ax, and squeezed it until it shattered.

Thar's eyes went wide as he watched his ax fall to pieces. "You ugly bastard. You can go to hell. You go straight to hell!"

Thar drew his dagger and thrust it through the Doya's throat. It happened so quickly that the Doya jerked in surprise.

"This dagger here is called Wench's Mother." Thar grabbed the Doya by the skin of its bald head and started to saw at its neck. Blood gurgled out of its throat.

"Do you have something to say? Wench's Mother doesn't care. She's a spiteful, angry bitch, and if she gets the chance, she'll take your head off."

The last Doya leaped at one of Mathus' swordsmen. His claws slashed and ripped open the swordsman's chest armor. He slashed again, this time at pink flesh, and blood spurted out. The man screamed and dropped his sword. The Doya slashed again and again until its claws came out of the swordsman's back.

Two soldiers advanced on him. They swung their swords. The Doya backhanded one. The force of his blow sent the soldier spinning through the air. The Doya flashed its claws into the other soldier's neck and ripped out his throat. The soldier gagged on a tangle of shredded muscles.

Mathus rushed to the Doya. The Doya expected him to slash and parry, but Mathus flung his sword aside and tackled him. The Doya drove its claw into Mathus' shoulder. His pauldron shredded and blood spurted out. Mathus clenched his teeth, but didn't lose focus. They rolled into the dirt. Mathus flipped the Doya over and pinned its arms under his knees. He balled a fist and punched the Doya across the face. The Doya's nose burst into a geyser of black blood.

"I don't need magic. I don't need claws." Mathus hit it again.

"You're nothing!" he hit it again.

Mathus brought his Aureate dagger to the Doya's neck.

"Wait—" the Doya choked and spit a tooth. "I have a message. We bring a message from Lord Sarod."

"Then speak quickly," Mathus said.

"Sarod's message is for the Archmage."

"Spit it out," Mathus insisted.

"Sarod proposes a truce, for a time. There is a greater enemy that threatens us all."

"I'd rather see you dead," Mathus said. His shoulder was starting to throb. Blood dripped off his elbow.

The Doya tried to pull its neck away from Mathus' dagger, but that only made Mathus press it harder against his throat.

"The Archmage can save us all, but I must speak with him. Sarod will send more messengers. Next time it will be fifty, maybe a hundred. Can your little band of rogues take a hundred of us?"

Mathus took the dagger from the Doya's neck and ran the flat of the blade across its cheek.

"This dagger is Aureate, steel mixed with gold. It's poison to your kind and sharp enough to cut through flesh and bone. If I cut you, that cut will never heal. You'll bleed until you dry up like a wrinkly, white raisin."

Mathus ran the flat of the blade over the Doya's other cheek.

"Now. Give me your message before I start cutting."

The Doya broke into a sweat that collected on the shiny edge of Mathus' dagger.

He brought the dagger back to the Doya's throat.

"I will die before I give this message to anyone but the Archmage. Those were Sarod's orders. Bind my hands and hold your dagger to my throat all the way to New Camelot if you wish."

"I haven't decided not to kill you yet," he replied.

The Doya inclined its head and gave Mathus a knowing smirk.

"Lord Marshall, you can't kill me. What I have to say could save your people. Isn't that your duty?"

Thar stood above them and scratched his beard.

"I say we take a big rock and crush its head. Their heads make a funny noise when they pop. Like a watermelon and a war hammer, but messier."

Willow pushed through the soldiers and crouched down beside Mathus.

"We could learn a lot from a Doya if we trapped it. We could find its weak spots, we could even make a poison."

A breeze made something dangle in the corner of Mathus' vision. It was the lock of Ele's hair. During the battle, it came out from underneath his armor to hang over his chest. The breeze lifted the cord and made the hair shiver. It dangled between them. Mathus' attention shifted between the favor of his slain sister and the knife pressed at the Doya's neck.

11

Avalon

Apollo couldn't sleep. How could he with Cat out there? He'd told the Night Guard that she knew how to break out of her cage, but they didn't believe him, nor would they admit they'd left her unattended. When he had told Vallan what happened, Vallan told him to keep an eye on the cage, and he did. By day Apollo rode on horseback over trails that were scarcely wide enough for a wagon and over rocky terrain that was so rough that they'd had to stop to cut down trees to make new axels and crude wagon wheels. At night, he watched the cage, and Cat watched him.

Vallan had said that it would take weeks to get the wagons to the Chasm. Now Apollo could see why.

The only sleep he got was on his horse. Exhaustion was making him sloppy. He'd stubbled on his last watch, and the hard ground had felt so comfortable.

His thoughts were never far from Cat. He had to get her to the Chasm, away from him, but he also wanted to talk to her again. She'd said his eyes were powerful.

Apollo walked through camp. The wagon drivers had already eaten breakfast and were packing up.

He saw Vallan hunched with his wide shoulders pushed forward and his arms folded. He looked strangely similar to a bird wrapped in his own wings. With an eagle-eyed stare, he watched the dying embers of the evening fire. As the fire faded, the near-invisible flames charred the logs, burning them into a dry, crumbly crust. Still and cheerless, Vallan watched the ashen snowflakes be whisked away by the wind.

The closer they got to the Chasm, the more Vallan retreated within himself. They'd scarcely spoken since Miriam, Rhean, and Wislan broke off from the group to head farther east to Atlantis.

"You'd better saddle up," Vallan said, irritated. The still, far off look in his eyes showed he hadn't slept.

Apollo still had his rusty broadsword drawn from being on patrol. He tucked it into his scabbard and located his saddle at the base of a tree. He shook off his horse blanket and laid it over his mare. Then he heaved the saddle over his horse's back and tugged on the straps until it was good and tight.

Apollo discretely turned away from camp and pulled his nicked mirror from his saddlebags. With it, he checked the marks under his eyes.

The Thetus Mud he'd applied the previous afternoon had cracked and fell off during the night. A distinct dark, almost black, skin pigment was visible. So much of the mud had flaked off, he could even make out the symbols.

He rubbed the last of the dry mud off. His bare cheeks held unmistakable symbols, half suns with branching rays that were discernible by anyone versed in the Garatha. Apollo took his container of mud from his pocket and applied a new layer of the brown clay-like substance over the marks. In moments, the marks that identified him as the Doomseeker were once again hidden.

Apollo straightened his full, long-sleeved robe. It covered everything but his hands and ankles. Its first wooden button fastened near his shoulder, closing the robe over his chest and the rest of the buttons varied in size and trailed down the right side of his torso. The robe was made of plain linen. Old and worn, the cloth looked and felt like wrinkled parchment. If it weren't for the Aurorean symbol sewn into the chest, the robe would be altogether hideous.

He stepped into his stirrup and pushed himself up into his saddle.

Finally, he could get some sleep.

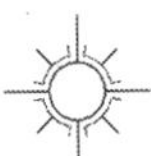

A hard slap across the face woke Apollo up. He jolted in his staddle and nearly fell off the side of his horse.

Apollo spun around in his saddle to see what had hit him. Cat's cage was rumbling down the uneven road next to him, but he was too far from the cage for her to touch him. He looked back and saw a tree branch hanging over the path, but it too looked far out of reach.

Cat was propped up on her elbow with her dress pulled up so her slender legs were showing, again. She was a prisoner, but her body language made her look like an empress being escorted in a carriage on a sunny afternoon.

She was still wearing the same white dress and crimson sash she'd been wearing when they'd left New Camelot. She should stink, but she was as clean as if she had bathed that morning.

"You haven't visited me."

Apollo blinked his eyes and wiped away drool that had collected on his chin. He opened his mouth to say something, but Cat beat him to it.

"You like to watch me don't you?"

Cat ran a fingernail down her thigh.

"Are we going to play this cat and mouse game all the way to the Chasm?"

Apollo looked around. He could only see the Night Guard driving the wagon and Cedric, her corrupted companion, lingering in the background. No one would be able to hear them over the pounding of the wagon wheels on the rocky path.

"I told them you can get out," Apollo said.

"Oh? Did anyone believe you?" She asked.

Apollo bit his lip. Suddenly, he felt foolish.

"Cat's don't belong in cages," she said.

"Why are you still here then?"

"I like it when you watch me." Cat grinned. "You have such powerful eyes. I haven't told you about your eyes yet. I want to."

"Then tell me," Apollo said, trying to sound uninterested.

Cat rolled over in the hay and laughed.

"I know you want to know, but I'm not going to tell you that easily. You're going to have to come to visit me. Tonight."

Cedric stood. Normally, he was a statue of solitude, but he was stepping toward them.

He pulled back his hood. His cheeks were sunken in and his head was bald and oily. A few strands of wiry hair hung from his upper lip. He bore his sharp teeth at Apollo.

"Back off." Apollo drew his sword.

Cedric growled a low grumble, part laugh the other disgust. Cat reached for Cedric and playfully hugged his knee.

"Cedric doesn't like games like I do. He's tired of this cage."

Cedric drew his hands out of his cloak. His fingers were mangled and oozed with Doya blood. He wrapped them around the bars.

"He won't hurt you. I won't let him," Cat said.

Apollo couldn't take his eyes from Cedric's hands. The tips were scraped to the bone. His fingertips were sharp boney things, and blood flowed so freely that it dripped down the bars he was gripping.

"Come see me tonight," Cat repeated. "I'll be waiting for you. I'll even wear my best dress."

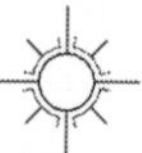

As the Chronos Mountains got closer, Apollo felt his aura shake.

Something was wrong. He felt as if he was traveling through a tide of hammers. Each pounded his aura. The impact created vibrations that twisted at his insides. The distortion created moments where he couldn't have touched his aura to cast even the simplest spell.

"What is that?" Apollo asked Vallan.

He could tell by the sober look on Vallan's face that he felt it too.

"Remnant."

The dense woods ended in a tree line. Beyond lay a small, waist-high ledge that led into a barren, dirt field. The ground was sun-baked and cracked. The forest looked like it had been torn right out of the ground. In its center were the mountain peaks that made the outline of the brow, nose, and sharp chin of the face of Chronos staring up at the sky.

Apollo examined the definitive ledge where the forest ended and the dirt began. It was such a short drop. A mere step down, but the foreboding pounding inside of him told him to stop.

Their horses froze on the ledge. Apollo coaxed his mare with a rasp of his heal, but the horse wouldn't budge.

Behind them, the horses pulling the wagons reared and kicked as if a lion were prowling the road.

Vallan didn't look the least bit surprised.

"Remnant is what is left after enchanted objects are destroyed. It's scentless and invisible. Plants will not take root here and animals will not enter the field."

Apollo dismounted. His horse retreated to the back of the group. Vallan's horse stood firm.

"The superstitious find Remnant haunting."

"Can it hurt us?" Apollo asked, waving an arm over the threshold between the field and the forest.

"No, but without a connection to your aura, you cannot cast new magic. Only enchantments work under Remnant's veil." Vallan dismounted and stepped past Apollo into the field. He cringed as if wading into icy water.

The Chronos Mountains dominated the sky. The stony peaks that made Chronos' face flashed in the afternoon light and their snow-covered peaks glistened, giving the titan's face a degree of godly beauty.

"Deep in the face of Chronos is the Chasm. We've arrived. When the suns set, Osirius, the leader of the Chasm, will address us."

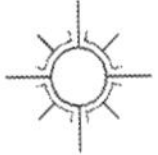

The dense canopy fortified the woods against the approaching moonlight. The trees held off the luminous invasion so that darkness blanketed the forest's interior. Thin moonbeams sliced through the canopy and touched the ground like long silver spears sticking out from the forest floor.

They'd set up camp in the woods near the field of Remnant. Apollo knew tonight was the last night he could speak with Cat.

He didn't want to go to her cage. It was a bad idea. He could watch Cat from across the camp. Yet, curiosity was driving his feet. He believed that Cat wouldn't hurt him. She was corrupted, and he'd even felt her absorb his fear. She was evil, but he sort of trusted her. She hadn't told anyone about him being a dark mage. It was a secret that he only shared with those he trusted. If she'd told someone, then they might start asking more questions and the last thing Apollo wanted was people prying into his secrets.

Apollo had his sword drawn. It was pockmarked with rust. He'd always imagined its previous owner to be a farmer. Its unsightly orange dilapidated blade and crudely chipped edges made it easy to imagine the sword shoved into a crate of farm tools and left to ruin in a leaky barn.

The weapon didn't carry the splendor of Vallan's sword with its gold-tinted blade and bone handle adorned with white and golden Opalite. Still, despite his sword's miserable appearance, it was heavy and sharp enough to cleave off a head.

That was how you killed a Doya. Cat was corrupted and so was Cedric. Stabbing them might stop them, but if they were corrupted enough, then their wounds would close. Could he cut off their heads if he had to? Mathus and Vallan wouldn't think twice. Could he cut off Cat's head? The thought damped his spirits. She was the enemy; why did it seem so wrong?

"You don't need your sword. I said that I wouldn't let Cedric hurt you."

"Cat?" Apollo spun around, but he was in the woods, alone, and surrounded by trees.

Movement caught his eye. A figure dashed through a moonbeam.

"Stop!" Apollo yelled.

Twigs and underbrush cracked under Apollo's boots as he ran.

"Come and get me," Cat purred.

Apollo ran faster. The camp was now out of sight. Even the light from the campfires was drowned out in the brush.

Apollo skidded to a stop. Cat sat above him on a tree branch. She leaned against the tree trunk and swung her bare feet above him.

"You came to visit me, *finally.*" Cat rolled her eyes.

"You shouldn't be out." Apollo pointed his sword up at her. Cat ran her toe up the flat of the blade.

"You're always so serious, like Cedric," she pouted.

"Where is Cedric? Is he out too?" Apollo demanded.

Cat's eyes glinted. "I couldn't let him rot in that cage."

A shiver made Apollo's sword arm shake.

"Where did he go?"

Cat slid out of the tree. Apollo still held her at sword point. She reached out and pushed the sword harmlessly aside.

"I can help you find him."

Apollo hesitated. He shouldn't go after him. He should go back and tell Vallan.

"You can see him. With those eyes, you can see everything." Cat took a step toward him. She tripped. Apollo dropped his sword and caught her. Cat pressed her body tightly against his. Apollo felt every curve and bump of her slender figure.

"You are such a gentleman," she groaned playfully.

Apollo tried to shake off a smile. Cat bent over and retrieved his sword from the ground and pressed it into his hand.

"We might need this. Cedric is angry." She took Apollo by the hand and led him deeper into the forest.

The farther they went, the thicker the woods became. Apollo had lost track of time. Still, there was no sign of Cedric.

"Your eyes are a gift," Cat said.

Apollo opened his mouth to argue, but Cat abruptly covered it.

"You talk too much," she said and continued.

"The corruption changes you. Cedric is growing his bone claws. You saw his hands. Once his eyes turn black, he'll be a Doya. Doya are children of the Darkness. They can see everything in the night."

"Darksight," Apollo said. He'd heard of it before.

"And you think I can see in the dark?" Apollo asked.

"You can," Cat insisted.

Apollo shook his head. Cat turned to face him. She leaned in close and brushed her nose against his cheek. Apollo thought to back away, but he wanted her to touch him.

"I like you," she whispered. "You're fun."

Her lips were black, and her skin was pale. She was corrupted, Apollo reminded himself, but it didn't seem to matter.

"Thank you," Apollo said.

Cat's big brown eyes looked into his black eyes. She was awestruck.

"Let me teach you," Cat whispered. She took his hand and placed it on her hip. His fingers tingled.

Apollo fell into a stupor. Part of him wanted to kiss her black lips, the other part told him to run. Let her go. Just leave.

Cat walked her fingers up his arm and across his shoulder.

"The darkness is the power that calls to us. Your eyes hear it. You have to learn to listen to the darkness. Once you know its voice, then your eyes are opened."

Cat pointed to a grove of trees off in the night.

"Focus on the void, the black, not what you're trying to see."

Apollo did.

Cat placed a hand on his chest.

"Breathe."

Apollo took a long breath. He could feel something, a whisper, no, a multitude of whispers. He flexed the muscle in his eyes and they became clearer. There were no discernable words, only confusion. His pupils dilated. The beams of moonlight spearing the forest split and blurred. His sight became nothing but a single splotch of light. For a brief moment, everything morphed into a fog as if a picture had been pushed against his face. Then as his Doya eyes started to focus, the whispers of the night touched him. The surface of his eyes felt mumblings of the darkness like millions of dull needles pressing against the sensitive bulge of his eyeball. As his mind interpreted the varying tones, the foggy picture pressed against his face drifted backward into his field of view. After a minute, the entire forest before him appeared in his mind as if it were carved out of stone.

The detail was breathtaking. What normal vision did with light and color, Darksight achieved with perfectly accurate textures. He could see each branch of every tree. The small ridges of every trunk, even the veiny spines of each and every leaf. However, despite the finely carved image rendered in his mind, the lack of light and color made a Doya's view of the world stone-like and cold.

"Now you see," Cat said.

Apollo saw her. His eyes saw her as a perfect sculpture. No black veins or oily skin, she was a woman without flaw. His heart pounded. He dropped his sword. Cat drew her arms around his neck. She licked her lips.

Apollo's aura shrieked. A jolt went up his spine, but before he could react, she pressed her lips on his. Apollo clutched her in his arms. It was wrong, he knew it, but it felt so good.

Cat squirmed and gently bit his lip, a sour taste filled Apollo's mouth.

Then he remembered the black tar that he'd seen oozing from her mouth. He tried to push her off, but she clung to him.

"What's wrong? I know you want this. I've seen the way you look at me."

"Get off." Apollo jerked his mouth away. His Darksight faded and he saw Cat, clinging to him. Black drool leaked out the corner of her lips. When she spoke, her teeth were covered in black ink.

Cat beat her fists on his chest. "You want me. I know you do."

"No I don't!" Apollo spit off to the side. He couldn't get the sour taste out of his mouth. His tongue burned.

Cat's mouth dropped.

"You're rotten, I should've let Cedric kill you with the rest of them."

"Kill them?" Apollo grabbed her by the wrists. "Cat, what did you do?"

Cat tried to pull her hands free, but Apollo had a firm grip.

Apollo thought of the last place he saw Cedric. He was in the cage. The Night Guards were watching him. Apollo felt a surge of panic. "The caravan!"

Cat blew out a stream of soot. She'd fed off of him again. She mumbled a word and Apollo's fingers went numb. He lost hold of Cat. The numbness spread up his arms, down his torso. His legs gave out.

He watched, powerless, as Cat turned back the way they'd come, toward camp.

12

Avalon

Thump. Apollo felt the pound of Remnant on his aura. He had to get back to camp. He didn't know how long he'd laid in the woods, immobilized by Cat's spell. It was before twilight, maybe there was still time to save them.

Thump. Again, the Remnant sounded, this time it was stronger. His legs still wobbled from Cat's spell.

He should've never left. Why couldn't he have listened to Vallan and just kept an eye on the cage. The suns hadn't risen, Vallan needed him.

Thump. This time it was so hard that Apollo's weak knees gave out. He stumbled into a tree, scraping his arm on a sharp branch.

Thump. He was going in the right direction. He knew it.

He could see now. The night was open to him. Every impression and detail of the forest was crisp and clear. The night held no secrets.

Apollo saw the field just ahead of him.

He hacked at tree branches and jumped over the ledge separating the forest and the field of Remnant.

A chill came over him. The pounding stopped. His connection to magic was severed.

A blur caught his eye. It was light. He couldn't see what it was. Apollo let go of his Darksight. He rubbed at his eyes as they struggled to focus.

An inferno raged where the camp had been.

"Vallan!" Apollo cried.

He ran across the field. A burning tree snapped and fell. It rolled off the rim and into his path. Its burning branches crumbled under it. Apollo took cover behind a boulder just as the tree split on the rockface.

Apollo looked over the boulder to the rim. Cedric was there. His cloak was partially burned off and his skin was blistering from the heat. Black drool drained out his mouth and down his chest. He flexed his oily muscles and roared into the night.

His eyes were marbled black and white. He was changing. A few more spells and his transformation would be complete.

Apollo looked down at his sword. It was all he had. The fire was erratic. Even if he left the Remnant, the fire blazed like the sun. It would be too hard to absorb the unstable shadows.

Apollo rounded the bolder and climbed over the rim out of the field of Remnant. His aura rushed back, knocking the wind out of him.

"Look out!" Vallan cried.

Apollo jumped out of the way. Cedric's mangled fingers, now sharp claws, plunged into the tree beside him.

Cedric's claw ripped open the tree. Flaming bark exploded over Apollo's head.

Vallan shoved Apollo away and caught the claw with his sword. He drew a pressure spell and released it into Cedric's abdomen. Cedric propelled backwards, tumbled, and slammed into a tree. His backbone visibly cracked and a tree branch jutted out his back.

"Where's Cat?" Vallan searched the burning forest.

Apollo saw the burning wagons and the men. Wagon men and Night Guards were strewn about the forest. Some burning, others were so mangled that they barely resembled humans.

"I don't know. I went after her. She tricked me." His insides twisted. He should've been watching the cage. Maybe then—.

"It's not your fault," Vallan said. He knew what Apollo was thinking.

Cedric pushed away from the tree. His backbone contorted and snapped back into place. Blood oozed from a tree limb sticking from his back. He pulled it out and the hole in his torso sucked shut.

"The wagons!" Vallan pointed to the lead wagon, loaded with the objects to be destroyed in the Chasm. The fire climbed up a longsword, the side of the charred wagon broke away. Shields, axes, and staves dropped into the burning forest.

"RUN!" Vallan shoved Apollo in the direction of the mountains. They hurtled the rim. Apollo looked back over his shoulder. A beam of light shot through the forest, overpowering the light of the fire. A relic broke and the power trapped inside of it was released.

A torrent of wind broke trees in half. They flipped end over end and shattered on the mountains. A dust cloud stampeded through the field.

The dust was too thick. Vallan and Apollo struggled for air.

"We have to get into the Chasm," Vallan said, trying to hold back a cough. "The mountain will protect us."

Ten more bursts of light. Immense boulders came loose in the field. The dry, cracked ground of the field broke up into chunks and lifted into the air. Rocks collapsed down the mountainside. Light from relics flashed in the dust cloud like bolts of lightning in a stormcloud.

13

Avalon - The Chasm

Apollo suspected that the suns had risen, but they were so deep in the mountain that he doubted the suns had ever touched these halls.

He'd expected the Chasm to be only a cave with a really deep hole. To his surprise, he found wide caverns that resembled the halls of a forgotten palace.

Water and time had taken their toll. The molding carved into the stone walls along with the sculptures melted, as it seemed, into the dripstones. Cracked reflecting pools were scattered and fragmented on the cave floor. Fountains gurgled water like cut veins and created muddy puddles for Apollo and Vallan to trudge through.

The ground shook. Vallan grabbed Apollo by the arm and pulled him into a narrow passage.

Vallan kept ahold of him as fist-sized rocks fell from the ceiling. Rocks splashed into the water and cracked against stone, sending a dull echo deep into the mountain.

"The relics are still bursting?" Apollo asked.

"The less damaged ones take longer to explode," Vallan replied, letting go of his arm.

They came to a dead-end where a pile of rubble obstructed the path. On one side of the cave was the statue of a pointy-eared elf almost fifty feet high. The elf held a leafy staff and was mostly covered by dirt spilling in between the cave wall. The statue looked as if it were struggling to pull itself from the mud. Apollo had seen a similar statue in the Aurorean Temple, it was Galandor; he was always depicted with a leafy staff. Galandor was Wythrin's father, and the first of the Elves to rule with the breastplate. Galandor was known to the Elves as the Peacemaker and so his statue held the symbolic, leafy staff of peace.

On the other side of the cave was another statue. Apollo was sure it was Wythrin, even though it was eroded by water pouring in from the ceiling. His form was a rounded clump of rock, the water left no detail, only a stone sword that the statue jutted triumphantly out of the small waterfall.

"Even the work of the Elves can't last forever," Vallan said.

The two sentinel statues guarded a pile of rubble that spilled from a mangled steel door. Above the door was writing in Primoris words of magic, the tongue of the Elves and dragons.

Primoris was a language of compound symbols. One simple symbol was drawn upon another to complete a thought. The symbols were rigid lines and angles. Only the powerful words had curves, and the rarer, the mightiest, used circles.

Above the door, Apollo could recognize simple symbols contained in the compound ones: "Ebgon" meaning "keeper", "Thrin" for "light", "Utha" for "command," and there were some that curled or contained several circles he didn't recognize.

Vallan located a steel wheel sticking out of the wall. It had the symbol "Ashborn," on it, the Primoris word for "fire;" a group of squiggles that flicked and curled upward like wild flames. Ashborn was the first symbol that Vallan had taught Apollo to draw using multiple fingers. Warlocks had a quick technique for the common words of power. They used them to cast spells faster than other mages. However, stringing them together was difficult. Conjuring a fireball was simple, but throwing it and making it explode required three symbols drawn to create a compound one, a feat that was quite challenging amidst a battle.

Vallan turned the steel wheel, jutting out from the wall. With each revolution, the steel squealed and the wall clanked.

Torchlight revealed more Primoris on the sidewalls as well. It was a story of some kind or a warning.

Apollo wished he'd paid more attention to Miriam when she'd tried to teach him the rarer symbols. The symbols used in spell casting were indistinguishable from the ones found in common writing.

He was eight and she'd taken it upon herself to instruct him in the stories and spells of the Garatha. When he'd seen her ancient leather-bound Garatha, with its wrinkles and crinkled pages, he remembered thinking that it almost looked as old as Miriam.

He had been determined to impress her. When she opened her leather book, and Apollo recognized some of the ancient symbols on the pages, he puffed out his chest and spouted them out randomly. Miriam clamped a hand over his cheeks and squeezed until his mouth scrunched into fish lips.

"These words are to be said with care," she'd dictated. "Their symbols carry power."

Looking back, he understood why she did that. He was a boy of eight and was still learning to control the energy in his Well. If he had absorbed power while verbalizing certain symbols, he could've cast any sort of spell.

Leaving New Camelot with Rhean, Miriam, and Wislan seemed like a lifetime ago. He wondered if they'd ever found their "Marked," and if they did, would they have taken the "Marked" before the Council? Being judged by the Council for prophecy was one of Apollo's greatest fears. If it ever happened to him, he didn't know what he could say. How could he convince them the gods were wrong about him?

They entered a pitch-black corridor. Apollo unfocused his eyes, and let a long breath as he switched over to his Darksight. It was easier this time. He wondered how he had gone his whole life not knowing he could see in the dark.

"Are you alright?" Vallan asked.

Apollo jumped. Vallan looked like a breathing statue under his Darksight. He could see the form of every wrinkle in his face and the tip of each hair.

"I'm fine," Apollo replied, pushing his worry aside. He didn't want to tell him about his Darksight, not yet. How would Vallan react if he knew that it was Cat who taught him how to see like a Doya?

Darksight uncovered the scratches and impression as if he could touch every part of the one hundred foot wall all at once. Words were cut in the walls, the same ones over and over.

Vallan struck a piece of fairy tinder on his boot and lit a torch. The flash of light forced Apollo to let go of his Darksight.

Apollo ran his finger over the scratches. "*He watches*," he read.

"They're writing about Sarod, aren't they?" Apollo asked, running his fingers through the scratch marks.

Vallan held his torch close to the wall for a better look.

"The Corrupted and the Doya say he knows things that only the gods could know," Vallan said.

"Does he?" Apollo asked Vallan.

"Sarod rose from the dead. I don't think there is much he can't do."

"Aren't they afraid he'll come for them?" Apollo asked.

"Sarod won't enter the Chasm."

"Why?"

Vallan stopped where the path split and considered each way.

"This was his first tomb millennia ago. His elven bones are at the bottom."

They passed through caverns, and though they were vast, they looked no different than any other cave. Then there were chambers that were mere shadows of a once-great palace. Chandeliers dangled crooked on the ceiling or lay broken in the ruin of the shattered ceramic floor. Stalactites punched through the ceiling murals like spears reclaiming what was theirs. The once-beautiful dwelling of the Elves had become a home to decay and a realm of darkness.

They cringed and covered their ears. The squeal of an iron crank grinding on stone reverberated throughout the mountain.

They followed the sound to a cavern containing a massive pit. In its center was a golden platform with a narrow bridge. Above the platform, hundreds and hundreds of elongated, dull, brass boxes hung from chains and were arranged in such a way that they resembled a giant chandelier. In the center of the masterpiece, a bright pillar of sunlight shone in from outside and reflected off the brass. It created a striking display of beams that shot out, illuminating the colossal cavern.

The iron shrieked as it rubbed against the floor. It was a constant wail, an iron scream that fell upon their ears like the high-pitched cries of a tireless child. Revolution after revolution, the crank loosed rope from a rickety wooden crane. At its end, lowered a square platform of blood-stained planks piled high with putrid meat.

A berserker, bound in thick iron chains, rotated the crane's crank and the pile of meat started to sink into the depths of the pit.

The animal had white fur and a gray mane along with the head and limbs of a great wolf. Hunching at a meager height of seven feet, the berserker was small compared to others of his kind. He had a frame like a muscular bear and black leathery hands that looked strangely human despite his sharp, jagged claws. Gelatinous slime slid off his canine teeth and collected in his chest fur.

"What is that?" Apollo asked, mesmerized.

"A berserker, a creature of the north," Vallan answered.

"Beware Aurorean, berserkers don't much like to be ogled," said a short gangly man. His pale skin made him a ghost in the darkness; when he moved, it was in the same way that an insect twitched and jerked. The man had bulbous eyes that jumped between Vallan and Apollo, while he scratched at a patch of flaky skin on the underside of his belly.

"Paranoid beasts. That one killed three men bringing him in here, and he's killed two curious fools since. We didn't mind much. They were the weird ones."

The gangly man took a bold step forward and held up five fingers speckled with dead skin. "That's five men dead. That's a lot."

He paused for a moment to count the fingers on his other hand.

"I had to mop them all up. That's ten arms, ten legs, and fifty toes. Ha! *Fifty toes*. I like toes."

Vallan moved toward the pit, but the odd, little man blocked his way.

"They call me Lurk. You can call me that if you want."

Vallan tried to step by, but Lurk blocked him again.

"That path only leads to death, or that's what everyone says," he said in a squeaky voice. "Walk down there and you're as good as dead. How many toes do you all have?"

Vallan ignored the question.

"I must speak with Osirius," Vallan said.

Lurk's big eyes flicked left and flicked right. He nodded and then shook his head.

"The Father?" Lurk said.

Lurk pointed to the pit. "We didn't go through all that trouble getting a berserker in here cause we like the smell of his sweaty hair. He has mean toes though. Spiky, sharp things."

"I'm going down there. Osirius will be waiting for me," Vallan said.

"I'm going with you," Apollo replied.

"You will remain here. Osirius knows me. This is not my first time into the abyss."

Lurk cocked his head as they spoke and politely waited for them to finish. "You come from the outside? Beyond the edge of the forest, beyond the Remnant?"

Vallan gave a hesitant nod.

"Will you tell me of my homeland?"

Vallan examined Lurk as if reading a passage in a familiar book. He didn't look old, no more than forty. Vallan's cold blue eyes followed the web of black veins in the man's milky skin. His tainted blood corrupted his hands, his fingernails had fallen off and the flesh on his fingers was cracked to the bone. Vallan noted the sweaty strands of hair on the man's nearly bald head and the black dribble leaking from the corner of his mouth. Each was a clear sign of corruption, yet he had the face of a man, soft and round. It didn't look like a Doya's face, and the man's dull eyes were sad and full of longing. In the spectrum between a human and a monster, Vallan knew that without Remnant's power to sever the man's link to magic, he would've changed to a Doya many years ago.

For a moment, Vallan pitied him, but only for a moment. In the forefront of Vallan's mind, he considered the others Lurk had wronged, the victims. Who had he frightened or tormented? Who had he killed to become such a monster?

Vallan tried to step past him, but Lurk only shuffled back in his way.

"I come from Hyperion, my town was called Anado, I think. Have you heard of it?"

Vallan stopped cold.

"You have!" The man grinned; his smile was a wet, slimy thing. He hopped forward and clutched Vallan's robes. "Tell me of it? How are my people?"

Vallan regarded Lurk with a burdensome stare.

"Dead. They're all dead." Vallan disentangled himself from Lurk's grip.

Lurk retreated back a step. "Dead? What? How?"

"Some years past, Sarod attacked the village...I'm sorry."

As he walked away, he heard Lurk creep up behind him.

Vallan started to pull his sword from its scabbard. The glint of the golden blade made Lurk stop dead in his tracks.

"I'll not harm you. I just want to know: the butcher, is he alive? He was my father. He'd be an old man now."

Vallan shook his head.

"And there was a schoolhouse. I had brothers there."

"No one survived," he said flatly.

Vallan stepped down into the Chasm.

"Apollo," Vallan called back. Apollo pushed off of the cave wall he'd been leaning on and walked to the staircase. "Keep your sword out and your back to the wall. These creatures are more monster than human."

For guidance, Vallan pressed his hand against the clammy stone wall. Slowly, he circled the vast staircase lining the walls of the abyss.

The Remnant was the strongest in the pit. Vallan's stomach churned at the chill it gave him. The light from the upper cavern dimmed. The pitter-pattering of Lurk's feet followed him.

Such a lonely man, Vallan thought. He almost pitied him, but no, his decisions had placed him here.

Those that sow terror harvest misery.

"My mother baked," Lurk yelled down. "She made the most delicious breads. Is she alright?"

Vallan didn't respond.

Vallan descended into the world below where his only companions were a steady shriek of the distant iron crank and the sound of Lurk's voice as he shouted questions from the safety of the last beam of cavern light.

14

Avalon - New Camelot

Clara walked out onto the balcony and ran a hand over the smooth granite banister. Beneath the Black Mountain's ebony shell was the gray granite that was used to reconstruct the ancient Elven walls and build Castle Caerlon as well as the Sanctuary. Clara pushed her finger over a perfect ridge where a chisel had carved a lip into the stone. This rock was quarried from the Black Mountains, yet they had shaped it precisely, despite the savage landscape of its origin. Each stone fitting into the next in symmetrical harmony.

If only they could shape the Doya like they shape the tough rocks from their mountains.

Clara leaned against the banister so she could admire the white marble angel carved into the keystone of the balcony's archway. It was accented with a sliver of gold on its head like a halo. Its arms were open for an embrace and on its back were outstretched wings.

An angel guarded every passage in the Sanctuary. King Arthur had overseen the construction of the temple, he'd placed them on the doorways to remind the people of how the angels of old delivered them from destruction.

Yet people would enter and exit the Sanctuary without so much as glancing at the angels. Time was clouding the past, and soon the people would forget them.

Clara turned and looked across the square to the Aurorean temple, a narrow pyramid of white marble that reached up into the sky. She suspected the Sanctuary was mostly granite because there was little marble left after the Elves had completed such a fantastic structure. From the Sanctuary, she could see over the temple's common brick wall and into the shimmering sunstone courtyard. A flood of warm colors reflected off the sunstones and onto the temple's white exterior, giving it an otherworldly glimmer.

"Isn't it magnificent?" asked Daynin from the archway. He stepped out onto the balcony to join her.

"Grandmaster." Clara raised her palm to her forehead and was about to bow when Daynin stopped her.

"Please, I've been a Grandmaster for over a hundred years. I think I've been bowed to more than most kings." Daynin leaned on the balcony beside her.

Clara pursed her lips. What was the Grandmaster doing talking to her? She was the black sheep of the Sanctuary.

"Sometimes I wonder: if the temple is so breathtaking, what did this city look like when the Elves were here? Do you think the whole city was paved with sunstones?" asked Daynin.

"I imagine Tarboroth like that," Clara said. She looked away from the temple through the corner of her eye. Grandmaster Daynin still stood next to her. She placed her hands in the balcony. She tried to fold them. Then she placed them at her sides. She couldn't help her fidgeting. What did he want?

"I don't mean to be rude Grandmaster, but why are you talking to me? No one ever talks to me," she asked.

"You aren't part of the Collective mind. Sometimes Healers forget that there is a world outside of the vastness of the Collective mind. Don't fault them for getting lost in it. The gods know I chastise them enough, but we were admiring the temple. Tell me, what is your favorite part of the temple?"

Clara squinted against the sunlight. She could see the golden bowl holding the smokeless fire burning on its peak. She scanned the ridges of the step pyramid and the hundreds of stairs until she got to the entrance, a great golden door.

"I like its shadow," she answered.

"Its shadow?" Daynin looked back, confused.

"The temple has a long shadow. When the lesser sun sets its shadow can reach the whole way across the city. It reminds me that even something as pure white as the temple has a darkness that it must live with."

Clara bit the inside of her cheek. Had she really just told the Grandmaster Healer that her favorite thing about the temple was its darkness? In what world would that be a good idea?

"I like it," Daynin admitted.

Clara let her cheek slip out from between her teeth and smiled.

"My favorite part is the heart of the temple, the Urim. I have seen it on occasion. Its light is as pure as sunlight and the energy from it invigorates. The Elves pulled it from the Breastplate, they couldn't destroy it, so they built the temple to protect it," Daynin said.

Master Ruben joined them on the balcony. He bowed to Daynin and then nodded to Clara. Daynin rolled his eyes.

"I've told him to stop bowing for gods know how long and he still does."

"Your title demands it, Grandmaster," Ruben replied.

"I doubt the Elves did so much bowing," Daynin muttered.

She tried not to stare at Ruben's crooked jaw. No matter how many times the Healers attempted, they never could quite fix it. She'd heard stories about how he'd broken it. All of them started with him chastising a drunken Warlock for not cleaning off his boots before entering the Sanctuary.

Ruben's scruffy face and tangled brown hair only made him look rougher. Clara never thought he was particularly interesting, but wherever he went there was always a crowd of Healers close behind. He was next in line to become the Grandmaster Healer when Daynin died and some of the Healers, especially those who didn't respect Daynin, were eagerly waiting for the change in power.

"Lord Mathus has been admitted with a stab wound. He's requesting that Clara tend to it." Ruben said.

"Good, he will be good practice for Clara," Daynin replied.

"You're going to let me heal a knife wound?" Clara's heart leaped.

"Grandmaster, I must respectfully object. She's not part of the Collective and he's lost a lot of blood. She doesn't have the power or the knowledge to tend to him."

Clara folded her arms and narrowed her gaze. "Master Ruben, I must respectfully say you don't know what you're talking about."

Ruben looked back, dumbfounded.

Clara had had enough of their criticism. She wasn't a member of the Collective; that didn't mean she was incapable. She couldn't perform the more complex spells, but not everyone needed to be pulled from the brink of death. They thought that just because she wasn't part of the Collective that she was a glorified errand girl. Well, that just wasn't true, and the next time a Healer asked her for a bandage, she was going to shove it up their nose.

Clara unballed her fists. Think, focus, you have a job to do, she said to herself.

Daynin and Ruben led her into a Healer's room. Sunlight came in from a row of open windows on one side of the room, and a table was set up where the sunlight was brightest. Along the edges of the room, Healers gathered to watch.

Healers are creepy, she thought. They looked at her and exchanged glances, but didn't whisper. A female Healer in the front snickered, yet no one was speaking to her. Then there was the nodding. Gods, she hated the nodding. She knew they were talking about her through their Collective mind. They were saying she was going to fail, and out of habit nodded in agreement. The woman laughing probably thought it was funny that she was even there.

Clara went to a corner. Her hands shook. She balled her fists and opened her hands to stretch her fingers over and over until they stopped shaking.

You can do this, she told herself. They don't hate you. They're not here to laugh at you.

Clara looked back at the gathering Healers. They were still nodding. Why did they have to do that?

She tied back her long, golden hair and took an apron from the wall. She dropped it around her neck and tied the waist, so it looked like a tent over her small, slender body. She doesn't even fit in the apron. She was sure that's what they were saying now. She's a seventeen-year-old twig in an apron.

Part of her wished she could hear what made them nod like that; the other part wanted to run out of the room and crawl under a rock.

Two soldiers escorted the Lord Marshall in.

"Lady Clara is all I require." Mathus bowed to Daynin, Ruben, and the crowd of Healers, and touched his palm to his forehead. He winced in pain and reached to where his pauldron was split and a blood-soaked bandaged could be seen between the torn leather and cracked iron plates.

Ruben opened his mouth to argue, but Daynin motioned him and the other Healers out of the room.

Clara could finally breathe. It was just her, Mathus and a couple soldiers in the room.

Mathus sat on the table, and his soldiers unclasped his red, leather breastplate and carefully removed the pauldron. Underneath, he wore a blood-stained tunic. The tunic was crimson, so it hid the blood well. The wet fabric clung to his skin. He'd lost the color in his face and his lips were as pale as clam meat.

Clara unraveled the bandage on his shoulder. When she reached the skin, she saw two jagged gashes across his shoulder.

"This is from a Doya claw," Clara said.

Mathus nodded but offered no explanation.

Clara took a pitcher of Blood Sap from beneath the table, poured Mathus a cupful and held it out to him.

"You need to drink this. You've lost a lot of blood. It will help your body compensate."

Mathus took the glass and grimaced at the smell. He took a quick breath and chugged it down.

"By the Gods that's horrible," he said, wiping his mouth.

Clara turned back to his ruined shoulder. She hoped she could remember what to do. If good deeds honored the sun gods, then surely they would help her now. Clara whispered part of a memorized prayer. "From the East, house of light, May wisdom dawn in us so that we may see all things in Clarity."

"You know what to do, Clara, don't overthink it," Mathus said.

Clara balled her fists and focused on the light around her. She could feel the warmth on her skin and the energy rushing to her heart. After a long minute, she summoned enough power to get her heart thumping hard. She reached out a hand and began a soft chant. Light surrounded her. She used her fingers to draw symbols over Mathus' wound. The light about her body flowed out her arms to the beat of her heart. Each thump made the torn flesh pull together. In moments, Mathus' wound pulled completely closed. Clara grabbed a towel and wiped the blood off his skin. There was no scar. The flesh was smooth and unbroken.

Sweat dripped from the end of Clara's nose. She wiped her face in a clean sleeve and took long deep breaths to calm her heart. She felt as if she'd been running. Her heart slowed down, but her body felt weary. Clara shook her robes to get some cool air between her sweaty skin and the sweat-soaked fabric.

Mathus moved his shoulder in a circle. He ran his fingers over where the Doya had cut into him, and the skin felt smooth.

"How are you feeling?" Clara asked breathless.

"Excellent, good work," Mathus said.

Clara went back to the corner and removed her apron. She looked back to where the crowd had stood bobbing their heads. She wondered what they would think if they'd seen her heal the Lord Marshall. They'd probably say something good about her for once.

"Clara, if you will excuse me for a moment," Mathus said and exited the room.

Clara went to the window. She always seemed to be at the window. She gazed outside so that she could see the Sanctuary's outer wall. The Sanctuary was colossal and completely round with stone walls and hundreds of balconies. From this window, she could see one of the two main entrances. It was so large that it was nearly the size of the castle gate. Almost a thousand pillars created the beautifully uniform outer walls. At times, at least in Clara's mind, they looked like the bars of a great cage.

The city square acted as a market separating the Temple and the Sanctuary. The shouts of merchants and patrons came up as whispers on the wind.

Clara wondered where she would be if she wasn't gifted. Maybe she would've married a merchant or a smith. She could've joined the army. The city guard was so desperate that there were often women archers. She'd even seen a female pikeman once. Her father wouldn't have heard of it. He had had plans to marry her off for money. He used to run his fingers through her blonde hair and call her his "little golden nugget."

Her mother was the dreamer. They'd played wizards together. Her mother would take her to gaze up at the temple and imagine what was inside. They would sit together and listen to Master Durakos teach the words of Taza, the Purist prophet, in the square.

Clara had prayed to the Sun God for the gift. To Purists, the most honorable calling from the Gods was to be an Aurorean Mage. She never told her mother that she wanted desperately to be an Enchanter like Durakos. He had the most interesting jewelry. Once, he even showed her a ring that could freeze water. Durakos put it on and touched his hand in a bucket of water, and the water froze so fast that the bucket burst.

Then in one night, her life turned over, and she chose to be a Healer, so she could save people. A part of that little girl thought that if she saved lives that it would somehow repair the gap in her soul. The one created when her mother died.

Now, she couldn't save anyone without losing herself to the Collective.

When the melding ceremony is performed and she is linked to the Collective mind, there is no going back. Her memories, her secrets, every image in her mind would spread between them. They would see the haunting scene she couldn't forget. Daynin, Ruben, and the Healers who laughed and scorned her would see the lifeless bodies of her two dead parents lying in pools of their own blood, and the whole Collective would know what she did.

Mathus brought her a washing bowl. “You should always wash the blood from your hands.”

Clara jumped. “What?”

She hadn’t heard him enter the room.

He set the bowl on the window seal and took the rag from it. He wrung it out and handed it to her. “Here, clean your hands.”

Clara took the rag and scrubbed her fingers. She dipped and rubbed and wrung again and again, but couldn’t get the blood out from underneath her fingernails.

“I need your help, I’ve lost some Night Guards. I can’t have people asking questions.” Mathus said.

Clara turned to the Lord Marshall. He was strong, lean, and taller than most men. He’d changed into a tightly fitted blue doublet with brass buttons. An elaborate blue cape with gold trim wrapped over his right shoulder and under his left arm. The fabric was fastened together over his right lapel with a large polished brass medallion engraved with a dragon head. The blue cape hung in a single-layered column from his right shoulder to his ankle.

Mathus waved his arm and the door swung open to fifteen of Mathus’ soldiers in red, boiled leather, blocking the Healers’ access to three stretchers.

“Let us through, we must tend to your wounded,” Ruben demanded.

“That’s enough, Ruben.” Daynin’s voice came from somewhere in the crowd of Healers. “This is the Lord Marshall’s concern.”

The soldiers filed into the room with the stretchers. Ruben and the crowd of Healers remained outside.

Mathus addressed the Healers. "The City Guard thanks you for your hospitality." It was a dismissal, but not a rude one.

The Healers gave Clara sidelong looks and unsettling stares. They wanted to be in there with her. With all that knowledge in their heads, they couldn't stand the unknown, especially when this mystery was under their own roof.

Clara knew it wasn't just about secrets, they didn't think she was capable without the Collective, the Healers wanted to whisper in her head, guide her thoughts, fill her with their *wisdom*.

Ruben's condescending words repeated in her head. *I must respectfully object. She doesn't have the power or knowledge to tend to the Lord Marshall.* He didn't have any faith in her, none of them did.

Just as the door closed, Clara stuck her tongue out at Master Ruben.

Protests erupted outside, but Mathus answered them with the heavy metallic rattle of the door's iron lock.

Willow, the captain of the group, took post at the door. She was taller than the other troops and her stern look never seemed to leave her face. Clara didn't know much about her, just that she was the one person the Lord Marshall seemed to trust more than anyone else.

"No one enters until we've finished here," Mathus commanded. Willow answered in a salute by pounding a fist to her chest.

The Lord Marshall rounded the three stretchers in the middle of the room.

"What happens here will never be spoken of. Not to the Healers, not to your fellow guards, not to your husbands or wives, not to your sleeping babes." His stare patrolled the room. He measured the look on every face.

"There are those in power who would disband the Night Guard. One day, the Doya will attack, and without the Night Guard, New Camelot will fall."

Clara didn't know if that was truth or paranoia. With the Aurorean temple at the heart of the city, she doubted Doya even considered attacking them.

Mathus waved for Clara to pull back the sheet on the first stretcher.

Clara covered her face when she saw the body of a young man covered in swampy green blisters. He'd died several hours ago, yet the blisters still glistened from sweat and seeped an acrid, vomit-like odor. His neck was shredded and his chest torn open. Splintered rib bones mixed with bits of his leather armor, and clung to his entrails.

"He was killed by a Doya. I can still smell vile magic on him," Clara said.

"Yes, but if you can mend him, we'll say he died on patrol." The Lord Marshall pushed the boy's eyes shut. "A bandit shot him in the heart." One of the soldiers pulled out an arrow and snapped off the golden fletching before handing the point to Clara.

"I can't hide these blisters. He must've been right in the Doya's face when it spewed its spit on him." Clara winced and examined the blisters closer. "Wounds created with Doya fluids are difficult to mend with Light Magic. If he were living they would heal in time, but without the help of the body they might be impossible to hide."

The Lord Marshall gave her a calculated look.

"Very well." He turned back to Willow, who was still standing guard at the door. "When we are done here, see that this man is burned. I will personally take his ashes to his family."

He pulled the sheet from the next stretcher. "This man was attacked by a bear."

Clara scanned the body. Claw marks ruined the man's face and throat. Her stomach turned when she saw where a Doya had reached in and pulled his throat out the front of his neck.

She covered her nose; the smell of dead flesh wasn't common in the Sanctuary. The Lord Marshall confronted the gore with a face as hard as a millstone, but in his eyes she saw that his grief was grinding away his resolve. Clara, like many, knew the story of his sister's death. When he had been appointed Lord Marshall, the tale of how he rebelled and broke his leader's nose crossed every tongue in the city. Some whispered that his sister's death was his own fault, but Clara didn't know what to think. She knew Apollo and Vallan trusted him. Vallan told her he was once a gentler man, but she couldn't see it. She could only see the Lord Marshall, the city's champion of swords, a man brimming with vengeful ambition.

The Aureate dagger at his waist said it all. Its hilt was leather-wrapped wood, but the blade was Aureate. Most men would trade it. With the small fortune, he could live a quieter life. But instead, he hunted Doya, and now he expected her to dress up the corpses to hide his mistakes.

Clara brought her hand to her mouth. The last stretcher held a man cracked in half by some sort of spell. His skin was moist and the cut was clean. The bleached white color of his skin made Clara wonder if there was a single drop of blood left in his body.

"Dirk." Mathus looked down at the broken man. "We'll say he was bitten by a Timberbelly in the swamp. Their venom will make your skin turn as pale as sheep's wool."

Clara pulled the sheet back over Dirk's head. She didn't like dealing with dead bodies, but it was good practice and she was desperate to feel part of something. Mathus had his flaws, and she could never trust a vengeful man, but he wanted to include her, and if she knew his secrets, it might be enough to save her from joining the Collective mind.

"How many Doya was it?" she asked.

Mathus scanned Clara's face. "Four," he said evenly. "You're all lucky to be alive."

"Not all of us," Mathus said. He gave the stretchers one last look and then went to the door. He stopped and looked back.

"Do you believe in what we're doing?" he asked, pointedly.

Clara scanned the man with the open throat, the next one with the shredded chest, and finally Dirk's pale, cracked body.

She didn't and she did. She took a breath and let it out. She could lie, but Mathus was clever, so she told him plainly.

"I've lost people close to me. I wish I'd been spared the truth. The families of these soldiers don't need to know the gruesome way they died. Sometimes we must lie. Even to ourselves. It's the only way to make things right."

Mathus nodded thoughtfully. "Through deception, anything is made perfect."

"You've read the Garatha?" Clara asked, surprised. Then she remembered he was trained by Vallan, of course he had.

"Clara, do you know the art of apothecary?" he asked.

"I mix all of the natural remedies used here in the Sanctuary."

Mathus nodded his approval. "When you are done here, Willow will bring you to the catacombs to meet our guest."

15

Avalon - New Camelot

A crack of thunder sent the merchants and townsfolk scurrying out of the city square. The warm months of Yielding had come to a close. The season of Sow arrived, and with it came colder months of rain, frost, and mud.

Just as the torrential downpour began, Mathus pulled on a sheepskin cloak and crossed the square. The last of the merchants tied down their booths and retreated through the streets. The gaps in the cobblestone flowed with water. The dips in the square filled and water receded off the bumps, so the square became a pond speckled with hundreds of stony islands. Children laughed and screamed as they jumped from island to island.

"Look at me," cried a little, round boy. He skipped across two stones and stomped in a puddle.

"I can do that," said a water-logged young girl.

"Oh, yeah? So can I," challenged another boy.

To Mathus' left was the Sanctuary. The giant circular building turned into a waterfall as the rain ran steadily off the dome roof. On his right was the Aurorean temple with its unblemished white marble that seemed to glow even in the gray afternoon. At the temple's peak, the ever-blazing torch burned true in the fierce gusts and heavy rain. In front of him was the castle; with its great stained glass window just above the entrance its face resembled an old cathedral. Beyond the gate were the courtyard and the main hall of the castle. It was a large building, smaller than the Sanctuary, but bigger than the temple. Of the three, the castle was the tallest. Its seven gray towers stretched to a dizzying height, the tallest of which seemed to scrape the belly of the churning storm clouds.

Mathus stopped to look up at the stained glass window. The temple's torchlight glinted off the thousands of yellow, black, and red shards of glass. The black glass was fitted together to form a dragon with outstretched wings. Along the edge of the window in aged, green copper read an inscription taken from Arthur Pendragon, New Camelot's first King:

Wisdom to those that seek it,
Peace to those that make it,
Strength to those that protect,
And above all Honor to those who forgive.

Mathus loved and hated that window. He could remember how his sister, Ele, used to stare at it for hours. She had said if you looked at it long enough, the dragon would look back. As a child, he'd wasted a lot of time staring that dragon down. Even now, some thirty years later, he caught himself staring at it, but for different reasons. The window was always repaired, polished, and washed. It looked the same as it had when he was a child, when Ele was still alive. She had been more than an older sister, she had been his only family. When their parents had died of the plague, Mathus and Ele lost everything. It was Ele who had stolen scraps to feed them, watched over him when he was sick, and even protected him until he could swing his own sword. They slept in the gutters of Westport, yet she had turned every day into an adventure. Some days they'd swim in the sea, or sneak up the city walls to be chased away by soldiers, or even skip through the rain puddles in the square. The timeless stained glass window was an anchor to his past, one he longed to return to.

The moist air became pungent near the window. The smell of dung and vinegar stole Mathus from his thoughts. The horrid smell was so overpowering that townsfolk chose running through the rain over the protection of the castle's wide roof. Mathus covered his nose in a handkerchief and stepped out of the rain and under the forsaken roof.

Two of the City Guard watched the castle entrance. They pinched their noses and armed themselves with sour expressions. Somehow, they looked even less pleased when Mathus approached them. Both had been late for morning drills the week before, so they had been given the honor of guarding the smelly castle gate.

"Good evening, Lord Marshall," one said sullenly. Both men saluted.

Mathus nodded as he stepped by. He crossed the gardens and entered the castle.

A servant took Mathus' cloak, while the rest of the castle staff bustled about, lighting candles to prepare for Sow's early evening. Somewhere behind the dark veil of purple clouds, Omega, the lesser sun, was setting. The castle and its long corridors turned into a shadowy maze. Lightning flashed, and jagged shadows shone through the castle windows. With each flash, the sky groaned thunder. When Mathus finally reached the heavy wooden door of the lesser throne room, he saw a mage in yellow and a mage in brown walking toward him. Between them, Mathus saw the Archmage. His red robe made him hard to see in the dark. When the Archmage got closer, Mathus could make out his white beard. It was as white as the snowcap of a mountain, though Archmage Lorad was no mountain. He stood at half Mathus' height, but his hunch made him look even shorter. At the Archmage's sides were Grandmaster Creator Gibnar in his yellow robe and Gibnar's twin sister Master Warlock Leteah in her brown robe. Leteah was new to the King's Audience and was only filling in during Grandmaster Rhean's absence while he was in Atlantis.

Both of the twins had long hair and strong masculine features. The only way to tell their faces apart was to look for the stubble on Gibnar's chin; though in her advancing age, Leteah had grown stubble as well, so it was better to remember that Gibnar wore yellow and Leteah brown.

The Archmage greeted Mathus. "The suns set and the city looks forward to another day, thanks to you and your men, Lord Marshall."

Mathus thanked the Archmage with a proper Aurorean bow.

"Thanks to all of us, Archmage," he replied.

Mathus liked the Archmage, as did just about everyone. As head of the Order, Archmage Lorad directed the other five Grandmasters, half of which were as cynical as any lonely crone. Luckily, Mathus only had to deal with them a few times a month.

He'd learned from Vallan that asking the Council for help was more like negotiating with an alligator to let go of your hand. They wouldn't be satisfied unless they got something, so you had to offer them a more tempting piece of meat, or be ready to gouge the gator's eyes. Either way, someone always lost, so like alligators, it was best to keep the Council at a distance.

Mathus had always thought the analogy was funny. Especially after he'd first met the Archmage, who resembled a wrinkly grandfather, the kind Mathus often saw playing chess in the square in the late afternoon.

Master Leteah yanked the wooden door open and led them into a windowless hall with a round table in the center. The King's banner hung from the wall, and below it King Amr the fourth sat in a tall wooden chair elevated just above the table. His ancient face, with its sunken cheeks and gray pigment, made him look like a dead man dressed in satins. He wore a blue cape over one shoulder like Mathus, but the King's cape was so long that it stretched out in front of him on the floor.

King Amr choked on a cough. He didn't cover his mouth. He pounded a fist to his chest until mucus dribbled down and he wiped it in his sleeve.

"Sit," he wheezed.

Mathus and the three mages took a seat at the round table.

"I'll hear your reports now," the King said.

Leteah stood and looked around at Mathus, her twin Gibnar, the Archmage, and finally back to the King.

"The Council has heard reports of a group of soldiers hunting Doya."

Mathus gritted his teeth behind his calm, uninterested expression. He knew he'd have to face this sooner or later.

"Is this true?" The King asked.

Mathus frowned back.

"My soldiers do what is needed to protect the city," Mathus said.

"I have forbidden you from attacking the Doya, we have enough enemies without provoking Sarod," the King said.

"He has lost several soldiers," Leteah added.

"Soldiers die, it's unfortunate," Mathus admitted. "I can't protect them from everything. I had one clumsy soldier fall over the wall and another two toss a cat into a privy. We are at war, and I command ten thousand soldiers, they're bound to get into trouble."

Mathus' face tightened as he turned to face Leteah.

"In case Master Leteah was concerned, the cat my soldiers commissioned to the privy survived. Though I doubt she'll wander into a barracks again."

Leteah's face turned a shade of red that matched the Archmage's crimson robe.

"You're making us a target," she blurted. "Sarod's last attack was nearly five hundred years ago. He wiped out half the army with only fifty Doya. We, the Order, saved the city from destruction. "

"Sarod attacked the city fifteen years ago," Mathus corrected.

Leteah spat as she spoke. "You're foolish if you think your sister's death was Sarod marching on the city. It wasn't until she shot him that he lashed out. She provoked him. Your personal quest for vengeance is going to put us in a war we can't win. You'll get us all killed, just like you got your sister killed."

Mathus lurched to his feet. His blood turned hot, and for a moment, he wished he wasn't Lord Marshall. He wanted to be that brash young man from years ago.

A vein bulged out of Mathus' tense neck.

One of Vallan's lessons came to the forefront of his mind. Each lesson had a rule that Vallan had made him repeat over and over: We are weak, we bleed, we mourn, we weep, but in the eyes of our enemies, we must be invincible. The phrase repeated over and over until he felt the tension in his neck loosen.

"The city guard has only attacked intruders," Mathus said.

"Intruders? You expect me to believe that?" Leteah balked.

"Enough!" The King commanded. "Mathus, you have your orders. Doya are not to be engaged unless they try to breach our walls, or harm our people. Gods help us if one ever gets into the city. If they do not threaten us, then Leteah and her Warlocks will handle them."

Mathus nodded stiffly. He wondered how Leteah would react if she knew he'd captured a Doya with a message for the Archmage. He would have to find a way to tell the Archmage without alerting the rest of the Council.

"Mathus," the King continued. "Do you have a report?"

Mathus took a calming breath and clasped his hands behind his back.

"We've spotted red dragons on the border. They're bolder than usual and there are more of them by the day. My scouts believe they're flying in from as far as Mount Scorpio to hunt. I've taken some precautions by having a portion of our pikeman trained in the Cog bow."

"New Camelot is protected from dragons." The King waved a hand dismissively.

"As you've said before my King, but should they attack the city—"

The King cut him off. "You needn't waste your time. Dragons fear this castle. His Majesty King Arthur put that fear in them, and they still remember his warning."

Mathus nodded, but he wasn't convinced. Dragons were the only enemy he had no protection against. If one should fall on the city, he didn't even know if his archers could bring it down. If many attacked, they only had the gods to save them, and Mathus wasn't about to rely on them.

"Thank you, your Majesty." Mathus bowed and sat.

Grandmaster Gibnar helped Archmage Lorad stand.

"Archmage, the floor is yours," the King said.

Lorad's eyes were framed with wrinkles. He licked his lips and spoke plainly.

"I have lived too long. When one younger than you dies that is how an old man feels. The longer you live, the more you realize how terribly unfair this world is."

The Archmage's voice turned raspy. He paused to swallow.

"Grandmaster Rhean, our Small Giant, is dead; slain by the Marked."

The King rose to his feet. "God have mercy."

"He wasn't alone," Archmage Lorad continued. "Miriam, the Grandmaster Oracle, was with him. She was a relic in her own right and as much a part of the temple as its marble walls. Some say she was as hard as them, too, and if you knew her, then you knew it to be true. She died at Rhean's side, fighting for the salvation of Haven."

"How did this happen?" the King demanded.

"As you know, we sent Rhean, Miriam, and Wislan to find the Marked. One of our trusted men in Atlantis told us there was a young man there with markings on his face that he'd had since birth."

The Archmage waved to Gibnar, who let a young blonde haired mage into the chamber. He wore a brown robe and walked with the grace of a noble. The King recognized his nephew at once.

"Wislan" The King greeted, sternly.

"Wislan was with them when they died. Go ahead, tell them what you told me."

Wislan's crystal blue eyes glanced about the room. He took a moment to inspect Mathus. His lip curled in disgust. Mathus was neither mage nor of royal blood. His presence offended Wislan. He'd never understand why his uncle, the King, thought it appropriate to replace Wislan's father with Mathus as Lord Marshall. Mathus was a rag boy of Westport, who'd been found guilty of blatant and deliberate disobedience to his superiors. How long would it be before Mathus started disobeying the King's orders?

Wislan gave Mathus a spiteful look. "Does the commoner need to be here?" he asked.

"That *commoner* is Lord Marshall," the King scolded. "Come now, boy, spit this story out. I haven't the time for old quarrels."

Wislan tossed his hair over his shoulder. He turned his back to Mathus, so that he was only facing the King and the Archmage.

"Our journey started with the envoy sent to the Chasm, Vallan and his black-eyed apprentice, Apollo.

Vallan tried to stop us. Somehow he'd learned of our journey and openly told Rhean to defy the Archmage and return to the temple, but we were diligent. We split at the border and traveled to Argos and took a ship to Atlantis. When we arrived in the city we went to the place where we were told we could find the 'Marked', but when we reached the spot, a man was already there, waiting for us. Rhean knew him and so did Miriam, but he was a stranger to me. They called him Alaric, the turn cloak."

"Do I know this turn cloak?" the King interrupted.

"He was one of Grandmaster Durakos' early apprentices, now an Enchanter for the Emperor," Gibnar replied.

"He left before Your Majesty was king," Leteah added.

"Continue," the Archmage urged Wislan.

"Rhean and Miriam exchanged words with the turn cloak. A boy approached them with a pair of crescent moons just under his eyes. The boy couldn't have been older than twelve. He knew Alaric by name, he'd been protecting him. Rhean commanded Alaric to hand the boy over, but he refused. Rhean drew his sword. He swung at Alaric, but some magical force blocked his blade. Then a man appeared. He just materialized out of the air. Rhean turned his sword on him, but he vanished. When he reappeared, he'd driven a blade through Rhean's back."

The King sunk in his chair. "And Miriam?" he asked, wearily.

"When the Marked boy saw Rhean die, he tried to run away. Miriam went after him, but the man, a thief whom some call the Shade, laid her outright beside Rhean."

"And how did you get away?" Mathus asked.

Wislan's lip curled up into a tight-lipped sneer. With his back to Mathus he could tolerate his presence, but not his questions.

"Answer him," the Archmage commanded.

Wislan rolled his eyes. "The Grandmasters died, so I had no choice but to retreat. Had I stayed, you wouldn't have known of Alaric's trap."

"I'm sure saving your own skin had nothing to do with it," Mathus remarked.

"Are you calling me a coward, commoner?" Wislan puffed out his chest and turned to face Mathus. His hand drifted over the hilt of his sword.

Mathus looked back, unimpressed. He had the robe of a Warlock and an Aureate sword, but Wislan was no warrior. Mathus had turned far too many boys into soldiers to be tricked by confidence and a mage costume.

"You are convinced this was only a trap set by this traitor Alaric?" King Amr asked, ignoring Wislan's quarrel.

The Archmage scratched his beard. "Alaric is known for his tricks. We can't say for certain, but our source in Atlantis is insistent that a marked is among them, so we will continue the search."

"Continue? That's madness!" The King's voice echoed. "Two *grandmasters* are dead."

"I must agree with the King," Mathus interjected. "As his Majesty stated with Sarod, we have enough enemies on our doorstep, we needn't create more. And these mages you're sending into the Empire, if they're captured, they could put the whole city at risk."

Archmage Lorad shook his head.

"My apologies, my King and Lord Marshall, but this is a matter concerning the Order. We need not even tell you of our plans; we do so by our own choosing. Don't forget that the Temple was here long before your King Arthur settled here. Be it two grandmasters' deaths or two thousand, we would pay such a price for the Marked."

The King stepped down from his chair. He walked on his old, wobbly legs so that he stood over the Archmage.

"When a gifted child is born in this city and you take him into your Order, is he not first a Citizen of New Camelot? Do you think if the Emperor took the city that he would let you take the gifted into your fold? It's foolish to think you're safe behind the magic of your temple when the Emperor needs only to starve you out."

The Archmage motioned, and Gibnar and Leteah took their positions at his sides. The King watched as the hunchbacked Archmage hobbled to the door.

The King wouldn't let it go. "We have been at war for hundreds of years. Our farms are destroyed with every slave raid. We haven't been able to produce enough food to feed the city since the Emperor's first attack. We don't need more enemies. Day to day we live a lie that is catching up with us."

"What are you saying?" Mathus asked.

The mages almost looked bored.

Amr lowered his head. His attention went to a gold bracelet around his wrist.

"The city was rich once, we had a treasury overflowing with gold, but the years of war have depleted it. If the Emperor attacks us again and destroys the few farms we have, then it will not matter if we defeat the slaves' raid. We don't need to fight Doya or these 'Marked.' We should be taking back our lands before we starve to death." he said.

Mathus searched King Amr's expression for a hint of hope but came up empty. "Can't the pirates smuggle in food?"

King Amr laughed. "Oh, they'll bring food. They've nearly emptied our treasury selling us food. For God's sake, I've made their leaders Avalonian Royalty. I've even given them the whole of Westport."

"Westport? You gave them a third of the city?" Mathus remarked.

The King leaned heavily on the round table.

"That deal fed us for the past fifty years. I thought time would've killed the Emperor by now. Our cities Winchester, Tristan, Uther, and York still sit in ruin. Glastonbury is a shack, invaders burn it while our people hide in the mountains waiting for them to leave. Now the pirates are docked in their ports, they've even started to rebuild. The Emperor is destroying us, and the pirates are taking over. They have our cities. Bards sing sonnets of Arthur; can you imagine what they will sing of me? King Amr, the spindly, moth-eaten king who watched his kingdom fall and sold his throne to pirates for bread?"

The Archmage patiently waited at the door for the King to finish. "You might think us foolish," the Archmage said. "The Order has a higher purpose beyond the needs of just your kingdom. We fight to save the Sun God. Without his light, Haven will transform into a cold, dark place. A realm of regret and sorrow where death is bitter, daily trial. How will your crops grow without the Sun God? Your Elven walls and your great armies will not save us then. When the Marked has killed the Sun God, who will hear your desperate prayers?"

The door swung shut and the mages were gone. Mathus went to join the King at his side.

"What would you have me do?" Mathus asked.

"Protect the city. Pray that this war ends soon, ask for a shorter Sow, a longer Yielding, and the death of the Emperor."

Mathus bowed his head. "I don't put much faith in prayers, sire."

The King nodded wearily.

"The Aurorean hunt these Marked. They have great power and they waste it searching the corners of the world for the Doomseeker, they call him the God slayer. Sometimes I wonder if God is already dead."

16

Avalon - New Camelot

Willow led Clara from the heart of the city east into Old Town. There the homes were built on the remains of ancient Elven buildings. It was the wealthier part of the city, and each house had its own gardens. In the late hours of the night, Moon Flowers opened their silver petals to show prickly red filaments. They were beautiful up close, but at a distance they looked like bloodshot eyes. Clara felt them watching her, and if flowers could think they would be wondering what a Healer was doing creeping around in the middle of the night.

Was she really that desperate to get away from the Sanctuary? It seemed like forever since Apollo had left. He would at least visit with her. Without their walks to break up the day-to-day happenings at the Sanctuary, Clara wondered how long she would keep her sanity.

They entered Shallot Street, the main road that led through Old Town. They passed several mansions; some of the builders had tried to rebuild the Elven homes, while others had followed traditional Avalonian construction.

The Elven buildings were many-sided with symbols and art etched into their walls. They had wide windows and narrow doorways. The stairs were never inside; they twisted up the exterior of the structures. The human buildings were grand stone mansions with slate roofs and thatched windows.

Clara had only been in Old Town a few times since her parents died. She'd lived in one of those Elven houses once, though not on the prestigious Shallot Street.

They went down a garden path. On the sides of the path were the tombs of the Pendragons. Each tomb was the size of a small house, and the stonework told the story of their life.

"The Path of Kings. Remember your way here. I will not escort you next time."

"Next time? I'm coming back?" Clara asked. Willow ignored her question.

They turned through the tombs until they reached stairs that led down to a wooden doorway. There were no elegant depictions, no tales scribed in the wood. The door was half-rotted and the iron holding the planks together bubbled from rust.

Above the doorway was Lancelot's crest, a shield freshly painted with white and red stripes.

Willow pointed to the crest.

"Lancelot's tomb. It is the duty of the Lord Marshall to see that soldiers are laid to rest here."

Willow descended the stairs and pulled open the door. The iron hinges moaned and Willow went inside.

Clara didn't like this. What sort of guest would you keep in a crypt? That was simple enough. One Mathus wanted to hide. Mathus seemed to be hiding a lot of things.

"Must I go down there? Can't you bring your guest out here?" Clara asked.

Willow looked around at the night. The moon was dim and even the stars lacked luster.

"Out here? In a dark and lonely graveyard?"

Willow laughed louder than Clara thought was appropriate.

"I've never liked crypts."

Willow placed a hand on her hip. She looked down the dark passageway and then back to Clara, who just stood there, biting the inside of her cheek.

"You can go back to your Sanctuary with the rest of your Collective," Willow said.

"My Collective?" Clara bristled. "They aren't *mine*. Not until I perform the Melding ritual. Everyone thinks Healers are so good, but they live in another world, and if you aren't part of that world, then you don't belong."

Willow raised her eyebrows. Clara could tell she'd said too much. She bowed her head and tried to think of something more proper to say, but nothing came to mind.

Willow took a burning candle from inside the crypt. "Mathus is waiting for us. I'll tell him you didn't come because you're afraid of a little hole in the ground."

A hole in the ground full of rodents and dead people Clara wanted to say, but with Willow's muscles and quiver of spears, she doubted that would mean much to her.

Clara looked back over her shoulder. She could find her way back herself.

"How deep do we need to go?" Clara asked, but when she turned around Willow was already through the doorway. The light of Willow's candle shone under the door, and it was fading.

"Wait!" Clara yelled. "I'm coming."

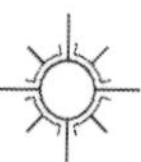

"Mathus sees that the tomb is cleaned daily. If soldiers must die, he believes that they should rest in a place fit for heroes," Willow said.

Willow's candle was dim, but Clara could still make out some of their surroundings. The catacombs had a high roof. Clara expected to see spider webs strung about, but the stone floor was swept and even the ceilings were clean. There were no bones on the floor, nor did she see any rats. Rainwater dripped down the walls and puddled in corners.

At the end of a hallway, they came to a torch-lit chamber. Willow placed her candle on a pedestal and approached two soldiers standing guard at a gate.

One of the guards, a plump man with a dimpled chin, greeted Clara with a mischievous smile.

"Who's she?" he asked.

"She's a guest of the Lord Marshall, so keep your eyes to yourself if you want to keep them," Willow spat.

"We should check her for weapons," said the other soldier.

Clara stepped back nervously and nearly stumbled on a rock.

"I don't have any weapons," she admitted.

Willow intercepted the soldier and prodded a finger into his throat.

"Grim, if you touch her with those gropey hands of yours I'll cut your little commander off. I've said it before, but Gods, I mean it this time. She is to be treated with the same respect as the Lord Marshall himself. Would you grope the Lord Marshall?"

"Aye Captain, I mean no Captain. I mean, as you wish." Grim tried to shake off the confusion. He turned to his comrade. "Mel, close those eyes, I think she's fixing to do us in this time."

Mel closed his eyes, but his smile still lingered.

Clara didn't like his grin one bit. "Why does he smile like that?" she asked.

Grim bowed to Clara. "Excuse my comrade. He is a pig, but we guard a hole in the ground, and that seems to be the proper place for pigs."

Grim gave Willow a disgusted frown.

"We don't see many ladies down here except for Willow, but she isn't much of a lady."

"That's enough." Willow snatched the keys from Grim's belt and unlocked the door.

The catacomb widened to a large chamber. Fires burned on pedestals throughout the room. Willow's and Clara's shadows danced as the flames flickered. Dead soldiers were placed on stone beds cut out of the wall. Each bed had another above it, stacked six high, the beds went along the walls and off into the darkness. Hundreds of clay pots lined the base of the wall.

"How many are there?" Clara asked.

Willow nodded to the pots. "We had to cremate some. There are many chambers like this. No one has counted them. Some served Arthur, but nearly all of them were killed during the Emperor's reign. In the early years, when we tried to hold the border, we lost whole armies."

They stopped at the white and red painted shield again. This time it was over an iron doorway.

"Is this Lancelot's chamber?" Clara asked.

Willow nodded.

The door to the chamber was made from rusted iron. It might have been a wonder several hundred years ago, but time had reduced it to a craterous, orange plate. Willow knocked, and flaky crumbs of metal trickled to the floor.

"Speak your name," commanded a voice from the other side.

"It's Willow, I've brought the Healer."

The door jerked and the flaky rust fell off the door like dirt off the side of a sheer cliff. A metallic squeal followed and the door rolled to the side.

Mathus greeted her with a solemn expression.

"It's good that you came," he said.

Clara wasn't sure how to take that. What good could come from a secret meeting in a catacomb?

Mathus assessed her. There was innocence in her face, a child-like ignorance in her eyes. She believed in a fair world where bad things only happened to the foolish and guilty. There were definitive paths for right and wrong. Mathus missed that peace of mind, the certainty. There was no going back to that ignorance. For Mathus, it had died with his sister, and just as he couldn't raise the dead, he couldn't bring back that treasured innocence.

Why did he have to take that from Clara? Somehow that felt wrong, but sense dictated that she see the world for what it really was. It wasn't hopes and dreams. There was darkness in it that preyed on the unaware and swallowed the naive.

"What?" Clara asked when she noticed Mathus staring at her.

Mathus swallowed. He glanced at Willow. She stood with a hand on her sword and another ready to snatch a short spear from her quiver. Her focus wasn't on Clara or Mathus. She looked beyond them into the room.

She was a weapon, a woman who couldn't enjoy an evening walk without a sword in hand and her eyes on the shadows.

Mathus spoke soberly. "You can't forget what I'm about to show you. Night will have a face, and it will frighten you."

Clara rigidly folded her arms. "I've seen more than you might think, Lord Marshall. I am a Healer," she replied.

Mathus nodded and stepped aside. Behind him, a figure was chained to the stone wall. Its body was limp and its bald head hung so its face wasn't visible.

Clara stepped through the doorway. Her mouth dropped. "Your guest is a prisoner? When was the last time he's eaten?"

"Don't get too close," Mathus warned.

Clara took a bold step toward the figure. "He's too thin and his skin, it's so pale. How long has he been down here? I doubt he's seen the sun in months."

"Longer than that, I'd wager," said Willow with a smirk. It was the first time Clara had ever seen her smile.

"This isn't funny. This could kill him."

"Look closer," Mathus said.

Clara saw a string of black drool leak from the prisoner's chin and puddle on the floor. She thought that was odd. Could it be blood? Vomit perhaps? Around its neck was a metal collar attached to a chain. A short, stocky soldier in red leather armor held the end of the chain. The prisoner wore nothing but a loincloth and a necklace of bones and tufts of hair.

Then she saw its hands. It didn't have flesh on its palms or fingers. Instead, it had sharp, boney claws.

Clara trembled. She backed away and bumped into the wall. "No, you wouldn't. You couldn't. You brought a Doya into the city?"

Clara's eyes moved around the room. There were so many shadows, so much power. And her fear, she would help it, unwillingly. If it was awake, it would rip them apart.

"We all have to get out of here." Clara gasped. She wanted to run, but her legs had fixed themselves to the floor.

"Calm down. It can't hurt you," Mathus said.

"It could," Willow corrected, "but it would be the last thing it did, isn't that right, Snails?"

Snails, the heavyset soldier holding the chain, nodded. Around the Doya's neck was a mechanical collar with springs depressed against two blades aimed inward at the Doya's throat. The chain that the soldier held linked to a small piece of steel holding the two blades open. One tug and it would pull free, release the blades, and cleave the Doya's head off.

Snails boastfully waved the chain in circles.

"Willow's right. I got this collar here and I just tug this chain like one of those fancy curtains, but instead of cloth falling over the windows, his head pops off like an apple from a tree. Oh, and the bugger's blood gets everywhere. Eh, I guess it's nothing like curtains, but you get what I'm saying."

Clara just blinked.

"You're mad. You're all mad," she said.

There was Devil from the Garatha right before her. Evil built of flesh and magic. She'd read about them her whole life, mended wounds they'd created, but she'd never seen one. As a Purist, she should grab Mathus' dagger and drive it through the creature. It would be the right thing to do, yet she couldn't. The Garatha taught that killing Doya was the justice of the gods. "*Send the fallen to me that I may reward them for their toils of terror and let them reap the fields of endless sorrow*," she'd read the verse a dozen times in worship.

And she couldn't muster up the courage to kill a devil? What sort of Purist was she? Durakos would toss her out of their prayers. He would've killed the creature six different ways while she was still reciting scripture in her head.

Clara straightened her shoulders. She sucked in a breath and said a silent prayer: "From the West, House of Transformation, may wisdom be transformed into right action so that we may do what must be done."

"He should be killed. You should've killed him."

Mathus pulled his Aureate dagger from his belt and held it out to her. "If you cannot keep this a secret, then it would be better for all of us if you killed him now."

Clara took the dagger by its crude handle. The leather-wrapped wood was soft and the blade was impressively sharp.

She turned it over so the point was down. It would be easy, she told herself. One quick jab right into the heart and the creature would die. She didn't even have to cut off its head. This was Aureate, a good cut was all it would take.

Clara took a step toward the sleeping creature. She could stab it. It would be as easy as slamming down a book or giving a shove, but it wasn't that easy. Her mind kept drifting to the past. When she looked at the knife in her hand, it made her think of her father. Was this how he did it? Did he hold the knife like she was? Had she gotten that from him? Like she'd gotten her eyes from him and the way she laughed? Would she stab the Doya like her father had stabbed her mother? How many times had he cut her? Would blood go everywhere like it had that night?

Clara gazed at the knife in her hand again. It dripped with blood. She hadn't stabbed anyone, or had she? She couldn't tell. The blood wasn't black Doya blood. It was scarlet red. Then the blood was on her hands. It leaked through her fingers. It was on her clothes. What had she done?

"Clara! Clara!" Mathus was shaking her and shouting her name. The dagger was back in his belt and she was frozen in the middle of the room.

"I'm alright, I'll be alright," she said.

Mathus let her go. Clara looked up and beyond Mathus. The Doya was awake. Drool leaked down its neck and chest. It bared its sharp teeth and growled.

Clara saw her reflection in its black eyes. She was teary-eyed in a void of nothingness.

Her voice shook. "Why have you brought it here?"

Mathus regarded her sternly. His gaze was intense. When he was convinced he could let her go, Mathus turned to the Doya.

"It says it has a message for the Archmage. We would like you to contact him and bring him here, alone. If the King or the people find out we're holding a Doya in the city, there will be hell to pay."

Clara pursed her lips and, after a moment, nodded. "I can do that, but in the Sanctuary you asked me if I know apothecary, not if I could get a message to the Archmage."

"I did. I have another task to ask of you as an apothecary. Our weapons are weak. We can't mix iron and gold." Mathus said.

"The secret of forging Aureate was lost with the Elves," Clara said. Mathus nodded.

"Aureate is costly, too costly to arm an army. I need poison to give our steel bite." Mathus turned to his soldiers. "Snails can help you. He apprenticed as an apothecary."

The soldier holding the Doya's chain gave her a clumsy bow. He was a scrap of a man with brown teeth, a patchy beard, and somehow he carried the foul scent of snails.

The Doya spoke, and a chill entered the room. Gooseflesh spread over the back of Clara's neck.

"Clara." It tasted the word in its mouth, "Clara. Clara."

"Stop it!" Clara shouted.

Her frustration only inspired the Doya.

"Clara, the Healer, Clara, the keeper of secrets, Clara, the outcast, Clara, the witch."

17

Havilah – Enoch

The tails of the Emperor's black and gold vest trailed behind him as he marched through the throng of Mayan slaves. His white silk shirt rippled and a strand of his long black hair escaped from his ponytail. The Mayan slaves were mostly naked, with cracked lips, and callused, sun-baked skin. What clothes they did have were made from patchwork pieces of rough spun cotton. Bones pierced their ears and the bridges of their noses. Their ribcages were bulky on their starved bodies, and their sunken cheeks were flat so that their angular faces were mere skulls covered in a thin layer of skin. Vega passed row after row of slaves. Each spoke the prayer.

"Lord Vega, I take every breath by Your Grace."

"Your breath is mine to give," Vega shouted in response.

The slaves continued. "If I am to die this day, let it be in your name. For both my body and soul are yours to command."

Vega held up his arms and spoke with authority.

"I am here to bless you. Follow my commands and you will not be punished. You will *never* be asked to give more than you're able."

"From eternity to eternity, I follow your command with an open and willing heart. I heed every command of you and your servants the Branded. Let your wishes be carried out with exactness, for on the throne of heaven sits Lord Vega and he is my judge."

Vega stopped at the head of the throng. He looked out at the slaves who filled a wide path through the ruined Forest of Eden back to the walls of Enoch. The Mayans knelt on the stumps of the trees they'd chopped down. Where they knelt was once a dense forest alive with wisps and fairies, but their stampede of axes had reduced the area to a path of stumps, a hollow swath of dirt cut into the heart of the forest. The trees along the edge of the path drooped in despair at the ancient ironwood trees felled before them.

The Emperor drew his arms high above his head. "I can open the gates of heaven and the pit of hell. Let your deeds honor me so that I will remember you on the Day of Judgment."

The slaves didn't cheer, nor did they rise from their knees. They were living statues in the Emperor's presence.

The Emperor ran his hand along the trunk of the Evertree. Four immense trees wrapped together to create the massive trunk. A steady glow came from between their seams. Carved into the wood, the oaths of the Wisps and Fairies glowed sapphire, the symbols so tiny they could be mistaken for the work of termites.

The slaves pressed their heads to the ground as Cain passed. They'd seen him take their women, beat their men, force their children into labor, even demand impossible tasks just to watch the Mayans die under the punishment of the Mind Curse.

Cain joined Vega's side.

Sheets of moss hung off the tree limbs. Vega cradled a lock of moss in his hand and took an intimate, savory whiff.

"There isn't a woman in all of Haven that smells better than the moss of the Evertree," the Emperor said.

Cain grabbed a clump of the moss and ripped it off the tree. He smelled it, grunted, and tossed it.

"It smells like moss," he said, unimpressed.

Cain held out a rolled parchment. "There has been communication from Lady Black."

The Emperor pushed the parchment away and turned down the path he came. Cain stopped him.

She gave a message, but she's no longer using the Witching Bone. The transcriber gave me this parchment.

The Emperor seethed. "What is the use of the Witching Bone if we don't converse? I could've sent a messenger to deliver parchment."

The Emperor snatched the parchment and ripped off the wax seal. He frantically scanned the page. When he reached the bottom, his face soured.

"She has taken the Branded to Avalon, but they can't steal the Urim."

"Why?" Cain asked.

"The boy with the black eyes hasn't entered the temple. Sarod can't cast the spell without him."

Vega ran a finger through the two open sockets in the jeweled breastplate around his neck.

"Inside this tree is the key to my immortality. Only the breastplate knows how to open it."

Cain shook his head. "It's a tree. Each of these slaves has cut down hundreds of trees."

"You," Cain called out to one of the larger slaves. His arms were spindly and his head was a mess of woolly hair that tangled into his beard. Branded into his forehead was his number: 9009.

Cain showed the slave the brand in his palm.

"Cut it down," he ordered.

9009 looked up the tangle of the Evertree's horse-sized roots, to its trunk as thick as a small castle, and finally to the upper branches where a rainbow of millions of leaves seemingly reached into the clouds.

9009 shrugged. "Need a bigger ax."

"I want you to chop that tree now," Cain insisted.

The Mind Curse ripped into 9009's head. With a cry, he lurched forward, clutching his ax.

9009 aimed for the small gap where the trees came together. He swung his ax. The dull thud of iron on wood made the Emperor shiver with excitement. Before 9009 could pull the ax free, the Emperor was already inspecting the cut. The ax wedged itself clean in the wood.

"We may not need that breastplate after all," he remarked.

The Emperor took a step back and waved for the slave to continue.

9009 tried to pull the ax free. It didn't budge. He planted his feet on the tree and pulled. His gaunt body strained. Still, the ax head wouldn't come loose.

"Out of the way," Cain said, shoving him aside.

Cain heaved on the ax with both hands. The slave numbers tattooed in his arms swelled. His arms became a mountain range of muscles wrapped in a web of throbbing veins.

The ax creaked. The handle snapped in two. Cain staggered backwards.

"Damn this ax."

He flung the handle at the slave. 9009 ducked as it whizzed by his head.

"Get me another!"

The Emperor watched eagerly as 9009 hurried through the ranks of Mayan slaves and returned with another ax.

Cain drew the ax high above his head and landed a ground-shaking *thunk* in the side of the tree. The ax head bore deep in the wood. Cain tried to pull it free, but it too wouldn't budge.

The Emperor shook his fists, his voice seethed with anger. "What sort of trick is this?"

A clump of the Emperor's black hair fell out. His face took on a yellow pigment and crow's feet appeared in the corners of his eyes. An old muscle in the Emperor's cheek started to twitch. Vega tried to massage it away. A pain shot up his back, forcing him to hunch. The Emperor's arm jerked as he reached for a glowing pouch hanging around his neck. The skin on his face drooped and wrinkled. He forced his hand into the pouch and he pulled out a short male fairy with turquoise hair. The fairy shrieked as he toppled into the Emperor's mouth.

There was a bone-snapping crunch. The Emperor's hair grew back, his crow's feet were gone, his youth returned. Still, he wasn't satisfied. There was a mad, desperate look in his fuming face.

"The fairies hide in their tree!"

"That's because we chopped down their forest," Cain added.

Vega reeled. "I only have a few left. Where can I get more fairies?"

9009 shuttered. The Emperor was staring right at him with the dead fairy's purple and white-flecked wings hanging from his chin.

"We hear things here in the Ironwood," 9009 admitted. "Some of my brothers speak with the fairies, and they have told us stories of the Oathbreakers."

"What are Oathbreakers?" The Emperor demanded.

"The fairies value promises. The Oathbreakers are the outcasts, the liars who fled to Tarboroth," 9009 answered.

The Emperor looked from 9009 to Cain, who'd planted a crop of axes in the side of the Evertree.

"Cain, prepare your dragons, we sail for Tarboroth immediately."

18

Avalon - The Chasm

The Chasm stairs seemed to go on forever, but Vallan knew they ended. Seven hundred steps, that's all there were before the staircase ended in a deadly drop.

Vallan paused to take a breath. The feeding platform was still lowering, the iron crank still squealed. He'd reached step six hundred, or was it? The uneven stairs and the darkness made them difficult to count.

The golden blade of Vallan's sword was made of the rarest of metals, Aureate. Forged from a mixture of Elven steel and gold, the special metal made it nearly indestructible, and the gold acted as a poison on Doya flesh. The precious metal also had the properties of flint when struck against stone. One rasp and the whole cavern would flash with white light.

The darkness played tricks on him. In his mind's eye, he could see Sarod's ghastly stare with eyes darker than the Chasm itself. Vallan had seen kingdoms rise and fall. Great fortresses built and crumble in time. And still, he could remember Sarod's elven face as if he'd killed him yesterday. Here he had sent Sarod, the dark Elven prince, to the afterlife, yet Sarod had come back wearing a man's face. He'd always come back. Every time he was killed, he'd return wearing a different face.

Vallan dragged his sword against the wall. Sparks shot out, lighting his path. In that flash, he saw a much different Chasm. The stairs remained constant, but the walls opened up like a beehive with adjacent cliffs and caves.

Six hundred and fifty steps.

Vallan could feel eyes on him.

Six hundred and ninety.

Vallan froze.

The unmistakable sound of a claw scraped across a stone. A hiss came from the black. Vallan turned. Hot, acrid Doya breath blew in his face. He flinched and backed into the wall. His heart pounded in his ears.

"I've come to see Osirius, the Father," he said.

Vallan rasped his sword on stone. A flurry of spark-light opened his eyes to the nightmare before him.

Dozens of starved, gangly Doya surrounded him. They'd given themselves over to fear, misery, hate, the dark emotions, and in doing so the lost their last few strands of humanity. They were neither man nor woman. Their red blood had turned black, and their once pink mouths were now pale and oozing black tar. And their eyes…

Their beetle, black eyes gleamed with excitement.

Vallan was a fly in a nest of spiders.

"I've come to speak with the Father," Vallan repeated, but none of the Doya seemed to care.

will be in your throats. When you crawl on me and start ripping, I will lash back. My swing is a mighty wind, and my steel carries the biting chill of death."

Vallan shouted out into the pit. "Osirius! I will kill your pets."

His heart pounded. He dropped his shoulder to charge up the stairs.

A small torch flickered alive. Osirius walked out of a cave that opened to the stairs and toward Vallan. Osirius wore a black hooded feather-cloak and leaned on a walking stick made from cast iron. Its skin was as pale and its eyes were as black as any of the other Doya. But unlike the others, its face was a grossly misshapen thing. It looked as if the head of a man was joined together with the larger head of a reptile. The lower parts of its face, its cheeks and nose, were smooth and human-like, while the others its ears, brow, and the skin around a large eye were black alligator skin. When Osirius spoke, the hard lizard parts remained still and dead, while the Doya parts animated. The Lizard-Doya spoke with a subtle hiss, but in a tone of reverence that made every word seem precious.

"Do not fear, old one. We can be gentle creatures."

Vallan rotated in a circle with his sword held high. One twitch from his enemies, and he was ready to loose heads from their shoulders.

The Osirius stretched out its arms. It spoke so its voice echoed throughout the cavern. "Look upon those the Gods cannot love. The Sun God deems we wander the Otherworld.

The One God would cast us into a fiery hell, and the Atlantian Gods would trap us in Tartarus for all eternity."

"Foul deeds cannot go unpunished," Vallan said.

Light reflected off the hard, lizard skin on Osirius' face.

Osirius spoke to the whole cavern. "The Aurorean says our choices are scribed on our very souls, so the gods may judge us. I say this is true, but not for the sake of justice. Where you see a god, I see a tyrant. I see the limits of the *all*-powerful. The gods can't change the past, they can't erase *evil* deeds, and so they seek to control the present. It's the limits of their power that create the laws that damn men."

A few of the Doya growled in agreement.

Vallan grimaced at the drooling Doya surrounding him, then to the bottomless pit before him, and finally to Osirius, the lizard-faced Doya walking along the edge of the pit. Osirius approached Vallan until Vallan's sword was pointed at its head.

"Lower your weapon."

The Doya around him growled a low, gurgling sound that brought tar bubbles to their lips. One straightened its back like a bear and rose from its hunch to attack.

"Be calm, Drail," Osirius commanded.

Vallan was about to hack Drail in half when Osirius gently ran its hand over Drail's scalp.

"Drail will not harm you."

Drail closed its eyes. The skin on its face fluttered. In a brief moment, Drail calmed, lowered its claws, and hugged tightly to the lizard-faced Doya's leg.

"Are my children so difficult to forgive?"

Osirius scratched the back of Drail's head. It swooned and drooled ink onto the Chasm stairs.

"Does even the worst of us deserve to burn in an everlasting fire?"

"I didn't come here for your lessons Osirius."

"No, you came here to dispose of your corrupted and destroy your Enchanter's mistakes. The relics you destroyed have now created a crater on my doorstep."

Osirius took a heavy whiff of the air through the slit in the lizard side of its face.

"Even in the depths of the mountain, I can smell the new remnant you've created. Soon much of our forest will die, and when the game is scarce, and we're starving, we'll curse the Auroreans."

"Just as the widows and the orphans curse the Doya who've broken their families. There is a greater lesson here." Vallan returned.

Osirius didn't give his words a thought.

"We require food and supplies. The Emperor comes and takes my children away and the great city of New Camelot, home to the Auroreans, brings me destruction. I have spent too many years in this mountain, the world must be in a dire state."

"The Emperor took your children?"

"Lady Black gave them a promise of freedom. If they agreed to serve her. She promised them protection from Sarod's vengeance and a pardon from all crimes, both past and future."

"Black was here?" Vallan asked.

"You know she visits me as you do. This is bigger than your quarrel with Black. The Emperor and Sarod have come to an agreement. My children don't know Sarod like I do. I spent years under a dark curse and a knife. Sarod has ways of breaking people. He's a god. A vile one. He plays the creator. It was he who did this to me." Osirius used his large black eye to examine Vallan. It was surrounded by lizard flesh, and as large as a fist. The eye was watching him, touching him, yet the monstrous eye didn't so much as blink.

"Lady Black needed no introduction here. Some of my children were her loyal servents, she protected them from the Mind Curse by hiding them from the Emperor."

"Do you serve Black as well?" Vallan asked.

"Lady Black has joined Sarod." Osirius ran his black tongue over his rough, lizard cheek. "I will not serve a pawn of the master. Nor will I ever join Sarod in sorcery."

"What sort of sorcery?" Vallan asked.

"Old magic. Lady Black's Doya are gathering in the Black Mountains and joining with Sarod's followers, more than ever before. The Emperor has sworn to release all the Doya he's captured with the Mind Curse to Sarod in exchange for something far more valuable."

"What is the Emperor after?"

"Immortality," Osirius said. The word echoed above and below them.

Osirius' Doya eye narrowed on Vallan.

"There is also talk of the Doomseeker. It's said he is the key to Sarod's sorcery."

Vallan tried to hide his surprise. "What do they say of this...Doomseeker?"

Osirius cocked his head. A wry grin crossed its face.

"Before I was changed by Sarod, my mind was part of the Collective. I remember when you first showed Apollo's marks to Daynin. I know his secret, and Sarod has known about his marks for many years. With his powers, he knows things that normal Doya cannot."

Vallan felt his blood turn cold. He knew Sarod's powers affected the Doya. He'd always hoped that Apollo was out of his reach.

Vallan swallowed dryly. Osirius could see the concern on his face.

"You are right to fear for him. Apollo cannot enter the Black Mountains. He should be kept in the temple, under the protection of its barrier. Power has always been Sarod's desire. To have once been so great and to have fallen so far as to not even have a body of his own makes him more dangerous than ever. These bodies of men he uses will not serve. He wants the power of a god. They say he found a way, before he was cast into this very pit."

Vallan shifted uncomfortably. This conversation made him feel old. The world was a barbed vine of greed, and power, and death, and it was wrapped around his shoulders with thorns prodding at his heart.

"What does he want with Apollo?" Vallan asked.

"It's said in scripture that Apollo will take the dark throne," Osirius answered.

Vallan grit his teeth. "Apollo will never—"

"I don't care who sits on the dark throne, as long as they don't want me and my children dead," Osirius interrupted. "Sarod might fear for his throne. He might want him to kill the Sun God. I can't say. I can tell you that Lady Black and Sarod are gathering their power and Apollo is the key. You must protect him, he's not ready to face the Prince of Darkness."

Vallan's jaw locked firmly. Osirius sighed and gestured to his followers.

"Evil can be tempered. Destruction is in Doya's nature, just as it is the nature of men to war. But just as men have learned to stay the sword, my Doya have learned to quench their thirst for death. There is still hope even in the darkest hearts."

Vallan sneered.

"You do not believe me, but look around you. My Doya haven't harmed you."

Vallan scanned over the drooling faces of his enemies. In their corrupted, black eyes and their dark dribbling lips, he saw the taint of sin. The screams of children. The murders of the innocent. The slaughtering of families. The choices that made even the worst, wicked, ungifted men call themselves devils and feel their souls shrink.

"I have lived for many years, Osirius. Where you see a creature to save, I see a creature that cannot, *will not,* be saved. Keep your spiders in the shadows, and the deeds written in their souls can wait for the final judgment."

Osirius took a step back and turned the dead lizard side of its face toward Vallan.

"When you look at my children, you see damnation. Do you see that same damnation when you look into the eyes of the boy you call a son? When Apollo falls, will you bring him to me? Or will you send him to hell yourself?"

Vallan's expression was sullen. "Apollo is a good man. His eyes are black but not from magical corruption. He has the heart of an Aurorean."

Osirius ran a forked tongue over his face. "Long ago, Sarod had the Breastplate of Decision for many years. It taught him magics only a god could know. He has the power to change men. I was once a Healer. I took the oaths. I protected life."

Osirius ran a claw over the rough ridges of his lizard skin.

"Look at me now."

The horrid smell of rotten meat stole the Doya's attention. The faint squeal of the Chasm crank stopped somewhere high above. The Berserker had finished his task. Low growls came out of the darkness as the prospect of food made the Doya turn on one another.

"Wait, my children," Osirius tried to calm them.

None seemed to listen. All eyes turned to the wooden platform where a pile of fly speckled meat was just a short step out over the abyss from the Chasm staircase.

"There is plenty for all," Osirius said.

The Doya closest Vallan growled so that black spit leaked down his chin. Another flexed its claws as it sized up the other Doya closer to the platform.

When Vallan saw their interest turn from him, he kept his back against the wall and started back up the stairs.

"There is no need to flee, old one. They are gentle creatures, my children; they're only excited for their meal. Stay, you'll see."

Then, out of the shadows, a Doya leaped onto the wooden platform and bit into the raw, festering meat.

The fragile peace shattered.

The Chasm erupted with the cry of demons as dark figures created a black waterfall that poured down the pit walls.

"Calm yourselves!" Osirius commanded, but his commands were lost, and the lonely light of his torch extinguished, leaving the Chasm in total darkness.

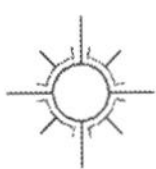

Lurk tottered down a narrow passage. He scratched at the skin under his gut, it flaked off and floated behind him. Apollo tried to keep his distance without losing him.

"You said you knew where she was," Apollo grumbled.

"I do. I do," Lurk announced, waving their only torch above his head.

"You also said it wasn't far." Apollo folded his arms.

"It's a lot closer than a lot of things," Lurk shrugged.

"It's the third time we've passed this pillar," Apollo said, pointing to a stone pillar carved into the wall.

Lurk spun and examined the pillar up and down. The harder he looked, the more he scratched his belly.

"I like this pillar," he said.

"Where is Cat?" Apollo asked.

"Cat, the women, yes. This way." Lurk turned back the way he was going and walked off into the darkness without even a glance back. Apollo watched as the light twisted through the cave until it and Lurk were gone.

Apollo kicked a rock. He was lost in the tunnels of the Chasm and any sort of creature from Berserker to legions of Corrupted were in here with him.

"Stay where you are," Apollo repeated Vallan's words. He rolled his eyes. Why couldn't he have listened just this once?

He looked off to where the last of Lurk's light had vanished, but there was nothing to see, only black. He thought back to what Cat had shown him. He took a breath, let it out, and unfocused his eyes.

The textures of the stone walls were vivid. As was the foot dangling just above him. Apollo's eyes followed the leg to the hem of a silky smooth dress and then finally up to a face he recognized.

"You don't look happy to see me," Cat said from an alcove above the path. Her foot was a pendulum dangling back and forth.

Apollo remembered their last meeting, the acidic taste in his mouth from her kiss, the spell that had frozen him.

"You can't cast any more of your tricks on me in here," Apollo replied.

Cat opened her left hand. Her index finger's skin had fallen away and only a sharp, boney claw remained. She ran it over the stone.

Apollo winced at the sound.

"I belong here now. The Father will take care of me."

"Who is the Father?" Apollo asked.

"The keeper of all of us. He looks out for the Corrupted. He even looks out for you."

"I don't know who you're talking about."

"I told him about you, but he already knew. He gave me something. He said it would save you. It will save all of us."

Cat held out a vial that she'd been clutching in her other hand.

"Take it," Cat ordered.

Apollo retreated a step. "I don't trust you."

Cat grinned as if he'd just complimented her. She pushed herself out of the alcove and landed gracefully in front of him.

Her eyes were wild, not angry, enthralled.

She pressed the vial into the center of Apollo's chest.

"I could've killed you in the forest when you spat my kiss on the ground. I saved you from Cedric's rampage."

Apollo nodded and then abruptly shook his head. Cat pressed the vial harder against his sternum.

"There will be a sword, unlike any you have ever seen. It has an ancient power. You must mix your blood with the dragon blood in this vial and cast the sword into a fire. The sword will then lose its power." Cat's face was tight, her expression was soberer than Apollo thought possible. This was a message, Lurk had called Osirius "Father," but he'd never met Osirius. Why was he giving this to him?

"The Father says this will save us all. The sword cannot fall into the wrong hands."

Apollo looked down at the vial with newfound wonder.

"Dragon blood?" he took it and rolled the vial back and forth in his palm.

When he looked up again, Cat was gone.

"Cat?" Apollo spun around, unsure if he should block for a kiss or a kick, but she was gone.

Apollo heard a whisper in the still darkness.

"You will come back to me. The Father has seen it."

19

Chasm

Vallan had no idea how long he'd been climbing the stairs of the pit, or how many times he'd looked over his shoulder into a wall of sheer black. When he reached the top, he stepped onto a golden walkway adjacent to the stairs and followed it to where it widened into a round platform containing the altar.

The berserker had finished raising the feeding platform, so he rested with his belly on the floor and pulled soft flesh from his reward, a leg of lamb.

Vallan crossed the golden walkway and leaned against the altar in the column of full-bodied sunlight. He closed his eyes and focused on the warm light on his face.

He didn't know how long he stood there.

Footsteps echoed up the Chasm stairs. Had a Doya followed him? Vallan looked out over the altar. To his surprise, it was Osirius.

"Time is of no use to us here. I tally my years by your yearly visits," Osirius said.

Osirius walked to Vallan and stretched his arms to the corners of the altar. The sunlight made the skin on his lizard arm glisten and his other arm sweat. He stared down into the infinite blackness below.

"How do you count your years?" Osirius asked.

The lizard Doya looked from the pit back to Vallan, his reptilian eye had a murky yellow tint in the sunlight.

"I count my years as you do," Vallan said. His face was rigid.

"You come under the flag of New Camelot with the authority of the Council, but you're really here for whatever is in that box."

Vallan didn't answer.

Osirius looked up at the dazzling display of brass boxes above them. Beams of light reflected off of them, stretching through the darkness, illuminating the rocky walls of the grand chamber.

"It was wise for Wythrin to create this bank of sorts. What shouldn't be destroyed is stored. I often wonder what the ancient world hid inside those boxes."

Osirius placed his hand flat on the altar and mumbled a word.

Chains rattled above as one of the containers lowered right above the altar.

"I've learned to call a few down with their words of power."

Osirius mumbled a second word and the bottom of the case opened.

"I've even guessed the second word to open a few."

A battle-worn, iron war hammer engraved with ancient symbols hovered out, and with the grace of a feather lowered to the altar.

"The Hammer of Tarbor. Wielded by the first Elven king."

Osirius brushed his hand across the altar and the hammer propelled back up into the bottom of the box, the brass container snapped shut, and reeled back up into its place among the others.

"Some things are better kept locked away," Vallan replied, unimpressed.

Osirius flexed the fingers of his lizard hand. A wet crack came from each knuckle.

"Your box has puzzled me," Osirius said.

He placed his hand on the altar and bellowed a word that echoed throughout the cavern.

"Ashborn."

A container dropped to hang just above the altar. Vallan knew the box, the size, the imperfections in the metal, he'd checked on the box more times than he cared to count.

Vallan took a step toward him.

"You can sense what is inside, can't you?" Osirius ran its lizard tongue down its cheek and over its chin.

Vallan placed a hand on the box. The touch made his hand tremble, but he didn't let go.

Osirius watched fascinated.

Vallan knew how to kill Doya. He understood how they moved, he could predict their decisions, even counter their magic, but these weren't simply Doya. They'd been starved both magically and physically. Their bones pushed against their thin milky skin so that it stretched like stringy mucus. Their veins coursed with stale magic-less blood, numbing their minds to a wild, primal state. Vallan was one sword against dozens of bone claws, and each yeared to tear off a chunk of his ripe, warm flesh.

Vallan pressed his back harder against the wall. In front of him, a void opened up to the depth of the world. If he went that way, he'd fall into a realm of empty space. There would be no light, only darkness, and nothing to feel but the air rushing by until his body shattered on the rocks far below.

He turned left and right. The Doya's breathing quickened. Under a veil of darkness, all Vallan could sense was his cold, sword hilt in his fingers and the rancid breath of the demons in the darkness.

He couldn't rasp his sword again, but the burst of light might provoke them.

He could shove a few in the Chasm. That might distract enough of them for him to cut more down. He would not live through it. One of the Doya would rip him open. Starved as they were, they would eat him. If he were lucky, he'd be dead by then.

Vallan raised his sword high and bellowed into the crowd. "When your claws are in my back, my sword

Just above the winged guard, the dragon sculpture's mouth opened upward to spew out a golden blade. One edge of the blade was straight and sharp like any common sword, however, the other side was crude and jagged as if the smith had only shaped one side.

When Osirius saw the sword, a tremor surged up his neck. His forked tongue flickered out and up his cheek. His awestruck tone was unmistakable.

"Ashborn's blade. Do the dragons know we have this?"

Vallan snatched Osirius by his black robe, ensnaring him in a stone-faced stare.

"If the dragons knew you had this, they'd rip the mountain open and take it." Vallan held his stare for a moment to let the words sink in.

"I am the Father to all in this mountain. You've endangered my children. That belongs at the bottom of the Chasm."

Osirius reached for the sword.

"No!" Vallan pushed his hands away. "Should Ashborn rise again, it will be our best chance at defeating him."

The human side of Osirius' face was a stone-like as the lizard side.

"The sword has no place here."

Vallan waved a hand and the empty brass box drew back up to its place in the ceiling. "It goes with me. When I leave the Chasm, the red Dragons will be able to sense the sword. It will bleed magic. They'll come looking for it."

Osirius looked past Vallan to where Apollo emerged from a passageway. He saw him stuff the vial of dragon blood into his pocket. It's working, just as Black said it would, Osirius thought. The lizard Doya's attention turned back to Vallan, who still wore a dire expression.

"Take it and Apollo to your temple, away from here and beyond the reach of the Dragons, Sarod, and Black."

20

Avalon

Desolation.

Apollo couldn't believe his eyes. There was no sign of the caravan they'd traveled with. Not a body, or splinter of wood from the wagons. The destruction of the relics had erased it from existence. Their final campsite looked as if a titan had reached down from the sky and pulled out the forest, creating a deep crater.

Beyond the crater, were fallen trees, uprooted, cracked, and scattered into a charred forest, burnt black as far as the eye could see.

"Nothing will grow back, will it?" Apollo asked.

"No." Vallan moved his hand through the air. "The Remnant has settled. This will all be a field of dirt soon."

Apollo looked down into the bottom of a smaller crater where rainwater had gathered.

He saw his reflection in the water. Apollo didn't recognize the man looking back. He had a patchy beard and his hair was as tangled and matted as a bird's nest. His robes were torn rags and his arms were bruised and cut. If he were on the streets of New Camelot, he wondered if anyone would recognize him. Would his closest friend, Clara, see him for who he'd become? Or would she toss him a coin, thinking him a beggar?

Vallan walked up next to him. Apollo spotted the peculiarly misshapen blade of a second sword hanging from his belt.

"Look," Vallan said, pointing into the blackened woods.

Apollo saw Vallan's white quarter horse walk up to the edge of the crater.

"We won't be walking home after all."

Vallan and Apollo took the narrow road back along the Hyperion border. It was a faster path, but the narrow passageways through rocks and over ridges made the route impassable for wagons. As the hours passed, the face of Chronos formed by a cluster of gray-blue mountains disappeared behind them.

Apollo twisted his back, it was terribly uncomfortable to share a horse.

He'd tried to talk to Vallan a dozen times, but he was more reclusive than ever. Had something happened to him in the Chasm?

Apollo couldn't get his mind off the sword hanging from Vallan's belt. Was that the one Cat had warned him about? He could feel the vial of dragon blood press against the inside of his pocket.

Vallan noted the change in the forest. When they'd left for the Chasm it was blazing with the yellows and reds of early Sow. Now the leaves had abandoned their trees, fallen in the mud, or gathered in heaps on the ground. The bare tree limbs seemed to shiver in the cold wind.

When he'd started this journey, Vallan had been in an argument with Rhean. Vallan respected him. Rhean was usually a reasonable man. He was strong and had an unwavering sense of duty.

That sense of blind duty to the Council would get him killed. At least that's what Vallan told him before Rhean ordered him silent, ending their discussion that day.

Miriam had never been good at keeping secrets. That's one of the many reasons Vallan hadn't told her about Apollo's marks.

The night before the caravan was planning to leave, she and Harthor, her most trusted Oracle, paid Vallan a visit. They'd told him the Council had learned that there was one marked with the symbol of a moon living in Atlantis. He wasn't the Doomseeker, but as one of Marked, their destinies were linked. The Council believed if they found this Marked, he would be able to lead them to the others. Vallan postponed the trip to the Chasm, it only took a few days before Rhean was on the road. He did everything he could to stop him.

Vallan had once believed the Council would learn to accept Apollo as he had himself. But many of them were Purists now; believers of the Garatha down to the letter. Purists were without compassion, quicker to judge than to forgive. Miriam, Rhean, and Lorad were the only members of the Council who weren't. If a Purist was ever chosen as the Archmage and they took the majority of the Council—

He didn't want to think of that. Lorad still had his health, and both Miriam and Rhean would have to die to be replaced. Rhean was a fighter and he doubted the gods would let Miriam die. She'd never let the gods hear the last of it.

Vallan rested his hand on the handle of the dragon sword. Holding it reminded him of his lost love, old magic always did.

Her eyes had a green glow, they'd sparkled with excitement, desire, and danger. She was wild. With her, he felt alive and for the first time, he felt whole.

When they were alone, he would call her "Green Eyes" and she would smile the wicked smile that said, "I love you" and "I want you" at the same time. His pulse quickened at the thought of being with her again. Like she was then.

The sword was a lure to a past he'd tried so desperately to forget.

The light of the lesser sun tangled in the trees and fell under the horizon, leaving them in the twilight.

"We'll camp here tonight," Vallan said.

"In the road?" Apollo asked.

Vallan didn't answer. He was consumed once again by his own thoughts.

Apollo gathered tinder from the forest and piled it in a mound in the middle of the road. He reached for a box of fairy tinder to light them.

"No fires tonight," Vallan said.

"No fire?" Apollo dropped his arm. "It's going to be freezing."

Vallan looked up into the starry sky. "Better to freeze than face a dragon."

"A dragon?" Apollo squinted to look for movement in front of the stars. There were no clouds, so he looked for a flash of darkness in what seemed to be an endless sky of stars. It was like searching for stones missing from a river. A lowborn dragon would be near impossible to spot at night.

Apollo put his hands on his hips, "Now we have to be on the lookout for dragons? What aren't you telling me?"

Vallan looked down at the sword he'd laid across his lap.

It had to be the sword Cat warned him about, Apollo thought.

Apollo reached into his pocket to take out the vial of blood but stopped. Why hadn't the Father or Cat given the blood to Vallan?

Vallan took a breath as if he was going to say something, but when he couldn't find the words, he just sat there quietly.

"What's so special about this sword?" Apollo pried.

Vallan lifted the sword from his lap and held it out to him. "See for yourself."

Apollo took it and gripped it in one hand. It was surprisingly light.

Dragon bone, it had to be, he thought as he marveled at the bleached bone hilt carved in the shape of a dragon.

Two dragon wings that made up the guard, they were gold, Aureate most likely.

Apollo ran his hand up the flat of the blade, a dragon's head opened upward from the guard to breathe out the ruined Aureate blade.

He couldn't tell how it had happened, but the blade was melted on one side. It looked as if it had been dipped in a furnace until the metal started to drip off. Strangely enough, the other side remained sharp and undistorted.

"What would anyone want with a ruined sword?" Apollo asked.

Vallan scratched his back on the tree he was leaning on and shifted for a more comfortable position.

"I can't tell you the value of this sword without telling you of a dragon named Ashborn."

Long ago, in the meridian between the disappearance of the Elves and the arrival of the humans, in a time before the Kingdoms of Avalon, Hyperion, even before Shem, there was one Kingdom, Havilah. In that time, Havilah stretched over what now is Hyperion and all the way to the Black Mountains. The Black Mountains were much different then. They were lush and green and the land was still wild with all types of magical creatures. Among those creatures, there lived a great red dragon.

He was the first dragon born into Haven. His father was Raiden, the greatest of the Aurorean dragons, and his mother was Pandora, the greatest of the Aphotic Dragons. His parents were the same Raiden and Pandora who created the world so long ago.

Vallan took back the sword and rested it across his lap.

"Life is rich with both good and evil. That's because we have free will. For life to be created, the creators must have a portion of both magic. Otherwise, freedom wouldn't exist. Without freedom, life would follow a set chain of events, making the universe stagnant. Happiness and sadness would have no meaning because one cannot exist without the other. Therefore, great magic, like the formation of life, requires both the power of the Aurorean and the Aphotic. The great dragons, having created such a magnificent world and having lived among its inhabitants, were compelled to create once more."

Pandora bore a son. He was the first red dragon, which gave him great power over the flame. They named him Ashborn. Years passed, and the dragon grew into adulthood. Other Aurorean and Aphotic dragons saw what a magnificent creature he'd become, so they too created dragons of all types.

Aurorean and Aphotic dragons are born with the universe. Like the universe, their lifetime is beyond comprehension. Highborns, offspring of the Aurorean and Aphotic dragons, like Ashborn, were the smartest and the strongest. They inherited more of the natural 'Witching Magic' of their parents. As offspring of the immortals, Dragons inherited near-immortality and soon outnumbered humans.

It was then that both human and dragon claimed dominion over Haven.

The constant conflict between humans and dragons brought an era we now call The Dragon Wars.

Dragons burned human cities to the ground and humans hunted dragons like animals. Through lies and deception, humans convinced the wisps to fight against the dragons. They knew if they could bring the wisps to battle, their numerous fairies would follow. Though they were small, they were deadly adversaries to the dragons. The wisps knew of the dragon's greatest weakness.

A dragon's most powerful weapon is its breath. When a dragon exerts itself, as it does in battle or flight, a part of its throat fills with potent fluid that it then breathes out to create fire.

No human can reach this weak point. It's too deep in the throat and requires precision to seal. Because of this, wisps and fairies are the perfect dragon slayers.

The fairies fell upon the dragons like locusts. Their unquestionable obedience to the wisps gave them the courage to fly down the dragons' throats and seal up the dragons' breath.

The dragons' greatest power became their greatest weakness. Once sealed, the neck swelled until it burst.

Races fought and died in great numbers. Dragons ripped men to pieces. Humans retaliated with all sorts of war machines. Fairies fell like rain from the sky. Ashborn watched from the top of the massive volcano, Mount

Scorpio. He chose to be a peacemaker like his father, Raiden. He landed between the two armies and put an end to the bloodshed.

Some humans resisted; Ashborn consumed them with his fire. Other dragons challenged his authority; Ashborn coiled them and snapped their necks. When the fairies saw the fury of the dragon prince of the world, they laid down their weapons and took an oath to never to raise them again. Henceforth, Ashborn became the mediator between the races.

Humans, wisps, fairies, and dragons nurtured decades of hate. To unite the races, Ashborn had a sword crafted from his prized horn and gave that sword to a worthy human. Other dragons did the same, and with the power of their bone swords, valiant humans fought with dragons to keep the peace.

Vallan turned the dragon bone hilt over in his hand.

"This is Ashborn's horn. That is why this sword is so dangerous. It was used to share Ashborn's power with a human."

Vallan reverently handed the sword back to Apollo. He took it with a newfound respect.

Why didn't we leave it in the Chasm? Wouldn't it be safer there?"

"Lady Black has been to the Chasm. She was close to breaking the magic that protected it. Now that it's out, the decedents of Ashborn will sense it and seek to reclaim it."

Vallan ran his fingers over the horn outlining the carving of the dragon.

"How did you know the sword was in the Chasm?" Apollo asked.

Apollo's aura revealed a tide of emotion. Vallan was a master at hiding his emotions, but this story had crippled that power. Something happened long ago and that event had bruised Vallan's soul.

Vallan's chin twitched and his face tightened. He released the smallest breath. His voice turned raspy.

"This sword was my son's."

"You had a son?" Apollo couldn't hide his surprise.

The ground thundered. Vallan's white stallion whinnied. Apollo searched the sky for black thunderclouds, but there were none.

The rumbling went unbroken and grew louder.

Apollo hurried to the middle of the road. He unfocused his eyes. The world before him turned foggy and then the textures came into view as he switched to his Darksight.

The road shivered.

A hunched, vaguely human creature with rough skin, tiny mole-like eyes, and a third arm curling out of his back came sprinting down the road. Then another prowled by on all fours. He spotted a third and fourth with an extra, lifeless head on their shoulders, another had four ears, and a crowd of them had only one eye. The Goblins had a variety of disformities, but what made them common to each other was their tiny eyes and baggy skin. All at once, a mass stampeded toward Apollo and Vallan.

Apollo only stared into the rushing horde.

"What is it?" Vallan demanded.

"Goblins," Apollo managed through a quick breath.

Vallan jumped to his feet and drew his sword. "How many?"

Apollo looked away. His heart thumped to the beat of the Goblin feet shaking the ground.

"Too many," he said.

"We need to go! Get on the horse," Vallan ordered.

Apollo hurried to the white stallion. He tried to mount it, but only managed to flop clumsily on top.

He'd heard the stories of Goblin hordes. To a horde, Apollo and Vallan weren't humans, they were meat.

Vallan turned back down the road, toward the mountains. He kicked his horse, but before he could get to a gallop, a Goblin jumped and sunk its teeth into the horse's hind leg. Vallan's stallion screamed and stumbled. Its eyes bulged in pain. It bucked, nearly flinging the Goblin off, but its teeth were planted firm. Apollo jumped into the dirt.

"Into the woods. Run!" Vallan screamed.

"Toss me the sword," Apollo shouted.

Vallan tossed the Sword of Ashborn.

Apollo caught the sword by its bone handle. He swung for the Goblin, but before steel met flesh, the Goblin tore his bite out of Vallan's horse. Apollo cleaved its head off with the horse flesh still in its mouth.

"Run boy!"

Another Goblin leaped on the stallion's head. Vallan pulled his sword back to hack the Goblin off. The Goblin sunk its teeth clean through the bridle.

Vallan's horse cried a final desperate squeal before its head rested lifelessly in the dirt.

"Let's go! More are coming!" Apollo yelled.

Like flies to a corpse, the Goblins clustered on the horse's body and gobbled down whatever flesh they could bite.

The horde was closing in. They weren't going to make it.

"We won't be fast enough," Vallan said. "You need to go. I'll hold them off. Take the sword to the Archmage, he'll protect it."

"I won't leave you." Apollo insisted.

"Look at them," Vallan pointed to the Goblins ripping and tearing his horse apart. "Do you see the colors they wear?"

Apollo blinked away his Darksight. He could see each goblin had a cord around their neck with a piece of metal painted black and gold, the colors of the Emperor, and on it, in red, was the outline of a bull's head.

"The Emperor has Goblins?" Apollo gasped.

"Yes, now go. Warn the city before it's too late."

"GO!" Vallan screamed.

Apollo turned and bolted into the woods.

Vallan clenched his teeth. He cut the first Goblin clean in half. He dashed his sword against a stone. Sparks shot out into the underbrush.

The Goblins looked up from the gore of Vallan's horse. More of them were rushing from down the road.

"Black stands here for hours on end, reading from ancient books. She has read this box a stack of tomes just to find the right word to open it. A few times, the box would crack open and I thought she might actually have figured it out. I've listened and tried a few myself. An ancient word unlocks this box. One so old that the world has forgotten how to say it."

"What's in this box belongs to me, not you or Black." Vallan shouldered Osirius out of the way.

Osirius scampered a step to the side.

Vallan ran his fingers over the brass box. He had a faraway look in his icy, blue eyes.

"What are you hiding from Black?" Osirius asked.

Vallan ignored him. His eyes were locked on the box.

"It has been safe here for a long, long time." Vallan swallowed hard.

He whispered a word that took all of his breath. The box jolted and seams appeared. Osirius watched anxiously as the bottom of the case opened and a long object wrapped tightly in aged yellow linen lowered to the altar.

The linen crumbled as Vallan touched it. Underneath was the hilt of a sword. The sword-guard was a golden cast of outstretched dragon wings. The hilt extended the sculpture to encompass the dragon's torso carved out of a dragon horn. At the bottom, the tail coiled around the pommel to hold a grape-sized ruby.

Vallan dusted the linen from the blade.

Another Goblin was upon him. He thrust his sword through it and slashed the stone again. Sparks rained into a pile of dry leaves. It caught and flames curled through the forest.

Vallan looked down at his magnificent stallion now covered in blood with its ribs jutting out and its guts scattered.

"You vermin!" he cried.

Vallan ran at them. He cut two in half. One jumped at him, clawing. Vallan lobbed off its talons. He drew power from the fire and hit another with a spell that sent it spiraling backward.

The thumping of feet stopped. Vallan spun around. The horde of Goblins surrounded him. Firelight put the gray skin of the mole-eyed creatures in an unsteady, crimson glow. Each had a different mutation. One had an extra leg, while another had one or two extra arms. Some had two elbows and a few even had a second headless neck. They all bore their flat, bone-crushing teeth.

At their rear, Vallan saw a human in a black cloak on horseback whispering orders.

"What do you want?" Vallan called out.

The human didn't answer. The Goblins started to chant. The word started rough, but gradually it came together.

"Mat, Me-ath, Me-at, Meat, Meat."

Vallan took in the firelight and drew his sword back. Using the light, he made an impossible leap into their mass. He slammed the ground and a ripple of pressure sent a wave of Goblins out in every direction. Vallan roared a battle cry and sprinted deeper into their ranks. Hacking and slashing, he cut through them like reeds.

He worked his way toward the back. With each step, his sword flashed. He was paces from their leader. The horde of Goblins was closing in. He couldn't hold them off for long. His only hope was to reach their leader. If he could only—.

A blow hit him in the temple. Vallan whirled to confront his attacker. Then a club cracked him across the back. He stumbled. Deformed fists pounded him down. Goblins pulled at his arms and legs. A club whizzed through the air and everything went dark.

21

Hyperion – Atlantis

Alaric couldn't stop scratching his fingers. His skin was strangling his bones. He looked longingly at the dagger hanging from his waist. His bones itched. He wanted to carve the skin off.

Sarod's spell was preparing him for what came next. Alaric shuttered.

He watched from the Agora of Atlas. In the thick mist, he could see the Emperor's carrack drop its sails off the shore of Tarboroth.

A sleepy mist hovered above the water. The sea looked dull and choppy. As the first sun Alpha, broke over the horizon, and the mist gradually dissipated.

Alaric liked the mist. There was privacy to it. Blindness that made everyone strain simply to see. He could focus on what was in front of him, and guess what possibilities were hidden in the fog.

Alaric had tempered his mind to do just that. When he wore the vial of Bane blood around his neck, to dampen the power of the Mind Curse, he could peer into the unknown for possibilities; ways to end the Emperor's reign. When Alaric took the vial off, he forced himself to only see what was in front of him; the wishes of the Emperor. It was a means to thwart the Mind Curse, and it had served him well.

Always look forward; never look back. It was the key to his trick. What a man could do was uncertain, but what a man had done was inescapable. Guilt was a weakness, a rotted beam in the structure of his mind.

Alaric was a murderer. He couldn't escape that. It was in the past and those he'd killed were stepping-stones to his ultimate goal.

He'd even forgotten their names. If his victims came back to haunt him and he saw their faces, Alaric doubted he'd even recognize them.

But he would recognize Bendri.

His death was the one event he couldn't forget, or forgive. He could still hear his screams echoing in his mind. Even if he exacted his revenge, would his grandson's wails still ring in his ears every time he saw a child?

Alaric had moved to Atlantis for the boats. His grandson, Bendri, loved to watch the Trireme coast through the water. He'd laughed at the ship's paddle wheels. He'd said the warship looked like a wagon rolling over the water.

"How do you think they move?" Alaric had asked.

"Dragons," Bendri had said.

"Dragons? I don't see any dragons."

"That's because you're not looking." Bendri had then pointed to the paddle wheels.

"They're in there. That's why smoke comes out the top. It's dragons huffing. Dragons do that."

Bendri would be nineteen now. If that damn Mayan slave hadn't broken her curse and escaped to New Camelot, the Emperor wouldn't have made him prove his loyalty. Cain wouldn't have given the order.

Sometimes he could still feel Bendri's warm blood on his hands.

Alaric couldn't dwell on what might have been. The past made things certain. Sinners suffer for their crimes. He had bought his passage to hell, but he wasn't going alone. He would drag Cain and the Emperor down with him.

He felt a mild shiver of pain pass over his mind. The thought of murdering the Emperor was too bold for even the Bane blood to block. He clutched the green vial dangling about his neck and waited for the pain to pass.

The Emperor couldn't die. Not yet. If it were that easy, Rinn could've handled it years ago.

Alaric had to know how the Mind Curse worked. He wasn't even sure what would happen to those under the Emperor's spell if the Emperor died.

The rushing waters of the Agora of Atlas were soothing at times. Alaric had spent many evenings meditating on the balcony. The Agora was blocky with pillars and peaks in near-perfect angles. Pumps below the structure drew water from the Sarthrin Sea and then purified it and diverted the water into four small rivers that coursed through the structure. Water rumbled outside, but inside the many hundreds of waterfalls resounded scarcely above a whisper.

Alaric raked at the skin on his fingers. There was no stopping the itching. He pulled a pair of leather gloves over his scabby hands and pushed through the curtains to enter the shadows of his study.

Miriam slouched in a wooden chair in the corner of the room. Her hair was tangled and her dark skin had turn pale brown. Her cheeks sagged with her scowl as she stared at the pile of books at her feet.

"Have you found anything?" Alaric asked.

Miriam looked from the pile of books to the iron shackles anchoring her ankles to the floor.

"Yes."

Alaric's frown softened. Miriam held up an empty page.

"I found what appears to be an ancient recipe for nut bread."

Alaric expected such an answer from the crone. She'd been nothing but a pain since he'd captured her.

"The Emperor has come to Atlantis." He paused for a moment.

Miriam pushed her books to the side. She saw Alaric nervously itching at his hands.

"If he finds that you're looking for a way to break the Mind Curse, then we're both dead," he finished.

Miriam examined her wrinkly hands. They had been smooth once, though she could scarcely remember those days. They seemed as distant as the histories she read in the tomes at her feet.

"Then, the Emperor will have to kill me. Death collects us all. To die a Grandmaster at the hands of a great evil, that would be a fitting end to my tale."

"Your Order thinks you died with Rhean," Alaric said.

Miriam folded her arms and cocked her head. "Even better, I'll be known as the Oracle who fought alongside the Small Giant and died weaponless facing an invisible foe. I might even get a statue."

Alaric cleared his throat and spat a glob of black spit on the handmade carpet.

"You are a wretched creature," Miriam said.

"Can I reason with you, or will I have to kill you?" Alaric asked.

"If you were going to kill me, you'd have done it by now."

That was true. She was the Grandmaster Oracle with more knowledge than he could ever comprehend, yet every time they spoke, she made him so angry that it took all his power to keep himself from driving his dagger through her.

He had to reason with her somehow.

"If the curse outlives us, who will stop it? What if it outlives the Emperor, or worse: what if the whole Empire is pulled into death when the Emperor dies? Have you considered the boundless power of the Mind Curse?"

Miriam slipped a finger between a shackle and her ankle to itch at the raw skin underneath. She didn't know how she'd gotten there. All she remembered was watching Rhean die and a blue dart pricking her shoulder.

He wanted her silence, and she wanted answers.

Miriam leaned back in her chair. "Your bait was clever. You knew the Order wouldn't pass up a chance to capture one of the Marked. The boy with the moons under his eyes. You painted his face, didn't you?"

Alaric ignored her question. He approached her and stood just out of reach so that the candles in the dark room cast his shadow over her.

"You're my prisoner and you're going to keep your mouth shut when the Emperor arrives," he pressed.

Miriam didn't seem the least bit intimidated by Alaric's posture or words. In fact, she found him irritating. Miriam wanted to reach out and grab him. If there had been enough light, she could have made him put his dagger through his own black heart, but the windows and doorway to the balcony were covered with thick tapestries. The two candles that lit the room weren't powerful enough, and in three hundred years, Miriam had never met a creature so barren of positive emotion. She also suspected that with a dagger in his heart, Alaric wouldn't be in any sort of mood to answer her questions.

"What did you call your henchman? The Shade? There is no spell that can make a man invisible, no relic, not even one made by eleven hands. Yet I saw it. I saw the man vanish into nothing before my eyes. These old eyes have never seen anything like that. I know what he is. I know *who* he is."

Alaric leaned in closer. His teeth were clutched together, and black spit leaked between them.

"You will be silent, or I'll kill you, and it won't be quick. You aren't going to say a word."

Miriam's scoffed.

"I haven't decided what I'm going to do. The Emperor would execute you if he knew what you were doing, and I would *really* like to see you dead. I'm just not sure how badly I want that yet. Now, are you going to tell me of your Shade, or do I need to start threatening you?"

Alaric released a growl of frustration and shrunk back. "I hate you. Had I known I would be trapped in a room with you for this long, I would've *never* tricked you into coming to Atlantis."

Miriam's wrinkly lips turned up into a crinkly smile.

"Finally, some honesty. If you want my silence, then you will have to answer my questions."

Alaric spat to the side, eyed the old woman, and gave a curt nod.

"Sitting here in the dark, I've had a lot of time to think. The boy with the moons on his face, he couldn't have been the second of the Marked. With marks as obvious as that he wouldn't have gone unnoticed this long. You painted his face, didn't you?"

Alaric nodded. "It was the perfect trap to ensnare an Oracle."

"No, it wasn't," Miriam snapped. "I can think of several better plans, easier ways that don't involve battling Warlocks."

She rubbed her chin. "So I asked myself: why would a foul, deceptive creature like you go through all of that trouble to get the Order to come hunting for the Marked? And if you were going to impersonate one of the Marked, why wouldn't you paint the broken suns of the Doomseeker on the child's face? The second of the Marked might tempt the Council, but the real prize is the Doomseeker."

Miriam looked Alaric square in the eye.

"Why did you paint the moons instead of the broken suns?"

Alaric hesitated. "I—"

"Shhh, it's a rhetorical question. I already know the answer."

Alaric's face was full of apprehension. She could see it in his tight grimace. The way he looked in her eyes and then looked away. He wasn't prepared for her, she'd blindsided him, and she loved every minute of it.

"My capture had a dual purpose. The most apparent reason is that you need the knowledge I have locked away in my head. I have most of the Aurorean Temple's tremendous library between my ears and you want access to it. The second, less apparent reason, was to demonstrate to the real Marked what the Council was prepared to do to catch him."

"What real Marked? You think I have the Doomseeker here?" Alaric balked.

Miriam rubbed her temples. "If you had the Doomseeker, then you would've painted the broken suns on that boy. Pay attention."

Alaric ran a hand over his dagger. His fingers tingled on the cold steel. It would only take a moment to put an end to her arrogant quips, but then all of her knowledge would die with her. Every book she'd read, all the understanding she'd gained in the Temple's vast library would be lost, along with his chance to learn more about the Mind Curse.

Alaric took his hand from his dagger and placed it on his hip. "What is your question? What do I have to tell you to spare me your insolence?"

Miriam ignored him again and continued her rant.

"I didn't see it at first, but then I thought. What could make a man invisible? And I remembered an old scripture from the Garatha: *The Doomseeker's right hand is swift and unseen. One man will stand by another, and one shall die and the other shall live. For death is a shade marked by the gods to be the unseen reaper.*"

Alaric was speechless. The long strands of hair bordering his bald head stuck to the sweat on his brow.

"By demonstrating the hate the Order has for a Marked, you've proven to this Marked that the Aurorean Order, the symbol of good, truth, and light wants him dead, and if they want him dead who can he really trust? You."

Miriam paused to give Alaric a moment to digest her words. The dark room was so silent that Miriam could hear Alaric breathing.

"Now, what do we call your Marked? Rinn, the Shade, or the Reaper? There is also a scripture that calls him the Wind of Peril, but that title is too long-winded."

Alaric stood and walked to the curtains blocking the light from the balcony doorway. He peered through the crack at the Emperor's carrack. The Emperor would be ashore soon, and Alaric's life would be in Miriam's hands.

"This is the part where you answer my questions," Miriam said.

Alaric pushed up his sleeve and wiped the sweat from his forehead. He looked reluctantly at Miriam. She was staring at him, eyes narrowed and full of spite.

"The Emperor will be here soon and if you don't want him to know about your little scheme to overthrow him—"

"His name is Rinn, but he is also called the Shade," Alaric conceded. "I found him here in Atlantis. He was a thief. He's always been a thief."

"How does he vanish?" Miriam pressed.

Alaric turned back to face her. "He takes in light and that light shines through him," he answered.

Miriam nodded as if she already knew the answer.

"Does he have a family?" she asked.

"His family is dead. All he has left of their memory is a Sand Horse. Now are you satisfied?"

"What happened to Wislan? Where did your Shade take him?"

"I sent him home," Alaric said. His mood shifted and he smiled a grin that made black dribble come out the corner of his mouth.

"To New Camelot?" Miriam asked.

Alaric nodded. "Of course, his passage came with a price. I require the Urim. The White Stone of power that you keep locked away in your temple. Only Auroreans can enter, and it seems with the help of Wislan that I'll even beat Lady Black and Sarod to it."

Miriam pursed her lips.

"No arguments? No: 'Wislan would never betray the Order' or something heroic like that?"

Miriam folded her arms and narrowed her gaze. "Wislan is an idiot. He'll bring you back a sack of stones and not a one will be the one you're looking for."

Miriam asked her final question.

"What do you want with the Urim? It will do you little good in your condition."

Alaric thought for a moment. If he told her the truth, maybe it would motivate her to help him. After all, he could still kill her.

"I'm building the Breastplate of Decision to discover how to dispel the Mind Curse."

Miriam waved her hand dismissively.

"Wythrin had all knowledge of the enchantments of the breastplate destroyed. It's impossible."

"He couldn't destroy everything. He never defeated Sarod."

Miriam's eyes flickered. "That's foolish, you'd be trading one world terror for another."

"Then help me," Alaric pleaded. "I don't want to bring it back, but if I'm going to defeat the Mind Curse, I might not have a choice."

A green light leaked through the fibers of Alaric's purple robe. He reached under his collar and pulled out his vial of Bane blood. It pulsated a green glow.

"The Emperor is coming," he said.

"You're nervous."

Alaric opened his mouth to argue, but Miriam was too quick.

"There is no point denying it. Your aura is shaking like a little girl with a spider in her hair."

Alaric gritted his teeth. He flexed his hands. He wanted to slap her. There had to be an easier way to get the knowledge he needed.

Alaric removed the vial, rolled it up in a cloth, and tucked it away in a drawer. He leaned back on a table to calm his nerves.

"Bane blood, the Breastplate, the Mind Curse. You're meddling in magic you don't understand. I knew a boy who did the same thing. He struck himself dumb and got himself stuck to a ceiling for a whole night. He ended up wetting his pants right over Grandmaster Durakos."

Miriam's mouth turned up into a smirk.

"I'll never forget Durakos' face." Miriam chuckled. "He was so horrified. You were his apprentice. I'm sure you know the face. His eyes were wide and his lip trembled between anger and horror."

Alaric had seen the face a few times. Durakos had always taken himself too seriously.

"His lips did tremble when he got mad." Alaric's scowl softened.

Miriam's smirk buckled into a contemptuous grimace. "Did they tremble when you shouted the words that burned the flesh from his face?"

Alaric pushed himself from the table. His bald head flushed red. "You're a deceitful bitch."

Miriam laughed. "That's Grandmaster Oracle 'deceitful bitch.'"

22

Avalon - New Camelot

When Clara joined the Healers, she had tried to be truthful. She was young, and she wanted to escape the hurt. Clara never wanted to harm anyone. Had she been naive? She sowed lies. The world was a garden of lies, and she was growing with the rest of the deceivers, the sinners. There were things in her past that she never wanted to share with anyone. That was the past. Now, day by day, she couldn't even tell Grandmaster Daynin where she spent her time.

Ruben had already confronted her half a dozen times. Suddenly, he needed her help in the Sanctuary. She wasn't sure if they actually missed her, or if Ruben wanted to pry into what she was doing. She wasn't about to go crawling back to mixing potions in the Sanctuary basement. Not when Mathus had given her the freedom and resources to create a poison to kill Doya.

Not only was it a noble cause, but it was also fascinating, and what would the other Healers say when Clara put an end to their greatest enemy? Then she might get some well-deserved respect. If she did that, then they'd be making her potions.

Clara worked diligently at a table piled high with bins of herbs, vials of acids, and metal dust. A few gold coins laid on the table. The Night Guard helped her grind up and collect ingredients. They even ground up the gold coins without so much as stealing the dust on their hands. If Mathus could be praised for anything, he was excellent at choosing loyal soldiers who shared his passion for their cause.

The Doya was staring at her again. She could feel the spite in its black eyes. When she glanced up at the Doya, it snarled back.

Soldiers were posted on either side of the Doya. It was shackled to the stone wall with the bladed metal collar still tight around its neck. The pull cord, to decapitate him, never left a soldier's hand.

At Clara's request, the Doya's fingers were restrained in mage shackles, two iron blocks molded specifically to contain the Doya's claws. The two blocks were then screwed together, to prevent its fingers from moving to cast any silent spells. Even with all of their precautions, the creature still made her nervous.

"Will you kill me today, *witch*?" the Doya asked with a wicked grin. She'd come to know the Doya as Farum, but the Night Guard had other names for it that she wouldn't repeat.

"No, Farum. Not today," she replied.

"You must have a soft spot for me, *witch*," Farum snorted.

"I told you, I'm not a witch."

Farum's sharp teeth stuck out the side of its mouth as it grinned even wider. It ran its oily tongue along the ridge of its black gums. Clara hated it when it did that.

"Clara, the Healer that mixes poison."

Clara returned to her work. Farum spat a wad of black phlegm on the floor before continuing.

"You were a Healer, but now you're a *witch*."

Clara looked down at her hands. She held a mixture of gold dust, bloodroot, crushed Hawthorne, red moss, and Linden root.

Farum was right. She didn't think she could call herself a Healer anymore.

The iron door creaked and Willow appeared with a plate of bread and pork.

"It's feeding time," she muttered.

"Pork and bread? No babies? We Doya love to nibble on baby flesh," Farum snarled sarcastically.

Willow dropped the plate of food on Clara's table. "We're fresh out of babies your *highness*, but if your delicate palate objects, I could always feed you my spear instead."

Farum ran its black tongue over its teeth and billowed a laugh. Syrup dripped from its mouth and slid down its bare chest. Farum's neck jerked as the soldier holding the cord to its collar pulled it taut. Farum's laugh soured.

The room was lit by firelight, except for a small gap where a mouse sided hole opened up to the outside. Clara took in the sunlight and cast a small spell, pulling the contents of the vial together until the ground up roots and leaves bound with the liquids.

The door opened and Snails, her assistant, entered. Clara didn't have to look up. She'd learned to identify the inept alchemist by his lingering smell. She held out the vial. Snails was content to just hold it.

"I'll need some blood." Clara took a pin from her table and a small tin cup.

Farum growled as she approached.

"I'm just going to give you a prick that's all," Clara said. She hated Doya like other Auroreans, but she didn't see a point in making this one suffer any more than it needed to.

"Let me," Willow whipped out her serrated dagger. With two quick paces and a thrust, she jammed it into Farum's stomach. The Doya let out a shrill cry and black blood poured out.

Willow looked Farum dead in the eyes. "Taste it. That's good steel," she said.

Clara gave Willow a disgusted look and put the tin cup under the knife. Willow pulled her serrated knife free so that it ripped Farum's flesh. The cup overfilled with blood. Clara and Willow watched as the strands of torn flesh squirmed around clumsily until they finally interlocked and knitted together.

"I'd like to see it dead as much as you, but it doesn't need to suffer," Clara protested.

Willow wiped her dagger off and tucked it away. With a disapproving grunt, she left the chamber.

Clara took the bread from the plate and held it up to Farum's mouth.

"Don't let it bite me," she said to the soldier with the leash in hand.

Farum opened its oily, black mouth. With unprecedented gentleness, it used its sharp teeth to pull the bread out of her hand.

"That wasn't so hard, was it?" Clara asked. Farum answered her with a glare.

She pulled off a strip of pork and held it up. Again, Farum ate with surprising placidity. For the first time, Clara could see a shadow of humanity in the creature.

"Why? Why would you do this to yourself?" she asked.

"Mathus did this to me." Farum rattled its chains. "The Lord Marshall and his merry band of misfits."

"No, why did you become a Doya?" Clara corrected.

"Darkness speaks to us. I am one of the chosen."

Clara glanced down at its collar. "And look what it's brought you."

"Bread, pork, a roof, and a woman to feed me?" Farum licked its gums again.

Clara gave Farum a disgusted frown and returned to her table where Snails had prepared a flat plate for their experiment.

She poured a spoonful of Farum's blood onto the plate. She then took the fresh poison and dripped a single drop to mix with the blood. She pushed the plate under an Atlantian table glass, a contraption with a half dozen magnifying glasses, to get a closer view of the poison as it mixed with the black blood. The blood turned grey and started to bubble. Clara bit her lip. It was working; it just needed to keep boiling.

The reaction stopped and the blood went black again.

"That's good, right?" Snails asked.

Clara huffed in frustration. "No, that's not good. Just a sliver of Aureate can boil a bucket of Doya blood dry." She took the rest of the poison and tossed it into a barrel with the other failures.

She looked at Farum, who wore a sharky grin. "The witch is angry. Go on, let me feel that frustration."

Clara looked down at the white plate she clutched in her hands. It took everything she had to keep herself from smashing it on the floor.

"I need some air," she said.

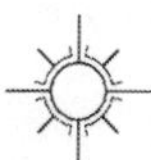

The warmth of the suns brought a smile to Clara's face. Her Gods were up there on their powerful thrones watching over her. It was their warmth that gave her peace, and their power that gave light to life.

Clara said a short prayer. "*From the South, House of the Eternal Sun, may right action reap the harvest so that we may enjoy the fruits of planetary being.*" She then added to her memorized prayer. "*Give me guidance and strength. Shine your light through the dark tunnel of my life. Give me wisdom to defeat my enemies, and peace to know I am subject and guided by your will. Deliver my friends from danger. Please, protect Vallan and Apollo from evil.*"

The Council reported Rhean and Miriam dead. They'd already begun to appoint their successors. No one had heard from or seen Vallan and Apollo, but it wasn't uncommon for Vallan to leave for months at a time. He was aloof, and Clara always thought him to be withdrawn from everyone but Apollo. She hoped he hadn't gotten Apollo killed. Being pulled between the Healers and Mathus, Clara needed her friend now more than ever.

She could see the red dome of the Sanctuary just over the buildings of Old Town. The Order, the Healers, even the most righteous of the Purists, believed killing Doya was not only permissible but a duty. Apollo had Doya eyes. What would he think of her poison? When Farum had arrived, she had tried to kill him herself, but couldn't. There was a part of her that would do anything to not be like her father, the murderer.

That was then. Now, she'd gotten to know Farum. Terrible as the Doya was, she couldn't help but think of Apollo when she looked in its eyes.

Clara had never met a Doya before. She didn't expect them to be so intelligent, so human-like. She felt foolish for thinking that. After all, they were Dark Mages before they transformed into Doya. They were human once.

Did Farum deserve to die? The Purist in her knew killing Doya was just, but the Healer in her saw a sickness. She felt a dangerous sympathy for the creature. Taze, the prophet of the Purists, said all Doya were abominations before the Gods; Farum was an abomination if she ever saw one.

A swarm of soldiers in blue and gold tabards gathered at the barracks at the end of the street. Clara went in for a closer look.

"Mathus!" cried a bearded man with brown skin. He was Mayan, and his eyes, there was no mistaking his eyes.

"Apollo!" Clara called out. "APOLLO!" she yelled after him, but her voice was lost in the crowd of soldiers.

Mathus came out of the barracks to meet him. Apollo's legs wobbled, he propped himself up on a peculiar sword.

"Apollo?" Mathus slung his arm under his shoulder to hold him up.

"Get him a chair," Mathus ordered. Almost instantly, a soldier emerged with one in hand. Mathus helped Apollo down into it. He tried to pull the sword away too, but Apollo wouldn't let it go.

Mathus considered Apollo's ripped robes, dirty skin, and scruff. Apollo had black eyes, but Mathus still recognized the look in his face. He'd seen it too many times. There was a fight, and someone close to Apollo was dead.

Mathus scanned the courtyard. "Where's Vallan?"

Apollo couldn't answer that. The words just wouldn't come.

"Come now, spit it out," said Thar.

"Take your time," Mathus said. Apollo winced. His legs ached and his mouth was dry. He couldn't remember when he'd last eaten.

The crowd of soldiers pushed in around them.

"Give him some room," Willow commanded.

Apollo searched the faces of the soldiers. He felt camaraderie with them. At least for this moment, they didn't see him as a monster.

"We were attacked by an army of Goblins wearing the Emperor's sigil. It was—"

Apollo stopped. He couldn't remember if it was a couple days or a week. He'd been walking forever. He'd left Vallan back there for the Goblins. He couldn't get the image of Vallan's mangled horse out of his mind.

"I don't remember. Within the week, I think."

"Where?" Mathus asked.

"On the road along the river Bassas, a few leagues from the Chasm."

Thar turned to a nearby soldier. "Saddle the horses and fetch my armor. And bring my new ax."

Thar yanked a flask from underneath his blue high captain's cape. He popped the cork off and took a long swig. Cheeks full of meade, Thar caught Mathus' disapproving look.

Thar emptied his bulging cheeks in a single gulp.

"What? You don't expect me to fight Goblins sober, do ya?"

Mathus spouted off orders to another soldier.

"Light the signal fire. I want our gates closed, our archers in place, and our people inside by nightfall." The soldier saluted with a fist to his chest.

Mathus turned back to Apollo. "You've done well. I couldn't ask for more from my own soldiers."

Willow was already suited up with a quiver of short spears hanging over her shoulder and a serrated sword at her belt.

Mathus starting issuing orders. "Willow, I need you here. We must prepare the city for an attack. Thar, take a hundred of my best soldiers, go to the road and see if you can find Vallan. A horde should be easy to track. Take fifteen scouts; send one back every four hours. I want to know where this horde has been hiding."

"I'm coming with you." Apollo blurted. He tried to push himself out of his chair.

Both Mathus and Thar were about to object when Clara beat them to it.

Clara shoved and squeezed her way through the soldiers. "You're not going anywhere!" she scolded.

When she reached Apollo, she wasn't sure if she wanted to hug him or slap him, so she just stood there, pointing an accusatory finger.

"You, you look like hell," she said.

By the look on her face, Mathus half expected her to grab him by the ear and drag him out of the barracks. Mathus watched the angry, young girl snatch Apollo by the collar. Despite the circumstances, it made him smile.

For a breath, he thought back, and he wasn't in the courtyard of the barracks anymore. It was a different time, a different place, and that concern on the bold, young girl's face was for him.

Apollo opened his mouth to argue. Mathus could see some of his own stubbornness in him.

"My men will manage without you," Mathus said. "You best stay here, we can't face a horde of Goblins and the Wrath of Clara."

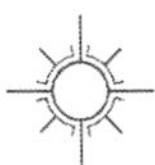

Clara practically dragged Apollo to the Sanctuary and into one of the washrooms. The place was simple with a small hearth by the window, a wooden tub of tepid water, a short oak stool, and a pile of fresh towels and bandages folded on a table.

Apollo hadn't spoken since they left the barracks. Clara was starting to get worried. When she looked into his eyes, they didn't just look black; they looked empty.

Clara sat him down. He was a head taller than her, but on the stool, he was just a little shorter. She gently placed a hand on his cheek and tilted his head to look up at her.

"Let it go, everything is going to be fine now."

Apollo searched her concerned face. He wanted to forget the Chasm, Cedric's massacre, Cat, the sword. He needed Vallan back. Apollo recognized her locks of golden hair, soft skin, and sweet face. Her eyes were teal, with flecks of the lightest blue around the edges. They were beautiful.

Apollo surged out of the stool and captured her in an embrace. Startled, Clara sucked in her breath.

It was a long embrace, longer than it should've been. Apollo seemed content to stay that way, but Clara finally pulled away.

"Vallan is dead."

"What?" Clara gasped.

"I left him with the Goblins. I saw them eat his horse."

"Did you see him die?" Clara asked.

"No."

"Then you mustn't lose hope," Clara said. She'd heard that once, in the Sanctuary, when a wife saw her soldier husband pulled over the wall in a slave raid. Hope didn't help him.

Clara looked away and swallowed the lump in her throat.

"Arms up," she ordered. Apollo raised his arms and she pulled off his torn shirt. He was stronger than she remembered. She covered her mouth when she saw cuts scabbed over across his chest. His arms were dotted with old yellow bruises and brush burns.

What had he been through?

Clara washed the dirt from his neck and shoulders. A chill came in from the window. Rather than block out the fresh air, she tossed another log in the hearth.

"You made it to the Chasm?" Clara asked.

Apollo nodded.

"Did they do this to you?" she asked, pointing to his bruises and cuts.

"The caravan was destroyed. One of the Corrupted got out. I tried to help, but the relics started exploding. We took shelter in the Chasm."

The clean water was helping. Apollo was starting to feel a little better.

Clara hung on every word. "What was the Chasm like?"

"Imagine sitting in a cave, always. No morning or night, no light. Nothing changes. There's no happiness there. It's hard to believe, but some of the Corrupted choose to be locked away."

Clara selected a new towel and a straight razor from the table. She took a glob of soap and rubbed it over his neck, and followed up with a swipe from the razor.

"The Archmage has been asking about you."

"Me? "Why?"

"I don't know. He told me to bring you to him if I see you."

Clara dipped the razor in water and ran it carefully up Apollo's neck again. She wiped soap over his cheeks, Apollo felt her fingers brush over his Thetus Mud.

"I can do the rest," Apollo said graciously.

Apollo took the razor. A splotch of red on Apollo's pants caught her eye.

"You're bleeding," she gasped.

Apollo saw the blood, but he knew he hadn't been cut.

"I'm fine." Apollo gingerly put his hand in his pocket and ran a finger over the vial of dragon blood. It was cracked.

"You're not fine," she said.

"It's not my blood. Give me some time to clean up," Apollo stood and opened the door to the washroom. Clara reluctantly left.

Apollo pulled the vial of Dragon Blood from his pocket. It was cracked on top. He must've landed on it somehow.

He went to the closet and found a vial of Blood Sap among the piles of Healer's herbs and potions. He emptied the Blood Sap out the window, dipped the vial in the bathwater, swished it around to clean it, and dumped the vial out again.

He carefully poured the Dragon Blood from the broken vial into the new one and pressed the cork down tight.

When he finished, he took his pants and the vial and tossed them into the hearth. Apollo watched his pants burn, he waited for the blood to boil away, but instead, it started to glow, shimmering as if made from a thousand crushed rubies.

Apollo grabbed the hearth shovel and collected the blood. He searched around the room for somewhere else to put it. Then he saw the privy door. He yanked it open and dumped the blood down the shaft.

He hurried to the window. Eventually, the sword would draw dragons to it, Vallan had said that. It was one of the reasons they had to lock it away. But everyone knew dragons could smell blood for a league, especially dragon blood. He'd carried that cracked vial from the border all the way to the center of the city.

Apollo squinted at a group of creatures in the distance. They were hard to make out. Their bodies moved with every flap of their wings. They got closer and closer. Apollo dug his nails into the side of the window.

The cry of an eagle settled his nerves. They were birds, only birds.

23

Avalon - New Camelot

Willow walked through the ranks of swordsmen and pikemen along the North Wall. She passed the City Guard in breastplates shimmering in torchlight and rows of Night Guard in their blood-red, leather armor.

Soldiers saluted her with a fist to their chest as she passed.

Willow's thin eyebrows tightened on her brow as she peered out over the wall and across the fields surrounding the city, searching for Goblins. They would rush the wall and then the killing would begin.

Soldiers parted to make a path for Mathus as he marched down the wall. Candlelight reflected off his freshly polished plate armor, giving it a bronze glow.

He briskly passed Willow. She had to jog to keep up.

"Are the archers prepared?" he asked.

Willow cleared her throat.

"Yes, my Lord, we have near eight thousand Cogbows and another ten thousand longbows in position."

Willow nodded to the throng of archers dispersed evenly across every rooftop within bowshot of the wall. Anyone who could shoot a bow was positioned on the nearby buildings. These men, women, even some stronger children, could create a volley of arrows that could black out the sun.

"How many swords and pikes?" Mathus asked.

"There are two thousand pikemen on the North Wall and another eight hundred on the East Wall. The North wall is strong with two thousand swords and we have another seven hundred on the East wall."

"And my ballistas?" Mathus continued.

"Eighteen of the twenty ballistas are battle-worthy. We're piecing together another with some old parts. We might even have a few of the old catapults working. We don't have much to fire. We could get some stone from the quarry, but it will take a few hours."

"Keep the soldiers on the wall," Mathus insisted. "If we get reports that the horde is far enough out, we'll start bringing stones in."

"My Lord," a soldier cut into their path. He smelled of horse and sweat, and his armor was made of sheep leather. He was a young, scrawny scout with the face of a boy and hair tied back in a ponytail.

"Did Thar find Vallan? Did he locate the horde?" Mathus demanded.

The scout lowered his eyes. "We found the hip bone and skull of a horse, but that's all. The Goblins even ate the small bones."

Mathus looked out into the darkness. The scout couldn't tell what Mathus was staring at, but Willow knew. The surrounding hills were empty, but the enemy would come, as the Emperor's army had come many times before, but this time with Goblins. Soon the horde would stare back and Mathus couldn't flinch. Hell could open up its gates, and the Lord Marshall would have to lead them through it. His conduct held the whole army together.

The scout continued. "The horde came from the Black Mountains, when they returned they took the same route. It's impossible to tell their number by their tracks. I can only guess."

"How many?" Mathus asked.

"The roads along the border are trampled with footprints. I'd say more than thirty thousand and less than fifty."

Mathus still stared at the dark hills, yet despite all his battles on the Wall he couldn't picture an army of that size.

"But they returned to the Black Mountains?" Mathus asked.

"I left Thar's men nearly two days ago. The horde could be anywhere."

Mathus swallowed hard and waved the scout away.

"Do you have orders for me, sir?" the scout asked.

Mathus looked at the youth. He was a scout and knew little of battle, but what choice did he have?

"Sword or pike? Which do you prefer?" Mathus asked.

"Pike, sir," the scout said.

"Good, find one and fill in a gap on the wall."

Mathus scanned the horizon again and again.

"We can't defeat that many," Willow said, plainly.

Mathus didn't answer. He straightened the brass medallion pinned into his long, Lord Marshall's cape.

"In the battle of Asher, the Emperor marched on Salem with forty thousand slaves and five dragons. When they reached the city, the tribe of Asher was ready for battle. They were a third their number and no dragons, yet the tribe slew twenty thousand and all of the Emperor's dragons. The Emperor was forced to retreat. It took him a year before he returned with a large enough army to defeat the tribe and take the city. Do you know why?"

"They had good bowmen," Willow answered.

Mathus shook his head. "The tribe offered positions of power to Warlocks. As much as I don't like magic, it can tip the scales of any battle. Warlocks can feel the flow of battles, they use that sense to move and attack. They move through an army like a river through stones, a current of death, unified."

"Will the mages help us?" Willow asked.

"Lord Marshall," Harthor called out, interrupting their conversation.

Mathus and Willow turned. Harthor's dark green Oracle robe was out of place among the armored men. The Aurorean sunburst on his chest earned him a few glances from the stationed soldiers. A broom of straight brown hair hung in his face, divided by his pointy nose.

He pushed his hair out of his eyes and waved when he saw Mathus on the other side of a crowd of soldiers.

"Excuse me," he said and awkwardly picked his way through. "Pardon."

"Will the Council hear me?" Mathus asked.

Harthor nodded. His expression was grim. "They've already deliberated on the aid you requested, but haven't voted. The vote will be split. Master Leteah has been chosen as the Grandmaster of Warlocks to replace Rhean. And I've been chosen to replace Miriam the Grandmaster Oracle. Leteah sides with the Purists: Durakos and her brother Gibnar. They don't believe this is their fight."

"What about the rest of the Council?" Willow asked.

"The City Guard has my support, but there are only a few Oracles and none of us are any good in a fight. Daynin and the Healers believe the city needs to be protected. They'll tend to your wounded, but they won't shed blood."

"And the Archmage?" Mathus asked.

"Night is upon us, Sorcerers are no use without the Suns, and Archmage Lorad will not send his Sorcerers to battle without the support of the Warlocks."

Mathus was growing irritated. "Then have the Archmage order the Warlocks to fight. There isn't time for this. My scouts are tracking the horde; they could be on top of us in a matter of hours."

Harthor raised his hands in a helpless gesture. "Grandmaster Leteah controls the Warlocks. She will not help you, and with the Council evenly split, the Archmage can't seize command of the Warlocks without the support of the majority."

"I must speak with them," Mathus said.

"Durakos is a bitter man; he will not hear you. Gibnar and Leteah await you in the Gatehouse. They might change their minds, but it won't be easy."

Harthor led Mathus down the stairs to the street. Mathus stopped when he saw a soldier leaning on the portcullis. He was standing in the same place he had been when he'd taken Ele's bow the day she died. That morning was nothing like tonight. The soldier didn't even resemble him, but the way he looked out the portcullis, with dread in his youthful face, reminded him of that terrible day fifteen years ago.

They descended the stairs. Mathus still stared at the gate. It was so long ago, yet the moisture in the air felt familiar.

"Lord Marshall," Harthor said, jolting him out of the memory.

Mathus swallowed the lump in his throat as Harthor lead him into the Gatehouse.

An iron candelabra sat in the center of an oak table. Wax dripped down the iron and collected in a creamy pool that dripped between the loose boards of the tabletop.

Gibnar's yellow robe drank in the light, while his twin sister's brown robes looked dull. She was his living shadow. They had the same hair and features, but Gibnar's shoulders were slightly broader, and Leteah glowered.

Leteah spoke first. Her voice shook with aggravation.

"The Council has made its decision."

"We have yet to vote," Harthor said.

"Voting is a ritual. If our minds are made up, the outcome will be the same," Leteah argued.

Mathus pushed his fists into the table and leaned over it.

"I beg your pardon, Grandmaster Leteah. There are a lot of lives at stake. Many good soldiers, some of them Purists, will die tonight if we don't have your help."

Leteah's face flushed with anger.

"Don't you think we considered that? Just because we didn't come to your *rescue* doesn't mean we took this decision lightly."

Gibnar raised his hand. "Leteah, that's enough," he said. "Mathus has been good to us. Better than the last Lord Marshall to hold his rank. Show him some respect."

The door burst opened and what looked like a skeleton in a lion skin cloak stood in the doorway. Mathus and the mages squinted against the candlelight to peer into the darkness. Upon the man's brow, a glint of candlelight flashed in the gems of the skeleton's crown.

"Your Grace," The mages abruptly rose to their feet.

The King entered, leaning heavily on a cane. His face entered the light, a frown ruled his wrinkled expression.

The King spoke with an inner strength that betrayed his frailness. "I've been told that we sent *one hundred* of our garrison after the horde to save a mage."

"I sent a group with some scouts to locate the horde. They're going to save a lost mage if they can. If he's even still alive," Mathus said.

"I know the mage, Vallan. I blessed you with your calling as Lord Marshall to protect the city, not use our defenses to save your friends."

"Your Grace, I sent scouts with those soldiers to report on the size of the horde and their intentions," Mathus replied in a measured tone.

"They mean to attack us. The Emperor wants the city. He's always wanted the city," the King blurted.

Mathus sucked a loud breath through his nose. "If that's the case, we'll be prepared for their attack."

"We would be more *prepared* with the one hundred soldiers you sent away."

Mathus gestured to Gibnar and Leteah across the table. "Sire, the Council and I are in negotiations for their assistance."

The King ignored Mathus' words. "If you want to remain Lord Marshall, you won't be so cavalier with our garrison."

Mathus' jaw tightened. "Yes, sire."

Gibnar spoke carefully. "The Archmage instructed me to speak with you. The rest of the Council hasn't been told of your prisoner or its message."

"Prisoner?" the King said. "I haven't been informed of any prisoners."

Leteah and Harthor's ears perked up.

Mathus folded his arms. "We're here to discuss the protection of the city and the temple, not the fate of my prisoner. If we're defeated, the city and everything in it, including the temple, is lost."

"The barrier protects the temple. It has for thousands of years. It doesn't need *your* protection," Leteah said.

"Even the barrier has its limitations. It has a weakness," Harthor corrected.

Gibnar scratched the stubble on his chin. He took a thoughtful moment to choose his precise words.

"What prisoner, Mathus?" the King interrupted.

Mathus spoke with reluctance. "Some time ago, we captured a Doya approaching the city. We've been keeping him in the crypts."

"A Doya in the city!" the King exclaimed.

Mathus closed his eyes and nodded.

"I ordered that no Doya be allowed within the city walls." The King's voice echoed in the small room. "If we live through the night, you will be a foot soldier. I will personally see your cape torn from your shoulder!"

The King turned and marched out the door, slamming it behind him.

Mathus kept his attention on Gibnar. Leteah and Harthor shared a look of outrage.

"We're consorting with Doya?" Leteah spat.

Gibnar shrugged off her question. "The Doya you captured warned us of the Doomseeker. He has been hiding here in the city for several years."

The room turned cold.

Mathus and Gibnar slid back into their chairs. Leteah and Harthor chose to stand.

"The Doomseeker is in the city. Why weren't we told?" Leteah demanded. Harthor nodded his emphatic agreement.

"The Archmage believes there is a traitor on the Council helping the Doomseeker. It was necessary to keep it from everyone until the traitor was found."

Gibnar turned his attention back to Mathus. "We do not share faith. You pray to the god of Arthur, the One God, do you not?"

"I pray to no gods," Mathus said.

"Have you heard of the Doomseeker?" Leteah asked.

"I've heard a few of the prophecies," Mathus replied.

"And you know that prophecies are never false?" Harthor asked.

"They wouldn't be very prophetic if they were," Mathus said.

Gibnar leaned forward in his chair. He pushed the iron candelabra out of the center of the table, so he could meet Mathus' firm stare. "Sarod's message was a warning. In one of the prophecies, the Doomseeker is foretold to take the Dark Throne. Lord Sarod fears for his seat of power, so he has been generous with his information."

Mathus grit his teeth. "You're trusting Sarod? I brought the Archmage to our prisoner to warn him of deceit, not to be Sarod's messenger boy. You can't trust anything—"

Gibnar interrupted him. "We can trust that the Dark Prince wishes to keep his throne, and with the Doomseeker alive, it's only a matter of time before the prophecy comes to pass."

"I won't side with the Doya who killed my own blood," Mathus said.

Gibnar interlocked his fingers and placed his palms on the table. "Using Sarod's information is no sort of alliance. You need our help. I'm prepared to change my vote so that the Council will add Warlocks to your ranks if it means the capture of the Doomseeker."

"I will even lead them," Grandmaster Leteah added.

Harthor didn't like the sound of this, and he could tell by Mathus' disagreeable grunt that he didn't like it either.

Mathus searched Gibnar's face. It was still and his gaze was steady. Leteah wore the same look. Their resolve was pristine. He remembered what Vallan had said of the Council and their deals. They were like alligators: greedy, stubborn, and ready to snap.

There was hesitation in Mathus' voice.

"What do you want from me? I don't have the Marked locked up in some catacomb somewhere."

Gibnar shook his head. "We do not need your help. We know where the Doomseeker is hiding. It is a matter of consent. The Archmage would like to capture the Doomseeker without complicating our relationship with the King."

Mathus pulled out a chair and sat. "Then, I assume the Doomseeker is under the King's protection."

"He's in the Sanctuary, a safe haven for the sick and protected by royal decree."

"And you want my permission to remove him from the Sanctuary?" Mathus asked.

Harthor was putting the pieces together. He could tell the Archmage had looked at every angle. "King Amr puts no faith in Aurorean prophecies. If we were to take the Doomseeker from the Sanctuary without his permission, he would consider it an attack on the city itself. The King could make life very hard for the Order."

"And he has threatened such measures in the past," Leteah said.

Mathus watched a glob of wax break off one of the candles. It slithered down a channel until it stiffened on the candelabra's base.

"If I give you leave to take this man, what will you do with him?" Mathus asked.

"We will perform a purification ritual to cleanse him of evil," Gibnar answered.

"What makes you so sure he's evil?"

"Along with the Marks, he has the corruption of a Doya," Harthor answered.

Mathus felt relief wash over him. Any man that is corrupted could have no good in them. The Council would show less mercy than the King, who would send him to the Chasm. He could have his Warlocks and see proper justice done.

Gibnar continued. "We will offer you Warlocks to help in your fight, but you must help us in ours by not interfering. When we enter the Sanctuary, it will be according to the law. As Lord Marshall, you can give us the authority to arrest him in the name of the King."

Mathus didn't know this man. If the man was corrupted, he would eventually become a Doya.

Mathus thought of Ele and gave a rigid nod.

"Take him," Mathus said.

A horn blew outside. Mathus jumped to his feet. He shoved the door opened. There was shouting on the wall.

"They're here! It's too soon!" he exclaimed.

24

Avalon

A high-pitched shriek woke Vallan. The hairs on the back of his neck bristled. He knew the sound. The cry of a young dragon was hard to forget.

Vallan's eyes sprung open. He was on his belly, flung over the back of a horse. Dried blood flaked off his neck. His head was throbbing. The suns would set soon.

"Shlama, Vallan mighty Warlock," said a soldier who rode alongside him. He had the dark, olive skin of a Sheminite, and wore a surcoat with the bull's head, the sigil of the Emperor, on the breast. In one hand, he held his reins, and in the other, he carried a broad sickle-sword.

"You've been out for many days. I almost gave you over to the horde, but the suns shine on you."

"You're my captor?" Vallan asked.

"No, they're your captors."

Vallan looked beyond the Sheminite at the horde of Goblins gathered around them. The closest one kept creeping nearer. It had a misshapen head and its third arm scratched a pimple on its nose. It got too close. Another Goblin grabbed it and yanked it back.

The horde ate creatures, even if they weren't hungry. Goblins were fiercely competitive. They respected those who had the shiniest treasures, could run the fastest, crush the hardest, or eat the most.

They were confused, greedy, stupid creatures. No one knew where the Goblins had come from, or their history. Hundreds of years ago, they'd crawled out of the ground. If the world were an apple, Goblins were the worms that hid underneath the peel.

"Hordes can't be tamed. You're a fool to think you can control them."

"It isn't Goblins that scare me." The Sheminite inclined his head to look up at the sky.

A shadow engulfed them. The heavy flapping of wings filled the air. Vallan glanced over his shoulder and his eyes went wide.

The sky above him glittered with red scales. He counted five, then seven, no, ten dragons. Leading them was King Marbor, a massive Highborn dragon. His scales burned with an inner light and he was three times larger than any of his companions.

They didn't even stop to look at the horde. Instead, they continued their route west towards New Camelot, Apollo, and the sword.

Vallan thought Apollo would be safe until he reached the Archmage. The Dragons could sense the sword, but they couldn't track it. Dragons weren't good trackers; their noses were only good for smelling blood.

"The city will be destroyed!" Vallan exclaimed.

He shouldn't have given Apollo the sword. Marbor wasn't to be trifled with. If he found Apollo with the sword, Marbor would punish the entire city.

Vallan had to get back. He knew King Marbor, and he hoped he could reason with him. Then again, anyone that knew Marbor knew that he was unreasonable.

Vallan's arms were tied behind his back. With a silent spell, he undid his bindings. He glanced around and rolled off the horse.

Before he could get to his feet, a young Goblin was on him. Vallan tried to get him off, but the creature had three mouths. Two bit his robe, while the third wailed.

"Get off!" Vallan growled.

Vallan spun to fling it off when a club cracked him over the head.

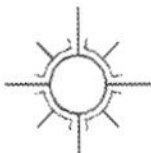

When Vallan opened his eyes, the room around him was shadowy and cold. He tried to remember where he was. He had the feeling he'd just woken from a nightmare, but the soft touch of the fingers going through his hair made him want to forget. When he looked up, he caught his breath. He recognized the woman looking down at him. Her skin was as white as porcelain. Her fierce green eyes sparkled, and a soft nostalgic smile tugged at a corner of her perfectly shaped mouth.

He lay with his head in her lap. His head ached, but for a moment, the world, the pain, and all his concerns melted away. He lost himself in those green eyes. Her hands felt so wonderful in his hair.

"Am I dreaming?" he whispered and reached for her.

Vallan ran his finger up her long slender neck, over her ear, and pulled her in for a kiss.

Lady Black gave him that mischievous grin. He felt her breath on his face, his heart pounded in his ears and just when their lips were about to touch, she stopped short.

"I missed you," she whispered.

Vallan pushed a lock of her long ebony hair out of her face and tucked it behind her ear.

"How long has it been? A decade? A century?" Vallan asked.

Lady Black leaned back and stiffened. She took a moment to survey his face. Her lips pursed in thought.

"There's never been anyone else. It's only ever been you." She raised an eyebrow and gave him a scrutinizing look.

Vallan nodded, his eyes still focused on her lips.

"Have you, could you, love anyone else?" Her voice had the faintest trace of suspicion.

"No one. Ever," Vallan insisted.

Lady Black's green eyes flared and her smile turned bitter.

"What about the Doomseeker's mother?"

Vallan felt the chill in her words. "She—" Suddenly, he realized the lie he and Daynin had fed the Council had made it far beyond the walls of New Camelot. The dream of her lips was gone. Her trap had sprung and he was helpless to escape it.

The world came back into perspective. He remembered saving Apollo's mother, raising Apollo as if he were his own son, training him, protecting him, doing everything in his power to keep him from becoming the Doomseeker. He looked around at his cell made from a small cave. He saw the shackles on his wrists and their loose chains tethering him to the ceiling.

She wasn't the love he'd once known. She had the same face and the same green eyes, but her quest for vengeance had changed her into Lady Black, a general in the Emperor's Army.

She shoved him off. Vallan thumped to the floor. He reached for the power coming from the faint torchlight. He pulled it in and tried to break his chains, but they only shook. It wasn't enough. He needed more power.

Vallan turned back to her. A blow caught him across the jaw and another in the eye. Vallan whipped his arms up and wrapped her in his chains, hoping she'd break them. Instead, she pulled in darkness and cast a pressure spell and they both tumbled across the room.

Vallan slammed into the wall. She crashed into him. They both hit the floor.

Lady Black was up first. Her eyes were green fire. She untangled herself and kicked him in the stomach. She raked him across the face with her nails.

She reeled back her foot and landed a flurry of savage kicks.

"You lying—"

Kick.

"Cheating—"

Kick.

"BASTARD!"

Kick. Kick.

Vallan caught her last kick. He took power from the torch and shouted.

"Far utha wy thrin."

Lady Black knew the spell. She shielded her eyes. A burst of white light filled the room. Vallan dropped his shoulder and barreled into her. He pinned her to the cell door. Lady Black cast a spell and flicked her wrist. The door hinges cracked. The cell door fell outward and crashed into the floor. Lady Black fell just out of the reach of Vallan's chains.

Lady Black panted and rose up on her elbows. A trickle of blood came out the corner of her mouth. She licked it and grinned at him. A chuckle escaped her lips.

"What happened to you?" Vallan asked.

Lady Black's smile faded. Angry tears filled her eyes and she drew her sword. Its serrated obsidian blade glistened in the torchlight; it was razor-sharp. She held it to his throat.

"I lost a son. My only son."

"I can't change the past." Vallan's shoulders sagged. He made no move to escape.

"Which past?" she sniffled, looking more and more vulnerable. "The one where you made a new child with another woman, or the one where you failed our son?"

The sting of her words hurt more than the cuts in his face or his bruised ribs. He sank to his knees and bowed his head.

"Not a day goes by that I don't think of him."

"Liar!" Her green eyes burned. Her sword point pressed against his throat.

"You have no right! No right!"

"He was my son."

"Silence."

"The Doomseeker has the sword." Lady Black lifted Vallan's chin with the tip of her sword. "And thanks to Osirius, he has the blood."

Vallan felt a chill go down his back.

"Ashborn's blood," she said. A smile crossed her lips. "You would've never let him perform the ritual. That's why you're here. You've done everything we expected you to do."

"You weren't after the sword?"

Lady Black's smile widened.

"Why would I need the sword when I can have the Doomseeker? You know the prophecies, the power he'll have. The justice he'll bring to the Sun God. Why would I want a sword when I can have it all? He only needs to arm himself with a proper sword. The only sword with the power to kill a Sun God."

Lady Black dabbed her bloody lip. Then she pulled her sword back and slashed it across his breast. Vallan's robes tore and blood ran down his chest. He cried out and fell to the floor.

A malicious smile crept across her face.

"We're all after something. Osirius wants the Doomseeker to fulfill a prophecy by killing Sarod. Sarod wants to use the Doomseeker to bring your Order to its knees, and the Emperor wants the breastplate so he can unlock the mysteries of immortality. And your boy is in the center of it all."

"The Seer Stones." Vallan moaned, clinging at the cut in his chest. "They were hidden to save us from ourselves."

Lady Black sheathed her sword and tossed her hair back triumphantly. She reached down and put her fingers through Vallan's hair again, but this time Vallan pulled away.

"I'm nothing to all of them. A shadow of a shadow, watching, waiting. When the Doomseeker reaches the peak of his power and kills the Sun God, the old laws will die with him. Haven will be governed by new laws. Then, I will need the breastplate to bring our son back. I already have the horde searching the mountains for the Aphotic Temple. When our son is returned to us, you may even thank me. If you live that long."

A pair of Goblins picked Vallan up from the fallen door. They dragged him through a narrow hallway and tossed him unceremoniously into another cell. Vallan rolled onto his back. The door bolted shut and the clumsy footsteps of the Goblins turned to a whisper.

Warm blood trickled out of Vallan's chest wound. He reached between his split robes to feel the cut. It would leave a nasty scar, but it would heal.

Vallan leaned his head back against the cold, stone wall.

She'd played him like no one else could. And now Apollo had the sword of Ashborn and Ashborn's blood. If he were to perform the binding ritual—

The first prophecy of the Doomseeker came to the forefront of Vallan's mind.

"The fire will know him. The throat of hell will swallow him, and in hell, he will face one of the lost children of the Gods. He will battle that fiend, and when his blood is spilled on the ground, what was strong will become weak, and what was prized will be lost. In that day, you will know that it is the beginning of the end of the laws of the Great Sun God."

He'd read it a thousand times, but only now was it starting to come together. Vallan had done everything in his power to keep Apollo from that path, but everything he'd done had been in vain. Each step was in the wrong direction. He'd given him the means to kill the Sun God. The universe was against them. His enemies would be Apollo's allies. Apollo's destiny wasn't a road or path. The world would create him. He would be molded by evil and put on a pedestal of power.

25

Avalon - New Camelot

Mathus rushed up the stairs to the top of the city wall. It was an impressive forty feet tall and nearly half as wide; the carapace of the great city, the hard skin, the people's main defensive position.

The stars hid their light. The moon peeked through a shroud of clouds and the wind ran over the hills, combing the cut blades of harvested rye.

Chilly moonlight reflected off the steel of thousands of swordsmen positioned in rows on top of the wall. Pikemen stood at their sides; the army bristled with polearms.

Sweat rolled down Mathus' brow. He scanned the hills of farmland surrounding the city, they would run red tonight.

Mathus squinted to see the tree line in the distance. A lone fire burned. At first, Mathus thought the forest had been lit on fire, but the flames weren't spreading; they were floating, slowly, just skimming the tops of the trees.

Mathus reached into a barrel and pulled out a torch. It dripped with oil. He drew his Aureate dagger and dashed it against the wall. Sparks sprayed the torch and it took flame.

Willow ran down the wall, between the ranks of soldiers. She was in heavy steel armor that clanked with each long stride. She reached Mathus' side, huffing.

"What sort of magic is this?" Mathus asked.

Willow already had a golden tipped spear in her hand. "The Branded have Doya. This could be one of their tricks."

"A distraction maybe," Mathus agreed.

Mathus couldn't see them, but somewhere out there was an army. Slaves, or Goblins, or both, he couldn't tell, soon they'd come rushing at the wall. Their only hope would be to hit the enemy with volleys of arrows before they could climb the wall to challenge New Camelot's thin line of pikes and swords.

"ARCHERS DRAW!" Mathus shouted and raised the flaming torch above his head.

Behind them, atop each roof, along the interior of the wall, were the archers. The city moaned with the sound of eight thousand Cogbows tightening. The clicking of the cogs echoed off the nearby mountain.

All he had to do was lower the torch. One swift swipe downward and eight thousand arrows would disappear into the black night to rain down on the invaders.

The timing was everything. Too soon or too late, and the soldiers on the wall would have too many enemies to fight off. If they breached the wall and got to the archers, the battle would be lost.

Mathus couldn't take his eyes from the cloud of fire. It was out of place yet moved so naturally across the sky.

He squinted and saw the edges of the cloud wave up and down like wings.

As it got closer, Mathus made out a distinct shape. He saw what appeared to be a tail and a neck.

"My God!" Mathus cursed.

"What? What is it?" Willow insisted.

The shape was clear now. There was no mistaking the rhythmic movement of the wings and the whip of the tail.

The other soldiers saw it too. Suddenly, the wall erupted with shouts.

"Dragon!" squealed a soldier.

"Marbor!" cried another.

This dragon was unlike any Mathus had ever seen. His body was a masterful sculpture of red-hot coals that rolled together into blazing muscles. His scales were dark rubies and behind them came a fiery glow. Flames trailed from his burning wings and streaked across the sky. Jagged horns jutted from his head, down his back, and over his tail.

The flaming dragon closed his wings and dropped like a meteorite crashing from the sky. He landed in an explosion of turf that made the ground convulse.

A smaller red dragon came out of the darkness. It shrieked a blood-curdling scream and slammed down next to the first dragon. It wasn't nearly as large as the flaming beast, but it still had a faint glow to its scales. Another dropped down behind it with its muscles rippling as it folded its wings away. A fourth thud followed, and a fifth.

Mathus, Willow, and the garrison watched, dumbfounded. The boom of the dragon landings echoed off the wall until the tenth slammed into the ground.

Mathus' pulse was a battle drum in his ears.

The ranks of soldiers were now a clump of men crowding on the edge of the wall to get a better look.

"Arm the Swordsmen with bows, as many as you can," Mathus ordered, and Willow sprinted back down the wall, shouting out commands.

The dragons gathered in a group. The flaming dragon turned on the city and took a heavy step toward the gate. The magnitude of his step shook the wall. He lifted his talon, leaving a burning claw print behind. He took another heavy step toward the castle. The smaller dragons struggled to keep pace.

"Retreat!" cried one of the Swordsman. He turned and fled.

Mathus heard a few follow him, but he didn't turn to look. The volley had to be timed just right.

Mathus held the torch high, but some of the archers had already released their arrows. A swarm of arrows launched out of the city, and over him to fall terribly short of their target.

Mathus turned back to the building tops and the thousands of his archers. They were fleeing; others were firing arrows as fast as they could load them.

"WAIT FOR MY COMMAND!" Mathus screamed. Swordsmen ran down the wall. Some to grab bows; others to search for cover. Arrows zipped by.

Mathus hoped there were still a few archers watching his signal torch.

He waved the torch.

A long heartbeat passed and the twang of bowstrings broke through the air. A swarm of arrows followed.

Marbor, the flaming dragon, turned an ear. He perked his head toward the hum of arrows, speeding towards him.

"That's right, you son of a bitch," Mathus hooted. "Look up."

The dragon took a deep breath. The flames licking his wings turned from red to blue. A surge of white light flashed through his scales. He opened his jaws and a fountain of blinding white flames burst from his mouth.

The hail of arrows collided with the fire and disintegrated into bits of falling ash.

The flaming dragon turned on the city and bellowed a deep, rumbling growl.

"What do you want?" Mathus thought out loud. "Why now? Why are you here?"

Mathus looked to his side to see Willow, once again, standing next to him with a Cog bow in her hands.

"What do they want?" Mathus asked her.

Willow strung an arrow. "Maybe they're hungry?"

"Highborns can eat whatever they choose," Mathus contested. He'd studied them. They were a threat, yet the King had told him the city was protected, and now Mathus had nothing to fight them with. What were bows and arrows, swords and pikes to these flaming monsters?

"That burning one, he's King Marbor, a Highborn, and one of the few that remain alive. The lesser dragons worship him. They would bring him anything he desires. Why is he here and why now? They've never attacked us before. What do they want? And more importantly, what do we have that they've been so afraid of?"

"They don't look afraid of the city," Willow said.

"The Emperor has an army of dragons, yet they've never attacked us. They've raided cities of Hyperion and Shem. This is the dragon's first attack on this city.

The ten dragons marched forward, led by Marbor. Hissing and huffing, they were a wall of smoke and scales. The lesser dragons burned the arrows shot at them, while Marbor let them bounce off his stony skin.

"They've never attacked us. Ever. There must be something about this city that dragons fear, and its been protecting us for a very long time."

"What good will that do us now?" Willow asked.

"I don't know," Mathus admitted.

The dragons' footsteps shook the ground. Mathus glanced up. They were in reach of the dragons' breath. A few breaths, from them, could consume the entire army.

Mathus issued Willow an order. "Have the ballistas target Marbor. I don't know if it will work but on my command, give him hell."

"What will you do?" Willow asked.

"I'm going to try to reason with King Marbor." Mathus realized how incredibly stupid that sounded.

Mathus' stomach churned. The dragons were getting closer. Marbor had a crown of horns. Each spire was the length of a pike.

"Don't be afraid." Mathus declared, trying to convince himself he wasn't. The Wall Captains repeated the words down the wall. The soldiers stopped to look up at the Lord Marshall.

Mathus couldn't tell them they'd take their last breath tonight. They couldn't kill ten dragons. All he could give his soldiers was a good death.

"New Camelot is not afraid. My soldiers are not afraid," he shouted.

Mathus pounded a fist to his chest. The army watched, astonished.

"Tonight, we are what the city needs. Tonight we are dragon slayers!"

Marbor held his wings open in a threatening posture. His glowing red shoulders rose and dipped as he approached the wall. Hot steam billowed out his nose and mouth. Burning saliva dripped from his teeth to sear the ground.

As Marbor got closer, heat from his body turned the night air sweltering hot.

The other dragons dropped their heads low. The scales on their necks bristled, and guttural growls rumbled between their clenched teeth.

One of the lesser dragons kicked off the ground. It ascended into the sky and darted along the wall. Soldiers cowered as it passed.

"They're going to cook us in our armor!" cried a soldier.

"Stand together!" Mathus pulled a few of the soldiers off their knees. The crowd of soldiers started to form back into ranks.

Marbor opened his burning wings. They spanned across a line of two hundred soldiers, illuminating the wall. Mathus examined the dragon's torso for weak points. Between the scales, maybe? An amber glow of hot coals came out.

In that heat, a sword would be useless.

The fiery dragon looked over the wall and down at Mathus, who still held the torch. Its big yellow eyes glinted in amusement. Hot breath made clouds of steam stream out between the gaps in its sharp, wicked smile.

Mathus glanced at his soldiers. Everyone was watching him. He was their strength. If he ran, they all would. Mathus' hand was shaking. He gripped the hilt of his Aureate dagger. He pulled it free and squeezed the handle until his hand steadied.

The dagger brought back memories of a headstrong young man who'd gotten his sister killed. It was here on this very wall that she was shot for his mistake. He had been weak then. He couldn't protect her.

A demon came and took her away.

Mathus glared up at the dragon, eyes kindled with rage. His fear was gone.

"King Marbor!" he screamed.

The dragon's scales lifted, flames licked out from beneath them. The Highborn beast roared an earsplitting hiss.

"This is my city. I've paid for her in sweat and blood," Mathus roared back.

He marched to the edge of the wall and stepped up on the ledge. Marbor leaned in; hot steam blew out his nose. Mathus met his fearsome gaze.

"King, dragon, demon, or god, you will *not* harm her."

26

Avalon - New Camelot

A man bumped Apollo's leg. He looked down and saw Vallan sitting on the ground, staring up at him. His arms were chewed down to stumps.

"You killed me," he said.

"No. No, I didn't. I tried to help. You wouldn't let me," Apollo argued.

"I wish I'd never saved you. Demon."

"No!" Apollo screamed, clutching his head. "I tried—"

"Wake up, Dragons!" Vallan shouted in Clara's voice. Apollo jumped back.

"All hail the Godslayer, All hail the Doomseeker," Vallan cried.

Vallan grabbed Apollo's hand.

"There are Dragons at the gate!" It was Clara again. Apollo could feel the dream slipping away.

Apollo's eyes popped open. Clara had him by the hand, she was trying to pull him up. Her hands were shaking.

"What's wrong?" Apollo tried to steady her hands, but she yanked them away.

"The city is under attack!" she exclaimed.

Apollo jumped out of bed. He was in the Sanctuary. He'd been so worn out from his journey that Clara had insisted he sleep, but once he'd laid down, it felt almost impossible to get back up.

Apollo reached for the sword at his side. It wasn't there. All he felt was the waistline of his underclothes. He was nearly naked.

"Where are my clothes?" he gasped.

"I tossed those rags in the fire."

Clara went to a closet and returned with a white Healer's robe.

"It's all I have," she said.

Apollo pulled the robe over his head. It was tight around the shoulders, but it would have to do. He pulled on the pants, which only came down to his knees. Apollo wiggled his feet into his boots and tied the laces. He gathered his Thetus Mud and the vial of dragon blood from where Clara had placed them on the nightstand.

The Sword of Ashborn was leaning against the hearth. For the briefest moment, Apollo felt as though the sword was a beast basking in the warmth of the fire. With the one side of the blade ruined and the dragon carved in the hilt, there was viciousness to the weapon.

Clara hurried to the balcony, and frantically searched the sky.

The wall was lit with torches and dressed with ranks of soldiers. Long-distance Cogbowmen had taken positions on the rooftops and bent their bows at an enemy beyond the wall. A clicking sound resounded throughout the city. Apollo knew the cry of Cogbows, the mechanical snap that gave their strings deadly tension. Apollo grabbed his sword and ran out to join Clara.

Apollo's mouth dropped open, and hairs perked up on the back of his neck. "My gods, what could kill that?"

Clara didn't answer. She held her trembling hands over her mouth.

The dragon was a fiend of horns and flames, a raging inferno of muscle and heat. The Highborn dragon was big enough to fit a wagon in its jaws. Its shoulders spanned the width of the main gate. Arrows were mere twigs to the colossal creature.

It opened its wings. Clara gasped. The wings burned so brightly that the whole Northern wall lit up as if it were midday. Many of the guards were retreating. Whole sections of the wall were abandoned.

"There's more," Apollo pointed to a shadow just below the clouds and at the dragons on either side of the Highborn.

The square was in chaos. The refugees from the nearby town and farms stampeded into shops. They broke windows and kicked in doors. Families pushed into the Sanctuary. Apollo spotted a few climbing down into the sewers. There wasn't enough cover; half of the mass was still out in the open air. One puff of dragon fire and a human forest would go up in flames.

Clara pointed to the helpless crowd. “There are still people out there. What do we do?”

“What about the chamber below the Sanctuary? Can we fit them all inside?” Apollo asked.

“We can’t keep that many. What if the dragons don’t leave?”

Apollo hadn’t thought of that. Dragons could nest in a place for centuries. Why were they here? They’d never attacked the city before. What did they want?

A chill shot up Apollo’s spine. He remembered the vial of blood he’d cracked and brought here. He’d traveled from the border here. Was it possible that they could’ve followed him?

Apollo took the vial of dragon blood from his pocket. Was this his fault? Would all of these deaths be on his head?

“Can dragons smell their own blood?” Apollo asked, but he knew the answer.

Clara glimpsed the vial. “You wouldn’t be that stupid.”

Apollo grimaced.

“By the Gods, you are!”

“I meant to get rid of it, but—”

Clara snatched the vial from his hands and went inside to the hearth. She held the vial up to the fire until the blood shimmered. “This is Highborn blood. They could smell this for leagues. Where did you get it?”

Apollo kept his mouth shut. What was he to say? It was a gift from a Doya?

"The dragons will kill for this. Dragons know blood even better than we humans recognize faces. If this Highborn dragon is dead, and you have its blood, they've come for revenge."

"What can I do?" Apollo asked.

"That dragon out there is King Marbor. How do you not know of King Marbor? He is a direct descendent of Ashborn. This Highborn blood could be from his own brood."

Apollo felt the smooth dragon bone hilt of the Sword of Ashborn between his fingers.

"They respect Ashborn?" he asked.

"Respect? Don't you know anything of dragons? They worship him."

Apollo rubbed the sword's hilt between his fingers and palm. If they worshiped Ashborn and he gave them a sword made from Ashborn's horn, he might be able to get them to leave.

Apollo went back to the balcony with Clara in tow. He looked out across the city to the Highborn still looming over the gate.

Could he face a Highborn? He didn't know if he could look into that face of flames, horns, and teeth, but if there was a chance that he could save the city, he had to try.

"I can stop them." Apollo turned for the door.

Clara cut him off. "You? Face the dragons? Are you mad?"

"Someone has to try. Get out of my way!"

"There is a whole army out there trying!" Clara blurted. "You must stay until Daynin arrives."

Clara winced. She'd said too much.

"Daynin is coming here? Why? What does the Grandmaster Healer want with me?"

"He said you would be safe here." Clara bit her lip. "I promised him I wouldn't let you leave. The Archmage is looking for you."

"Safe? There are dragons swarming the city. No one is safe!"

Across the square, Warlocks poured out of the temple. Some turned down the main road toward the dragons and the city gate, others looped around the crowd cowering in the square.

"Why are they coming here?" Clara asked.

When the Warlocks got closer, Apollo and Clara saw that they wore modest steel breastplates over their brown robes, and each had a pauldron over the shoulder of their sword arm, with the Aurorean Sun cast in bronze.

"They're dressed for battle," Clara said.

Apollo counted twenty Warlocks lead by Grandmaster Gibnar. What were they after? Were they coming for the sword? Did they even know about it? Or was it something else?

Apollo barred the door.

"What's going on?" Clara demanded.

"They're coming here."

Apollo glanced back out at the flaming dragon at the gate. Was the City Guard going to try and fight the creature? Didn't they know that Marbor's breath could melt stone?

Gibnar shouted from the hallway. "Apollo, come out and you won't be harmed."

"What do you want?" Apollo demanded. If they were after the sword, maybe they could help him get it to the dragons.

Gibnar tried to shove the door open, but it only jolted against the wooden crossbar.

"Clara?" Gibnar shouted. "You're in danger, Apollo is not who he seems. You must open this door. We have authority from the King to detain him."

Clara looked at Apollo and Apollo watched the door.

"I don't understand," Clara said.

No answer came from the other side.

Apollo paced the room and tried to untangle his thoughts. He walked from the hearth to the bed and back again.

"I didn't ask for any of this!" He threw up his arms.

"Stop pacing," Clara ordered. "What did you do?"

"I was born! That's what. I don't know who to trust or what to believe. I don't even know if I can trust what I do."

"You aren't making any sense," Clara said.

"It makes perfect sense. I'm in a fight with destiny, and I'm swinging in the dark. It doesn't matter what I do. I tried to do the right thing with the dragon blood and the sword, and look where it got me."

Clara went to the door. She was about to pull up the bar when Apollo dashed to block her. "What are you doing?"

Clara folded her arms. "You're going on about nothing. I'm sure whatever you did can be explained. Gibnar is a Purist. We believe that all deserve a trial."

That was too much. Apollo clutched his head between his hands and let out a shout of frustration. How could she put so much trust in the Purists, a group that hunted for him, and even prayed for his death?

"All men will get a trial? Do you believe that?" Apollo seethed.

Clara put a steady hand on his chest. "Calm down. You're scaring me."

"You think we are only judged for *our* crimes?"

"That's how it has always been. We reap what we sow."

Apollo turned to the balcony. The dragon was still at the gate and Warlocks were at his door. There was no more time for secrets. The Thetus Mud on his cheeks was dry. In a wrathful fit, he scrubbed off the dry flakes and spun around to confront Clara.

"Look at me! Look at what I've done. I was born cursed! And now they're here to judge me for crimes I haven't even committed."

Clara stepped away. Then she reached out to feel the marks. They were real. She gasped and yanked her hand back.

"How? I don't understand."

Gibnar's muffled voice came from the hallway.

"Take the door down!" he ordered.

The door jolted.

"Do you think I'll get a trial now? Tell me your Prophet Taza would give the Doomseeker a trial and I'll open that door."

Clara's heart burned. She grabbed her chest and gasped for breath. She could see it happening again. The dark room, the shouting. It felt too much like the night her mother was taken from her. She was going to lose Apollo. Would they kill him in front of her? She couldn't watch. Would they at least spare her that?

Clara slumped against the wall and slid down to the floor.

Apollo crouched next to her. She looked up. Her eyes rested on his marks again. Her expression was blank and dizzy.

Apollo glanced back out the window. The Highborn dragon still had its wings open and the whole North Wall lit up like midday.

"I can fix this. The city can still be saved. If I give the dragons this sword, they just might leave."

All Clara heard was the door reverberating on its hinges. The wooden crossbar barring the door cracked. He would get through, she thought. He always did. Would he kill her too? No, he would beat her bloody, but he couldn't beat her anymore. Clara had made sure of that. She'd taken his dagger and put it in her father over and over until he'd stopped screaming. She'd cut him until he was just as dead as her mother.

"Clara? Clara?" Apollo cried, but it was no use. Her face was blank.

The vial of dragon blood slipped out of her hand and rolled across the floor. Apollo dashed after it. The vial rolled down the floor's uneven boards. It was going toward the hearthstone. It was moving too fast. The vial would shatter, and the blood would be lost.

Apollo caught it between his fingers just before it broke into the hearthstone. He knelt by the fire.

Apollo spoke to Clara's blank face. "I don't have a choice. If we don't give up the sword, they'll burn the city to the ground."

Apollo looked down at the vial of blood. It was half full, but it would have to be enough. He grabbed the sword by the blade and winced as he ran his hand up it. The sword's rough ridges cut deep into his skin. His blood dripped down the yellow steel.

The Warlocks split the door. Clara jumped to her feet.

"They're coming through," she cried.

Apollo uncorked the vial with his teeth and dumped the dragon blood over the hilt. He let it run down the dragon bone and drip over his hand. It burned to touch it. He endured the pain until the dragon blood mixed with his. Then he cast the sword into the hearth.

The flames licked the blade. The blood glowed. Red light filled the room. The mixed blood seeped into the Aureate and stained it. Apollo kicked it out of the fire.

Red light reflected in Clara's wide eyes. "What sort of sword is that?" she asked.

"It's the Sword of Ashborn, and now it's powerless."

Clara saw the cut in Apollo's hand, and then the empty vial. She snatched the sword up off the floor and tried to scratch off the bloody fingerprints that had soaked into the steel.

"What have you done?" she asked.

Apollo took the sword from her. "If the sword is disenchanted, its power can't cause any harm."

Clara sunk her fingers into the front of Apollo's robes and shook him.

"Why do you think they built the Chasm? Relics have to be destroyed. Ashborn's sword is cursed. He's damned. He betrayed the whole world. That sword is the tool the Doomseeker will use to kill the Sun God. Don't you see what you've done?"

The door broke in half and fell apart. Gibnar burst through the doorway; armored Warlocks piled in behind him.

Apollo raised the sword.

Gibnar regarded Apollo with disdain. "I'm instructed to bring you before the Archmage, preferably alive."

"This is the Sword of Ashborn. If I take it to the dragons, there still might be hope for the city."

The firelight was dim, there were still shadows in the corners of the room. Apollo drew in the darkness. He counted seven Warlocks, champions with the sword, and Gibnar, a Grandmaster.

His only escape from this room would be death. Apollo's eyes went up the blades of the eight swords. Which would go through him? Would the blade be cold?

A tear escaped from the corner of Clara's eye. She placed a hand on his and pressed his sword down. "Please, don't make me watch you die."

Clara leaned into him. She whispered in his ear. "The balcony, there is another one below it. You could make it if you jump."

Apollo's nose brushed against her hair. He smelt the lavender in it and he felt calmer. The battle seemingly stopped.

Apollo drew Clara's hair out of her eyes. The strands of golden silk slid through his fingers as he tucked it behind her ear.

Clara looked up at him, her eyes were turquoise in the firelight. They glistened with tears.

"I—I don't want you to die," she whispered.

Apollo ran his hand over her cheek. Clara leaned into his hand. It felt so good to have him touch her.

There was no deceit in her. She wasn't like Cat. Clara was right, everything about her was right for him.

Apollo pulled her closer. He could feel her heart beating. He leaned down and pressed his lips into hers. Her lips were firm on his. Apollo drew them in gently, he closed his eyes and savored her touch.

Clara didn't pull away.

"You're coming with us," Gibnar said.

Apollo slipped a hand behind her and drew a silent spell. He let the energy flow from his heart to his hand. He thrust his arm out at Gibnar. A blast of pressure erupted from his hand. Gibnar and the front line of Warlocks fell backward. Chunks of the floor broke free and pelted them.

Apollo dashed for the balcony. He climbed on top of the railing. Apollo's knees weakened. The lower balcony was a leap and a drop, a long drop.

Gibnar was back on his feet and rushing toward him with two Warlocks in tow.

"Kill him!" he shouted.

"Jump!" Clara screamed.

The Warlocks raised their swords. He had to jump. He looked down at the lower balcony again. Could he make it? If he missed, it was a straight fall right into the crowd on the Sanctuary stairs.

Gibnar was at his heels; there was no more time. Apollo sprung from the balcony out into the open air. The wind rushed by. His white robe flapped and his stomach flew up into his throat.

Apollo screamed.

He hit the lower balcony. His feet were knocked out from under him. He rolled and crashed into the balcony's stone railing.

A pair of hands grabbed him under the arms. Apollo was too dizzy to fight back.

Someone was pulling him inside the Sanctuary.

"Come on, don't you want to get out of here?" said a voice.

Apollo looked up, Grandmaster Daynin was pulling him inside.

"Boy, on your feet, they're nearly upon us."

27

Avalon - New Camelot

Daynin's short, portly frame bumped against the sides of the curling staircase. He wheezed, and streams of sweat traversed his double chin. Despite his size, Daynin moved at a brisk pace without complaint.

In Apollo's early years, he'd spent time with Daynin trying to develop a remedy for the Mind Curse. Daynin was a gentle man. Whether he saved a dozen lives or had a dozen slip through his fingers, Daynin was never jubilant or bitter. The Grandmaster Healer was a man of composure. His kindhearted smile could even calm those who'd lost loved ones.

Daynin's own concerns for Apollo's destiny remained hidden under his peaceful facade. Apollo didn't know why Daynin had opened the doors of the Sanctuary to him. Daynin had even created the Thetus Mud to hide Apollo's marks. Once Daynin had thought to use him to break the Mind Curse, but that quest was abandoned years ago. Now, in his hour of need, Apollo had nothing to offer the Healers, yet Daynin still extended a helping hand.

"We're almost there." Daynin raised a candle and peeked over his shoulder at Apollo. "Why the glum face? You're not dead yet."

"A group of Warlocks is hunting me, Clara thinks I'm a demon, I have to go face a dragon, and to top it all off, these pants are too tight." Apollo adjusted his pants again, but they kept riding up his backside.

The staircase ended at a heavy, wooden door. The only way was forward. The Warlocks raced through the Sanctuary, searching every room for the Doomseeker.

Apollo had fled from the Goblins and left Vallan behind. He was escaping from the Warlocks as well, this time he'd left Clara.

He could still smell the lavender oil she'd used to scent her hair, and his mouth had the fading memory of the kiss they'd shared.

It was rash, but was it? He'd known her since they were children, she'd looked him in his black eyes and seen a person when others couldn't. Now she knew his secret, all his secrets, and he was afraid, not of the Warlocks, even facing a dragon wasn't as frightening as losing her.

What had the Goblins done to the man he'd called 'father?' The thought kept creeping up on him. They'd devoured Vallan's horse. He was dead. No, Clara said not to give up hope.

Vallan was eaten by Goblins.

Apollo pushed the thoughts away. He had a duty, and this time, he wasn't going to run from it. He would look that beast in the face.

"If a prophecy has never been false; I will not die tonight, will I? Apollo asked Daynin.

Daynin's eyes looked tired, nestled in bags of age. He was out of breath, but that didn't stop him from wheezing out an answer.

"Prophecies are never fully understood. They will come to pass, but that knowledge is only known by the gods. What will unfold is uncertain. I suspect there are ways to appease the prophecy; do not think words on a page will make you immortal. Scripture can be interpreted in many ways."

Apollo frowned and looked down at the Sword of Ashborn clenched in his bloodied hand and then at the door in front of him. "I led them here. The city is in danger because of me."

Apollo pulled the tin of Thetus Mud from his pocket and placed it in Daynin's hand. "I'm done hiding, It's time to show the world that the Doomseeker is a force for good."

A flash of torchlight came from the top of the stairs.

"They've found us," Daynin gasped and fumbled through his pockets for a key.

Footsteps hammered down the stairs. Daynin pulled a key out and thrust it into the lock. With a twist, the lock clicked and the door flung open.

"Run!"

"They'll know you helped me," Apollo said.

"They already know." Daynin shoved Apollo out the door and locked it behind him.

Apollo sprinted to the square. He pushed through the wall of refugees bunched up at the Sanctuary doors.

"Hey now! Watch where you're going," a man cried.

Apollo gave him a chilling look.

One glance at Apollo's marks and the man scampered backward. "Get away from me!" he screamed and pushed his way through the crowd.

A wood splitting crash drew attention to the Sanctuary. The door Daynin was guarding splintered, and Warlocks came pouring out with Gibnar at their head.

"Stop him!" he shouted.

The square churned as refugees gathered to watch the group of Warlocks flowing out of the Sanctuary. Apollo ducked down low and pushed his way through the crowd to the edge of the square.

When he looked up, Master Durakos stood in front of him. His purple robes glistened like black oil in the lucent city lamps. His burned face was more like tree bark than skin. His face contorted. Only two round holes remained of his burned nose. They flexed and he huffed a bullish snort.

Before Apollo could raise his sword, Durakos held his Aureate short sword at Apollo's chest.

"Surround him!" Gibnar shouted from somewhere in the crowd of people.

Durakos glimpsed Apollo's marks. His face twisted into a knot of anger.

"Gibnar, what is this? Why wasn't I told?"

Apollo tried to step away, but Durakos only pressed harder on his sword.

"I need to save the city Durakos, you have to let me go."

"Shut your foul mouth, traitor." Durakos punctuated his words with a prod of his sword.

Apollo slapped the sword away. He balled his cut hand up into a fist and cracked it across Durakos' jaw. Apollo cried out in pain. Durakos staggered backward. Apollo grabbed Durakos' sword guard and ripped the weapon out of Durakos' hands. He threw a second punch and Durakos fell to the cobblestone.

Apollo jumped past Durakos, narrowly escaping a swipe of Gibnar's sword.

"You'll never escape the city," Gibnar cried.

Apollo spotted a farm horse tied outside a shop just beyond the square. He ran to it and mounted the steed. Apollo gave the horse two swift kicks and its legs blurred into a gallop.

"Thief!" a woman cried. "Help, my horse. He's stealing my horse!"

Apollo peered over his shoulder at the Warlocks behind. Gibnar trailed him, spitting out orders.

"Get to the horses. He's heading for the gate!"

Apollo turned the corner. His horse sprinted in full gallop past fleeing soldiers. A dragon flashed by overhead. In the distance, he could see the tower of flames that was

King Marbor over the main gate. His glowing form was a shattered sun rising over the city wall.

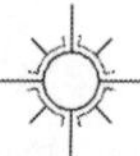

Marbor stood over the main gate. His body crackled as flames roared off his back, across the brim of his wings, and leaked off his boney horns. White steam vented out his nose as he glowered down the Lord Marshall, who stood as a sentinel above the gate.

"I will speak to your King," Marbor bellowed in a tone so strong that it made Mathus' plate mail rattle.

Mathus took a breath and squared his shoulders. He had a torch in one hand to control the archers, and in his other, he gripped his golden dagger.

"I am Mathus, commander of the city garrison. I speak for his Majesty."

Marbor's amber eyes glossed over the Lord Marshall's scowl to the small dagger he held between them. There was a glint of amusement in the dragon's eyes.

"Do you mean to threaten me, son of Earth?" Marbor rumbled.

The other dragons made a guttural sound that sounded almost like laughter.

"We are the children of Ashborn, the sons of the Dragon Gods, and you threaten us with steel."

Marbor dipped his head over Willow and bore his spiky teeth. Willow's muscles stiffened as the dragon's boiling saliva dripped around her. Marbor's head swung over her to the Night Guards beside her. The leather-clad soldiers met the dragon's fiery stare with spite. Marbor passed over them to the common soldiers. He stopped at a young man shaking so violently that his armor clanked together like cooking pots.

Marbor flicked his forked tongue. It was a whip of flames that wrapped around the young man's sword. He screamed and pulled back a burned hand. As he did, the sword came apart. It sloshed out between the coils of Marbor's tongue into a metallic puddle at the young man's feet.

Marbor glanced at the other dragons who'd taken positions at the ballistas. Their snouts flexed, and their scales bristled at a smell in the air.

Marbor's nostrils flared as he, too, sucked in the night air.

Mathus could only smell the smoke from his torch. The dragon nearest Marbor bore his teeth. It growled; a fiery light flickered in its throat.

Marbor's mouth curled up into a snarl.

Whatever scent they picked up, Mathus noticed, it was clear they didn't like it.

"Your city is protected," Marbor growled.

"What do you want, Marbor?" Mathus demanded.

"Man of Earth, how do your people sleep with a viper in their city?"

Viper? Mathus thought. Could that be what was protecting them? What sort of snake did Dragon's fear? Did it matter? If it frightened them, he had to use it.

"They sleep knowing dragons cannot harm them," Mathus replied, but he couldn't hide his look of uncertainty.

"They don't know?" Marbor's mouth crept up into a devilish, spiky grin. "You don't know what power protects your city. Ask yourself, man of Earth, what terror has the power to ward off the Children of Ashborn?"

Marbor turned his gaze to the torch in Mathus' hand. Squinting, the dragon concentrated on it. The torch surged with flames that collected in the center, creating a thin column of fire. One side of the fire burned as steady as an oil lamp and the other flickered and burned in waves. Then flames started to lick outward and Mathus saw that the pillar of fire was sculpted into a sword.

Marbor's voice turned disgusted as accusations fired out his mouth.

"I sense the Sword of Ashborn in your city and your streets *reek* of the blood of my grandfather."

Marbor slammed a claw into the wall.

"This sword belonged to Ashborn, my grandfather, the only son of the gods Raiden and Pandora." Marbor dropped his head low. Steam whistled out his clenched teeth. He leaned in so close that Mathus had to shield his face from the heat.

"Protected or not, I will turn your city to *ash* to find it."

The clouds began to weep; rain fell sparsely on the soldiers. Apollo pulled up the white hood of his Healer's robe as he slipped past Grandmaster Leteah and her lines of Warlocks. He ascended the Main Gate stairs to the top of the wall, and moved toward Mathus and Marbor when a Night Guard blocked his path.

The Night Guard suspiciously eyed Apollo's tightly fit robes. "This is no place for a Healer."

"I'm not a Healer." Apollo looked up so the Night Guard could see his marks. The Night Guard examined his face but said nothing.

Apollo held out the hilt of the dragon sword.

"This is what the dragons are looking for."

The Night Guard took the sword. Marbor's attention flicked their direction.

"Bring me that sword," Marbor demanded.

The Night Guard stepped toward the dragon.

"No, you. The Healer."

Apollo reluctantly took the sword back and walked to Mathus. Apollo stood before Marbor, in the dragon's presence the air turned dry, and the rain dried up before it hit the ground.

Mathus drew back Apollo's hood.

"Apollo?" he said. The light from Marbor's skin was so bright he could just make out Apollo's dark hair and black eyes.

"What are you doing here? Where did you get that sword?"

"You will be silent," Marbor ordered.

It took everything Mathus had to keep the torch above his head. Marbor might be a Highborn, but this was his city and those were his archers, ready to fill the self-important lizard with arrows.

In the heat, the sword took on a glow of its own. The dragon blood Apollo had poured on it had a brilliance to rival even Marbor, and the ruined blade took flame, like the edges of burning parchment.

Marbor inspected Apollo with one great eye. His attention moved from the sword to the cut on Apollo's hand.

The flames in Marbor's crown shrank and the glowing ambers in his face dimmed.

"Begone, Mathus, son of Earth. I am finished with you."

"I am the Lord Marshall. I speak for the King."

Marbor shot a burst of steam out his nostrils. Mathus jumped away. With his torch still held high, Mathus stood as close as Marbor would permit.

"Where did you find the blood you spilled on this sword?" Marbor asked.

"It was given to me by Osirius," Apollo admitted.

Marbor hissed when he heard the name.

Apollo held the sword out to him. Marbor once again glanced down at Apollo's hand. Then he pulled his head up out of his reach.

"You think to trick me, thief?"

The scales on Marbor's neck bristled. His chest filled with air. Steam erupted from his nose, and in a single heartbeat, his mouth shot open.

White flames gushed out.

Apollo fell to his knees; blinding white flames enveloped his entire body.

"Nooo!" Mathus cried.

He swung his torch. The garrison released a wave of arrows.

A dragon circling above shot a ball of fire into their mass. The fireball crashed into a rooftop filled with archers; they were thrown from their posts. The archers screamed, flailed, burned, and died.

The other archers from adjacent rooftops looked on horrified. They turned their bows on the dragon above. They drew and released, but the dragon disappeared into the clouds.

Wood cried out as the ballista bolts loosed. One caught a dragon by the wing, but before they could reload to deal a killing blow, the dragon bit the machine in half. Another two shot at Marbor, one whizzed over his head, the other ricocheted off the hard spikes on his back.

Marbor's column of fire roared down on Apollo. When he was out of breath, he looked down at the round black patch of melted rock. The army stopped loosing arrows, and the dragons gathered behind Marbor.

Both human and dragon held their breath.

Apollo cowered in the center of a ruin of melted stone, the sword in his white-knuckled grip.

"Hold your fire!" Mathus shouted, but his order wasn't repeated. No one was paying attention. All eyes watched in astonishment as Apollo stood back up, unburned.

Mathus sprinted toward him, but the heat from the melted rock was too much. Mathus called out from the perimeter of the scorched ground, "Are you alright?"

"I don't know," Apollo replied shakily.

Apollo looked himself over. Not a hair on his head was singed. His white Healer's robes were unscathed. The sword of Ashborn shone with inner power, blade ablaze.

Apollo stared wide-eyed at the burning sword. It had to be blistering hot, but the steel was cool in his hand. He looked past the fiery blade to Marbor's ferocious stare.

Marbor spoke so all of his dragons could hear. "Our sacred sword has been bound. There is only one way to break a binding."

Flames licked Marbor's face. They spread thickly up the tips of his horns and elongated his crown of fire. He looked more devil than dragon.

"Kill the boy. Crush the defiler!" Marbor commanded.

Marbor's eyes flared and he snapped his jaws at Apollo. Apollo rolled to the side. Marbor's arm came crashing down. The melted stone cracked under his weight.

Mathus tried to draw the dragon's attention. He threw his torch. It flew end over end and bounced harmlessly off Marbor's face. The archers responded with a volley of arrows that splintered on Marbor's hard skin.

Both of Marbor's feet slammed down on the wall. It strained under him.

"Bring him down, men!" Mathus ordered. Willow led the charge. She threw a spear into the dragon's side. It hit square between two scales. The steel struck true, but the spearhead bent and fell away.

"Swordsmen, attack!" Mathus charged with his sword high. He aimed for the dragon's tail.

The dragons behind Marbor leaped into the sky. One rained fire into Westport. A whole city block burst into flames.

Another dragon slammed down on a group of archers on the top of House Uther, the oldest inn in New Camelot. Archers drew their swords, but the whole building collapsed under the dragon's weight.

Mathus glimpsed the rubble, but only the dragon emerged with an archer in its mouth.

Dragons ripped ballistas off the walls, letting them shatter on the ground below.

Mathus swung for Marbor's tail, but Marbor dodged and swept his tail into Willow and the approaching Swordsman. They screamed as the burning tail threw them backward.

Heavy raindrops beat against the street.

Apollo ran down the main gate's stairs to the street. He turned up the main road and skidded to a stop. Gibnar and his pack of Warlocks galloped toward him. He turned back. Marbor stomped over the wall. The main gate rumbled. The street convulsed, and the gate collapsed. The iron portcullis groaned and folded in half under the weight of the falling stone. A cloud of gray dust ripped through the street.

Archers sprinted through buildings and side streets. Townsfolk screamed and ran blindly through the dust cloud.

Apollo could feel Marbor's breath on his back.

The rain picked up and the dust cleared. The main gate was a pile of rubble. Marbor stood on top of it. Rain fell and screeched as it burned off his blazing skin.

"You've stolen a most sacred honor. I am the blood of Ashborn. I choose who carries his power."

Apollo couldn't run toward the dragon. He looked back toward the Warlocks. They were lined up in an impassable wall with Gibnar at their head; Durakos was at his side with a blooded jaw and a face fuming with rage.

Gibnar's determined voice rang through the street.

"Our quarrel is not with you, Marbor."

Apollo looked between the wall of Warlocks and the approaching dragon. The sword was still aflame in his hand.

Marbor's head shot up.

A monstrous shriek echoed throughout the city, but it wasn't the roar of a dragon. It was something else, a shrill, wild cry. Part beast, and part demon. The sky glowed with the faint light of red dragon scales.

The other dragons were fleeing.

The shriek resounded through the streets again. The Warlocks looked back toward the castle. Durakos and Gibnar searched the sky. Both soldiers and townsfolk cringed as if a giant was above them, ready to smother them with its boot.

Marbor didn't waste a moment. He kicked off the ground. The street shook. Apollo stumbled and Marbor launched into the air. The sky above them burned as Marbor retreated over the ruined wall.

Mathus and a group of soldiers charged into the street. Each carried a Cog bow. Mathus gave Apollo a hand up and watched the sky. "Where did he go?"

"That sound scared them off. Did you hear it?" Apollo asked.

"There is something here in the city, some sort of demon," Mathus said.

Mathus turned to Gibnar and his line of Warlocks.

"Come, I need every hand. We need to get the injured to the Healers."

"You will manage," Gibnar replied. He waved his hand and the Warlocks surrounded Apollo.

"What's going on?" Mathus demanded.

"Apollo, by decree of the Order and with the permission of the Lord Marshall, you are under arrest for crimes foretold by the prophets."

Apollo turned his sword on Gibnar.

"This is your Marked?" Mathus erupted. He looked at Apollo and for the first time, he noticed the marks under his eyes.

Mathus shoved a Warlock out of his way and marched to Gibnar.

"He's a boy, the son of one of your Warlocks!" Mathus positioned himself between Gibnar and Apollo.

"We are acting within the law. We have honored our part of the agreement. See that you honor yours."

"Agreement? What's going on?" Apollo turned his sword on Mathus.

"Put your sword down," Mathus said.

"Why? So you can give me up to them?" Apollo shot back.

Apollo scanned the dark street puddling up with rain, he had power here. He could fight, he'd lose, but he would go down fighting.

"Your hour of judgment is here, Doomseeker," Durakos said. He pulled back his hood, revealing a bald head of stringy scorched skin. His cheek was bleeding where Apollo had struck him.

The Warlocks advanced.

Mathus raised his arm and Cogbows clicked around them. Mathus' men had taken position on their perimeter.

"At close range, a Cog bow can shatter dragon scales," Mathus said.

The Warlocks grudgingly raised their swords.

"You may take Apollo and detain him, nothing more. That was what was promised." Mathus instructed.

Mathus sidestepped Apollo's sword and grabbed him by the arm. He pulled him close enough for a whisper.

"Be strong. I will do what I can. I'm sorry—I didn't know."

Mathus felt Apollo's forearm tighten in his grip.

"Give your life. Don't let it be taken." Mathus whispered.

Apollo lowered his sword. Vallan had said that. Mathus and he weren't brothers, but they'd shared a mentor. Now, he was the closest thing he had to family.

28

Avalon - New Camelot

Peet Moss grew between the granite bricks of Pendragon Abby. The ebony doors leading inside came to ridged points at their peaks. They were carved with a tangle of two massive dragons wrestling in a magnificent display of might. Each pulled away from the other so the dragon heads reached outward to offer doorknobs in their throats. Wislan had placed his hand in the dragon's mouth and turned the handle for as long as he could remember. It was different now: he'd seen a dragon face to face. Wislan had felt Marbor's scorching breath and watched raindrops boil off his back.

Even in his life of spells and swordplay, the night was too fantastic.

Wislan reached his frantic fingers inside the dragon carving's mouth, past the dulled wooden teeth, and clutched the doorknob. He turned it, and the door creaked open.

Pendragon Abbey was a realm of shadow. The whole of King's Gift, a section of the city for royal blood, was deserted, and the fires of Westport shone in a bronze haze over the rooftops. The screams in the streets were a stark contrast to the still empty halls of his father's house.

"Father?" Wislan called. "Is anyone there?"

Wislan drew his sword. This was his home. It felt foolish to arm himself in the Abbey, but the leather grip of his sword bolstered his courage.

Wislan stepped through the threshold onto a porcelain floor of red, yellow, black, and white tiles laid in the form of the Pendragon crest, a black dragon encircling itself within a breath of flames.

At the end of the hall, he saw a pinprick of candlelight coming from the study. Could it be his father? Why hadn't he taken refuge in the castle with the other nobles?

Wislan crept toward the light. The city was in turmoil, but the chaos couldn't penetrate the abbey's stone walls.

The hushed hall made the hairs stand on the back of his neck.

Wislan crept into the study. Fat wax candles sweated on the mantle. Bookshelves wrapped the walls of the room. He'd read nearly all the books in the years he'd lived with his father. Here he learned the history of the Pendragons. Before he was a Warlock, he spent time in the finest academies in New Camelot, but that wasn't enough for his father, Loholt Pendragon.

Loholt was a Prince, knight, scholar, philosopher, mathematician, and the former Lord Marshall. Wislan was convinced his father would even have been King if he didn't like his brother so much. King Amr and Prince

Loholt were twins. Loholt's only failure in life was being born moments after his brother.

As the former Lord Marshall, Loholt knew Rhean, the Grandmaster Warlock, quite well. He'd asked him to take Wislan as an apprentice, he'd even told Wislan it was his duty to honor his blood in the field of battle.

What would his father think if he saw him trembling under his own roof?

Wislan peered into the mirror above the mantle. His eyes were glossy and the whites were red and cracked. His long blonde hair was tangled and his face drooped.

He'd forgotten how to sleep. Every time he closed his eyes, he saw the Shade shoving a blade through Rhean.

The Shade stalked him. He was in every crowd. Every street. Every thought.

The floor creaked. Wislan whirled around, but the room was empty.

"Who's there? Come out!"

Wislan shoved a table over. He looked under a chair. He dashed into the hall but saw no one.

He buried his face in his hands and sank to the study floor.

"I'm going mad." Tears trickled down his cheeks, and he started to laugh. "That's it, I can't take anymore. Go ahead Shade, kill me."

His words bounced off the walls of the study.

He said a prayer to his Sun God to pull him out of his pit of sorrows.

“From above House of Heaven, where star people and ancestors gather, may their blessings come to us now.”

Wislan saw movement above the mantle, in the mirror. He peered into it, but only he looked back. A window was open. Wislan walked over and closed it. He looked back up into the mirror.

The Shade stood behind him, his black cape was a storm cloud that filled the room. His voice shattered the silence.

“Have you brought the stone?” the Shade asked under his drawn hood.

Wislan’s sword slipped through his numb fingers and rung on the floor.

“I—”

The Shade’s gauntlet clicked and a blade folded out to his hands. It was the same blade he’d plunged through Rhean’s back.

“I came here for the Urim. You said you could steal it,” said the Shade.

Wislan couldn’t steady his quivery voice. “I…I can’t—”

The Shade shoved Wislan against the mantle. He touched the point of his dagger to Wislan’s forehead. “You were spared because you said you could steal the Urim.”

“I tried, I got to the chamber where it was kept, but Gibnar ordered all Warlocks after the Marked,” Wislan blurted.

The Shade lowered his dagger. “What did you say?”

"We've captured one of the Marked, the Doomseeker," Wislan said.

"You're sure it's not a boy in face paint. It would be awfully embarrassing if you fell for that trick twice."

"They plan to purify him before the Lord Marshall can intervene."

"What do you mean, purify?"

"The Urim can be used to dispel some powerful curses. He has the corrupted eyes of a Doya. Old law permits purification. The stone sits on a pedestal. There it gives power to the temple—"

Wislan conscience screamed for him to be silent. Without the Urim, the temple and all of its treasures would be unprotected. But he didn't have a choice. His life, the royal life of a Pendragon, was more valuable than any rock. "During purification, the stone will be removed for a short time. The temple's torch will burn out and the temple's protective barrier will be down. You could enter the temple, and steal the Urim, you could take whatever you wanted."

The Shade drummed his fingers together. His curiosity peaked. No one had ever broken into the temple before. If a thief got inside, it would be legendary.

"And when I'm inside, where can I find the Doomseeker?"

29

Avalon - New Camelot

A mother held the face of her dead son, she wept as she kissed him and cradled his head in her arms.

"He was a good boy. He never hurt anyone," she cried.

Clara looked beyond the woman down the stairs of the Sanctuary. A queer light came from the West. It almost looked like a sunset the way the amber and crimson hue lit up the sky, but it was near midnight, and the suns had set hours ago.

A cloud of smoke rose over the horizon. At first, Clara thought it was another storm cloud, but she could taste the ash in the air.

Westport was burning.

Clara searched the desperate faces of the afflicted pushing toward the Sanctuary. She saw a man crying. His arms swelled with burns, yet he cradled his little one. A splinter of wood had lodged in her leg, she had lost too much blood.

She would die tonight. The father was burned so badly, he'd lose his arms. Scores of Healers were scattered throughout the crowd, immobilized.

In the darkness, Clara didn't have the power to heal the man's burns. Some of the Collective knew how to draw power from fire. As a Purist, she didn't agree with the practice, but if it could save a child's life, could it really be that wrong?

Apollo had cast a spell just that evening with the power of the darkness. As a Purist, she knew that was wrong. Power should only come from the suns. She didn't know Apollo had such power, Vallan had been so strict with his magic. He'd used it to push Gibnar and the Warlocks back, so he could escape and save the city. He had to take the sword of Ashborn to Marbor, or at least that's what Apollo intended, but it wasn't any sort of deal that had made the dragons flee. It was the shriek that came from the castle.

If there was a devil, like the One God claimed, Clara had heard his voice.

The Dragons had wounded the city. The Healers were surrounded by afflicted, yet they stood frozen and watched them suffer and die.

Clara didn't have her magic, but she had training, and she could clean wounds and bandage up the afflicted. She couldn't help very many, or the severely injured, but it would be something.

Her bandages and ointments were in the Sanctuary. Clara turned to hurry back inside when she found Grandmaster Daynin behind her.

"Grandmaster?" she said.

Daynin's eyes rolled under his eyelids.

"Grandmaster? Can you hear me?"

Clara grabbed him by the shoulders and shook him. She'd seen him meditate before, but not so deeply.

Daynin's eyes shot open. He looked right at her, but he didn't see her.

"Grandmaster, the people need you. We need the Healers."

Daynin's took a quick breath and started to shout. "I had to do something. You were going to bring the wrath of the Council down on all of us."

Clara jumped back.

"I swore an oath to save those in need," Daynin said in a calm voice.

"Who are you talking to?" Clara asked.

Daynin's voice rose again. "You're our Grandmaster and you've led us to ruin. I told you your callous decisions would catch up with you. We couldn't keep Apollo's secret forever."

Clara spotted Master Reuben walking through the temple gate on the other end of the square.

"Master Reuben," she called, but he was too far away to hear her.

A hand grabbed hers. Clara turned to a woman Healer who looked blankly back at her.

"We cannot decide the Doomseeker's fate," the Healer said.

Clara pulled her hand from the Healer's grasp. "What's going on?"

A child clung to the Healer's leg, and a man stood before her clutching his broken arm, but the Healer was blind to them.

Clara looked between the Healer and Daynin. They were speaking the words of others. The Collective was broken.

Clara pushed deeper into the crowd until she got to the next Healer. His expression was as blank as the others. His white robe was bloodied. He held a bandage out, but the woman he was tending laid dead at his feet.

"Daynin is no longer Grandmaster. The Council has appointed me to fill his seat," he said.

He turned his head away, and his voice changed. "You bought the seat by giving them Daynin and branding him a traitor."

A hand grabbed Clara by the shoulder. She turned around and saw Master Reuben. His voice was full of anger. "Daynin would let the Collective crumble and for what? The life of the Doomseeker?"

"You led them to us," said the Healer.

"The Council needed someone to blame. We hid the Doomseeker under your request," Reuben said to no one Clara could see.

A group of brown cloaks collected in front of the temple. Clara pushed through the afflicted until she emerged on the other side to face Durakos.

"Master Durakos, the Healers need our help. They're stuck in some sort of trance."

Durakos' sunken eyes watched behind Clara. She turned and found all of the Healers. Every white cloak in the square clumped together with Daynin and Reuben at their head.

Durakos' lipless mouth curled up on one side. "Grandmaster Daynin has been removed from the Council. Master Reuben has been put in his place. Some will be true to the Order and others to Daynin. I do not pretend to understand the Collective mind, but if they can't agree on a leader, then they can't think as one."

Clara saw the dragon sword tucked into Durakos' belt. She could still see Apollo's bloody fingerprints in the Aureate, and from the rhetoric of the Healers, she could only assume he'd been caught.

"What are you going to do with Apollo?"

Clara looked from Durakos to the Warlocks filing through the temple gate. At their head was Apollo at sword point. He was still in the white Healer's robe she'd given him.

"I convinced the Archmage that as a Purist, you would've brought Apollo to us if you knew of his markings. It's best for you to forget about him and the traitors that protected him."

Durakos snapped his fingers and a pair of Warlocks grabbed Daynin by the arms. In a blind stupor, Daynin was directed through the gate, across the sunstone courtyard, and into the temple.

The square was filled with afflicted and Healers, yet Clara felt as if she were standing alone. She recognized the feeling inside her. She'd felt it when she'd brought her father to justice. It was a determination, a dire state where evil could only be stopped by evil. She couldn't pray Apollo out of the temple. No matter how long she begged, the gods wouldn't take his marks away. Righting this wrong could cost her everything. All she had to do was nothing and she'd be safe, but nothing was the one thing she couldn't do. He was the Doomseeker, but he was also Apollo. When she was a child and lost everything, he'd befriended her.

The Healers spoke each other's thoughts at random.

"The Council will save the boy."

"They will destroy him."

"The Council will cleanse him of evil."

"Purification will bring him back to the light."

"Purification is evil."

"Purification?" Clara grabbed the cloak of the last Warlock. "What is Purification?"

The Warlock pushed her off and went through the gate to join the others.

"The Doomseeker will be dead by morning."

"He will not last the night."

"Gods spare him the pain."

"Gods spare him the knife."

"The Gods do not hear the prayers of the damned."

"If they purify an innocent, we're all damned."

Clara watched until the last Warlock vanished beyond the temple doors.

Apollo was to be purified. Was it a cleansing of sorts? What would happen to him? The Order wouldn't speak to her, the Council didn't answer to her. She had to get her answers elsewhere.

If the Order wouldn't tell her what purification was, then maybe someone else could. She needed to speak to a Corrupted or a Doya.

She needed Farum.

30

Avalon - New Camelot

Clara thought of going back, but her feet kept moving forward. She crossed the city and was in the catacombs before she gave a thought to those left behind.

In the darkness, she could only bind wounds and apply ointments, but she could've helped some of the afflicted.

She abandoned the Healers as well.

Clara thought of the man in the square who had held his wounded child in his scorched arms. His child was probably dead by now. How many more would die tonight? How could she leave them when she was a Healer sworn to preserve life?

Perhaps Farum was right, maybe she wasn't a Healer anymore. She spent most of her time in the catacombs, trying to make a poison to kill Doya. What was she? What sort of person turns her back on those she can help? In the whole of the city, Clara was the most experienced Healer, free from the Collective's debilitating trance. She could help the living, yet now she was in the halls of the dead.

Apollo needed her, but if she helped him, would she be helping Apollo or the Doomseeker?

Clara had believed the best of Apollo all of her life. She'd never questioned his integrity. His black eyes were a deformity he'd been born with, but now she even questioned that. Could he have committed some great offense? Had he corrupted himself? If he could hide his marks in plain sight for all these years, what else could he be hiding?

The Healers had said he was to be purified. Was his body or his soul filthy?

Clara pushed against the doubts coiling her mind. After all, she'd grown up with Apollo. She'd missed him. He'd kissed her.

Part of her had felt a rush of excitement in his embrace. It was a quick kiss, too quick. Then there was the other part of her who still saw Apollo as a boy, a brother, and that made it all wrong.

Clara knocked on the crumbling iron door to Lancelot's chamber, and a deep, iron groan escaped out the empty corridors.

"Speak your name," ordered a man on the other side.

"Clara, I've come to see the prisoner."

The bolt retracted. The hinges squealed and the door swung open.

Farum, the Doya, had been slouched against a wall for several weeks, yet his frame remained as strong as it had been the day she'd met him.

The bladed, spring-loaded collar remained open around Farum's neck. The chain that released the blades always remained in the hand of a Night Guard.

The room usually held four or five Night Guard. Clara only saw a soldier at the door and another holding Farum's chain.

"Where is everyone?"

"Lord Mathus has every available hand putting out fires in Westport, and the Night Guard is searching for what scared off the bloody dragons," said the soldier at the door.

"They say a Healer stood in Marbor's breath. Snails said he wasn't burned or nothin. Snails said the Healer told the dragon his breath smelt like a pig's ass. Did you see anything?" asked the other soldier.

Clara shook her head.

Farum's voice was cool and even. "People are dying. The children are burning, yet Clara, the Healer, has come to poison her captive. Twisted. The world is a twisted place."

The corner of Farum's mouth turned up to show his sharp teeth, and his black eyes glinted with a fiendish light that Clara had learned to interpret as a playful expression.

Clara walked over the crooked flat stones in the floor. The stones were straight once, an example of perfect symmetry, each stone in its proper place to create a pattern, but as time passed, and the ground shifted, what was once a perfect floor had become distorted with dips and loose stones.

She stopped at her mixing table. It was cluttered with bowls of herbs and an assortment of potions. Water collected on the glass bottles from the moisture in the air. The soldiers had left a half bottle of wine in the mix. Clara pulled off the cork. It smelled strongly of cedar with a hint of sweetness that was so slight Clara almost mistook its fragrance for vinegar. It wasn't altogether horrible, so she emptied out a bowl of dried wolfsbane and filled it to the brim.

"Do Doya drink wine?" Clara asked.

"We don't give wine to Doya," the soldier holding the chain blocked her path to Farum.

"He's my experiment, I'll give him whatever I wish."

Clara stepped around the soldier and held the bowl up to Farum's lips.

Farum regarded the offer with suspicion. At first, he turned away, but the aroma drew him back to Clara's offer.

"Let us drink to the carnival of death above us." Farum took a sip of the wine, swished it around to collect syrupy saliva, and swallowed.

"Leave us," Clara commanded.

"We can't abandon our posts," said the soldier at the door.

Clara took Farum's chain from the soldier at Farum's side and wrapped it around her fingers. "I know what to do if it tries anything. You can guard the door. There is no other way out."

The soldiers reluctantly stepped outside.

"Close the door," Clara ordered.

The door creaked shut. Farum and Clara were alone.

Farum's eyes were voids. Two dark holes into a rotted soul. She told herself that Apollo's eyes were different, but now she wasn't so sure.

The room was lit by a mere lantern hanging from the ceiling, ushering in an audience of heckling shadows.

"You can feel the dead can't you?" she asked.

Farum took another sip of wine from the bowl, swished, and swallowed.

"Clara, the girl with questions."

"What is it like?" she asked.

"You cannot stand in the light and see into the dark. You must step inside the darkness and let your eyes adjust. How do I explain lust to one as innocent as dear Clara? But how innocent can you be when you cut me to make your poison?"

Goosebumps raised from Farum's pale scalp.

"Even now, I feel the terror, sorrow, death. It's sweet, as sugar but this sweetness I can savor with my whole body. You should be up there helping, but no, you're here with me. Could Clara not be that innocent? Can you feel the pleasure that I do? Clara, what sort of pleasures do you long for?"

Clara thought of Apollo. She didn't want him, not like that, or at least she didn't think she did. His kiss had caught her by surprise. Why hadn't she pushed him away?

"Is that why Doya kill? For pleasure?" she asked.

Farum gulped down the rest of the wine and Clara used the limit of Farum's chain to reach the table.

She returned the bowl to its place and leaned against the table.

"You are tormented tonight. I can feel it in you. Clara, the girl with the fleeting heart. The child lost in confusion and I'm the voice of reason?"

Farum belted out a laugh. Black drool sputtered from his mouth.

"Why do you kill? Is it for pleasure?" Clara repeated.

"The city is burning. What about the afflicted, the Healers, your family? You've abandoned them to ask a demon about evil?"

Clara couldn't think of all of the people she'd failed. Apollo needed her now. She had to know if he could be helped or if he was on the path to becoming like the monster before her.

Clara left the table and moved as close to the lantern as the chain would permit. There was solace in the light, strength.

"Why do you kill?" she pressed.

Farum's toothy grin widened.

"There is great power in standing over the bodies of the dead, knowing it was you who chose their destiny."

Farum cupped a claw and held it out to her.

"Have you ever held a flower in your hand, looked at its beauty, and wanted to crush it? Why? Why would innocent Clara want to crush something so beautiful?"

"I, we all have thoughts. They're the whisperings of the shadows," she said.

"Are they? How can you be so sure, Clara? What if deep down, you're not as pure as you want everyone to believe?"

Clara shook her head, but Farum continued.

"Murder changes destiny, maybe even fate. What other power can do that?"

Clara understood that. How different would her life be without murder? She never quite understood why her father killed her mother. It wasn't important. Why then was it so important for her to remember why she killed her father? Did her mother's death somehow wash her hands of her father's blood?

Clara couldn't be haunted now. This wasn't about her.

Apollo had Doya eyes. Had he corrupted himself? Was it his own fault that he was the Doomseeker or was he a victim of destiny or chance? Who had he preyed upon for the Gods to curse him?

"Do you have to do evil to become Corrupted? Can you be born with it?"

Farum ran his wet, black tongue over his lips. A knowing grin made his chin quiver.

"Clara, the girl with a heart for the boy with Doya eyes."

"What?" Clara took a quick step forward. "It's a simple question, nothing more."

Oily drool dripped out of the corners of Farum's grin.

"You want to know if the boy is evil. Clara, the pure, can't get a stain on her white soul by helping the wicked.

She can't stick her neck out for a friend, or maybe even a lover?"

Clara clenched her teeth and tightened her grip around Farum's chain.

Farum could sense her anger.

"You save lives, but not evil ones. No, the evil be damned. All hail Clara, the Healer; Clara, the righteous; Clara, the judge; Clara, the executioner."

One tug was all it would take to wipe that grin off Farum's face.

"Go ahead. You can do it. Passion is the strength behind the sword that kills. Is Clara capable of murder? But if you kill me, I won't be able to answer the question you've come to ask."

"What's that?"

Farum's lip curled open, exposing his black gums. "What is purification?"

"What? How do you know that?"

"Clara, I was sent with a message from the Prince of Darkness. I delivered it to the Archmage. You should know, you brought him to me, but he didn't trust you, so you had to wait outside. Poor Clara can't even be trusted by her own kind."

"The message was about Apollo?" Clara asked.

"Sarod has eyes everywhere. Lord Sarod gave the Council what they've been searching for all this time, he gave them the Doomseeker."

"Why?"

"For the Purification. Lord Sarod will take great pleasure in watching the Aurorean mages, disciples of the Sun God, *butcher* one of their own."

"*Butcher*!" Clara exclaimed.

"They'll blame his marks on the Corruption. Then they'll try to dispel the curse with the Urim. When that doesn't work, and it won't, they'll turn to more *primitive* methods, starting with his Black Eyes. They don't need to kill the boy. Instead, they'll remove his corruption and set him on the righteous path."

"Blind him? No, they can't. Apollo hasn't ever been anything but kind. I…I have to do something." Clara bit her lip to keep it from quivering.

"Clara, the frail, you needn't worry your heart. You didn't know you were betraying him by bringing the Archmage to me." Farum licked his lips as if the words had a rich flavor. "The Dark Prince and Lady Black have plans for your Doomseeker."

"Is that what this is? You came here to tell the Archmage about Apollo so he could blind him and toss him into a dungeon?"

Farum gazed at Clara's long shadow, and then up her body. Clara stirred.

"The Doomseeker is a boy. A troubled boy. If Lord Sarod wanted him blinded or dead, he could've sent one of his servants. Clara and her ignorance of the darkness. Lord Sarod is everywhere. Even now, he watches the Council. He watches you. Clara, can you feel him? I can. I am his vessel. My senses are his. The Dark Prince watches you now through me."

"Sarod can see me through your eyes?" Clara stepped closer to examine Farum's black eyes again. She could smell the wine on his breath.

"Not just through mine. Sarod gazes through the corrupted eyes of any Doya."

"What about Apollo? His eyes are black, like yours."

"The Doomseeker has taken Sarod's gaze where it could never go.

"The temple," Clara said to herself. Still, she didn't quite understand. "If Sarod can see through Apollo's eyes, why would he turn him in to the Council?"

"Clara asks a question when she already has the answer."

"Sarod wanted the Council to purify him," she stated.

Clara bit the inside of her lip. What couldn't Sarod's followers do? What was the purpose of Apollo's purification?

Clara felt a chill. The stone. They were going to try to dispel the curse with the Urim. If it were removed from the pedestal, then the temple's protective barrier would fall. If Sarod knew when the temple was vulnerable…

"Take this chain," Clara yelled to the soldiers outside.

The door swung open and the two soldiers burst in.

"Take this chain!"

"You're too late. My dark brothers have gathered. They've patiently awaited tonight. As one, they will destroy your temple, and your great Order will be nothing, and your precious Urim will be lost."

"What's going on?" demanded one of the soldiers. He grabbed Farum's chain, while the other drew his sword and pressed it against Farum's throat.

Clara didn't hear the question.

"I can stop it, there is still time," she said.

"Clara does not see the prophecy being fulfilled."

Farum started to shout. *"The fire will know him. The throat of hell will swallow him, and in hell, he will face one of the lost children of the Gods. He will battle that fiend, and when his blood is spilled on the ground, what was strong will become weak, and what was prized will be lost…"*

"That's enough!" growled the soldier with his sword at Farum's neck. The other was at his side with the chain taught.

Farum glared down at the blade. "Mathus and his band of insects."

The Doya looked down at the mage shackles binding his claws.

"Far-utha-sither" Farum commanded. The shackles exploded into a dozen pieces.

Farum drew a hasty symbol and the soldier's sword slid across Farum's throat and into the neck of the soldier holding his chain.

The flesh in Farum's neck pulled back together.

Clara gaped as the dying soldier, dropped the chain and reached for the cut in his neck. He staggered and fell dead.

Clara turned to run. She stumbled over an uneven stone in the floor. She tried to catch herself, but her trembling hands were too slow.

"Pull the chain!" she screamed from the floor.

She turned on her back and saw Farum stick his bone claws through the other soldier's head.

Farum's voice turned guttural. "The fire knows the Doomseeker. He stood in Marbor's breath. Now your Order will become weak and your prized Urim will be lost. Clara, how can you stop prophecy? How do you hope to turn the tides of what's foretold?"

A silent spell cracked the chains holding Farum to the wall.

The iron door sucked shut.

"There is no escape. No poison to kill me."

Farum walked toward her with the chain to his collar trailing behind him.

"No soldier to pull my chain."

Clara scooted back toward the door.

"Stay away," Clara gasped. She held up a hand as if she could push him back, but Farum kept coming.

Farum's chains rattled on the crypt floor.

Clara clambered to her feet. She grabbed the door bolt and pulled it back, but it wouldn't come open.

Clara slammed her palms into the door, but only chunks of rust crumbled off.

Farum leaped at her. He soared over the table. His chains whipped behind him. His bone claws itched for a taste of Clara's soft, exquisite flesh.

The chain to Farum's collar slid through the lantern hanging from the tomb ceiling. The metal on metal rumbled like a lowering portcullis.

Farum's claws flexed. Clara fell back on the floor. He was coming too close. One swipe of his bone claws would open her up.

The lantern swung as the last of Farum's collar chain slid through it. If only it would catch and release the blades in Farum's collar, but even if it did, would it be enough? Farum was right above her.

Clara screamed and drew her arm to cover her face. His claws came down. She heard a crash and bones snap. Warm blood splashed in her face.

Clara could taste sulfur. The lantern had fallen from the ceiling and its faint light was burning out on the floor. Attached to it was Farum's chain. Clara followed it to Farum's headless body.

The lantern flickered out. The room went completely black, and Clara felt a soggy object roll up against her leg.

31

Avalon - The Black Mountains

A foreboding wind howled through the cracks on the mountainside. The peak of the volcano was a severed black finger that reached toward the misty, gray clouds.

Vallan stepped over thick, hairy briar curling out of the ground with vicious barbs long enough to punch through a man. He had a Doya behind him with a claw point in his back.

Vallan knew the Black Mountains, he remembered when the forest at the base of the mountains covered the whole mountain range. The place teemed with life. He'd roamed this volcano then, through forest trails dense with underbrush and Cyprus trees. He'd waded through rivers, and even watched the white-tailed deer drink from the water.

But that was long ago, after the Elves had vanished. When humans were new to Haven, and the Highborn Dragons were born.

The Elves had left behind empty cities and humans staked their claim in them. Then came the Dragon Wars.

If Ashborn hadn't ended the bloodshed, Vallan wondered if the fighting would still be raging now millennia later.

The dragon swords were the key to peace. The swords gave the just humans the power to keep order, and they gave those same humans the power to speak for the dragons. A bond existed between the wielders of the dragon swords and their dragons. Humans became the voice of reason, and Dragons the power that kept the order.

Vallan had told Apollo the story, but only in part, before the Goblins took him.

He felt foolish now. He should've started with Ashborn's betrayal. Then maybe Apollo would've have known why the Sword of Ashborn was so dangerous.

But Vallan liked to think of times before Ashborn's fall. The era of peace between the Dragon Wars and the Armageddon was bittersweet.

Haven was a place of retreat for lost humans, a refuge, but the Gods couldn't stop humans from their wars and their greed. The humans wanted to own everything, the land, the mountains, the rivers, the world that was not theirs to own.

It was so long ago, to Vallan, the memory seemed more like a dream, or a folk tale that he'd heard a hundred times, but the desolation of the Black Mountains was a testament to the validity of the story, and here he was ascending one of their peaks.

Haven would be whole if an Aphotic Dragon hadn't betrayed the laws of the universe, and taught the humans the forbidden magics. If that knowledge had remained lost, Ashborn might still rule, and the world would still have order.

After the Dragon Wars, the Doya craved war, and many dragons wanted revenge. They went to Ashborn's cave atop Mount Scorpio and found his mate Tesh. The Doya performed forbidden magic on her and twisted her flesh. Creation magic was not made for Doya. They only used the dark half, the part to bend and mold flesh, they couldn't control it. Tesh became a creature of blood, lust, and rage. Evil magic seeped into her skin, turning it black. Her teeth splintered, creating hideous fangs. They split her legs like a great spider and molded her arms into thick claws capable of pinching a man in half. With their magic, they twisted her tail and perverted it into a scorpion-like stinger. When they were finished mutating her body, they imbued her blood with darkness until it could hold no more. Her blood became liquid Remnant, and she became the first Bane, the world's most vicious creature.

Then the creature they created devoured them.

Black shale cracked under Vallan's boots. He scanned the mountain, it was rotted, like the dark blood that ran through Doya veins.

The Black Mountains were the corruption of the world. The deeds of Ashborn's vengeful heart, for when he found his mate mutated, with his hatchlings in her jaws, he lost his mind.

Ashborn, in a fit of blind rage, barreled down the throat of the volcano, Mount Scorpio, and scratched at the heart of the world until the world bled. The volcanoes of the Black Mountains erupted, lava flowed into the Glimmering Sea, and created the Obsidian Ocean. The mountains were sheathed in hot lava, and the sky filled with ash.

The whole world would choke to death on ash, all because Ashborn, the ruler of the world, wanted his revenge on humans and Dragons.

When Pandora, the Mother of Haven, saw the whole world dying in the ash cloud, and Armageddon her own kind created, she used her power and pulled the ash from the air and returned it to the mountains.

The Sun Gods, stewards to the world, banished the Aphotic dragons from the world for the treachery of the one who gave the forbidden magic to the Doya. But the Aurorean dragons couldn't stay without the Aphotic, so both abandoned Haven.

The Sun Gods couldn't banish Highborns. To punish Ashborn, they took his dragon sword from its wielder and trapped him and Ashborn deep in the ground where they would remain for all eternity.

Vallan had taught his son justice. He'd wanted him to be a symbol of peace. He'd told him it was his duty to make the world better. If it weren't for him, his son would've never gotten involved. His son would've lived a normal life, but instead, he was buried. Dragon and man were placed in the ground together, and the sword was taken from them.

Vallan paused, he was standing in what used to be a riverbed, but now it was nothing more than a shale-covered trench. His soul felt as ruined, as dry, and purposeless as that forgotten riverbed.

Then Apollo was born and Vallan had purpose again.

The Doya behind Vallan pressed its claw into Vallan's back to urge him forward.

Vallan circled the crater rim. Doya were spaced evenly throughout the crater, but the shadows made it difficult to see them all. He counted at least three hundred with soot leaking from their mouths. The only light came from a green fire that reflected off a lake at the center of the volcano's crater.

The Doya were humming a low tone that made the air vibrate.

Vallan's captors led him through the ranks of evenly spaced Doya. Each focused on the emerald fire.

Vallan was prodded toward the flames. He covered his mouth. The blaze was kindled by a pyre of bones. They licked up leg bones and danced out of the eye sockets of human skulls.

Vallan saw a man on the other side of the pyre. His eyes were bruised shut and his broken jaw hung open. He stood on two shaky legs and his wrists were bound and bloodied with rope.

The rope was attached to a woman beside him. Her hands were also bound, and her half-naked body was littered with purple welts.

Her rope led to another captive, and the next captive led to another. Each was tied in a circle around the fire.

An overwhelming sense of terror leaked from them. It hit Vallan's aura, nearly knocking him to his knees.

Lady Black stood just outside the ring of captives. She wore a black silk cloak, and her wicked green eyes glowed in the shade of her hood.

"Leave us," she said to Vallan's captors.

"Flesh flames kindled with the bones of virgins. This is corruptive magic," Vallan said.

A wry grin crossed Lady Black's angular face. "Yes, there is at least one virgin in there. You never know these days."

Vallan turned from the flames to Lady Black's haunting eyes.

"Don't do this," he swallowed hard. "This isn't you. This magic corrupts."

"How benevolent," said a voice from the crowd of gathered Doya. "The immortal wants to save the damsel from corruption."

A Doya pulled back its raven feather hood. Vallan gaped at the monstrous creature. His shoulders were as wide as an ox and his arms bulged with black veins. Black blood tears ran out his eyes and down his pallid chest.

"Sarod."

Vallan saw his sword on Lady Black's belt. If he shoved her in the fire, he could wrench it free, but he couldn't; no matter how badly he wanted to send Sarod back into death. Every time he looked into Black's eyes, he saw what she was before all this, and he still loved her.

Sarod snatched the welted woman from the group gathered around the fire. He ripped off her bindings and cast her into the fire. Before she could scream, her flesh burned off, and her bare skeleton fell apart to join the bone pyre.

The wails of the captives echoed off the crater walls. Sarod threw his head back and lapped his oily tongue at the sky.

"There is nothing sweeter than fresh souls in the air."

Sarod turned up his stump. Vallan had severed Sarod's hand the day he'd saved Apollo's mother. More of his wrist was cut off than Vallan remembered. Most of his forearm had been amputated and a steel short sword was attached in its place.

"You cut off your wound," Vallan said.

"I survived. I will always survive. I am the darkness, even you cannot destroy the darkness," Sarod said.

Vallan looked around at the Doya in the crater. There were hundreds of them, he hadn't seen such a gathering since the days of the elves.

"Why do I still live?" Vallan asked. "I cut off your hand, I've killed you again and again over millennia, now is your chance to kill me, yet I still breathe."

"Killing you would be merciful. How would I repay my many deaths with your one?" Sarod prodded Vallan in the chest with his broad sword. Vallan felt the steel scratch against his breastbone. "Your world is about to crumble and I wanted to see your face when that happens."

Sarod grabbed Vallan by his silver hair and dragged him to the fire. Vallan grunted and flailed, but he was no match for Sarod's strength.

Lady Black took up the rope that was binding the woman and tied it around Vallan's wrists. She shoved Vallan to his knees. The man to his right, with his eyes swollen shut, was prostrated on the ground in prayer. The woman to his left saw Sarod at her side and screamed a shrill, earsplitting cry.

"Now, I want you to feed me, Great One. I want to taste your fear," Sarod said.

Vallan spat out his words. "You're dead. The Elves have vanished. The throne you once sat on has crumbled. You are a shadow and I could never fear a shadow."

As Sarod spoke, the flames burned higher.

"The Gods only know how long you can live. You will live your days in an eternal night beneath these mountains. I will see you cry my name. You will curse the heavens, immortal. I will see your hope wither and die when you cannot. "

Vallan's eyes flickered to Lady Black's callous stare and then to his Aureate sword hanging from her belt.

"Apollo, the Doomseeker." Sarod's words were daggers in Vallan's ears. "He is the key to a trove of fear and dread buried within you. I sent one of my servants to your city. I spoke with my servant's tongue and saw through his eyes."

"What?" Vallan lurched toward Sarod, but his restraints held him back. "What did you do?"

"My messenger told the Archmage who has been hiding under his nose all this time."

Vallan grit his teeth. He'd sent Apollo back to the temple with the sword, right into the hands of the Archmage. The veins in his neck bulged. "I'll kill you!" His eyes were blazed with rage. "I'll cut off your head and wait for you to rise so I can do it again and again."

Vallan's fury made Lady Black quiver. A mischievous smirk slid across her lips.

Sarod walked to the fire. "Is that anger or anguish I sense? Fear comes next. Once you know you're powerless the fear will bleed out. I may not be able to control Apollo like a Doya, but through his corrupted eyes, I can watch. Tonight the Council plans to purify him, but he's a pawn, my gambit."

Sarod took in a heavy breath and closed his eyes. He fell into meditation. His eyes moved under his milky white eyelids, and his black tears quickened.

"I see the temple. The Council is gathered around the Doomseeker. The Archmage will approach with the Urim. It is time."

Sarod hummed. His low pitch was matched by the hundreds of Doya in the crater. They were linked. Vallan couldn't guess how long they'd been drawing power, or when the Doya had begun the spell.

Corrupted magic flooded over Vallan's aura. The feeling was so potent he felt as if he couldn't breathe. Vallan sucked down a deep breath, but it didn't help. The corrupted magic was so dense, so absolute.

Sarod shouted words of power. Rare words, Vallan knew them. Such a spell hadn't been cast since Elven times.

The whistling howl of the wind stopped. The air stilled. Sarod waved his arms over his head, and the wind obeyed him.

32

Avalon - New Camelot

Clara burst out of the Catacomb. Her heart pounded in her ears. Her legs ached, but she couldn't stop.

In the distance, high in the night sky, she could still see the temple torch burning in its golden bowl atop the temple. The Urim was still on the pedestal. She still had time to save them.

The wind at her back surged her forward.

She reached the edge of Old Town. Clara could see where the road converged with the city square, and beyond that the temple.

Trees bowed in the bounding winds. A clay shingle broke off one of the Elven houses and shattered in the street.

"Clara!" shouted Mathus. He was at the entrance to the Sanctuary with his Night Guard crowded around him. They were wrapping bandages and splints around the afflicted's wounds. One was even administering Blood Sap.

Mathus saw Farum's black blood splattered in her face and soaked into the front of her windblown robes.

"Are you alright?" he asked.

"Farum is dead," she answered quickly. Clara looked around at the throng of people in the square. She saw refugees from nearby towns who'd taken shelter behind the city walls for the attack, injured from Westport, catatonic Healers, and soldiers.

"Keep them back, we can't help them all at once," Mathus ordered his soldiers, but the injured still crowded in. "Block the stairs, keep these people back," he repeated.

Clara looked across the square to the temple. Her instincts told her they were too close.

She yelled over the wind. "We have to get everyone away from the temple."

The wind stung her face. Clara wiped her watery eyes, and Farum's blood smudged on her knuckles.

"The temple is going to be attacked," Clara yelled.

Mathus surveyed the mass of people.

"How long do we have?" he asked.

Clara pointed to the East Wall. The clouds along the Black Mountains folded over and came pouring toward the wall. The wind smothered the torches. The Wall and Old Town vanished into darkness.

The temple torch flickered. The crowds in the square went silent. Clara's heart stopped. The torch was out, would it come back on? The square was faintly illuminated by the candlelight from the city's street lanterns. The temple torch flickered aflame again. All eyes watched the beacon of light paramount in the night sky.

The Purification. Clara had to get to the temple.

Mathus spouted out orders to his Night Guard. "Get these people out of the Square. Force them into side streets. Clear the area around the temple."

Clara plunged into the dense crowd. There was no space to move. There wasn't time to go around. Clara shoved through a Healer, afflicted farmer, even soldiers. She was so close, the temple was just on the other side of the square.

The temple torch went out. Only the dim street lanterns remained. The cries of the crowd turned to a whisper. They watched, waited for the torch to flicker aflame again.

A scream ignited the tension, the people in the square panicked, and Clara was caught in a current of terror.

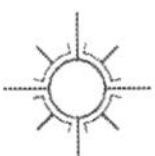

The Lord Marshall was shouting orders from the Sanctuary stairs, but Wislan couldn't hear them over the frenzied crowd in the square. Several Healers, lost in their minds, were trampled underfoot, and the injured who couldn't escape the stampede were crushed into the cobblestones. Those who couldn't flee into the side streets tried to kick in the doors of shops. Some smashed windows, while others tried to scale the Sanctuary walls to climb in through the balconies.

The horror Wislan knew as the Shade was beside him. His spider silk cloak was tucked into the back of his blue leather armor, and his chestnut hair parted in the winds.

In the lantern light, Wislan could see the gauntlets the Shade had used to kill Rhean. Would the Shade kill him before the night was over? He'd done everything he'd asked.

Wislan shouted over the crowd. "The barrier is down. It's safe to enter."

The Shade ran a gauntleted hand over the gap in the archway as if petting an invisible beast. One of his eyes was covered with a silver eye patch; the other he turned on Wislan.

"Prove it."

Wislan threw up his arms. "How am I supposed to do that?"

"It's your enchanted wall of death. You figure it out."

Wislan stormed into the frenzied crowd and returned with a flimsy, freckle-faced boy.

"Let me go!" the boy cried, and Wislan shoved him past the Shade and through the temple gate.

The boy cried out and stumbled into the dim stones of the sunstone courtyard.

Wislan pointed to the boy, who curled up in a ball on the ground. "He wasn't eviscerated. Satisfied?"

Wislan watched the Shade step through. He prayed to the Gods that the Urim would be put back in place and reduce his living nightmare into a gust of ash, but the Gods didn't answer his prayer.

Screams turned to shrieks, a dense black cloud flooded in from the East. It poured over the Sanctuary. Wislan watched the cloud consume the Lord Marshall and his men. It silenced his orders and flowed down the Sanctuary stairs.

Wislan couldn't follow the Shade inside, he was finally free from him. He tried to shove his way north of the square to the castle, but the crowd was too thick, he'd never make it. The black cloud pooled into the square. Street lanterns snuffed out. Townsfolk tripped over each other to get away, but the cloud marched over them. Wislan cried out and dropped to his knees.

"I can't die like this. I'm a Pendragon, I'm nephew to the King, son of Loholt. Third in the line of succession."

The wave of darkness enveloped Wislan. It broke on the Temple wall and leaked over the brim.

The Shade saw mages beyond the gate, taking shelter from the storm. He counted a score of Warlocks with their swords out and a few Sorcerers and Enchanters break away from conversation.

"How did you get in here?" one of the Enchanters demanded.

The Shade needed a distraction, and the frenzied crowd was perfect. He cupped his hands around his mouth and shouted into the choking fog. "Everyone, take shelter in the temple!"

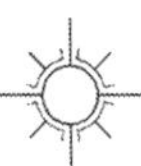

Apollo should've told Vallan about the dragon blood. Vallan would've known what to do, but he was gone now, and

Apollo hadn't shed a tear for him. He'd seen Vallan charge into the Goblins. One against the horde, yet Apollo still hoped against reason that he would see Vallan in the halls of the temple, or walking the walls of the city with Mathus.

Apollo was alone, all he had to guide him were the lessons from a mentor, a father he'd left to die with the Goblins. Remembering Vallan's precious words was like catching rain. He could only hold a little, while the rest slipped through the cracks of his mind.

When would he mourn the man who'd held his hand and brought him out of the shadows, the hero who'd saved his mother, and the man who was willing to be his father?

Warm tears ran down Apollo's cheeks, he swallowed the lump in his throat.

The Archmage approached to face him. "Tears will not help you, Doomseeker." He checked the ropes, binding Apollo's hands.

Apollo shook away his tears, but the lump in his throat returned.

The Archmage's shaggy, white beard hung over the folds of his crimson robe. He was a tiny, gentle man, yet Apollo felt a chill from his sharp gaze and a warning in his aura that was so palpable that it made his throat dry.

Beside the Archmage, Harthor read a tome aloud, but Apollo wasn't listening. It was the usual death and damnation speech he'd heard all his life.

The three purists were next: Durakos, Leteah, and Gibnar; in purple, brown, and yellow robes. The colors of their robes were different, but they all wore matching wrathful faces.

The room was pale marble. Torchlight illuminated the prophecies written on the walls. Apollo could see the first prophecy over Lorad's head. It was the verse Vallan had been studying.

Why hadn't he listened then? Vallan knew the Garatha better than anyone, and this prophecy plagued him. What was in it that was so important?

Apollo tried to pull the sentences apart.

The fire will know him. Apollo had stood in Marbor's breath. He'd felt the fire in his hair. He'd tasted the warm, sweet rosewater flavor of the dragon's flames.

The throat of hell will swallow him... Apollo didn't like the sound of that. He'd always thought "hell" was such a strange word in the Garatha; its translation from Primoris never seemed quite right. Any place called hell was never good.

Harthor's methodic tone of reading the scriptures grated on Apollo's nerves.

"Do you have to read all of that?"

Harthor paused, looked at the others, and continued. "You will know him by the marks on his face..."

Was this what his life was going to be? So long as he lived, he would witness prophecy. The riddle of his life would unfold before him and he would live on as a victim of fate.

Unless the Urim had the power to lift his burden.

Apollo saw his mark, the broken sun, under each prophecy on the walls. He'd never seen it in the temple before, nor did he know of this room. Wythrin had built the temple millennia ago, knowing that Apollo would one day stand in this very place. He belonged there, despite his hands being bound by cords, Gibnar's glower and Durakos and Leteah's scorn, despite the damning words on Harthor's tongue. Apollo didn't want to escape. If anyone ever had the knowledge and power to cure him, wouldn't it be Wythrin, the legendary Enchanter? If the stone could remove his marks like the Archmage had explained, then he welcomed the Urim's prickly touch.

Apollo was finished hiding. He'd fought Warlocks and bathed in dragon's breath. What man could say that? He'd hid as a child, but now he was a man. No more lies, no more secrets. The Urim would take away his marks and then Clara would look at him like she had before. Everyone would see him, accept him.

Lorad pulled a leather bag, the size of a coin purse, out from a pocket in his robes and emptied it into his hand. A blinding light burst outward. The light overpowered the torches and filled the whole room.

"The Urim created and imbued with power by Raiden the highest of the Aurorean Dragons, the father of the Universe," said Lorad.

The Purists bowed their heads. Durakos used his hand to shield his eyes. "Please be quick Archmage, it is a sin to look upon the White Stone."

Archmage Lorad shook his head. Harthor rolled his eyes.

Lorad held the Urim between his thumb and forefinger. He touched it to Apollo's marks. It crackled with power.

"Historically, the Urim dispelled curses for the Elves, even a few blood curses," Harthor said.

Apollo felt the warmth of the stone on his face.

"Its power is immeasurable. It truly is a gift from the creators," said Leteah.

"Do not look sister," said Gibnar, "The Urim's power is too great for mortals."

Archmage Lorad touched the stones to Apollo's cheeks again.

Lorad's face tightened. "Why isn't it working?"

"Try again," Apollo insisted.

"Being marked is not a curse." Durakos lowered his hand but still kept his eyes away from the stone. "The Doomseeker is a demon. The Gods would never damn a child. Life and death are the only powers that create or destroy destiny."

Harthor snapped his book shut. "So we should kill Apollo as if he's just another Doya? Is that what you're saying?"

"What! How did this go from tapping a stone on my cheeks to execution? That's a little drastic, don't you think?" Apollo reeled.

Leteah drew her sword and prowled along the perimeter of the Council. Her muscular face flexed. Her eyes locked on Apollo's throat.

"I will make it quick. He won't feel a thing," Leteah said.

Apollo's attention turned to the steel door, there was only one way out. He could knock the Archmage down, but could he pull the door open before Leteah made him a head shorter? He needed a sword. Even with his bound hands, he could grab the Sword of Ashborn from Durakos' belt, but Gibnar would hack him in two before he could swing it.

"No," Lorad said.

"Why? Because he looks like a boy?" Durakos spat.

"I saw him stand in dragon fire!" Leteah insisted.

"What you saw was the power of the Sword of Ashborn, no feat of Demonic origins." Harthor took out his dagger. "Can I have a lock of your hair?"

Apollo frowned. "Sure."

Harthor cut a lock and took one of the torches down from the wall.

"Watch, if he isn't holding the sword, he can burn just like the rest of us." Harthor dropped the lock of hair into the torch and it burned up. Harthor covered his nose against the smell.

"What does that prove?" Gibnar asked dryly.

"That his power comes from the sword," Durakos clarified.

"And that we can burn him," Leteah added.

Apollo jerked at that. "I tried to save the city, and you want to burn me?"

Lorad shook his head. "I'm not turning the noble cause to save the Sun God into a witch hunt. We aren't going to kill a boy."

"Boy or not, he's still the Doomseeker," Gibnar said.

Harthor prodded his finger into the sweat-stained Aurorean symbol on Apollo's chest. "He's also one of us."

Leteah still circled the perimeter. "He's a traitor and a deceiver."

Harthor shook his head. "He was the Doomseeker before he became a mage. How do we know he didn't betray his nature to become one of us? If that were true, we'd be executing one of our own, not a traitor."

Archmage Lorad and Harthor challenged three Purists. Through the years, Apollo had dreaded this moment, he never imagined the Archmage would be protecting him.

"If we aren't going to kill the Doomseeker, how do you suggest we deal with him?" Gibnar asked.

"We continue the Purification," Durakos cut in.

Durakos pulled out a sharp glass dagger and handed it to Lorad. Lorad held the Urim in one hand and the glass dagger in the other.

The Archmage lifted the glass dagger to his eyelid and held the stone above his head for light.

"What are you doing?" Apollo said, jerking his head away.

Lorad's voice changed to a whisper. "I can save your life, but we cannot abide corruption, not when it comes to the Doomseeker."

"So you're going to blind me? That's the alternative?" Apollo bawked.

The Archmage's ancient, wrinkled face would be the last thing he'd ever see.

"I'm not Corrupted!" Apollo shoved him away, the Archmage fell back to the wall, and Apollo ran for the door.

"Stop him!" Durakos ordered. Gibnar and Leteah grabbed Apollo by the arms.

Lorad re-positioned the knife. Apollo pulled away.

Harthor tried to comfort him. "Don't struggle. It's a delicate procedure. It will hurt, but not for long."

The door swung open.

"What are you doing?!" Clara screamed.

"Clara!" Relief washed over Apollo.

The Archmage turned. Clara's fierce eyes glared at him. The Council stared at the Doya blood splattered all over her face.

"What's going on? Who are you?" Lorad demanded.

"She's the Doomseekers' lover. They were together when I found him," Gibnar sneered. Leteah sized her up, and Harthor stood there with his mouth agape.

Durakos put his arm around Clara and pulled her away from the Archmage.

"What are you doing here? The Council has captured Daynin and they're searching for Vallan. I did my best to prove you weren't involved with this deceiver."

Durakos' words were nothing. She'd seen the fear in Apollo's face and the knife in Lorad's hands.

Clara pushed Durakos back. “The barrier is down. People are flooding the temple.”

“We have to put the Urim back,” Gibnar said.

Clara jumped in front of the door. “No! They’re still coming. If you put it back now, they’ll be rushing into the barrier and you’ll kill them.”

“Then we have to block the gate somehow,” Harthor said.

“That’s not all. Sarod cast a spell and it’s spreading over the city. We don’t have much time.”

“Sarod?” the Archmage grumbled. “He wants Apollo destroyed. He wouldn’t interrupt the purification.”

Durakos stepped away from Clara to join Gibnar and Leteah restraining Apollo.

“Apollo hasn’t done anything to deserve this,” Clara said.

Durakos, Leteah, and Gibnar gave her scrutinizing looks.

“If you believe in the Garatha, then you know what he’ll do. We should kill him, we’re being merciful.” Durakos said.

“He’s already started his path into the darkness. You saw him cast dark magic in the Sanctuary,” Gibnar added. “You’re a Purist, you should trust in us.”

Clara could see the scorn in their faces. “Save your pompous judgments for another lost girl without parents, or the afflicted, or whatever poor, vulnerable soul you can feed your lies to. I’ve had it with Purists, Healers, and Councils.”

Screams sounded in the hall. A puff of black smoke leaked in under the door.

"I met a Doya in the catacombs. His name was Farum." Clara wiped some of Farum's black blood off her face and held it out to them. "Is that proof enough? The Archmage knows him. He told me what Sarod was planning."

Lorad held out his hands to Apollo. "Sarod will lose his throne to the Doomseeker if he's not stopped. He wants him here."

Clara pointed to the stream of smoke leaking under the door. "They're using Apollo to draw their spell into the temple. We have to get everyone out."

"Sarod played you," Leteah said. "The identity of the Doomseeker should've been revealed to the Council."

Lorad stomped his foot. "Someone on the Council was helping him. I didn't know it was Daynin. It could've been anyone of you."

Lorad's face sobered. There were two ways to stop this spell. He had to sever the connection on Sarod's end, or here. Lorad looked helpless, defeated, his face pleaded for forgiveness. He lowered the glass dagger to Apollo's chest. One quick jab through the ribs and it would all be over. "There is no other way. I'm sorry."

"NO!" Clara grabbed hold of Lorad's arm, but his robes slipped through her fingers. Apollo cried out.

Clara turned her head. She sunk her face in her hands. "Monsters! Murders! You're no better than the Doya," she cried.

The glass knife smashed on the floor.

"What the…Who are you?" Durakos demanded.

"How did you get in here?" Leteah growled.

Clara looked back. A man wearing a silver eye patch and dressed in blue armor was standing between the Archmage and Apollo. The stranger gasped for air. Sweat ran down his face.

Apollo looked over the stranger's shoulder and down at the shattered, glass dagger Lorad had tried to thrust into his heart and sighed with relief.

"Doomseeker, what sort of trick is this?" Durakos shouted. Gibnar and Leteah held tight to Apollo and drew their swords.

Apollo's mouth hung open. He glanced around at the Council, who were looking at him for an explanation. "Everyone thinks that just because you're the Doomseeker, you have all the answers."

Archmage Lorad lifted the Urim to shed more light on the stranger's face.

Durakos drew the Sword of Ashborn. "Who are you?" he demanded.

The stranger caught his breath and dropped into a graceful bow. "Let me introduce myself. My friends call me Rinn; then there are those that call me the Shade. Those who know me as the Shade have usually lost something valuable, or are dead. In which case, they can't call me anything. Then there are the scriptures, which have branded me with a chilling title."

Rinn removed his eye patch. A crescent moon curled around his eyelid in perfect view in the light of the stone.

Rinn winked.

"The Reaper," Lorad gasped, his eyes flickered from Rinn to Apollo, the wrinkles in his face shook. "The Doomseeker and his Reaper together, by the Gods, kill them, KILL THEM BOTH!"

Durakos brought the Sword of Ashborn down on Rinn.

Rinn vanished. Apollo lunged forward and used Durakos' wasted swing to cut his restraints. His hands came free. Gibnar and Leteah pulled him down. He hit the floor and rolled. Leteah's Aureate blade cut into the stone. Sparks burnt Apollo's neck. Gibnar swung for his head. Apollo rolled out of his reach.

"We have to get out of here!" Clara screamed.

Smoke billowed from underneath the door.

Apollo drew a spell from a shadow in the corner of the room and threw a blast of pressure. It hit Durakos; he flew against the wall, hit his head, and fell unconscious to the floor. The Sword of Ashborn slipped out of Durakos' hands. Apollo snatched it up. He blocked high and caught Gibnar's advancing blow.

Leteah's attack followed. Apollo spun out of the way. The marble cried sparks as her blade slashed into it.

Harthor and the Archmage ran for the door.

Rinn appeared in their path. Clara didn't know which way to turn. Aureate swords splashed sparks in the back of the room as Leteah and Gibnar advanced on Apollo. Lorad and Harthor slid to a halt, Rinn blocked the door. Durakos was on the ground, still not moving.

The smoke was rising. Sarod's spell would envelop them all.

Rinn opened one of his gauntleted hands. "Give me the Urim. I want you to tell the story of how the Shade stole the impossible. No thief has even gotten through the temple barrier and here I am taking one of the Seer Stones from the Archmage. It doesn't get better than that."

"The Urim should be protected by the temple. It's not a gem to be stolen or a stepping-stone to fame. You can't fathom its power," Harthor said.

"Leave us be, Reaper," the Archmage commanded.

The corner of Rinn's smile turned up into a cocky smirk. He crouched down to Lorad's level. "To be honest, I thought this would be harder. I had to spook one of your Warlocks for a month just to get in here and I find the Urim protected by a bunch of…"

Rinn winced and gave Lorad a pitiful look. "You're not exactly in your prime. I mean, you're like a hundred years old."

Rinn stood back up and pulled a dagger from his armor. He pointed it at Lorad and then Harthor. "A thief is only as good as his reputation. I don't make it a habit to kill old men or librarians, but I will if I have to."

Clara coughed. Soot speckled the air. The door creaked and like a cloth dipped in water, the door soaked darkness from the floor so that it was stained black.

Harthor grabbed the Urim from the Archmage. He threw his tome at Rinn and ran for the door.

"No, don't!" Lorad cried.

Harthor's fingers crimped around the black door handle; his hand went numb. Blackness went up his arm. His green cloak turned an ashen gray. Harthor yanked his arm, and it crumbled off at the elbow. He cried out. His skin dissolved.

"What's happening?" he screamed.

Gibnar, Leteah, and Apollo took defensive stances and gaped at Harthor as he clutched the stump of his elbow. His severed arm broke from the door handle and granulated into a cloud of dust on the floor.

"Help!" he cried. Harthor stumbled toward Clara. "Oh, gods, help me!"

"Someone, do something," Leteah cried.

"Help him," Gibnar demanded.

Clara looked on, horrified. "What can I do?" She reached for his dissolving elbow.

"Don't touch him!" Lorad pulled Clara back.

Harthor coughed out pink sand. He fell to his knees. The White Stone fell from his dissolving fingers. His shoulder collapsed. He tried to scream again, but his head caved inward. Harthor's entire body crumbled to a pile of grains on the floor.

Clara looked back, shocked, and pointed at the door, now stained black. "How do we get out of here?"

Gibnar roared as he advanced on Apollo. Apollo ducked, Gibnar's heavy sword just missed his head. Leteah followed with a thrust, Apollo blocked.

"Stop it!" Clara screamed. "We have to work together, or we're all going to die."

She saw Durakos on the floor, his head leaking blood. She dropped to his side.

Rinn took the Urim from Harthor's remains. He tried to stuff it into a pouch on his belt, but Lorad blasted him with a pressure spell. Rinn flew backward toward the door, he hit a jewel in his gauntlet and a cord shot into the ceiling. Fiery red light dripped off the Archmage's hands popping and flickering to the floor. The light came out of his fingertips as a hundred snakes of red energy that intertwined and gushed toward Rinn. The power hit Rinn's cord and burned it to nothing. Rinn fell out of reach just as the slithering energy bored dozens of small holes through the marble ceiling. The Urim slipped from Rinn's fingers and slid across the floor. He dove and snatched it back up.

The red snakes curled to chase him. Rinn rolled out of the way, he pulled a knife from his armor and threw it at Lorad. The knife whistled through the air and nicked Lorad's ear.

The door rattled on its hinges and smoke spewed from every side of its frame.

Apollo still battled the twins in the rear of the room; Leteah was too fast and Gibnar was surprisingly strong. Leteah came down with an overhead thrust, teeth clenched, eyes budging with determination. Apollo drew a pressure spell and knocked Leteah's sword free. It spun end over end and plunged into the door. Blackness poured over the Aureate and reduced the sword to grains.

The ground heaved, the door vibrated as the mist sucked back through.

A loud pop came from the door. Like a bolt shot from a crossbow, a flash of metal whizzed by Clara's head.

Metal clanged against stone. Clara looked from Durakos toward the sound. A door hinge tapped against the stone wall. The doors were pulling outward. They were going to rip off.

"Look out! The door, the hinges are breaking." Clara cried.

Rinn was near the door, he threw every dagger in his armor, but Lorad created a tangle of energy in front of him that eviscerated his blades.

Gibnar came at Apollo with a crushing blow. Apollo met his fury. Their swords rang; sparks filled the air. Gibnar's sword cracked, and the point of Apollo's blade slammed into Gibnar's forehead and sliced into in his brains.

Leteah screamed.

Gibnar teetered, he slid off Apollo sword and sunk lifeless to the floor. Leteah dropped to his side.

Shocked, Apollo covered his mouth. "Gods, I didn't mean to—"

"Gibnar! Gibnar!" she called, but he was dead.

Another hinge broke free. The bolts holding the hinge to the wall flashed across the room at a deadly speed.

"You'll pay for this, Doomseeker!" Leteah screamed.

A hinge bolt popped. It zipped across the room. The bolt caught her in the side of the head. Leteah toppled over, blood soaking her ear.

The door bent in half and exploded outward into a swirling, purple vortex. Lightning cracked in the whirlpool of clouds that filled the doorway. Harthor's sandy remains pulled in. They circled the vortex until they disappeared beneath the darkness. The winds picked up. The fragments of the shattered, glass dagger vanished into the void and Gibnar's body slid toward it.

The winds pulled Rinn backward. He tucked the Urim into a pouch on his belt. Still, its light came shining through. Rinn tried to find something to grab on to, he was nearing the door, and his only grip was the tread of his boots on the slick marble.

He trudged against the pull toward the center of the room.

Lorad dropped his disintegrating power to cast a spell to hold himself to the floor. He stood firm with his feet in place with Rinn on one side and Clara and Apollo on the other. All his Grandmasters were down.

Clara left Durakos' side and fought the high winds to reach Leteah sliding across the floor. "She's still breathing. We need to get her to the Sanctuary, Durakos too."

The vortex consumed Gibnar's body. Apollo dragged Durakos to the rear of the room. Staggering against the force of the vortex's pull, Clara tried to push Leteah, but the winds pulled her back.

"I'm coming," Apollo shouted.

A surge of wind knocked Apollo from his feet, and he slipped past Clara. The Archmage was the only one in reach.

Apollo snatched his hand; Lorad's old muscles strained.

Lorad pried a finger out of Apollo's grip.

"No! Please don't!" Apollo cried.

Lorad screamed over the raging wind, "I have no choice. You can't live."

Lorad wrenched his hand out of Apollo's grip. The vortex drew him in. Apollo fell sideways.

Rinn caught Apollo by the forearm. Apollo's feet stopped just short of the swirling vortex.

"I've got you," Rinn shouted.

Rinn shot a cord into the floor. The winds pulled them off their feet. Apollo held on to Rinn, and Rinn the cord, as they dangled before the mouth of the vortex.

The Archmage started to draw a powerful pressure spell. If he could break Rinn's cord, the Doomseeker and his Reaper, and their prophecies would all be extinguished.

Clara grabbed his arm, but his opposite hand was still drawing symbols.

Lorad tried to shake her off. "Get off child!"

"Let them be!" Clara screamed.

Lorad's fingers still moved in a silent spell. Clara balled her fist and punched him in the gut. Lorad coughed violently, but he completed the spell. He turned to throw it. Clara grabbed his hand and it blasted between them.

Clara and Lorad flew backward. The pull of the vortex took them. Lorad flipped and twisted and vanished beneath the vortex's purple clouds. Rinn grabbed the back of Clara's robe and yanked her in. Clara clung to his armor. Apollo was just below her.

Rinn's cord loosened. Clara saw it fraying.

"The rope, it's going to break!" Clara yelled.

Rinn shook his head. "It's an Atlantean rope. It's stronger than iron."

Apollo shouted up to them. "We have to swing! The pull isn't as strong at the sides of the door."

"I don't think we should," Clara argued.

Rinn shouted above the whistling wind. "On three. One, two—"

The rope snapped, and Apollo, Rinn, and Clara were swallowed into oblivion.

33

Avalon - The Black Mountains

Vallan surveyed the crater. He'd spotted two hundred Doya before losing count. Too many were lost in the shadows of the rock outcroppings and huge boulders. The green light from the pile of burning bones was dim, and even though he couldn't see into the shadows, he knew Doya lurked there.

He could hear them, their hums, a profanity that made the shale on the ground rattle.

Vallan took a breath. His lungs prickled. Power traveled to Sarod as a weightless, invisible sheen that clung to Vallan's robes and snapped in his hair. Tiny bolts of lightning crackled around them.

The Doya were absorbing darkness and Sarod was taking the energy from them. Sarod's dark eyes were open and empty. Black tears, the symbol of Sarod's possession, bled into his open mouth.

Lady Black pressed up against Vallan. Her voice became wistful as she watched Sarod. "The breastplate made Sarod a master, he's defeated death." She marveled at the sky. "He commands the heavens."

Vallan felt her breath quicken. Her face was charged, alive. She was a lioness brushing up against him, lusting for the power of another pack.

Sarod held his claws outward and viciously squeezed them together as if he were strangling an invisible victim.

"Get off me," Vallan growled.

Lady Black smiled a wicked, pointed grin. She leaned in closer and bit his ear. "Always so noble, you never were much fun, but you were powerful. That's what drew me to you, but those days are nearly forgotten. The only power you have left is your name, but you deny yourself that as well. You were a ruler and now you're a pauper."

Lightning cracked across the crater. The sky groaned. Lady Black and Vallan watched Sarod's funnel cloud swirl over the crater. Clouds shredded in the force of the whirlwind. Sarod tightened his grip on his invisible victim. Vallan couldn't understand how a Doya could be lord of the winds. How did Sarod strangle the sky?

Vallan was a prisoner and had watched the other prisoners be thrown into the green fire. Flesh had burned to ash and what was a living, breathing person became cold bones to fuel icy green flames. Sarod had drawn every last drop of fear from them, and when they'd passed out, Lady Black used a wave of magic to pull them into the fire.

"Haven is going to change," she said. The wind pushed them backward, their feet slipped. Lady Black drew a spell to hold them in place.

The pyre of bones toppled over. A ribcage rolled past them. An arm bone twisted up into the clouds. A skull rolled to Vallan's feet. Its jaw swung open. Vallan thought he heard it scream, but it was only the wind howling in his ears.

"What's happening?" Vallan shouted.

Lady Black ran her fingertips through Vallan's beard. "A new beginning," she purred. "The start of the end of everything you hold dear."

Vallan searched Lady Black's green eyes for the love he'd known, but there was only poison in them.

Her mouth twisted into the playful grin Vallan had once loved.

"I lost what mattered when I lost my wife and my son." Vallan shouldered Lady Black away, but even his sharp words couldn't sour her mood.

Vallan squinted up at the whirlwind over the crater. The glowing bones from the pyre were caught in the current and became streaking green light through the funnel cloud.

Vallan needed magic, but it was too dark, and the light from the bones swirling above was too weak.

Lightning flashed. It was only a blink of light, but it was concentrated power. Vallan looked down at the cords around his wrists. He could use magic to sever them and the spell Lady Black had cast would help him keep his footing. His sword was in her belt. Could he kill Sarod if the timing was right? He'd only have a few heartbeats of freedom before Lady Black turned her magic on him. Seven steps and a swing: that's all it would take to sever Sarod's head and put an end to the spell forming above them.

White pebbles fell. Was it hail? No, the pebbles were too white. Vallan hunched over and picked up a tiny stone. It wasn't cold like hail, and its pure white was familiar, but Vallan couldn't quite place it.

"The show is about to begin," Lady Black said. She pointed up at a golden, metal circle in the sky. Vallan squinted as he watched it round the funnel cloud and crash into the crater wall. A deep dull note resonated from the metal.

The circle flipped, rolled down the crater, and splashed into the crater's lake. Vallan's breath caught in his throat.

It was the temple torch.

The pebble of temple rock rolled out of Vallan's hands. A wooden beam flipped and splintered on the lake's edge.

A boulder of white marble spiraled out of the clouds and plunged into the lake. Grimy lake water exploded into the air and the brilliant marble sunk into the depths.

Bodies twisted through the whirling cloud, some mages, some wearing the common clothes of peasants and craftsmen. From a distance, they were marionettes without strings and they were falling.

Vallan closed his eyes. The first hit the ground with the sloshing sound of a wet towel. The second was alive, and he screamed until Vallan heard his bones crunch. A third came so close Vallan could smell the body's sweat in the torrential wind. Then Vallan couldn't count them anymore, crunching and screaming surrounded him. Vallan wanted to reach for his magic; he had to help them. But he was too late. Sarod's spell would claim them all.

Vallan opened his eyes to a blood-spattered battlefield. Healers, Warlocks, farmers, merchants they were all pulverized into the crater floor.

They were all dead, life snuffed out by the Dark Prince.

The Doya threw their heads back and lapped their tongues at the sky.

Vallan grimaced at the Doya's gyrating tongues. "You're murdering them, this isn't a battle, it's a massacre."

Lady Black saw Sarod tongue sticking out of his mouth, dripping tar down the side of his cheek.

She folded her arms. "Their lives are so short. Haven won't miss a few insects."

Vallan clenched his teeth. His eyes narrowed. "Insects? Look at them. Don't you see the children? You've lost your child, yet you kill another as if you don't understand."

Lady Black closed her eyes. She couldn't look at the children, their empty, dead faces frozen like dolls. She wasn't doing this. It was Sarod. She didn't have a choice. If she was going to see her son again, she had to endure.

She needed the breastplate.

Vallan noticed a man's body in yellow robes twisting through the funnel cloud. The wind turned it over as it bounced off rocks and planks until his body slammed into the ground at Vallan's feet.

Vallan knew him. His face was a ruin of splinters and open wounds. A blade had split open his head.

"Gibnar!" Vallan exclaimed.

Lady Black pushed Gibnar with the point of her boot, but he was clearly dead.

Sarod sneered at Vallan's shock. "Look upon the first to die at the Doomseeker's hands."

Vallan dropped to his knees. He reached for Gibnar. His skin was cold, his face petrified in death.

Vallan's hands shook; it was happening, the nightmare had started. Death was all around him. He'd spent all of Apollo's life trying to guide him, and Sarod was about to undo all of that. If they got their hands on him, Apollo would no longer be his pupil. Vallan would have to put down the boy he'd thought of as a son, but how? Could he ever see Apollo, the child he'd cared for, comforted, the one he'd watched peer out the window at the great wide world, was it possible for him to see Apollo as a demon?

Lightning flashed again, but Vallan wasn't ready to take its power. He'd missed his chance to escape. Lady Black drew her obsidian sword and reached over Vallan's shoulder. She pressed the jagged edge into Vallan's throat.

Sarod waved his arms and the funnel cloud pivoted directly over the lake.

The sounds of the storm turned to murmurs as Lady Black nuzzled Vallan's neck and whispered in his ear. "It's time to introduce your wife to your bastard."

34

Avalon - The Black Mountains

Apollo cried out. He was falling. The surface of the water stung. He was underwater. His head was spinning. Apollo kicked his feet. He surfaced and spit out a mouthful of hot, sour water.

Temple rock peppered the lake around him, and then the winds went still. The night was silent. Lighnting flashed and Apollo saw the light glint off of the twisted metal of Rinn's gauntlets. He was in front of him, clinging to a floating door.

Apollo swam up beside him and latched onto the door. "Where's Clara?"

Rinn ignored his question. He grimaced at the stink of sulfur. "So this is what the Underworld looks like." He ran his fingers through the gritty water and stared into the utter blackness. "I thought it would be more crowded."

"We're not dead. Where's Clara?" Apollo insisted.

"The girl?" Rinn asked.

Apollo bristled. "Yes, the one that said your rope couldn't hold us, and you said—"

"Never mind that," Rinn interrupted. "Where's that fossil?"

Apollo furrowed his brow. "What's a fossil?"

"Gods, you Avalonians are primitive. The Archmage, the old man who got us into this whole mess."

A faint glow showed through the surface of the water. It gradually got brighter until they could see a shoreline.

Rinn checked the leather pouch where he'd stowed the Urim. It was empty.

"My stone!" Rinn exclaimed. He pushed off the door, but Apollo grabbed him.

"Get off!" Rinn tried to shake him off.

"Wait!" Apollo insisted.

Archmage Lorad surfaced with the Urim glowing brightly in his hand.

Rinn grabbed at Apollo's grip on his armor and tried to pry his fingers off. "He's getting away with my stuff," he squawked.

"Let him. Look."

The Urim's pure light illuminated the crater. Apollo pointed to the hundreds of Doya in positions along the crater walls. An imposing figure watched Lorad crawl up the shallows toward shore. The figure stood upright, with the shoulders of a warrior and the build of a quarryman. He looked like a titan compared to Lorad.

"Come forth, Archmage, death awaits you," the Doya bellowed.

"What's that thing?" Rinn asked.

"Sarod," Apollo answered. He didn't know how he knew, but he was certain of it.

Behind Sarod was a woman with a sword to a prisoner's throat, watching the Archmage approach. It was too far to make out anything more than their silhouettes.

Apollo and Rinn ducked low in the water and crept in closer. They could barely hear Sarod and his companions.

"Any magic and your Warlock dies," said the woman.

"It's Black, the Emperor's bitch. She's come for the Urim too," Rinn whispered to Apollo.

The Archmage held the stone up high, so its light dominated the crater. "In my hand, I hold enough power to cast whatever spell I wish."

The Doya positioned on the crater walls crept over rock and corpse toward Lorad.

Lorad's baggy eyes showed no emotion, his expression was weary, yet his voice carried a power that echoed through the mountains. "I am the Harbinger of Dawn. I've leveled armies with less power than I hold in my hand."

Sarod spat a wad of tar at Lorad. "Harbinger of Dawn, you've seen your last sunrise."

"We should get out of here," Apollo whispered to Rinn.

Rinn shook his head. "I came for that stone, and I'll be damned if I'm going to let Black or a wrinkly, old man take it from me."

Apollo searched the shoreline, but even with the light of the Urim, he couldn't find Clara. "Fine, you're on your own. I'm finding Clara and getting out of here."

Apollo pushed off the door and into the lake when he heard a man's voice. Vallan? Impossible, he thought. Vallan was dead, killed by a horde of Goblins.

Apollo took a stroke toward the other side of the lake. Debris had collected there. If Clara had fallen in the lake, she could still be alive.

The prisoner called out to the Archmage. "Lorad, give them the stone, we've lost this battle."

"Silence, I will not take council from the father of the Doomseeker," Lorad spat.

Apollo stopped, he turned toward the Archmage. The Urim illuminated the prisoner's face. Apollo saw the ashen beard, and the white-streaked hair, he recognized the prisoner's brown robes, and all at once Apollo's faintest glimmer of hope, the part of him that couldn't believe the man he'd called father was dead, surfaced. They were surrounded by an army of Doya, trapped in the Black Mountains, at the mercy of Sarod and his god-like powers; as dire as their situation seemed, with Vallan here, Apollo felt a comfort he couldn't explain.

"Change your mind?" Rinn asked as Apollo returned to the floating door.

"That man, my father, the prisoner, we have to save him."

Rinn cocked his head. "Black has a sword to his throat, I'd say *father Warlock* is the last person that's coming out of this crater alive. Even if we could get to him, there is the matter of being surrounded by Doya in the middle of the night. No, our only chance is to sneak out once we're figured out who's leaving with the stone. Then we follow them and rob them quiet like."

"Do your invisible trick and help him," Apollo said.

"Now wait," Rinn released a frustrated breath. "That sounds like hero talk, and I'm a thief. I stick my neck out for me, that's it."

"You saved my life," Apollo corrected.

"Are you going to make me regret that?" Rinn rolled his eyes. "Besides, there isn't enough light for me to do my *trick.*"

Apollo pointed to the Urim shining over Lorad's head. "Use the light from the stone."

"Gods, you're persistent, that light is too far away, and besides, Doya can see right through my disguise."

Lorad was still far off, and surrounded by Doya, at the mercy of Sarod. He used the light of the Urim to look to either side of the crater, the Doya were closing in.

Lorad's ancient face shook with spite. "Vallan, you've betrayed the Order, your place is with the fallen. If our paths cross again, you'll join Daynin in judgement. *Your* secrets have destroyed us."

Sarod's foot splashed into the shallows of the lake. He let his raven feather cloak slide from his muscular shoulders. The Archmage watched the giant approach. Sarod raised the broadsword sticking from his wrist stump. The bone claws of his other hand flexed. Each finger was a dagger that was long enough to push right through the Archmage. Lorad's shaky knees made ripples in the water.

“Get back, fiends of hell!” Lorad waved the White Stone over his head.

Sarod ran a claw down the blade of his broad sword. “Tame your hypocritical tongue before I tear it from your throat.”

The Doya crept closer. Lorad was surrounded. A few more steps and he’d be in reach of their bone claws.

Lorad weaved a spell but before he could get it off, a Doya jumped on his back. Lorad fell forward. The stone dropped from his hand.

Vallan leaned back into Black. His sword was still in her belt. He could reach it.

“Don’t try anything,” Lady Black pressed her sword deeper into Vallan’s throat.

Sarod snatched the Urim and threw it to Lady Black. It bounced on the ground. The light in the crater stirred. One of the Doya opened up a crude lead box and scooped up the Urim. The Doya took the stone to Lady Black, she peered into the box, and once she was satisfied, she tucked it into a pocket of her cloak.

“Now we can go,” Rinn whispered.

The crater was dark again. Rinn and Apollo could just make out the outlines of the crowd of Doya.

Sarod pressed a claw into Lorad’s forehead. “Do you want to know how the Doomseeker got his black eyes?”

Sarod turned and looked out over the lake to look directly at Apollo.

Apollo clutched the floating door. “He can see me. He knows we’re here,” he gasped.

Sarod lifted Lorad off the ground with only his finger. Lorad cried out. Sarod hissed a word of power and the Archmage tensed. He turned his head up to scream, and foam erupted from his mouth.

Sarod shouted over the lake. "I'm pouring corrupted power into him, but it's too much. His frail body can't take it all."

"Stop." Vallan pleaded. "He's worth more to you alive."

Lorad's eyes bled black tears. His limbs flailed. He shrieked. His cries filled every ear, and then all at once, he died.

"No!" Vallan reached for Lorad. His fingers curled in knots. He wanted to destroy Sarod, his mouth opened the words to kill him were on his tongue, but he didn't have that power anymore, so he just stood there with his mouth agape.

Lady Black lowered her sword to his collarbone. He was drained, she could feel the sorrow in him. The night's events had torn down the walls that guarded his emotions, and now, she could sense his every feeling. The connection reminded her of the time she'd loved him, long ago.

Sarod bore his teeth. His throat rumbled, he huffed and blew a heavy breath that squealed through his sharp, uneven teeth. Lorad's face cracked like glass, the shards of his nose and mouth slid apart and his head dissolved. Sarod pulled back his finger and Lorad's whole body crumbled into ashes that floated like moss on the surface of the lake.

The Doya growled a guttural cheer.

Rinn squinted at Lorad's powdery remains, blinked, looked again, and whispered to Apollo. "You're right, it's time to go."

The Doya watched Sarod, and Sarod locked his attention on Apollo.

"You absorbed all of the corruption from your mother, and it changed you. You became my eyes into the Aurorean Temple. You were the link to this spell." Sarod turned to his Doya. He opened his arms and proclaimed, "The Aurorean temple is destroyed. The Doomseeker has helped bring the Order to its knees."

"Apollo!" Vallan cried. Lady Black grabbed him by his scalp, her sword returned to his throat.

Vallan pulled against her grip. "Run! Get out of here!"

Lady Black drew a spell. Vallan's skin felt as if it were tightening, he cried out in pain.

A sizable air bubble rose from the depths of the lake. It surfaced near Apollo, pushed him aside, and popped.

"Time to go," Rinn repeated.

Bubbles surfaced and burst all around them. A rancid vinegary odor gave Apollo pause. "What's that smell?"

"Something just moved past my leg," Rinn said.

Apollo and Rinn shoved the floating door aside and swam toward shore.

Sarod and his Doya watched, they were the rulers of the night, and they were waiting for him. They wanted Apollo to come to them.

"Apollo, go! Get out of here!" Vallan screamed from the ground. Lady Black loomed over him, with her hood drawn and her emerald eyes radiating. "You struggle and I hurt you, you disobey me, and I hurt you. Now, scream for me, bring your boy here."

Lady Black twisted her wrist and Vallan shrieked again. He writhed. His hands came free, he grabbed at the skin on his face.

Apollo and Rinn reached the shore, Apollo looked wearily at the bodies littering the crater floor. In the dim light, he hadn't realized just how many people the storm had killed.

Apollo walked toward Vallan, Sarod, and Lady Black farther down the shoreline, while Rinn turned the opposite direction and started to climb the crater rim. The Doya were moving toward the shore, each wanted to get a look at the Doomseeker. Sarod and Lady Black stood over Vallan as he writhed in pain.

"It's best to let him go, that's a bad plan." Rinn called out.

Apollo stopped and threw his hands up in the air. "I have no plan, go escape, you owe me nothing."

Rinn climbed up a stone and then jumped to the next. The crater wall was steep on this side, but he could climb it. "Listen to your Warlock; this is suicide. I didn't save you from the Auroreans so you could die protecting one of them."

Vallan's cries echoed off the crater walls. The Doya were closing the space between Apollo and Sarod.

Apollo called back to Rinn just paces away. "I can't turn my back on him, not again."

Rinn crouched down and spoke so only Apollo could hear. "We are bigger then this, you and I. We're Marked, maybe the only two. Come with me. Don't you have questions? Don't you want to know why the Gods made us this way? I have a way, we can find the answers together."

Rinn offered a gauntleted hand to pull Apollo up the steep slope. Apollo gave the cold, steel hand a look of caution, and stepped away.

"If I live, I'll find you again. If I don't, maybe you'll be spared a few of the prophecies of the Doomseeker," Apollo said.

Rinn gave Vallan and his captors a grimace. "I'm not going to stick my neck out for an Aurorean. I told you I'm not a hero."

"And I'm not a coward," Apollo said.

"There is bravery, and there is stupidity, Doomseeker," Rinn said, but Apollo had already turned to leave.

The Doya were focused on Apollo and Sarod. Rinn felt invisible as he crossed the crater rim and stepped into irrelevancy. He was alive, but there was a ghostly hollowness to it. He didn't know if the feeling came from the lost loot, or from leaving Apollo at the mercy of the Dark Prince.

Small waves formed in the lake, the water bubbled furiously, yet the Doya watched the Doomseeker approach Sarod.

The shore was walled by the lake on one side and Doya on the other. The Doya were drooling, spitting, Apollo could see his reflection in their eyes. They were hollow inside, shells of humans twisted and corrupted, mutated into monsters. Unlike the Corrupted at the Chasm, Apollo couldn't see them as victims of circumstance, wayward souls. They were the audience of hell, the fallen, the damned.

Vallan's cries were haunting.

Apollo's aura screamed inside of him too. His instincts as a Warlock were crying out for him to turn back, but he couldn't. Vallan was alive, and if the gods had mercy, Clara was too.

A Doya swiped its claws at him, yet Apollo didn't flinch. What was there to fear? He'd faced a Highborn dragon. He'd looked into its burning face and lived.

Apollo reached the shore where Lorad had died. He held out the Sword of Ashborn to Lady Black and dropped to a knee. "Release him. Take me if that's what you want."

Lady Black drew a spell and Vallan's screams ceased. His arms clung to his chest, his legs slid inward, and he rose up to stand at Lady Black's side as still as a stone pillar. Lady Black reached out to touch the sword. Her fingers trembled as they crossed the dragon bone hilt.

"Do you like my gift?" she asked.

"Your gift?" Apollo contested.

"The dragon blood vial was filled when humans first stepped on this world. I gave it to Osirius along with what to tell Vallan so he would take the sword from the Chasm. You can't even begin to understand its importance. Its power is yours, and in your hands, you will wield this to bring about my will, so saith the prophecy."

"I won't. I'm Marked, but I'm not evil." Apollo pushed the sword toward her.

"You act as if you have a choice." Lady Black laughed.

Sarod was beside her. Blood dripped between Sarod's chest muscles. Apollo's attention followed the streams of blood over Sarod's wide, pale neck to his bloody chin, cheek, and a pair of eyes that resonated contempt. Apollo had to look away. Sarod's gaze was a disease to his soul. Apollo's aura knotted inside him. Dread, regret, remorse, anger, and hate entangled his aura. Had he done something wrong to feel this way? Who had he killed? What terrible evil had he done? His aura was a burden in the presence of Sarod's corruption.

"I am the Prince of Darkness. I sit on a throne beneath these mountains. I am the Prince of the unseen, the outcasts, the creeping things."

Sarod ran the point of a claw over Apollo's scalp. Sarod's words boomed over the bubbling lake water and the hissing of his servants. "The Garatha says you will take that away from me."

Sarod knocked Apollo's sword from his hands and gripped him by the throat. He pulled him off his knees. His voice turned to daggers. "You are to be an evil even greater than I. You will have the power to kill the Sun God. You're fragile, weak, you're a child."

Apollo twisted his neck. Lurching under Sarod's grip for a breath, he kicked his feet to find the ground, but Sarod only held him higher. "I could squeeze and your prophecy is over." Apollo tried to scream, but nothing came out.

"Then do it," Lady Black said. "Kill the Doomseeker and let the Sun God thrive. Live forever as the Prince of Darkness." Lady Black pressed her finger into Sarod's oily chest. "Be a roach that scurries from one dark corner to the next, knowing that you could've ruled everything."

Sarod backhanded Lady Black and she fell backward.

Lady Black hit the rocky ground. She rolled until she bumped up against the corpse of a Healer that had fallen from the sky.

Sarod started to draw a spell. Vallan struggled, but his arms were still bound in dark magic.

Apollo jerked, he opened his mouth wider, but it was hopeless, Sarod's grip was too strong.

Lady Black got back to her feet and wiped fresh blood from her nose. For a brief moment, wild anger raged in her green eyes. "You want the throne of the Gods. Killing this *bastard* will only hinder your plans."

Sarod grit his teeth. He looked into Apollo's purple face and dropped him to his feet. Apollo fell to his knees and gasped for air.

Sarod spat out a wad of black blood. "You will live, but you belong to me now. Body and soul, you're mine."

Apollo stared back, helpless.

Sarod turned on Vallan. "There is fear here, can't you feel it?" Sarod ran a claw over Vallan's shoulders. "Look at this *man* you call father. Pitiful."

"Vallan is this bastard's father," Lady Black corrected.

"Lies from an Order of Lies. I've tasted his mother's blood. Your father is of far lesser blood than this man you call Vallan."

Lady Black leaned in and took a heavy whiff of Apollo's hair. She recoiled on Vallan. "What sort of trick is this?"

Vallan tried to open his mouth, but Lady Black's spell still held it shut. His eyes traveled between Sarod, Lady Black, and Apollo, his face flexed and throat tightened.

"I want the truth," Lady Black demanded Sarod, but her demands went unanswered. Sarod was too focused on Apollo.

"Vallan can't hide his fear anymore. It's potent, and you're going to drink it. You want the darkness. I saw the way you looked at Cat."

Apollo jolted. "How do you know about Cat?"

Sarod pressed his bone claw against his bloodied chest. "There is nothing you can hide from me. I watch all Doya. I see all, know all; I am your God."

The lake water was rising. A wave splashed into Apollo as he knelt on the ground.

A horn echoed through the crater. Torches lit along the rim, and a group of soldiers in red leather jerkins on horseback advanced down the crater wall.

The Doya blocked their path.

At their front was High Captain Thar, a stocky man with a long beard touting a serrated battle-ax. He halted at the wall of Doya and nodded at Vallan.

"Looks like I won the bet," Thar announced, "I told the troops you were hard to kill."

Thar turned in his saddle to address Sarod, who was the same height as Thar on horseback. "I am High Captain Thar of New Camelot. I've been wandering around for Gods know how many hours looking for an Army of Goblins. I don't suppose you've seen them?"

"What is the meaning of this interruption?" Sarod hissed.

Thar continued. "We found Goblin tracks and they lead us to these mountains. I have short legs. I'm not too keen on climbing mountains, but when I saw half the bloody temple fly across the sky, I thought: let's go up there and see what that big, old, bleedy eyed Doya is doing, it'll be fun."

Sarod pointed his broadsword at him. "My Doya will rip the flesh from your bones."

Thar's red, bushy eyebrows went up. He looked around at the barren crater, the piles of bodies heaped on one another, and the bubbling lake. "This is why you don't have any folk living up here. You're a downright vicious lot."

Thar rested his serrated battle-ax on his shoulder. "This ax here; I call her Big Momma. I broke my last good ax killing your kind. I named this one after my own mother. She was a vicious hag, short, fat, and boy could she pack a wallop."

Thar nodded at his men on his right and left. “These here are the Night Guard, and we’ve come for our Warlock. I’d say give him up and there won’t be any bloodshed, but I’m a somewhat honest man. So I won’t be mudding my reputation.” Thar waved a hand over the fallen. “Hand our people over and we’ll show you the same mercy you gave these people. We’ll throw you off this mountain and see how long it takes for you to hit the bottom.”

Sarod bared his teeth. “Kill them, Kill them, KILL THEM!”

Doya leaped onto the mounted Night Guard, claws flashing. Blood shot into the air. Gold tipped spears flew over Thar’s shoulders. They caught one Doya in the chest and it toppled over. Thar’s ax split another in two.

Apollo rolled to where Sarod had knocked his sword. A wave of lake water crashed into the wall of Doya. The water knocked the Sword of Ashborn into the battle. Apollo crawled as fast as he could. Bone claws slashed at Night Guard and swords slashed for Doya necks. Apollo reached the sword and grabbed it. There was someone else crawling on the other side of the battle. It was Clara. Her white robes were drenched with grey muck. She was moving, breathing.

“Clara!” Apollo cried. A Doya saw him. Apollo raised his sword just in time to slice off the creature’s slashing claw.

Words of power echoed around him. The Doya were about to end this fight. A few spells were all it would take to put an end to Thar and the Night Guard.

Thar jumped off his horse. He whirled his battle-ax over his head and brought it down through a Doya's arm.

Clara coughed out gritty water. She looked out across the heaps of bodies on the battlefield. Her breath caught in her throat. She heard something behind her. A deep rumble. Clara turned over and shrieked.

An enormous creature with a deformed face emerged from the lake. It was covered in black scales and splotches of wet hair. Its snout ended with snake-like slits and a mouth that bent upward, containing row after row of needlelike teeth. It was part dragon and part scorpion. Its stinger swung wildly as it skittered on eight legs toward the shore.

Sarod waved his arms to summon a spell, but nothing happened. The Doya drew spells too, but in the presence of the creature, they couldn't reach their magic.

"Bane!" Vallan cried, as the spell holding him weakened. Lady Black watched dumbfounded. Vallan pulled his sword from Lady's Black's belt and ran toward Sarod. He swung for Sarod's throat and missed. Sarod responded with a mighty swipe of his broadsword, but Vallan slammed his shoulder into him, knocking Sarod into the dirt. Sarod's head clapped off the ground.

The Doya were watching the Bane rise from the lake, now was Vallan's chance, he drew back his blade.

"You don't belong in this world. There is a throne in hell for you built of fire and thorns," Vallan said.

Sarod climbed back on his elbows. "I can't die. Every time you kill me, I only get stronger. The prophecies will be fulfilled. You will fail him, just as you failed your first son. Take a good look at what he will become."

Sarod grit his sharp teeth. Tar oozed out between them.

Lady Black looked away from the Bane. She saw Vallan with his sword drawn back and Sarod on the ground.

"Nooo!" she screamed.

Vallan's sword rang through the air. In a flash of golden steel, Sarod's neck severed and spun off his shoulders.

Apollo rushed toward Clara. The Bane reached the shallows. It jammed its scorpion stinger into a Doya. The Doya screamed as its pale skin tightened. It muscles fatigued until he was skin over bones. The Bane whipped its tail and flung the Doya over the Night Guard. It hit the crater wall and shattered like chalk.

Another Doya leaped for the Bane's back, but the Bane snatched it out of the air and crushed the Doya between its crab claws. The Doya fell in two. The upper half still screamed and tried to crawl away, until the Bane drove its stinger into the Doya's shoulder. Two more went for the Bane's belly, but it whipped its tail and sent them spiraling to crunch into the crater wall.

The Bane scurried into the heart of the battle. It snapped its claws at two Doya, the claws caught them around the shoulders. The Bane pinched them apart; blood erupted from their mangled bodies. The Bane sunk its teeth into a Night Guard. The Guard tried to scream, but only blood came out. The Bane's stinger flashed down through a Doya's scalp and drained it dry.

A Night Guard dashed for the Bane's face, spear in hand. The Guard went for the Bane's eyes, but before the Night Guard could strike, the Bane's tongue shot out, wrapped the Guard, and pulled him into its mouth. The steel of his spear squealed as it crushed between its jaws.

Lady Black turned to flee.

"You don't have to run," Vallan said.

Lady Black looked at the cut she'd slashed across Vallan's chest and the bruises on his arms. His screams were still fresh in her ears. She'd caused him so much pain, yet he still wanted her. His persistence was the power that had chiseled away the stone around her heart, but that was another time, and this was a different world.

"You want me to come back with you? Is that it?" she asked.

"We are at war with the Emperor, you could provide valuable information. The Mind Curse can't harm you. You'd be the first dissenter to ever survive. Together, we could see the end of this war. The King could grant you amnesty—"

"No," Lady Black cut him off. Her face was iron, a wall of resolve, but her eyes, those green eyes, couldn't hide her feelings. Vallan saw the conflict, the pain, and longing all bound up inside her. He felt the love, the overpowering need to be with him, and a loneliness that only he could remove. Then he felt her push it away, deep down to the smallest corner of her heart.

"But, I know you don't want this," Vallan said.

"You think everything can be like it was when the stars were young, but it can't."

Lady Black turned and shoved a soldier aside. She kicked over a Doya in her path and marched to the crater wall.

Thar chopped through a Doya and emerged from the crowd next to Vallan with Sarod's dead body at his feet.

"Awe hell, I was hoping to kill that one." Thar shrugged. "Mathus would've bought me drinks for a moon's turn."

Vallan saw more Night Guard than Doya. The Bane was gaining ground, and its stinger thirsted for mage blood.

He could see Apollo had reached Clara. They were just on the other side of the Bane, within the range of the beast's stinger.

Vallan pointed his sword at the Bane. "Stay close enough to the Bane and the Doya won't be able to cast. We just might live through this."

"You want us to say close to the demon dragon, creepy-crawly thing?" Thar asked, doubtful.

Vallan didn't hear him. He spotted Lady Black's cloak flapping on the crater rim.

Lady Black looked over the battlefield. From the rim, the Bane dwarfed the battle. It was advancing. There was only one way this fight would end. The few remaining Doya were slipping through Thar's men. Soon it would just be soldiers against the Bane. She turned to escape when she saw a man in blue armor, standing next to her.

"You have something that belongs to me," Rinn said.

"You're a sneaky one, aren't you?"

Rinn flicked his wrists and blades slid out the top of his gauntlets. He swung for Lady Black's heart. She dodged and swung her obsidian sword. Rinn parried just in time to block her glass blade from cutting through his skull.

Rinn flicked a wrist and a dart shot out. It stuck harmlessly in Lady Black's cloak.

Lady Black responded with a blow across Rinn's face. He fell and his eyepatch slid aside, exposing the moon mark around his eye.

"The Reaper," Lady Black said. A smile crossed her face. "Everything is coming together nicely."

Rinn backed away. Lady Black waved a hand and her spell slid his eye patch back over his eye. She put her finger over her lips in a silent gesture.

"I'll let you go this time," she said and with another wave of her hand, Rinn was lifted to his feet.

"You have my stone. I want it back." Rinn complained.

The Bane shriek filled the whole crater.

"Your destiny is about to be gobbled up by a Bane. Whatever you hope to learn with the stone would be meaningless if the Doomseeker dies, your destinies are intertwined."

Rinn peered down at the Bane. Apollo had his sword drawn with Clara at his back.

"What are you doing?" Rinn cursed at them.

Rinn looked back over the crater rim. Black was gone. The Shade had lost.

Clara watched the battlefield. The Doya had fled. Many of the Night Guard were injured or dead. High Captain Thar and Vallan were running toward them.

Rinn yelled and waved his arms. "We have to get out of here. Banes crave mage blood."

Apollo didn't wait for an explanation. He grabbed Clara's hand and ran for the crater wall.

Rinn met them halfway. "The Bane sucks the blood from a mage with its stinger and stings a dragon. The dragon turns into an egg sac, until the spawn breaks out of the dragon's skin and eats it."

"That's disgusting!" Clara exclaimed.

Rinn nodded. "You don't fight a Bane, not without an army, and even then, you want to be at the back of the army with everyone you don't like in front of you."

They'd almost reached the wall. The Bane jerked its head and reeled and a pair of bat-like wings unfolded from its back.

Apollo glanced over his shoulder. "It can fly?"

A gust of wind lifted dust into the air. The Bane jumped away from Vallan, Thar, and the Night Guard. It crossed over Apollo, Rinn, and Clara and blocked their path with a ground-shaking thud.

They skidded to a halt. The Bane's claws snapped with such force that Apollo's ears popped.

"How do we kill it?" Apollo asked.

"How am I supposed to know? Do you think my luck is always this bad?" Rinn replied.

Apollo looked back at the Vallan and the Night Guard, they were running to join them, but they'd be too late.

Clara struggled to remember the little she'd read on the fallen dragons. "Cut into its temple. I think. Between the eyes."

The Bane's stinger flashed between Apollo and Clara. Its tongue whipped past Rinn's face.

"We attack it at the same time," Clara said.

Rinn retreated a step. "If we all run away at the same time, we might actually live to have nightmares about this."

"Spread out," Apollo ordered.

"Give me a dagger," Clara demanded.

Rinn clicked a ruby on his gauntlet and one of his blades fell out. He handed the flat end to Clara.

Clara gripped the knife, holding it point down. She could feel her heart play like a drum in her fingertips. It felt right, natural. This was what she was born to do.

The Bane's tongue flicked out and back in. Clara got an idea. She stepped in too close and the Bane's tongue wrapped her leg. It knocked her to the ground. Its stinger came crashing down just over her shoulder.

The tongue pulled her past the snapping claws and the thrusts of the Bane's stinger. Clara was almost there. The Bane's temple was nearly in reach.

Clara slashed her blade through the Bane's slobbery tongue. The Bain screeched a cry of agony. She was close.

She rolled to her feet and thrust her dagger into the Bane's forehead, but her dagger deflected off the creature's hard scales.

The Bane's severed tongue hung out its mouth. Rinn shoved a dagger jutting from his gauntlet into the Bane's underbelly. Apollo swung the sword of Ashborn clean through a back leg.

The Bane roared. Guttural rage shook the crater. It opened its wings.

"It's fleeing," Clara cried. "Get away from it!"

"I'm stuck! My arm, it won't come out." Rinn screamed and pulled on his gauntlet. He tried to pull it off, but his hand was wedged between the Bane's scales.

"I'm coming." Apollo rolled underneath the Bane. He plunged his sword into the Bane's gut, the Bane squealed, but its wings kept flapping.

"I told you this was a bad plan!" Rinn shouted back.

"I'll get you out!" Apollo cried.

Vallan reached them, Thar was a few paces behind trying to catch up. The Night Guard filed in around the Bane.

"Get out of there. It's taking off," Vallan ordered. He tried to move in closer, but the Bane snapped at him.

"We have to kill it now, he's stuck," Clara shouted, pointing at Rinn.

The Night Guard drew their bows.

Apollo grabbed Rinn's legs and pulled, but just as he did, the Bane lifted into the sky. They circled the crater.

Clara, Vallan, everyone below vanished into the darkness. The Bane tilted into a dive.

"Oh Gods, I hate heights." Rinn covered his eyes.

They dropped between a gap in the mountains, and into the mouth of a cave.

"My arm is coming loose," Rinn warned Apollo.

Apollo looked down. It was so dark, he couldn't tell how far down the ground was.

Rinn's arm came free. They both tumbled on the cave floor.

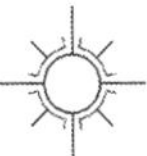

The pitch-blackness of the cave was a fog of uncertainty. A nightmare, but Apollo knew he was awake. His heart echoed in his ears and seemed to make the whole mountain shake underneath him.

Rinn's trembling voice found a way through the darkness. "It's in here with us."

"Where?" Apollo crouched down and felt the chilly cave floor.

Rinn panicked. "I can't see anything. Where's the door? I have to get out of here."

"Shhh, it will hear you," Apollo cautioned.

Apollo heard pattering feet on his right. "I can hear you. Stop moving!"

"I'm not a mage, I'm not even a soldier. I'm a thief. I kill people when they can't see me. I am the upper hand. I can't die like this, not here. Not in a cave in some mountain that no one knows. I can't be eaten, I can't be nothing, don't you understand? This isn't for me. I'm not supposed to be here."

"Quiet! I need you to get control. I can see in the dark, but I need you to get control of your fear."

"You think I'm afraid? I…I'm not afraid of anything," Rinn squeaked.

Rinn's fear was sludge, a quicksand that suffocated Apollo's aura.

"Think of something else," Apollo said.

"What are you talking about? We have to escape. We can't just will this beast away. We have to do something."

A rock clapped against the stone floor. The sound echoed off every wall. The Bane could be anywhere. Apollo didn't know where to turn.

"It's coming for us." Rinn's feet clamored against the cave floor. He bumped into Apollo and they both fell backward into a wall.

Apollo could hear Rinn breathing.

"Do you have any more tricks in those gauntlets?" Apollo asked.

"I have a dart, but it won't penetrate the armor."

A scraping sound came from the ceiling. Apollo unfocused his eyes; his Darksight took over. The textures of the cave rushed into view. The ground was cooled stone, layers and layers of dried lava. The ceiling was an open mouth, the dripstones were teeth, and Apollo and Rinn were at the back of the mouth, and there was no throat to escape to, no side passage, just a flat immovable wall, and they were pressed against it.

Then Apollo saw it, the Bane's stinger rubbing against the ceiling, bumping between dripstones, coming closer, but that didn't seem to matter. There was something else in the cave. A presence, a desire, richness oozing from Rinn.

Apollo could see Rinn's pulse in his face. Fear was ringing throughout the cave. The Bane was the bell clapper and Rinn's chest was shaking like a bell.

"Your fear is so rich, so strong."

"I told you…I'm not afraid," Rinn said.

Apollo tried to push the temptation out of his mind, but the power was so intense, and the darkness absolute, if he drew energy from them, he'd have enough power to bring the cave down on the monster.

The Bane was getting closer. He could feel the Remnant in its blood. It knocked against his aura. The Bane sniffed the air, it could smell them, and they had nowhere to run.

"I can see the Bane, it's coming for us." Apollo could feel Rinn's fear intensify.

"You're the Doomseeker. Do something!"

"I can use your fear," Apollo whispered.

"My fear? Like you're not afraid. You're the mage, did you see what it did to those Doya?"

Apollo didn't hear him. He was caught in Rinn's torrent of fright. He would have to use it soon. He was losing his connection to his aura.

Apollo remembered the pale flesh of Lurk in the Chasm. The black spider veins. Cat's rotting fingers. He couldn't use the evil power it would corrupt him, but what if he used it just this one time.

No one became a Doya from a single spell.

Rinn frantically pressed the jewels on his gauntlets, but nothing happened, he was out of daggers, and chords, and tricks. All he had was a knock out dart.

Rinn peered into the darkness. "I don't care what you do. I swear to the Titans, get me out of this and I'll never steal anything ever again."

Apollo didn't have a choice. He couldn't let Rinn die, not after he'd saved him from Purification. Wouldn't that be the greater sin?

The Bane snapped its claws at a thin bolder about the size of Apollo's head, it broke clean in half. The Bane smelled the cracked rock. It ran it's severed tongue over it, hissed and kept prowling.

There was only one way out of this. No. Absorbing darkness was wrong. Still, it could save them, but he had to do it now.

What would he become?

The Bane bared its teeth. Blood bubbled from its abdomen. Its two claws snapped blindly in the darkness. It had their scent. It was moving straight for them. It lowered its stinger to hover just over its head.

Apollo grit his teeth as he waited for his aura to slip away.

"I'm not a monster," Apollo whispered to himself.

"The monster is about to eat us," Rinn replied.

The stinger was just out of reach. Apollo held his sword up. He grabbed Rinn's arm and pointed his gauntlet in the Bane's face.

The Bane was just feet away, silently creeping. Apollo looked up to see the stinger overhead.

Apollo gripped his sword in both hands. "When I say, shoot."

Rinn's arm quivered. "Is it close?"

The Bane flexed its stinger. The point was just over Rinn's skull.

The prophecy suddenly made sense. Apollo spoke to the creature. "You are the one I'm to kill. The lost child of the gods, the Dragon Gods, and I am…I am the Doomseeker."

The Bane's stinger flicked over Apollo's head. It hissed, and its tail shot down. Apollo sidestepped the flashing stinger. It slammed into the ground, and Apollo brought the Sword of Ashborn down on it. The stinger sliced open. The Bane opened its mouth and roared.

"Now!" Apollo cried.

Rinn shot his dart. It flew into the back of the Bane's throat. The Bane choked and fell on its back legs. Apollo dashed toward its teeth. The Bane snapped its claw and missed. Apollo thrust the point of his sword into the Bane's temple. The sword split scale, bone, and brains, Apollo twisted his blade and the beast collapsed.

35

Hyperion – Atlantis

Vega reclined in a padded velvet chair on a pier. He placed his feet on a footstool, and a young Mayan slave, tied her hair back, and rubbed Castor oil on his feet. On her forehead, in her unblemished skin, was a sloppy brand that read 751.

"You've gotten better at that," Vega said as he flexed his toes.

"Thank you, Your Majesty."

"You are even better than my last house slave," Vega added.

"You are too kind, Your Grace."

Vega watched her press the oil between his toes. She had a purpose working. That should make her happy. What did it matter if she was a slave? He made her whole.

"Would you ever run away 751? If you could, would you leave me?"

"Where would I go, Your Majesty?" 751 asked.

Her answer brought a smile to Vega's face. "You haven't anywhere else to go." His smile rotted. "But neither did my last house slave and she abandoned me. She ran away to New Camelot. Their people have killed more Mayans than any of the other kingdoms. Wasn't her life complete by tending to my needs? Isn't your life complete?"

"Your Grace treats me better than any of the other slaves. I have a bed and I'm fed," 751 answered.

"The Scientists are ready, Your Majesty," chimed a short, bald, self-important man. Vega didn't know who he was. His wrinkly baldhead made the Emperor's lip curl.

"Hurry it up, and for Gods sake, send me someone I can stand to look at."

"Your Majesty?" the bald man asked, confused. "Have I offended you in some way?"

"Your bare head offends me. It's disgraceful for one so old to bare so much skin. Send me someone with hair, I want to see young people, attractive people, like myself."

The bald man's face flushed. "As…as Your Majesty demands."

Atlantis, the city of the future, that's what they called it, but Vega thought that sentiment was driven more by Atlantian arrogance than accomplishment. Each time he visited Atlantis, the Society of Science would try and dazzle him with their latest contraption.

Vega couldn't deny the magnificence of the city. It was second only to Tarboroth, but Tarboroth was cursed. Humans who had tried to inhabit the ancient city always died in their sleep.

Tarboroth was behind him, out across the channel, hidden in a cloud of mist that never receded. It was a confounding place, protected by the Elves even millennia after their disappearance.

The Oculus, the islands that made up the city of Atlantis, was placed between the Northern and Southern continents. It was the center for trade and a feat of human ingenuity.

At its center was the Agora of Atlas, a boxy building with an absurd amount of waterfalls. The Atlantians created bridges between several islands, so the city was a great bull's eye in the middle of the sea.

A younger man dressed in a tightly fitted coat and silver pants addressed the Emperor.

"Your Majesty, I want to present what I call the Sky Drifter," said the man.

He gestured to a brightly colored round tent of fabric on the edge of the dock. It was a large balloon with a basket on the bottom.

It looked like a giant multicolored pimple.

Vega didn't see the point of it. Why would he ever need a basket in the sky?

The man in silver pants climbed inside the basket.

"Your Majesty, we have developed a means to fly." The scientist looked quite pleased with himself, but Vega was more interested in his foot massage than any flying machine.

"I'll pull this cord, and this burner will create a burst of flame that will lift the basket off the ground."

Sure enough, the scientist pulled the cord to some metal contraption and the basket lifted a foot off the ground.

"Fascinating," Vega grumbled.

The scientist adjusted the pin on his lapel, the owl of Athena, and straightened his coat.

"Now, I will do what has never been done before. Today I will use my Sky Drifter to lift me into the heavens, and I will ascend above the clouds.

Vega blinked. Above the clouds of Atlantis swarmed his army of dragons. They were ordered to keep out of sight. This half-wit scientist would dangle from his balloon in his silver pants, and be served up in his basket as an afternoon snack.

Maybe his presentation wouldn't be that dull after all.

The scientist struck a triumphant pose and pulled the Balloon's cord. His basket gradually lifted up into the air.

Cain marched down the pier carrying a glowing sack.

"That man's a damn fool," Cain said as he watched the onlookers cheer for the scientist.

"With all of these dreamers about, I'm starting to think we're the only two sane people in this city," Vega looked at Cain. His shirt was open showing the slave numbers tattooed in tiny print all over his chest.

"That worries me," Vega added.

A Mayan slave came running down the pier. He reached the Emperor and dropped to his knees.

"Sire, there is a message, your Witching Bone calls for you."

The slave held out a small bleached knuckle bone leaking a steady stream of dark smoke that spread over the slave's hand and fell between his fingers.

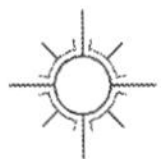

The Emperor led Alaric into a dark room. Alaric lit a candle and the Emperor took the bleached Witching bone from his pocket and placed it on the table.

The bone hissed out smoke and shivered against the table's surface. The cloud of smoke contorted like a black bubble until it morphed into the profile of a hooded figure, a woman with green glowing eyes, and somehow the cloud spoke.

"Your Majesty, I bring news that will please you," said the woman.

"Black, I am in Atlantis scavenging Tarboroth for fairies because you failed to bring me the Seer Stones in time. I have a path cut through Ironwood directly to the foot of the Evertree, all I need is the stones you've promised me." The Emperor turned spiteful. "If you've failed me, by the gods, I swear I will leave your punishment to Cain."

"I have the Urim," said Lady Black's shadow.

"And the other? Did you retrieve the Thummim from the Aphotic Temple?"

"The Goblins are searching for the Aphotic temple, but there have been complications."

"We don't have time for complications, Black—"

"Sarod is dead," Black interjected.

"What!?" Alaric shouted. "How? How was he killed?" Alaric turned to the Emporer. "Is she sure he's dead? Did she see him die? Your Majesty, if Sarod is dead then— "Alaric stopped abruptly.

"Then we won't have to kill him ourselves," the Emperor concluded.

Alaric's voice turned shrill. "No, he'll come back, he always comes back,"

"Calm yourself," the Emperor said, irritated. "Sarod would've betrayed us. He was after the Breastplate as well. It's better this way."

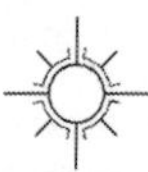

Miriam drummed her fingers on a book. She liked the sound it made, it kind of sounded like horses. She hated horses, but she'd be willing to ride about any horse if it was going in the direction of New Camelot and out of Alaric's grim study.

She'd even gotten tired of listening to the waterfalls. They were soothing, but now they only made her have to pee, and being chained to a desk was terribly inconvenient for one who felt like they had the whole ocean trapped in their bladder.

"By the gods, if that half-wit doesn't come back soon, I'm going to piss right here on—"

Miriam looked at the spine of the book she was holding.

"Wythrin's Poems Volume 2," she read aloud.

Volume two, she couldn't figure out why there was a volume one. Wythrin had no equal when creating enchantments, but when it came to rhyming, his lyrics were terribly awkward.

If it was half as bad as Volume 1, then it deserved to be pissed on.

Miriam tossed the book aside and slumped on the table. The Elves didn't have the answer. That much was certain, she couldn't find any reference to any Mind Curse in any of her memorized tomes or in the pile of books that she'd tossed to the floor.

The Mind Curse had been around as long as the Emperor, that's all she'd learned in a month of being shackled to a desk in a godforsaken study where the waterfalls never stopped, they just trickled all day, it was torture.

Maybe Alaric had finally figured out a way to get even. She'd been testing the limits of his sanity. Was he fighting back with trickling water and poetry?

Gods, he was an evil creature.

Miriam looked around the room. It was dark and there were several tapestries on the walls, and of course, the waterfalls. But there were also carvings. Stories etched into the stone above the bookcases.

On one wall, there was a particularly loud, obnoxious waterfall built into a carving. She'd given it stink eye for several hours a day and now she was staring at it, again.

Poking out from the wall was the carving of the Oculus. The ringed city of Atlantis, but the waterfall was running over it. Miriam had read about how Atlantis was destroyed. It's said that the whole city was swallowed in a day, and from the way the waterfall crashed into the carving, Miriam could believe it. After all, this was the second Atlantis, all of the cities on Haven were built anew on top of ruins of Elven cities.

Several of the kingdoms wouldn't accept it. Every kingdom was saved from some untimely demise. Atlantis was saved from the sea. Enoch, Camelot, and Salem were saved from wars, Mayans from extinction. They were all rescued by some higher power, a god perhaps, yet they wouldn't admit it. Miriam had learned that long ago when she'd arrived in New Camelot as a young girl and asked where Old Camelot was. The Grandmaster Oracle, at the time, had set her story straight. She'd told them that humans came from another place, another existence.

The last to arrive were the Mayans, they appeared as nomads at first, seemingly out of thin air. The King of Havilah promised them lands in Enoch. In return, he was immersed in a culture he didn't quite understand.

That's when the Emperor showed up. Miriam didn't know where he came from. He wasn't from Enoch, he wouldn't age rapidly, and his skin wasn't dark like hers, so he couldn't be from Shem. He could've come from Hyperion, or maybe Avalon. But Miriam suspected that somewhere in all of her history books covering the Emperor's rise to power someone would've mentioned his homeland, yet there was nothing.

The Emperor appeared near the same time as the Mayans, maybe he was Mayan? He didn't look Mayan, but from what she'd read, it seemed like Emperor Vega had an intimate knowledge of the Mayans when they first arrived on Haven.

Miriam looked back at the carving on the wall. The old Atlantis looked much like the new Atlantis. It had several docks and was surrounded by boats, the rings of the Oculus lead to a great building in the center that looked like the one Miriam was in now, and on the edges of the city, floating about as if they were protecting it were men and woman in white robes. They had wings that came out of their back and on their heads were golden crowns, halos.

Miriam had seen such figures before, they were never mentioned in Elven texts, but Arthur spoke of them in his journals.

Arthur called them his protectors, his deliverers.

Then it dawned on her, Miriam had seen these figures before, these angels. They were plastered all over the Sanctuary. Arthur had commissioned the building. He'd had them placed in every mural and above every door.

Every one of them wore white, and they too had halos, thin crowns on their head.

Just like the Emperor.

Alaric pushed open the door to the study. He had a far off look in his eyes, and he itched at one of his gloved hands.

"It's about time, I've had to pee for hours, and your cursed waterfalls aren't helping."

Alaric didn't hear her. He walked past and slumped in the chair at his desk. He opened the drawer and pulled out his vial of Bane blood and dropped it around his neck.

"Take me to the privy and I'll tell you what I've learned," Miriam was getting desperate.

Alaric still didn't seem to hear her.

"I know where the Emperor gets his power from, but I'm not talking until I get to take a piss."

Alaric itched his hand. Miriam snatched Wythrin's Poems Volume two and hurled it at him. Alaric batted it away.

"His power is in the crown on his head," Miriam said. "You've never seen him without it, have you? He always wears that thin gold ring on his head. It's what he's using to cast the Mind Curse."

"We're too late," Alaric said.

Miriam got to her feet. "Too late? Too late for what? The privy never closes."

Alaric winced and pulled off his glove. He held out his hand, Miriam didn't look the least bit surprised. The skin on his fingers from his knuckles to his fingertips was gone, scratched off, and his finger bones had turned sharp.

"That's what you get for meddling in Corruptive Magic," Miriam scolded. "What did you think would happen?"

Alaric still didn't hear her.

"I'm a dead man," Alaric's face was white. The few strands of hair he had were gone.

"Your eyes aren't black yet," Miriam said.

"No, you don't understand. I made a deal with Sarod. I paid the price for the instructions on how to construct the Breastplate. The price was me, my body."

"You sold your body to Sarod for instructions on how to build the Breastplate of Decision?" Miriam asked, aghast.

"It was foolish."

"It was a good deal, I'm surprised Sarod fell for—"

"It was foolish," Alaric insisted. He sunk deeper in his chair. "Now Sarod is dead, and I am his next vessel. He's going to take me, I'll be his tool, his next body.

Alaric looked wide-eyed into the dark corners of the room as if the shadows were a beast looking back at him.

"He's coming for me."

36

Avalon - New Camelot

"Where is the rest of the Council? Where is Apollo?" Mathus shouted.

Durakos opened his eyes. Through a haze of confusion, he looked up from the ground at the Lord Marshall. Healers weaved spells over him. Their rhythmic speech was a song that made him feel weary. He just needed more sleep, that was all. His eyelids slid closed.

"Where is the Council?" Mathus insisted.

Durakos jolted awake. The Lord Marshall was over him, in his face. His armored shoulders took up his whole vision.

"Where are they?" Mathus demanded.

Durakos' head throbbed. He scratched at the back of his neck. Dried blood collected under his fingernails. He'd hit his head. He could remember that. And the Doomseeker had stolen the sword. He had been in the temple. There had been darkness and the Doomseeker and his Reaper had attacked him.

"The Doomseeker attacked us," Durakos said.

"Apollo? You were beaten by a fifteen-year-old boy?" Mathus said.

"Clara betrayed us." Durakos spit out blood.

"A fifteen-year-old and a Healer?" Mathus frowned.

"There was a third, an invisible man."

Mathus rolled his eyes. "What about the Council?"

Durakos' jaw hung open. "I…I don't know."

A soldier emerged from the temple rubble with Grandmaster Leteah in his arms. He laid her down next to Durakos. The Healers swarmed around her. They drew frantic spells. Master Reuben pushed through the soldiers and took his place with the Healers. "We have to get them to the Sanctuary."

"I need answers," Mathus insisted. "Where is Grandmaster Daynin? He's on the Council."

Reuben motioned for a group of soldiers with stretchers to lift Leteah and Durakos.

"Daynin is no longer the leader of the Healers," he said.

"Why? Where is he, I want to speak with him," Mathus insisted.

Reuben cracked his crooked jaw as he thought of what to say. "He was trapped in the Collective mind like the rest of the Healers when Sarod's spell ripped the temple open. He was in the temple, but I cannot sense him anymore."

Reuben turned and left. Mathus watched the soldiers carry Leteah and Durakos through the square, a graveyard of bodies and blood splattered marble.

They reached the top of the Sanctuary stairs. He'd stood on those stairs not seven hours ago and watched helplessly as chunks of temple marble were thrown into fleeing crowds. He'd seen a boulder erase an entire family. Their shrill cries still echoed in his ears.

Mathus had sent a man to do a body count an hour ago. He still hadn't returned.

Mathus stood on top of a mound of crushed temple rock. Willow joined him. Her braid was undone, and her face was covered in soot. She had to be exhausted, but her demeanor was as hard and focused as ever.

Mathus took the lock of Ele's hair from around his neck and rolled it between his fingers.

"How can we fight a god?" he asked Willow.

He'd failed Ele. Her lock of hair was a token of his inadequacy and no matter how much he wanted to, he couldn't go back and change the past.

He'd failed the city too.

"How can we fight a god?" he asked again.

He surveyed the northern side of the temple. It had been torn open, exposing four floors to the open air. "Only a god could do that. I had walls, thousands of swordsmen and pikemen; I had eight-thousand archers. Tell me what demon must I barter with? What power can kill a god?"

"The Doomseeker is said to be a god-slayer. They even say he will take Sarod's throne," Willow said.

"Apollo? You think that boy has the power to kill Sarod?" Mathus asked.

"The Order fears him. Maybe there is some truth to it, but what is worse: the enemy we know, or the enemy we don't?"

The city was wounded, and he had to stop the bleeding. Sarod's spell had cut a hole in the heart of the city, the dragons had scorched most of Westport, and the main gate had been crushed under Marbor's feet. And the people, the lifeblood of the city, cowered in their homes, were trapped under rubble, or were dead in the street.

Where was the count? How many men, women, and children had they lost? How many Healers had been trampled or killed with debris before they broke out of their trance? How would they tend to all of the injured? Where would they put the homeless?

"Do I have a body count yet?" Mathus shouted from the mound. No one answered.

The King's Private Guard, Sir Lortan, approached the mound. His long Pendragon gold hair hung over his shoulders and he was still dressed in his full plate. "Lord Mathus, a word. It's about His Majesty."

Mathus frowned. "The King will have to wait."

"My Lord—"

"If King Amr wants my attention, have him send some of his nobles to help the people instead of hiding in their homes."

"But my Lord—"

Mathus marched down the mound. "Did you not hear me? Don't you see the people bleeding in the street?"

"Lord Marshall, The King hasn't sent aid because he can't."

Sir Lortan approached Mathus. His words were a ghost's whisper. "The King is dead."

Mathus grabbed Sir Lortan and pulled him away from the crowds.

"Dead? I have no reports of dragons or debris breaching the castle wall."

"I will show you."

Sir Lortan led Mathus between the boulders in the square. They past Healers and afflicted, and moved through the ranks of dead lined up in front of the castle. The Castle gate carried its usual horrid stench, but now it mixed with the salty stink of blood and flies hummed around them.

They passed through the castle gate and navigated side passages until they came to a solid steel door locked shut with three different locks.

Sir Lortan turned. "The smell is going to get a lot worse."

Sir Lortan unlocked each of the three locks with different keys. He pulled open the door and led Mathus inside.

Mathus could taste the acidic stench of what smelled like vinegar and filth.

Light poured in through the stained glass window, through the dust in the air to rest on a monstrous heap of gleaming onyx stone. The stained glass window took up a whole wall. It wasn't polished on this side, and the dragon depicted in the glass appeared backward, but Mathus still recognized it. He'd seen the window from the city square countless times.

A flash of silver light caught his attention. A sword stuck out from the heap of onyx.

"Excalibur, King Arthur's own sword," said Sir Lortan.

Mathus stepped onto the black heap.

"Careful!"

The onyx shifted. Mathus jumped back.

Mathus followed the ridges of the heap. He saw a huge black crab claw anchored to the floor. Then several hind legs curled up under a gut. His eyes trailed past the legs to a tail. At the end, there was a point, an insect stinger. Iron clamps and chains held the creature to the floor.

Mathus looked at the opposite side of the creature. A big yellow eye glared at him through an iron mask.

"It's a Bane," Sir Lortan said.

The beast was bound, Mathus was safe, but he still felt his blood go cold. He remembered the shriek, the cry that scared the dragons off. He'd sent his Night Guard throughout the city to find a beast capable of such a savage roar, but they'd found nothing.

The beast was hidden behind the stained glass window in plain sight.

"Arthur placed the Bane here, to keep the city protected from dragons," said Sir Lortan.

"It's lain there for thousands of years?" Mathus asked.

"The Pendragons have cared for it for as long as this castle has been standing. King Amr was its caretaker..."

Sir Lortan led Mathus around the creature's claw to its head. Its jaws were held shut in the iron mask.

"The mask can be opened with a lever. It's how the Bane is fed. When the dragons attacked, King Amr opened the mask and stabbed the Bane in the mouth. Its screech scared the dragons off, but when the King tried to close the mask, the Bane wrapped him with its tongue and pulled him inside its mouth."

"It ate him?" Mathus cringed.

Sir Lortan answered with a heavy nod.

"You're saying the King scared the dragons off? He saved all of us?"

"I was here. The King trusted me with all of his affairs. The Bane must be looked after. King Amr had a successor named, Wislan Pendragon."

Mathus nodded stiffly. Wislan cared for mages and nobles. The people bleeding in the street were nothing to him.

"I have not informed anyone of the King's wishes." Sir Lortan held out a piece of rolled parchment. It was sealed shut with the King's seal.

Mathus took it.

"Why are you telling me this?" he asked.

"Wislan is a mage, not a soldier. This Bane has kept us safe from dragons for centuries. Wislain is a Purist, he would have it killed on principle. The interests of his

Order would be put before our people. New Camelot needs a King, not an Aurorean puppet."

Mathus nodded. He grabbed a stool and set it in front of the Bane's large yellow eye. He stared at it and the Bane stared back. His eyes went to the parchment in his hands. It was all the proof Wislan needed to take the throne.

"You have the power of the army." Lortan continued.

"And that makes it right?" Mathus asked.

"In war, the best decision isn't always the moral one."

Mathus gazed out through a crack in the stained glass window. The square was pulverized with chunks of blood-spattered temple rock. The temple had a gaping hole in it, a cloud of smoke lingered over Westport, and the main gate was a mound of rubble.

How many had died? He still didn't know.

The parchment tore in Mathus' grip. Once, then again, he ripped until it was in bits on the floor.

"How will I gain the support of the nobles?" Mathus asked.

"The pirates King Amr appointed nobles, they'll need a demonstration of power."

"And Arthur's ancestors, the rightful heirs to the throne, how will I convince them?" Mathus asked.

"There will be opposition, Wislain has a strong claim, but you will have one thing that Wislain will not." Lortan nodded to the sword in the Bane's back. Mathus rose from the stool and stepped onto the Bane's claw. It growled and shifted, but Mathus kept his balance. He walked up its arm and onto its back to where Excalibur was sheathed between its shiny, black scales.

The hilt was yellow, black, and red; the colors of the Pendragon crest. The fine steel glistened almost white.

Mathus gripped the handle. He slid the blade out of the Bane's wound. The Bane grunted and jerked, but the chains held it in place. Mathus let the sunlight hit the white blade and glisten with power.

"My King." Sir Lortan dropped to a knee.

"You are now a High Captain in my Night Guard." Mathus declared. He looked out over the Bane and through the stained glass at the broken city. "First, we mend our people, then we rebuild."

"What about the Dragons and Sarod?" Lortan asked.

"We're safe from dragons, for now," Mathus answered.

"And Sarod? What if he attacks again?"

Mathus remembered the family he'd seen crushed under temple rock. The piles of dead in the square. Apollo's mother. And Ele.

Mathus swung Excalibur, the Bane flinched as the blade rang in the empty air.

"We'll give him the bloody battles he's dreamed of. We will drag him from his mountain. He will pay for his crimes against New Camelot. He will answer to me."

37

Hyperion – Atlantis

The suns came though the peach glass of the Emperor's bedchamber. He blinked awake. Another day in Atlantis, another day to live, he thought.

Cain had captured more of the Oathbreaker Fairies, but not enough for him to leave. Atlantis would be his home, for now.

Vega tried to push himself up to sit, but his arms buckled under him. He looked down, skin hung off his bones. His muscles were old bands of leather straining under his skin. He grabbed a glowing jar containing a fairy from his bedside table. Vega unscrewed the lid, reached inside, and stuffed the fairy in his mouth.

He let the creature struggle for a moment. The fairy ran over his tongue and pressed its hands into the sides of his cheek.

He bit down and felt the fairy's hands grab tiny handfuls of the inside of his cheek. Gradually, the fairy's fingers went limp.

In moments, Vega's arms were strong again. He flung his covers aside and looked out the window at Atlantis.

The peach window made the outside look like a moving picture drawn on parchment. Vega watched the paddles of a steamboat cycle as it turned out toward the mists of Tarboroth. Atlantians were walking the streets. The men strolled proudly in their tightly fitted clothes with walking canes. The women, the wealthy ones, wore straining gurtles and wide dresses. He saw a woman in a wig the size of a beehive and another fanning herself with a peacock feather.

Haven was a world of magic and dragons, and mysteries. Vega had learned to call it his homeland. Earth was so different. And Atlantis was even stranger. They did things, wonderfully impossible things, with machines that he only thought possible with magic, and that scared him.

Magic was easy to contain. Few could wield its power. Anyone could use knowledge against him. Ideas and contraptions were dangerous.

Slave 751 entered with her dark hair braided with flowers and a velvet dress wrapped around her slim frame.

Vega gave her an approving smile.

"My robe," he held out his arms and 751 took his robe from the wardrobe and draped it over his shoulders.

Vega sat down at a table facing a mirror that reached from the floor to the ceiling. He tossed his locks of thick, black hair over his shoulders and 751 reached for a brush.

"You look so young this morning," 751 said as she pulled the brush through his hair.

The Emperor took a hard look in the mirror. He did look young, but there was something different about him. He needed a shave, but that wasn't it. Maybe it was his hair. There was something about his hair, his brow. His crown.

The Emperor snatched the slave's wrist and squeezed.

His face boiled as he stared at himself in the mirror.

"What have you done?" he growled through gnashed teeth.

751 whimpered under his grip.

"Emperor, Sire." 751 winced. "I've done nothing, I swear."

Vega was still staring at himself. His crown was gone.

"Where is it? What have you done with it?"

He dragged her behind him to the bed and flung the covers back.

"It's not here. Where is it?"

She shook her head and Vega slapped her onto the floor. He looked frantically from one corner of the room to the next. It was gone.

He rushed toward 751. She crawled backward on her elbows.

"I want it back! Bring me Cain. I want him now!"

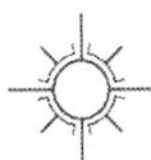

A sailor slid down the middle mast. He dropped to the ship's shroud and descended the ropes. When he reached the bottom, he jumped triumphantly to the main deck.

"Bring me some tea," Miriam ordered.

"What?" the sailor responded.

"Don't you know what tea is?" Miriam rolled her eyes.

The sailor scratched his shaggy beard. He looked down over the rough battle scars across his chest and the jagged sword hanging from his belt. He was sure that he was dressed the part of a pirate.

"I'm a pirate, not a serving boy," he spat.

"To me, you are all boys, and you're a sprite one at that. Now get me some tea before I tell the rest of the crew about the unsavory advances you've made on a kind, old woman."

"What? I never—"

"It doesn't really matter, does it? I wonder what sort of pirate nickname you'll have then."

The sailor stood there with his mouth agape.

"First Mate Biddy?"

The pirate swallowed.

"Bag boy, the Crone Catcher?"

The pirate hung his head. "All right."

Miriam turned triumphantly and walked up the stairs to the quarterdeck. Once she was sure that she was alone, she opened the pack slung over her shoulder.

"Soon, we'll be back in the library, beyond evil's reach, and the world will change."

Miriam looked down at the golden halo in her pack. The tool the Angels used to bring people to Haven. The Emperor's crown.

38

Avalon - The Black Mountains

The cliffs of the Black Mountains had a rugged, unnatural look that set them apart from the world. Looking out across the landscape at the first rising sun, Apollo felt as if he were standing on a thundercloud, looking down on the valley below.

Apollo turned to Vallan and Clara at his sides. "Can the darkness have beauty?" he asked.

Clara gazed over the ridges of the mountains. The light of the first Sun, Alpha, crossed over Avalon. They watched it cross the river Bassas, then through the Gaia forest, until it stretched to touch the distant walls of New Camelot.

Apollo and Clara could feel the sun on their skin, but the dark shale and black cliffs of the mountains were so lightless that they only permitted ghostly shadows.

Clara took Apollo's arm and laid her head on his shoulder.

"As a Purist, I would say that all darkness is evil, but I saw the Council try to cut you up. I found a glimmer of humanity in a Doya that I, a Healer, kept alive so I could create a poison. A thief who tried to steal the Urim, saved my life. The prophets say that you will kill the Sun God and I'm here with you even though I know prophecies are never wrong."

Clara released a heavy breath and looked up into Apollo's eyes. "Can darkness have beauty? What was right and wrong was so clear, but now I doubt; I have questions, and I can't figure out if that's more liberating or frightening."

Vallan lifted a hand so he could feel the sun's rays pass between his fingers. "I believe life is about seeking the answers we can't find in a prophecy, scripture, or our elders. Can darkness be beautiful? There can be no light without shadow, but there can be darkness without light. All good things have light and darkness to them. It's the duty of the Order to keep that balance."

"That's why there are Light and Dark Mages?" Apollo asked.

Vallan nodded. "Long ago, in the time of the Elves, the Aurorean and Aphotic were one Order, but that is a tale for another day."

Captain Thar and his men were camped at the far end of the ridge. Thar cupped his hands over his mouth and addressed the group. "I want to go home. What I mean to say is: I'm out of mead and I can't have a proper breakfast without it, so pack up your gear and let's get out of this godforsaken place. I owe a pint to every soldier who killed a Doya."

The soldiers cheered half-heartedly, they'd lost so many in the battle.

"When will Sarod return?" Apollo asked.

"He lost his body, it will take time to prepare another," Vallan said. "Last night, he suffered a great defeat, most of his Doya are dead. He won't command that kind of power again."

Vallan turned back to Apollo and Clara. "We will follow the Night Guard at midday. I've convinced Captain Thar that you and Clara carry a disease that could affect the army. We will travel separately, and when we get to New Camelot, I'll go into the city, alone, and retrieve more Thetus Mud for Apollo to hide his marks."

"What sort of sickness?" Clara asked curiously.

"Sweat Mites."

Clara pointed a finger in Vallan's face. "Sweat Mites aren't a disease, they're tiny bugs that crawl into your pores. They're gross—"

Vallan interrupted her. "Apollo can't march with the army. Not with his marks exposed."

Apollo couldn't do this, not again. He wasn't going to go from inn to inn hiding in empty rooms, watching the world thrive through windowpanes. It was cowardice, fear, defeat; the world knew he existed. His life had changed forever. There was no going back. Why couldn't Vallan see that?

"You think I can keep this all a secret?" Apollo threw up his arms. "I was captured by Warlocks. I killed Gibnar."

"Grandmaster Leteah saw the whole thing," Clara added.

Vallan's tone left no room for argument. "We can make it work. You killed Gibnar defending yourself. The Council will have to appoint new leaders. They will be more understanding. If not, we will travel to Shem. There are places we can hide you there."

"I don't want the approval of the Council, and I don't want to go to Shem. I'm done hiding," Apollo returned.

Vallan scratched at his beard. It was longer than Apollo had ever seen it. He couldn't help but think it made Vallan look old. How long had he lived? Centuries? Millennia? He didn't know. It was Vallan's well-kept secret, and if anything, it proved that Vallan could keep a secret forever.

If he followed Vallan back to New Camelot, he could be hidden away. He'd grow old, while Vallan never aged. He'd be a prisoner to his marks. The world would remember him as the Doomseeker who helped the Doya destroy the Aurorean temple and kill the Council, the fool who was tricked and brought the wrath of Marbor on New Camelot, and so long as there was scripture his name would be cursed. No one would see him as the hero who defeated the Bane.

Vallan's eyes traveled from one of Apollo's marks to the other. "I'll speak with the soldiers. In a few hours, we'll follow them back to the city." Before they could argue, Vallan turned and marched to the soldier's camp.

Clara let go of Apollo's arm as she watched the second sun break over the horizon. "Leteah and Durakos, they'll influence whoever is chosen to replace the fallen Grandmasters. Purists will replace Gibnar, Harthor, and the Archmage. Then they'll hunt you, and the other Marked. You're their devil, and they won't let you go."

"I know," Apollo replied.

With Omega, the second sun, came another shadow. Apollo looked down at his second faint shadow stretching out over the ground. His first shadow looked as if it reached down the path after Vallan. The other trailed off in another direction, into the unknown.

"The Doomseeker was never meant to be a Warlock's lapdog," said a voice. Apollo and Clara jumped. Rinn appeared next to them.

"You faced a dragon to protect a city. You killed a Bane, yet with all of your good deeds, you still fulfilled the first prophecy." Rinn propped his foot up on a rock and looked off into the distance. "You stood in the fire. You were swallowed in the wind and brought to this godforsaken place and fought a fallen dragon. The Order has become weak. The Urim, the most prized possession of the Aurorean order, was lost and there wasn't a damn thing you could do about it."

Apollo looked back down at his two shadows. "There's no escaping the prophecy. What's your point?"

Rinn folded his arms and drummed his fingers on his bicep. "What if you knew the result of every tiny decision before you made it. Wouldn't that give you the power to change destiny?"

Rinn's silver-gray eyes measured Apollo, and then Clara.

"I'm asking you to come with me. Together we can change our fates and prevent our evils from ever happening."

"How?" Apollo asked.

Rinn's mouth curled into a cocky smirk.

"First, we're going to steal very valuable trinkets from some powerful people, then we're going to build a breastplate."

"The Breastplate of Decision," Clara added softly, eyes not looking at the sunrise, but lost inward.

"Could it work? Could we control it?" Apollo asked.

Rinn grinned from ear to ear, "Let's go steal the greatest treasure in the history of the world."

END

About the Author

Joshua Hedges lives in Pittsburgh Pennsylvania. He is a writer, traveler, software engineer, dedicated partner, proud father, artist, and outdoorsman.

joshhedges.com

www.facebook.com/joshuahedgesauthor

Made in the USA
Middletown, DE
22 May 2022

66008795R00298